A diamond on her finger...

DIAMON
are for *Marria*

Three sensational, emotional ı
from Margaret Way, Trish W
and Jennie Adams

Diamonds are a Girl's Best Friend!

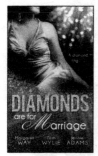

January 2013

February 2013

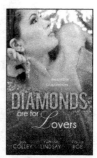

March 2013

April 2013

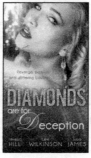

May 2013

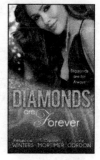

June 2013

DIAMONDS
are for
Marriage

Margaret
WAY

Trish
WYLIE

Jennie
ADAMS

MILLS &
BOON

Mills & Boon, an imprint of Harlequin (UK) Limited, Eton House, 18-24 Paradise Road, Richmond, Surrey TW9 1SR

DIAMONDS ARE FOR MARRIAGE
© Harlequin Enterprises II B.V./S.à.r.l 2013

The Australian's Society Bride © Margaret Way, Pty., Ltd 2008
Manhattan Boss, Diamond Proposal © Trish Wylie 2008
Australian Boss: Diamond Ring © Jennifer Ann Ryan 2009

ISBN: 978 0 263 90284 6

024-0113

Harlequin (UK) policy is to use papers that are natural, renewable and recyclable products and made from wood grown in sustainable forests. The logging and manufacturing processes conform to the legal environmental regulations of the country of origin.

Printed and bound in Spain
by Blackprint CPI, Barcelona

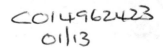

C01496242З
01/13

THE AUSTRALIAN'S
SOCIETY BRIDE

MARGARET WAY

Margaret Way, a definite Leo, was born and raised in the subtropical River City of Brisbane, capital of the Sunshine State of Queensland. A Conservatorium-trained pianist, teacher, accompanist and vocal coach, she found her musical career came to an unexpected end when she took up writing, initially as a fun thing to do. She currently lives in a harbourside apartment at beautiful Raby Bay, a thirty-minute drive from the state capital, where she loves dining *alfresco* on her plant-filled balcony, overlooking a translucent green marina filled with all manner of pleasure craft—from motor cruisers costing millions of dollars and big, graceful yachts with carved masts standing tall against the cloudless blue sky, to little bay runabouts. No one and nothing is in a mad rush, so she finds the laid-back village atmosphere very conducive to her writing. With well over a hundred books to her credit, she still believes her best is yet to come.

CHAPTER ONE

"LEO, YOU KNOW they don't want me, but they feel obliged to ask me," Robbie, her stepbrother said. As usual, he was making himself comfortable, lolling back on her brand-new sofa, dark head on a cushion, his long legs slung languidly over the other end.

This was a familiar theme between them, causing Leona, always the peacemaker, to answer automatically, "You know that's not true." Sadly, it *was* true. "You're good company, Robbie. You're an asset to any house party. Besides, you're on Boyd's polo team, which counts for a lot, and you're a darn good tennis player—my best doubles partner. We can and do beat the rest of them." The rest of them being the close-knit Blanchard clan, many of whom would be attending the weekend house party.

"Except Boyd," Robbie chipped in. "Now, Boyd is a man to marvel over—a business dynamo, IQ off the charts, superb athlete, a serious heartthrob with the women. What more could a man hope for? They could have cast him as the new James Bond."

"Forget Boyd," said Leona. "I rather like the new guy." As always, she was masking the deep feelings she had for Boyd— feelings she thought she would never get past—as she chucked a cushion at Robbie. "Though I will concede they don't come any more perfect than Boyd." This was said very dryly.

Robbie laughed, deftly fielding the silk cushion and depositing it on the floor. "Sure you don't actually love him?" He lifted his head to flash her a bright challenging look. Robbie was teeming with intuition and he frequently caught her out.

"Now, that would be a turn-up, wouldn't it?" she answered, hoping her white skin wasn't showing tell-tale bright flags of colour. "He *is* my second cousin."

"Well, not strictly speaking. You'd have to give or take a few 'steps'," Robbie reminded her. "There've been so many deaths, divorces and remarriages in the Blanchard family."

That was certainly true. Triumph and tragedy aplenty. She and Boyd, for instance, had both lost their mothers. She when she was eight. His beautiful mother, Alexa, had become Leona's honorary aunt after that until she'd died when Boyd was in his mid-twenties. Boyd's father, Rupert, Chairman of Blanchards, had remarried two years later, not to a nice sensible woman somewhere near his own age, as the family had dared to hope, but to a flamboyant divorcee, the daughter of one of Rupert's old cronies who sat on the Board of Blanchards. She was just a handful of years older than Rupert's only son and heir, Boyd.

The family had been reduced to a state of shock at the speed of the new alliance. Robbie privately referred to the newcomer as the Bride of Frankenstein. And he wasn't the only one in the family to gloat. Most expected the marriage would end in a ferocious court battle and a huge settlement. All had the great good sense to keep their opinions to themselves, except Geraldine, Rupert's older unmarried sister who didn't hesitate to speak her mind, as befitted her position. Despite that, Rupert had married his Jinty—short for Virginia—regardless. Rupert Blanchard was a law unto himself. And so, as it had transpired, was Jinty.

"Anyway, we're not talking about Boyd, we're talking about

you," Leona picked up the conversation. "Why you keep writing yourself off, I don't know."

"Ah, but you *do* know, Leo." Robbie sighed. "Low self-esteem." The unhappy, rebellious six-year-old he had been when Leona had first laid eyes on him fourteen years before glittered out of his dark eyes. "The problem is, I don't know *who* I am. Carlo didn't want any part of me. Didn't even bother to toss a coin for me. 'Heads me, tails your mother'. *Your* dad, my stepfather, is a good man, a gentleman of the old school, but he still doesn't know what to make of me. Just hopes things don't get any worse. Mother dearest has never loved me. No need to ask why. I don't make her proud and I don't look a scrap like her. I keep reminding her of Carlo and their failed marriage. To top it off, I'm *not* a Blanchard, am I, all these years later?" Robbie's intense young face took on a bitter cast. "I'm the misfit in your midst, the emotionally neglected adopted son."

In a way he was absolutely spot on, but Leona didn't hold back on the groans. "Please, Robbie, not again!" She allowed her still coltish frame to collapse into an armchair opposite him, feeling weighed down by constant anxiety for him and his well-being. "Do you really have to sprawl all over my new sofa?" she asked, not really minding. As usual Robbie was immaculate, very sharply groomed and dressed. Nothing scruffy about Robbie, not that it would have been tolerated. Robbie, for all his moans, well knew on which side his bread was buttered.

"How can I not?" he responded, not moving an inch. "It's so darn comfortable. You have superb taste, Leo. You're a super girl altogether. Best of all, you're as tender-hearted as you're beautiful. Lord knows how I would have made it in this family without you—my big sister, my most trusted confidante and supporter. You're the only one who doesn't think I'll turn out a rogue like Carlo."

"No, no!" she automatically denied.

"Yes, yes!" said Robbie. "They're all just waiting for me to prove it. Probably the best thing I could do, so far as the family is concerned, is fall under a bus."

And he didn't have it all that wrong, Leona thought dismally. For that reason, she couldn't let the opportunity go past. "You might consider your gambling is a worry, Robbie. You have to get a grip on that." She couldn't bring herself to throw in drugs again. Not so soon after their last confrontation. Robbie ran with a fast, moneyed, mostly mindless young crowd, hell-bent on pleasure, or what they considered pleasure, which didn't include work. She knew for a fact he dabbled with pot, like so many of his peers. She was fairly certain it hadn't gone any further than that. Not *yet* anyway. Like her, Robbie carried the burden of the Blanchard name, which meant pressure as well as prestige, power, mega-wealth. But, unlike her, Robbie wasn't the most stable of people.

The only person he seemed to be able to commit to was *her*, his "big sister." They hadn't used the "step" for years and years. Robbie just referred to her as his sister, as she called him her brother. It didn't seem to matter that there was no bond in *blood*. Her father had legally adopted Robbie directly after he'd married Robbie's mother, Delia. Newcomers who didn't know Leona and Robbie's background always commented with perplexed frowns, "But you're not a bit alike." Maybe the fact that Robbie—christened Roberto Giancarlo D'Angelo—strongly resembled his Italian father while she was a porcelain-skinned redhead had something to do with it.

"Pure art nouveau," Boyd had long since labelled her looks, consigning her to the romantic, overly sentimental Pre-Raphaelite lot—the willowy springtime woodland nymph with her loosely pinned mane of red-gold hair, flowing floral dia-

phanous dress, away with the fairies. Not his usual cup of tea—
slick, elegant, the perfect brunette, all long legs and womanly
curves, whereas she had as many curves as her ironing-board.

Don't think of Boyd.

It was excellent advice. She'd do well to follow it. Even
being around him was dangerous enough.

Robbie's voice brought her out of her discomfiting thoughts.
"I promise you I will, Leo. Have there been more whisperings
about me in the family? 'What else is Robbie doing'?" he
mimicked a female family voice.

There had been plenty of those, she thought. Shocked horror
from the older generation. Delia, his mother, reduced to fat
crocodile tears over her son's misconduct. "Remember there's
Boyd to consider. Nothing gets past him, Robbie. He has eyes
and ears everywhere."

"Spies, spooks!" Robbie laughed as if it was funny. It wasn't.
Robbie sustained himself with cynical, sometimes bitter banter,
when in reality Boyd Blanchard was everything he yearned to
be. "Scion of generations of multi-millionaires, now billion-
aires," he continued, dangling an arm to the floor. "Now there's
a man for you."

"Oh, I don't know." Leona pursed her finely cut, sensitive lips.

"Come off it." Robbie grinned wickedly and swung upright
with the strength and elegance of the university champion
gymnast he was. "Maybe he's the one to awaken you—"

"He is *not*!" Leona protested, uncharacteristically cross.

"Well, you do a good job of covering up, but I *know* you,
remember? You admire him as much as everyone else.
Problematic old me included. He might bawl me out from time
to time, but I know he means well by me. I'm simply not in his
league. He's cast in the heroic mould. I'm the one everyone is
waiting to see unravel. No wonder Boyd is worshipped by the

family. He's probably the most eligible bachelor in the country, all the women love him, not yet thirty—"

"He is. A month ago," Leona confirmed, not giving Robbie a chance to go on. Counting off Boyd's attributes was a sure way to madness.

"Fancy that! I wasn't invited to the party, then?"

"There was *no* party. He was much too busy."

"Well, that would be true enough." Robbie was always fair. "He's a workaholic. Just think what he's achieved. He's ready to step into Rupert's shoes right now. Boyd and Jinty— one of my least favourite women, as I've told you umpteen times—are the only ones in the entire clan who don't go in fear and awe of old Rupe. And there's *you*," he pondered thoughtfully. "The odd thing is, the ruthless old devil is very fond of *you*. That's the only thing about him I like. He despises me."

"Not true." Again Leona shook her red-gold head when she knew the autocratic Rupert considered Robbie "worthless". "He's ready to take you into the firm as soon as you complete your degree."

And why not? Robbie was very clever and he was right about one thing: Rupert had always shown a marked interest in her since she was a little girl. Intimidating with most people, he had always been very gentle with her, especially after she had lost her mother, Serena, in that fatal riding accident on the Brooklands estate. In those far off days Boyd, six years her elder, vividly handsome and clever, already at fourteen six feet tall, had made a special effort to take her under his wing as if she were a stray fluffy duckling. He had always looked after her at family functions and gatherings, without any need for prompting. He had just done it. In those days Boyd had been her hero. She told herself she had long run out of hero worship.

These days, Boyd affected her so powerfully, so painfully, she could scarcely make eye contact with him. He made her nervous and excited. He challenged her and honed her already sharp wits. It was torture to be physically near him, yet she couldn't seem to draw back. The fact was, she was mesmerised by his whole persona—those piercing, incredibly beautiful blue eyes that wooed as they wounded. She was a seething mass of contradictions where Boyd was concerned. He stirred her and she feared him. Any liaison between her and Boyd would never be accepted. Not that he had ever looked at her in that way. Well, how did he look at her, exactly? Sometimes he made her feel extraordinarily *beautiful.* Inside and out. Other times he seemed to go out of his way to alienate her. The cool tongue. The blazing eyes. Face it: it was *her* fantasy, not his.

Robbie broke into her errant thoughts again. "I expect I get invited because they want to keep an eye on me."

"Same way they keep an eye on all of us," she said with a smile.

"Just like royalty! At least they acknowledge you for the clever, creative young woman you are. The fact you're a genuine beauty is always an enormous help, and you have the wonderful gift of being able to get on with all sorts of people."

"Except Boyd." The fact she had voiced it aloud made her twitch with self-disgust.

Robbie laughed. "I expect there's a very good reason for that. I ask myself—all that sparring the two of you go on with. Are you both playing a part? Is it all a sham?"

"Funny sort of sham." She spoke as though the very idea of being secretly in love with Boyd was utterly ridiculous. "We bring out the worst in each other." How proficient she had grown at crushing down all other explanations. It was bad enough they lurked on the outskirts of her brain.

"Personally, I think you're a good match," Robbie announced as though he had given it serious consideration. "Boyd needs a woman with fiery red hair. You're good at keeping him in line. Well, I'd best be off."

"I hope that doesn't mean to the races." Leona stood up. It was Saturday and the Spring Carnival was underway.

A little colour rose to Robbie's olive cheeks. "I don't do much harm. I'm taking Deb. Barrington and his current squeeze are coming along. Just a fun afternoon and a chance for the girls to dress up. I'm surprised you're not going. Old Rupe's glamour two-year-old is bound to win its race. Shall I put a couple of bob on for you?"

Leona shook her head, her beautiful hair loosely caught back in a high knot. "I've never felt the slightest urge to gamble, Robbie. With money, that is. I certainly play my hunches. That's the right side of my brain. Money makes money for the likes of Rupert." She planted an affectionate kiss on Robbie's cheek. He wasn't tall and she was for a woman. "If I were you, I'd put my boot down firmly on what you've got." Robbie was on a generous allowance from her father but she knew he made short work of it. He often borrowed from her, promising he would pay her back. Sometimes he did. More often he didn't.

The two of them walked to the door of Leona's very attractive open-plan apartment, which took full advantage of its marvellous location overlooking Sydney Harbour. The apartment had been a twenty-first birthday present from "The Family". It was their way of showing their approval of the way she conducted herself and brought credit to the family name. No way could she have afforded it herself, although with her latest promotion to personal assistant to Beatrice Caldwell, a fashion icon and overall Director of Blanchards Fashion, she had now hit an income high.

"You deserve it, girl. Like me, you have the eye!"

High praise from the autocratic and incredibly difficult to please Beatrice.

"So you *are* coming to the house party?" Leona needed to double-check. "You're expected to reply." Good manners ranked high on the Blanchard expectations list.

"*Naturellement!* And that just about exhausts my French for the day. Just for *you*, Leo. No one else."

"Don't be difficult, sweetie." She hugged him in the sisterly, protective way she had with him.

"Maybe if Carlo had stuck around instead of abandoning me," Robbie suggested unhappily. "But he couldn't wait to get back to Italy, remarry, father several more children."

"Let's hope he's done a better job with them than he did with you." Leona's tone was uncharacteristically hard. Was it any wonder her heart ached for Robbie? How could she not recognise his *emptiness*? Delia appeared to feel little or nothing for her only child, incredible as that seemed. Perhaps, if Robbie had taken after Delia—blonde, blue-eyed…? Carlo D'Angelo had never contacted his first born over the years, much less invited him to visit and meet his half-siblings. "It's *his* loss, Robbie," she said, resorting to a brisk confident tone. "Believe in yourself, like I do." Robbie had to buck up. With her hand resting on his arm, she thought she detected an inner agitation he wasn't allowing her to see.

"Everything okay?" She frowned. "You would tell me if it weren't?"

"Everything's fine!" Robbie gave a brief laugh. "Well, then, Leo love, next time I'll see you will be next weekend at Brooklands."

She smiled back. "Bring your racket. We'll lick 'em, same as always."

"Satisfying, isn't it?" he smirked.

"Very."

If only everything *was* fine, Robbie thought dismally as he strolled off to the lift. All sorts of anxieties were settling heavily in his stomach. Leo was wonderful. He loved her dearly. The only one in the world he did love, actually. In the end he hadn't had it in him to ask her for another loan. Hadn't he already asked enough of her? In fact he still owed her. But he was desperately in need of money and, to be honest, becoming increasingly frightened of the people he had got involved with. Basically, they were thugs, even if they moved freely through high society. God knew what they might do to him if he couldn't keep them happy. Or happy enough. He had the horrible feeling a trap was closing around him. Leo was right. His love of gambling, yet another unfortunate trait he had inherited from Carlo—were there any good ones?—had pitched him headlong into a maelstrom of danger. Old Rupe's brilliant two-year-old—Blazeaway—was practically guaranteed a win this afternoon. He'd put the few thousand he had left on its nose.

Characteristically, Robbie shrugged off his nightmares and began to whistle an old tune to keep up his spirits.

CHAPTER TWO

ON THE FOLLOWING Saturday morning Leona decided to let the parade of Blanchards get away from the city before she started out on her drive to the Blanchards' splendid country estate. In one way she was thrilled to be going back—she adored the house and its magnificent gardens and parkland, spreading over several square kilometres—in another, meeting up with Boyd again left her unsettled in mind and body. It seemed an age since she had seen him, in reality, just over a month, but he had been overseas on family business. Since Rupert had reached his sixties with such a splendid heir, the older man was happy to spend a lot more time at Brooklands. The result was that the mantle of power and responsibility had fallen more heavily on Boyd's shoulders.

Then again, Boyd knew all about power and taking over the reins. He had been groomed for the role. There had never been the possibility, or even the fear, that he might not possess his father's brilliant business brain; or when the time came, that he might opt out of a lifetime of hard work and enormous responsibility. Such a life might not have appealed to him. With a lavish trust fund set up by his grandfather, Boyd could simply have walked away and enjoyed a life of leisure, doing anything he wanted—Lord knew he was clever enough—but Boyd had shown even in his early teens that he was more than capable of bearing the burdens of a great business empire. His ambition, to the family's immense relief, was to continue his forebears' achievements.

Everything Boyd tackled he did with brilliance and determination, she thought, fixing her eyes on the road ahead. He was far more than a chip off the old block. Boyd, if the truth be told, was Rupert's superior in every way. Certainly he had that wonderful *polish* he had inherited from Alexa, along with her stunning sapphire eyes. At just turned thirty, he was right on top of his game, on course to outperform Rupert and the original family fortune builders and their achievements. Boyd commanded genuine liking, love and respect, whereas Rupert was rather more famous for commanding fear.

Extraordinary, then, that Rupert had taken such a fancy to *her*. The one time Rupert had ever been seen to break down was at her mother's funeral, when a stiff upper lip at his own wife's funeral had prevailed. Extremely odd, that. She remembered Alexa, a close friend of her mother, always so poised, had been in floods of tears that day too. Even as a stunned and grief-stricken little girl she'd remembered.

A wonderful rider, her mother, Serena, had broken her neck in a freak fall, taking an old stone wall at the upper reaches of the Brooklands lake. It was a wall she had jumped dozens of times before. Only that last time she and her horse had taken a catastrophic tumble. It was later discovered the horse's hoof had snagged in a strong loop of ivy clinging to the wall.

Sixteen years ago, Leona thought with familiar sadness. Sixteen years I've been without my mother. She still remembered how her mother had bent to kiss her before she had gone out on her ride.

"Won't be long, my darling. When I come back, we'll all go for a nice long swim."

Serena didn't know—couldn't know—she wouldn't be coming back. Not alive, anyway.

The entire family had taken her mother's death badly. Serena had been so deeply mourned that it seemed there had been no love left over for Delia, her successor, her father's second wife. The family had considered no one good enough to replace Serena. Certainly not Delia, who had "ambushed" her grieving father, bringing with her a difficult small son to boot. Perhaps that was why she, Leona, was held close to the Blanchard core. She wasn't a member of the main family. But she *was* the image of her mother. That seemed to accord her a special grace.

The great wrought iron gates to the estate were standing open. A mile long private road led to the house. Magnificent trees of an immense height lined the way, their outermost branches interlocking so that the road beneath formed a wonderful golden-green tunnel.

Minutes later, she was out of the tunnel and driving over an arched stone bridge that spanned the shimmering green lake. Fed by an underground river, the lake, very deep in some places, spread out over three acres, dotted here and there with picturesque little islands, which had become the breeding grounds for wild duck and other waterfowl. Today a flotilla of black swans sailed under the bridge. The lake's calm waters, glassy green with a multitude of flashing silvers, were spectacularly fringed by deep banks of pure white arum lilies, Japanese purple iris and a wealth of other aquatic plants.

Up ahead was the house. Built in the style of an English manor house, with various extensions added over the years in the same style, it had evolved into a very grand property indeed.

A vast sweep of lawn and formal gardens lay before it, the whole estate surrounded by undulating hills and valleys, brooks and streams. When she was a child she had counted the rooms—thirty-two, including a beautiful big ballroom where many large family and charity functions had been held over the years. Alexa had made the annual Brooklands Garden Party one of the most memorable events on the social calendar, a feat Jinty had never attempted to emulate. The glorious grounds were ideal for the purpose.

No one could match Alexa, Leona thought. It was a tragedy she had died so young. She had often pondered her private belief that Alexa had not been at all happy in her marriage but the subject had never been broached. In public Rupert and Alexa had played the role of the perfect couple. It was only as Leona had grown to womanhood that she'd begun to sense the very real *distance* between the two. They'd practically lived their lives apart, although Alexa had obviously decided to make the best of her marriage, always looking out for her beloved son, and applying her considerable skills and energies to running a large estate and numerous charities close to her heart.

If a woman like that couldn't have her happy ever after, forget the romantics, she thought. Marriage was a *huge* risk.

The presence of water was everywhere at Brooklands. The many brooks on the estate had, in fact, given it its name. Water was magic.

Way off to Leona's right were the three polo fields, covering a huge area given that one polo field had an area equivalent to ten football fields. The boundaries of the fields were deeply shaded by massive plantings of trees, both natives and exotics weaving in and out of one another. A world-famous landscaper had been brought in by Boyd's great-grandparents, who had determined on and succeeded in creating a world class garden. Many years on, another celebrity landscaper had worked with Rupert when he'd decided he wanted polo fields on the estate. A splendid polo player in his day, Rupert now left it to Boyd to carry on the tradition. Boyd freely admitted he found the dangerous, fast paced sport great relaxation.

A match had been organised for Sunday afternoon with a visiting team. Though he was a marvellously dashing player, she always found herself praying that Boyd would not be harmed. It was such a fast, rough game, though very thrilling for the spectator, especially those who adored horses.

All of them desperately needed Boyd to succeed Rupert. None of the other male cousins, even the really clever ones, and there were quite a few, could possibly take his place.

Even as she thought of him, she was conscious of a kind of panic moving through her. Her heart was beating faster. She could feel its mad flutter. The big thing was not to allow her schoolgirl panic to ruin the weekend. Think positive.

Boyd.

Damn, damn, damn. Just his name did her in. Head and heart. She didn't want it. It wasn't right. The very strength of her feelings made her afraid. Did anyone realise how hard it was for her to act normal around him? Robbie, maybe. But then Robbie saw too much.

At twenty-four, wasn't it high time she started to move past her feelings for Boyd? Give other guys a chance? There were plenty of them standing in line—no doubt the Blanchard name was an added attraction. But she was no heiress. She was one of the worker bees. It was a terrifying feeling to be held in thrall, for that was how she had come to think of it. It was every bit as bad an addiction as Robbie's gambling.

She wondered if Boyd was still seeing Ally McNair. Ally

was lovely and great fun. There had been Zoe Renshaw before Ally. Jemma Stirling. Not to forget Holly Campbell. She hadn't liked Holly. Such a snob. And, of course, there was Chloe Compton, heiress to another great retailing fortune, therefore judged by Rupert as very suitable.

Everyone in the family liked Chloe, including her. Rupert had gone out of his way to give her his nod of approval. There had barely been a time when Boyd didn't have the most beautiful girls chasing after him. Some, like Ally and Chloe, turned out to be regulars, but Boyd didn't seem in any hurry to commit himself. In any case he was, as Robbie said, a workaholic. Come to that, she worked pretty darn hard herself.

Even her boss had been known to comment on the fact. And Bea hadn't signed her up because she was one of the Blanchard clan. She had been given the job on merit alone. Although many in the country's fashion world would have given their eye teeth to land the job, most of Leona's colleagues found Bea immensely difficult—some days she was chillier than a travelling iceberg—but all in all Leona liked and greatly admired her boss. Bea was a huge driving force in fashion, and her own personal guru, and Leona knew in her bones that one day—all right, it was years off—she would be able to take over from Bea.

Jinty made a theatrical business of greeting her—hugging and kissing her with practised insincerity. "Lovely to have you with us again, Leo," she gushed. "Your outfit is perfect." Jinty's large, rather hard china-blue eyes comprehensively studied Leona from head to toe. "You know precisely what fashion is all about. But of course you have that extraordinary figure. What I wouldn't do to be as skinny as you!"

"Give up the champagne, Jinty?" Leona suggested with a teasing smile, knowing Jinty's big show of affection was sadly all an act. Everything was an act with sexy, bosomy Jinty, including her marriage. In the very next instant, as expected, Leona was waved away as of no consequence as Jinty's eyes flashed towards the door, brilliant with expectation. Instantly Leona had the gut feeling that it was Boyd arriving. Boyd was of infinitely more interest than she could ever hope to be. Boyd, the family superstar. She realised he must have left Sydney not long after her.

As though someone was physically shoving her in the back, Leona hurried up the grand sweep of the staircase. She wasn't ready to meet up with Boyd yet. Maybe she never would be.

She was in the same room she usually occupied. It had its own bathroom and a small sitting room—more a suite than just a bedroom. She had loved this room in the old days but Jinty, once installed in a position of power, had decided that new brides had a pressing obligation to sweep clean. At least Rupert had stopped her from doing anything much on the ground floor, with its beautiful welcoming reception rooms and library, but she had been given carte blanche on the upper floor. As a consequence Jinty had suffered a wild reaction. She had gone about her task like a woman possessed.

To the collective family mind, a kind of chaos had broken out—a chaos nurtured by unlimited money. It had also laid waste to the true elegance and country comfort of what had gone before. Now everything was *sumptuous!* Her spacious, high ceilinged bedroom was a prime example of Jinty's love of the baroque. There were lashings of gilt, lashings of Louis, lashings of ornamentation, damasks and silks. She fully expected to one day see a reflection of Marie Antoinette in the ornately gilded circular mirror. What the revamp lacked in style it more than made up for in a superfluity of riches. Money was no object and Jinty didn't need a good reason to spend.

There was a tap on the door and Leona turned to see Hadley, a permanent member of the household staff, smiling at her. Hadley—Eddie to her—was a big, pleasant-faced man with hands the size of dinner plates and a shock of thick tawny hair only now turning silver. He was holding her suitcase and another small piece of luggage. "Where would you like them, Miss Leo?"

"Please…just beside the bed, thanks, Eddie. All's well with you?"

"No complaints, apart from my sciatica that comes and goes. I'm pushing sixty, you know." He deposited her luggage, then stood upright, looking around him with the kind of baffled awe that most people viewed Jinty's efforts.

"And you don't look anything like it," Leona said, which was perfectly true. "Was that Boyd I heard arriving?"

"Indeed it was," Hadley remarked dryly, trusting to Leona's discretion. "A great favourite with his stepmother is Mr Boyd." A conclusion the entire family and staff had long since arrived at. "Mrs Blanchard's sister, Tonya, is here as well."

For a moment Leona looked at him in complete dismay. "Not Tonya?" She felt a silent scream of protest start up inside her head.

"Someone must have thought it was a lovely idea," Hadley murmured, tongue in cheek. Tonya was a very demanding and unpopular guest at Brooklands.

It couldn't have been Boyd, Leona thought. She had once overheard Boyd telling his father after one particularly strained dinner party, for which he blamed Tonya's abrasive tongue, that he didn't want her in the house any more. Tonya was a born troublemaker, a malicious one at that, churning out gossip and a whole lot of misinformation at every possible opportunity. As Jinty's sister, she swanned about the estate, treating the staff as though they were invisible. Added to that, she made no bones about the fact that she found Boyd enormously attractive. What was more, she had deluded herself into thinking she had as good a chance as anyone of landing him. Not that she was getting much encouragement from her sister. Jinty disapproved of her as much as everyone else.

So who was it who had invited Tonya? With a thrill of horror Leona thought it just might have been Rupert. He had such an alarmingly perverse streak. He had to keep proving to his son that he was still Boss and could invite whom he pleased. Though Rupert adored his heir, in a strange way their relationship was fraught with hidden conflicts and dangers. Leona often thought it was the ghost of Alexa that stood between them—that and Boyd's superior capabilities. On the one hand Boyd's brilliance was a cause of great pride to Rupert, on the other it caused a somewhat irrational level of jealousy and resentment.

Rupert had a monumental ego. Boyd did not.

A buffet lunch was laid out in the informal dining room for those of the family who had arrived. When Leona walked in, golden sunlight was streaming through the huge Palladian windows which allowed marvellous views of the rear gardens. Although there was a terrace outside for extra dining, the informal dining room with so much glass gave Leona the feeling of being outdoors. As the ancestral home of the Blanchard clan, frequently visited by its members, the large room, decorated with a valuable collection of botanical prints, had been set with a number of glass-topped circular tables on carved timber bases, specially carved in the Philippines. Each table easily seated eight on handsome upholstered rattan arm-chairs, rather than having one very long extension table as in the formal dining room. It had all been Alexa's idea.

Leona, who'd had a light breakfast of yoghurt and fruit at around seven a.m., found herself hungry. She was at the fortunate stage of her life when she could eat as much as she liked without putting on an ounce of weight. Good to know, but she stuck pretty religiously to the right foods anyway. Fine dark chocolate was her one vice, but she was well on the way to achieving a New Year resolution of only eating a single wickedly delicious piece a day.

At least ten members of the family were there before her, helping themselves to a buffet so lavish that Leona started to think of the world's starving millions. The best restaurant in Sydney couldn't have topped this spread, delivered by a stream of staff from the kitchen. At least the staff got to eat what was left over; it was one of the perks of the job.

"Oh, there you are, Leo!" she was greeted on all sides. Lovely to know that people were happy to see her and she, for the most part, was happy to see them.

Geraldine, who was a fashion icon herself—albeit more than a touch eccentric—was wearing a striking high-rise red hat. She jumped up from the table to come towards Leona with outstretched arms.

"Don't you look beautiful, Leo dear!" They exchanged kisses, blessedly sincere. Shrewd grey eyes searched Leona's face. "Such a pleasure to see you. You grow more and more like your dear mother every day. Come sit beside me. I want to hear all you've been up to."

Leona smiled back. "Just give me a moment to grab some food, Aunty Gerri."

From behind them came a feline little comment, something Tonya was never short of, "Yes, *do*. You're dangerously thin, Leona. Sure you're eating right?"

"Oh, do shut up, Tonya," Geraldine said, as brusque when she chose to be as her brother Rupert.

"Shut up? For heaven's sake." Tonya pretended to gasp, then she fell silent as the atmosphere suddenly heightened.

The reason? Boyd had entered the room.

Here was a man dazzling enough to break any girl's heart, Leona thought.

This love of mine.

The words sprang from the well of truth deep inside her. She couldn't suppress her true feelings. She couldn't choose the time or the place when they surfaced. The one thing she *could* ensure was that they were never exposed. Not to Boyd, whose position alone allowed no access. And especially not to Rupert, who had his own plans for the Crown prince. It was she who had chosen to lay down her heart. That Boyd could love her back in the same way was just an impossible dream.

Nevertheless she couldn't stop herself staring at him. After all, everyone else was. Some inches over six feet, superb physique, a constant tan from the time he spent yachting on the Harbour, an enviable head of thick black hair swept back from a fine brow, elegantly sculpted bones—he would look good at ninety—and those beautiful magnetic eyes, as deep a blue as the finest sapphires in the Crown jewels. Those eyes, inherited from his mother, set him apart.

The big hush seemed endless. It had to be enormously flattering, Leona thought, but Boyd took it in his stride. Probably accepted it as his due. No, that wasn't true. Boyd was no attention seeker. He simply didn't notice it. It was like witnessing a medieval prince coming in from the hunt, the public adoration merely his due. Leona couldn't help a tightening of her facial muscles—a little flare of rebellion? Public capitulation to Boyd's splendid persona was not her thing at all. She enjoyed being the one not to swoon. Besides, she needed a shield to separate her from him. It was the paradox she'd had to live with for years. Behind the mask, the strategies and the countless diversionary tactics she had developed for self-protection, she felt constantly starved for the sight of him.

Where you are, I want to be.

Lyrics of a beautiful song. They were so true.

A smile flared white against the dark tan of his skin. He lifted a nonchalant hand in greeting. "Hi, everyone!"

"Great you're here, Boyd!" came the chorus from the tables.

"We're expecting a cracker game tomorrow!" This from one of the great-uncles. Playing polo was a release for Boyd and they all loved watching him.

Tonya seized the moment by going up to him and laying a proprietorial hand on his arm. A petite, sharp-featured but attractive blonde, she looked like a doll beside him, even in her spike-heeled shoes.

"Cheek of her!" Geraldine muttered, herself grabbing Leona's arm in a surprisingly strong grip. "Doesn't she know she drives him mad?"

"So who invited her?" Leona asked, gently easing her arm out of Geraldine's fierce hold. She had her own suspicions.

"My brother, of course." Geraldine had confirmed them. Geraldine, who often referred to her powerful brother as "the tyrannosaurus" humphed, "Rupert likes to throw a spanner in the works when we all know who the right gel is for Boyd."

The right gel for Boyd?

"Chloe Compton?" Leona hazarded with a profoundly sinking heart.

"Gracious, no!" Geraldine turned on her, almost indignant. "Go fill your plate, child, then come back to me. Is that stepbrother of yours coming?"

"He *was* invited, Gerri. And he is on Boyd's polo team."

"All right, all right, so loyal. Not that I don't admire it." Geraldine shook her elegant silver head so that the little quiff of feathers on the hat which matched her chic suit danced in the breeze. "Matter of fact I quite like him, even if he does have the makings of a bit of a rogue. His father had charm too, but what a dreadful man, running off like that and leaving the boy. Being abandoned doesn't make for little angels."

Words to live by.

And then he was beside her. "How's it going, Flower Face?"

Again the familiar contraction in her breast. The invading warmth in her blood. Even her tongue stuck to the roof of her mouth. For all her strategies, nothing worked. As always, his voice fell with dangerous charm on her too sensitive ears. Sometimes, not often these days, he came out with that moniker, *Flower Face*. Each time it made a flutter of excitement pass over her, as if he'd actually stroked her naked body with a feather. Flower Face was the pet name he had for her when she was growing up. When she was his fluffy stray duckling.

She made herself steady, astonished she could do so. She glanced up, seemingly casual, allowing herself to meet his gaze for mere seconds only. She couldn't for the life of her manage a smile. Within her all was excitement and confusion. Her eyes, had she known it, were a pure crystalline green, set as they were against porcelain skin and the scintillating reds and golds of her long, naturally curly hair.

Deliberately she focused those eyes on his fine cotton shirt, white with a blue stripe, the long sleeves carelessly pushed to the elbow. She could see the tanned skin of his chest, the beginnings of the mat of hair, black as black. Boyd's height and handsomeness was only the half of his extraordinary sexual radiance. She knew other handsome young men but, though they did their best to engage her interest, they were mere schoolboys beside Boyd.

"If you don't like this shirt, I can always change it," he said.

She wanted to slap herself alert. "Actually I was admiring it. Helmut Lang, isn't it?"

"If you say so, Leona, that's good enough for me. You're the fashion expert in the family."

"Don't put yourself down," she scoffed. "Didn't *Icon* magazine name you one of the most stylish men in the country?"

He stared at her in mock astonishment. "You saw that, did you?"

With an effort she ignored the mockery. "Anyway, how was the trip—a big success?" She was pleased she was able to speak so collectedly.

His expression of indulgence abruptly sobered. "In many ways. Deals were done, a few swung. Blanchards has a lot of clout, but nothing is as it seems these days, Leo. It's a dangerous world out there. And becoming increasingly so."

"I know." She bent her head. " Terror and suffering everywhere." She didn't tell him how she worried every time he flew off on one of his many overseas trips. For that matter, she suffered a degree of apprehension on her own overseas buying trips with Bea.

He nodded, looking down at her hair as it caught fire in the sunlight before focusing on the buffet table.

"What are *you* having?" he asked.

"The same as you," she answered tartly, another defence mechanism. One of the things she did to put distance between them because, oddly enough, they had many things in common. They loved horses, country life. They liked the same food, music, books, films, even people. They both shared a great love for Brooklands and they both derived enormous pleasure out of being successful at what they did, finding relaxation there.

He laughed, looking much amused. "Right then. Leave it to

me. I know what you like. Go back and join Gerri. Save a place for me on your other side."

Her shimmering eyes ranged across the large room, at the groups of laughing, chattering people, then back to him. "What, with Tonya waving a hand?" Tonya was indeed waving an unrestrained hand, trying to capture Boyd's attention. It was a wonder she wasn't banging a spoon on the table.

"Doesn't give up, does she?" he murmured dryly, blatantly ignoring the summons. "I love it, playing happy families. Do as I say, Leo." He spoke with a natural authority that had nothing to do with arrogance. "I don't get to see enough of you."

On track again, she spoke with a spurt of challenge. "That's an order then, is it?"

He laughed—so annoying, so devastating—before turning to glance at the lavish buffet. "You know what, Flower Face? You've made an art form of challenging me."

"Maybe I'm a rebel at heart," she suggested.

"How could you not be with that glorious red hair?" He picked up two plates. "By the way, do you want to go riding with me this afternoon?"

The offer was so unexpected that she just stood there, overtaken by excitement and shock.

"Well?" Boyd asked, his blue eyes moving lightly over her. What he saw was a lyrically beautiful young woman in an extremely pretty silk dress—pure, virginal and incredibly sexy, which he knew she was unaware of. And for once lost for words.

Silently she willed herself to answer. "I should check that Robbie is okay," she said, not enjoying the nervousness she heard in her voice. Exactly *how* was Boyd looking at her? Whatever was in his mind, it was very unnerving. "He hasn't arrived yet."

"How old is Robbie now?" He shifted his brilliant gaze to the buffet, as though aware of her inner confusion.

"He's still my little brother."

"High time he stood on his own two feet," he said crisply. "This little brother bit has gone on too long."

"And you don't like it?" She leaned towards him, aware that others might be watching—most certainly Tonya—deliberately keeping her tone low.

Boyd too spoke quietly, but forcefully nonetheless. "He uses you, Leo. That's the bit I don't like. He loves you. I'm well aware of that. But you're too vulnerable where Robbie is concerned. I intend to have a little chat with him this weekend."

Oh, God! She visibly swallowed. What had Robbie done now? "Please take it easy with him, Boyd." The minute she said it, she realised she had betrayed her own anxieties.

"Surely I never come down *too* hard on him?" Boyd asked, hardening his heart against the meltingly lovely *pleading* image she presented. It was high time to pull Robbie up, before he totally ran off the rails. He had received information that Robbie had been getting in over his head, gambling. He was even doing business with a very unsavoury character, suspected of money laundering. That had to cease.

"I thought we'd ride out towards Mount Garnet," he said, briskly changing the subject. "You've brought some riding gear, haven't you?" If not, he knew she kept clothes at the house.

She had hardly been listening, wondering exactly what he had learned about Robbie. The gambling, of course. The drugs? What else? Robbie could be wonderfully sweet—at least with her—but he wasn't as yet a really strong character. Nothing got past Boyd.

"You're trembling," he said, suddenly putting a strong hand on her bare arm, his thumb moving almost caressingly over the silky skin.

Instantly heat raged around her body. Her skin was melting

as the hot blood fizzed through her arteries, ensuring she shook even further. "Yes, I will come riding with you. I was just trying to remember the last time we went riding alone," she managed, hoping she hadn't turned scarlet. Both of them had been riding since they could walk. Both of them were very accomplished. Heavens, Boyd was a top class polo player. But she couldn't remember the last time they had been on their own.

He laughed, sounding particularly at ease, even happy.

It came to her how much she loved his voice and his laugh! It was a sound she adored, yet somehow it disturbed her. It made her bones turn liquid. Even the way he said her name was enough to turn her knees to jelly.

"I'm surprised you don't remember," he said, suddenly pinning her with his blue eyes. "You told me you hated me and I couldn't placate you."

Didn't he realise it had just been another outburst against the pull she felt towards him? She willed herself to speak calmly. "I don't hate you, Boyd. It's just sometimes I'm not at ease with you. Or you with me. I'm not a fool."

How could she possibly say: *You're the moon and stars to me. When you touch me I dissolve?*

Why did she become so erotically charged with Boyd and no one else?

He was looking at her intently. "I realise I make you sparkle with temper, revolt, whatever. I have a mental image of you at the age it all started. You were around sixteen. You'd been really sweet up until then."

You mean I was your little slave.

"It's called growing up," she said coolly. "Finding one's own identity. Sometimes you do make me very angry," she admitted. "You're so terribly…"

"What?" He pressed for an answer.

"Dominant," she flashed back with spirit. "The family idol, born to be worshipped. You mock me like I'm a—"

"Nonsense!" he cut in. "Why are you so unwilling to really answer my question? It's all evasion with you these days. That makes me sad. It's not any authority I might have that angers you. It's something else. So far as the mockery goes, it's the other way around. I see it in your face and in your voice. I can see it *now*." His eyes swept over her, marking the tension in her body, which looked so entrancingly fragile but he knew was in fact quite athletic.

"Boyd, everyone is watching us," she whispered a warning, her nerves exquisitely frayed.

"That's okay," he answered without concern. "They're well used to the friction between us by now."

"How can you call me evasive, Boyd? Did I not just agree to go riding with you?" she asked, pleased to have tripped him up. Then it struck her. "We *are* going on our own, aren't we, or are you getting up a party?"

"A party of *two*, Leona," he told her dryly. "I'm after your company *alone*. No need to bring in the rest of the family."

"Right!" She tilted her chin as she prepared to move off.

"You used to love me," he said, very, very gently to her averted profile.

It stopped her in her tracks. It was still so deliriously *true*.

She moved back to him in that moment, wanting to throw herself at him, clamp her arms around him. Never let go. Have his arms move to embrace her. If he kissed her she feared she might lose consciousness. Or maybe her soul would float out of her body into his. Instead, she raised herself on tiptoe to be nearer to that so dear yet so dangerous face. "I don't any more," she said.

There was safety in deception. Much better to be safe than horribly sorry.

* * *

For well over an hour they rode through a countryside that had never seemed so luminous to her. Along the eastern seaboard and even deep into the Outback the land had received wonderful life-giving rain and overnight the land had renewed itself. The light beneath the caverns of trees was jewelled, the display of blossom sumptuous, the air sweet with a hundred different haunting perfumes. Riding together so companionably was too precious to be described. Leona wanted to retain the memory for ever. The sight of him, the familiarity and the exciting *strangeness,* the profile she loved, that clean cut chiselled jaw. With his head half turned away one would have assumed his eyes would be very dark to match the black of his hair and his strongly marked brows. They were anything but—sometimes his eyes were so blue they looked violet. He really was a dream come true.

Out of the golden glare of the sunlight and down into the dappled green sanctuary of one of the many creeks that wound their way across the estate, he turned his head to smile lazily at her. His eyes, even in the shade, blazed. His wide-brimmed hat, a soft grey, was tilted at a rakish angle. Riding gear suited him wonderfully well. "Enjoying yourself?" he asked.

"I love it!" Leona responded with uncomplicated joy. "I especially love water. All the time we've been riding we've been in sight and sound of it."

"That's what's so powerfully attractive about the estate." He studied her smiling open face with pleasure. "You don't feel threatened by me when you're on horseback?"

"I'm secure in the knowledge I could gallop away from you." She laughed, one hand lightly holding the reins of her pure Arabian mare, as nimble and sure-footed as ever a mare could be. "Anyway, you've never really done anything to threaten me," she added.

"I think I have," he answered slowly.

The way he said it shook her to the marrow. She had to look away. Curly tendrils of her hair had escaped from her ponytail, glowing brightly against the cream of her skin. "You sound as though you care." She couldn't help the revealing tinge of sadness in her voice.

"Of course I do," he answered, almost roughly.

"Good!" she retorted, suddenly very tense. In fact she was starting to feel light-headed. "At least you know with *me* you can't have it all your own way."

"You think I do?" He leaned forward to caress the bay's neck.

"You're quite daunting in a way, you know."

"Leo, that's absolute nonsense," he said crisply.

Her breath fluttered. "No." She could feel the heat in her cheeks. She even felt like bursting into tears, he moved her so unbearably. That alone gave him a power she could never match.

"Then tell me," he demanded. "In what way?"

"In *every* way!" she said a little wildly. "Don't let it bother you. You can't help being like that." Despite the lovely cool of the creek, she could feel trickles of sweat run between her breasts. She had to stop this conversation before her emotions got right out of hand. That would be a very serious mistake.

"Maybe it's proved a pretty effective defence," he suggested, as though he had discovered the answer. His handsome, dynamic face was caught in a shaft of sunlight. She realised he looked unexpectedly serious, faintly troubled.

"Against what?" Horribly, her voice wobbled.

He turned a concentrated gaze to her. "Do you remember when you were a little kid you used to pester me with questions?"

"The miracle is you used to answer me." Despite herself, she gave him her lovely smile, her green eyes changing from stormy to dancing.

"You had such an insatiable curiosity about everything. You read so widely, even as a child."

"That may have been because I was so lonely after my mother died. You know, sometimes when I'm walking about the lake, I hear her calling to me," she confided with a poignant little air.

That didn't surprise him. Many times he had fancied he had seen his own mother near the little stone temple that stood beside a secluded part of the lake. "We never lose the images of those we love," he murmured gently, wanting only to comfort her.

"She was a beautiful woman, Aunt Alexa. She was so kind to me." She sighed deeply, in many ways still the child denied her beloved mother. "After my mother died—the way she was killed—I thought I'd never get on my pony again. *You* were the one who helped me through that. Not my father. He was too dazed. He went off to some distant planet. It was *you* who convinced me it was what my mother would have wanted. She loved horses. She adored riding. You made me understand that although peril can be anywhere, we have to go on with our lives; we have to hold our simple pleasures close."

"Then I was good for something," he said, a faint twist to his sculpted mouth.

"You were. You *are*," she said, unbearably conscious of his closeness and the fact that they were alone together. But did it really have to put her in such a frenzy? Why, for the love of God, couldn't she relax? Was it because she knew Boyd, heir to the Blanchard fortune, would always be denied her? Maybe she had to accept, once and for all, that he was much too much for her.

The silence between them had taken on a deeply intimate turn whether she wanted it or not. She had the strongest notion that the nerve fibres in their bodies were reaching out to draw them together. When all was said and done, he knew her better than anyone. Her eyes smarted with tears. To be together like this always. To have their relationship develop and flourish as she wanted.

She knew in her heart that it wasn't possible. It wouldn't be allowed. That was the reason she kept that side of her hidden. Now alarm bells were going off in her head. How easy it was to slip into a dream. But it wouldn't do at all. Boyd was so far above her she couldn't begin to calculate the distance. Resolutely she squared her shoulders. "D'you want a race? Let's say to the old ruin?" she challenged him. The old ruin was what they called an extraordinary rocky outcrop on a wilder part of the estate.

"Flower Face, you couldn't beat me," he answered, slowly coming out of his elegant slouch.

"Then I'm going to have a darn good try." Abruptly she turned the mare, spurring her into action. They were tearing up the fairly sharp incline, vanishing down the other side while startled magpies croaked their high displeasure and wild doves shot up into the blue, blue air.

He was giving her a start. She knew that, not sure if in plunging away she wasn't revealing what an emotional coward she was. What made her so emotionally insecure? Was it because she had lost her mother at such a tender age? In many ways she had lost her father to his grief. Lord knew Delia hadn't turned out to be a mother substitute. She couldn't even mother her own son. Galloping wasn't half as dangerous as getting into an intimate conversation with Boyd.

She travelled so fast towards the ruins that an old time Western movie posse might have been giving chase. She wondered excitedly when he was going to close in on her.

To her left was a thick copse of cottonwoods, the golden poplars whose foliage put on such a wonderful brilliant yellow display in the autumn; to her right Chinese elms covered in spring's delicate whiteish-green samaras. Beyond that an indigenous forest of eucalypts in a country where the gum tree was king.

Did anyone who didn't ride realise the wonderful exhilaration of being in the saddle? Her breasts beneath her cream silk shirt rose and fell with her exertions. The balls of her feet, encased in expensive riding boots felt weightless in the stirrups. Compared to the order of the rest of the estate, she was heading into near virgin country as she veered off to take the short cut to the ruins.

She sucked in her breath as the remaining section of an ancient weathered wall threw up a challenge. The wall was covered in an apple-green vine with a beautiful mauve trumpet flower. It would be a very small risk taking the wall. The mare was a good jumper; she rarely stumbled, never baulked. Leona felt completely safe. She had taken far higher obstacles than this. Taking obstacles had claimed her mother's life, but everyone had agreed it was a freak accident, not a miscalculation on her mother's part. Leona trusted to her own judgement.

They literally sailed over the wall. She gave a great shout of triumph, even though her breath had shortened and her breasts were heaving. The old ruins were dead ahead. They looked for all the world like tumbled stone masonry and pillars. She knew she could beat him. What a thrill! She absolutely revelled in the thought.

When Boyd realised she was about to jump the old weathered wall his heart gave a great leap like a salmon making upstream. He wasn't sure, but he thought he shouted, "No!" In an instant he was back in time, caught up in a terrible moment of *déjà vu*. Reining the bay in sharply, he sat stock still in the saddle, back erect, but driven into shutting his eyes. Nothing ever really healed. For a moment he was a boy of fourteen again, waiting for Serena to return so they could all go swimming. He didn't think he could bear to suffer a *worse* loss. He had a vision of Serena's body, brought back to the house on a stretcher. The sorrow he had seen. His mother, Alexa, her beautiful face distorted by grief; the pulverising shock and grief of the others. Leona's father had been unable to speak, totally gutted. Rupert had taken charge of everything, as was his way, his strong autocratic features set in stone.

He opened his eyes again as he heard Leona's shout of victory. She was galloping hell for leather towards the ruins. Like her mother, she brimmed over with life. He was over his fear now, but for several moments he sat on his quivering horse, trying to quell the sudden upsurge of anger that swept in to take the place of his enormous relief.

"Sorry, Boyd, *dear*, I beat you!" She waved an arm high above her head and, not content with that, pulled off her wide brimmed hat and threw it rapturously in the air, bringing home her victory. "Goodness, you're not mad, are you?" she asked in the very next second, catching sight of the bright sharp anger in his face. He had dismounted, too, and was stalking towards her.

"Why do you take risks?" he gritted with what she took to be hostility.

"I don't. I never do." Hurriedly she tried to defend herself. "Risks? Don't be absurd." This was Boyd. How could she be afraid of him? Boyd would never hurt her. "You're upset," she said as she quickly comprehended. "There's no need to be. I wouldn't do anything stupid."

His eyes burned with the blue intensity of sapphires. "Your mother didn't do anything stupid."

Now both of them were confronting the past. She remembered the horror everyone had felt on that tragic day. The utter disbelief that life, as they had known it, was for ever changed. Her father had been near catatonic. The tears had poured out of Aunt Alexa's eyes. Geraldine had had her arms around her, trying to comfort a loved child. A Blanchard uncle was there with a second wife. That marriage hadn't lasted either. She remembered the way she had afterwards clung to Boyd like some little monkey too scared to let go.

Now she tried desperately to offer conciliation. "We've had a lovely ride. Please don't spoil it."

"Spoil it?" He knew he was losing control, something that never happened. "What you had to do was *not* tackle that damned wall. It could have cost you your neck."

Would anything go as she hoped? Temper flashed. "What I did," she told him defiantly, "was jump a fairly low obstacle. I've jumped a lot higher than that."

"Not on *that* little mare you haven't," he said with a vigorous jerk of his head towards the pure bred Arabian.

She stared back at him in disbelief, forgetting all caution, missing the fear behind his grimness. "So she isn't the tallest horse in the stable, but I love her. In any case she's sure-footed. Who the devil do you think you are, telling me what I can and cannot do?" she demanded. "Who are you to rule my life? No wonder I resent you. No wonder I've fought you for years. No wonder—"

She was on such a roll she was completely unprepared for his explosive reaction. Sparks seemed to be flowing from him like tiny glittering stars. While the blood rushed in her ears, he pulled her to him in a kind of fury, locking one steely arm around her, his left hand thrusting up her chin. "Oh, shut up bleating about your resentments and irritations," he bit off with unfamiliar violence. "You irritate the hell out of me."

He had confirmed it at long last. She let out a cry of pain.

"I was wondering when you'd get around to admitting it," she said, small white teeth clenched. They were standing so close together all her senses were reeling. Her blood ran blisteringly hot in her veins. To her distress she knew she couldn't handle this. She was shaking with the effort to hold herself together. Dazzling sunlight spun around them like an impenetrable golden web.

"Let me *go*, you savage!" Even as the words left her lips she was shocked that she had said it. Boyd, a savage! Why couldn't she shout, *I love you*? Why did she for ever have to hold it in? It was agony. There was no hope of getting free unless he released her.

"Count yourself lucky I'm not!" He laughed, but that didn't lessen the bright anger on his face. "I'm not going to let you go, Leona, until I've taught you a necessary lesson. No point in struggling. I've been far too indulgent with you, taking all the little taunts you throw at me on a regular basis. Just how long do I have to wait before you call a ceasefire?"

How could she possibly demolish the defensive structure she had so painstakingly built up in a matter of moments? "For ever!" she shouted fiercely, not fully realising how wildly provocative she had become.

And that sealed her fate.

With a face like thunder Boyd lowered his head. He hauled her right up against him, her delicate body near breakable in his grip, intent on finding her beautiful, softly textured mouth. He felt capable of something monstrous, like picking her up and carrying her off into the forest like some primitive caveman. Sometimes she literally drove him crazy.

The impact on Leona was equally tremendous. Yet hadn't she always known that something like this would happen? This was the man she loved. And, from time to time, *hated*. Because he made her feel so…so what? Off her brain? She couldn't move. Her riding clothes seemed to have turned to gossamer. She had to tense her body so it wouldn't dissolve into his. She had never experienced such tumultuous emotions in her whole life. It was seismic.

His long fingers plunged into her hair, catching up handfuls of red-gold curls. "I get so tired of your fighting me," he groaned.

Her legs had given way to the extent that she thought if he hadn't been holding her so powerfully she would have slid down his body to crumple at his feet. "Open your mouth," he said. "I want to taste you."

The sensuality of the moment was ferocious. It stole her breath. Desperately she clamped her lips together. The utter senselessness of it. His tongue prised them apart. "This is something else you can resent," he told her harshly.

To save herself from going totally under, like a swimmer in wild surf, she closed her eyes and let the giant waves of emotion engulf her.

He was kissing her, devouring her, eating her, as if her mouth were a peach. To make it worse, she was so driven by sensation she began to eat him. It certainly felt like it. All she knew was desire. It was terrifying. So sensuous, so *natural*, so voluptuous, so God-given. To ease the strength of his hold on her, she thrust one of her legs between his, making her acutely aware that he was powerfully aroused. And *she* was the cause of it.

When he let go of her—all but pushed her away—she felt so disorientated, so weak-limbed, she actually fell down into the thick, honey-coloured grasses that grew in a wide circle around the ruins. "I don't believe you just did that," she said eventually, her hands pressed to her temples as if they were pounding.

"It happened all right." Forcefully, Boyd drew air into his lungs.

"I hated it," she said. An outrageous piece of lying. And it wouldn't help her.

"Don't lie to me, Leo," he chided her curtly. "It won't work." He gave them both a necessary minute of respite, then he reached down to pull her to her feet, keeping a hold on her swaying figure.

Her green eyes met his, huge with shock. "But I *need* to lie to you." The truth would involve love and *love* was a fatal word. "Don't you understand? We're *cousins. Family.*"

He gave a jagged laugh. "Second cousins, more or less. Less, actually, when you consider your grandfather and my great-uncle were half-brothers."

"Does that make a difference?" How could she possibly steal Boyd away from the family? She knew Rupert fervently wished for an alliance between him and Chloe Compton, who was an heiress in her own right. How could she challenge powerful, menacing Rupert? She would never be allowed to walk away from that one.

"A difference to what?" Boyd rasped, uncaring of his father's plans, his own man.

"You mean you were doing me a great *honour* kissing me?" She felt unendurably pressured, not even sure what she was saying. Whether indeed she was making any sense.

"I didn't think for one moment you'd admit to a passionate response," he said bitterly.

How was she managing to hide all her yearning? She was a woman, flesh and blood, not a pillar of ice. But she *was* managing. She saw it in his eyes.

He was waiting for something from her—something important—only she was in such a state of high arousal she didn't know how best to answer. She didn't know how best to handle a situation she herself had created. Instead, she concentrated fiercely on a distant copse of trees. "Let's set the record straight. That was an *angry* response, more or less." Anger was safe. It was what he was used to from her, after all.

His expression became hard and mocking. "That's it! Do another runner." His brilliant blue eyes darkened to cobalt.

"And just who am I supposed to be running away from?" Unable to help herself, she took the bait.

"Hell, Leo, we both know that."

How she felt the power of those blazing eyes. She was shaking all over, engulfed by raging passions.

"Oh, for God's sake!" Boyd, contemplating her extreme agitation, suddenly relented. He reached out and drew her against his chest as if she were still a child, allowing her to stand until she was quiet within the half circle of his arms.

"Here, let's get you home," he murmured, somehow preventing his hands from sliding all over her perfect body. A body he wanted to cover like a man sought to cover the body of the woman he desired.

To Leona's ears, he sounded near defeated. That was *so* unlike Boyd—but he kept a supportive arm around her. It was a measure of his very real affection for her, she thought gratefully. Affection was allowed. The family would allow affection.

Boyd must have been on the same wavelength because he asked in a very dry voice, "Anyone for a cup of tea?"

She fell into line. "I don't drink tea."

"Neither do I."

"I know." She dared to look up at him, seeking some measure of reassurance. "Was kissing me a game?" If he said yes, she thought she might die.

"If it was a game, it's one I'm not sure I know the rules to," he said grimly.

"Sometimes I'm afraid, Boyd." She tried to explain herself.

Without her mother, with a largely "absent" father, she had become used to keeping things in. It was all right to worship Boyd. He was the supernova in the family. She was part of the clan certainly, but still fairly low in the pecking order. For her and Boyd to become romantically involved would cause huge problems. She could even lose her job. Would Bea allow it? She badly needed time to consider the magnitude of what had just happened. Both of them had responded so passionately they might have been trying to make up for lost time. Would the force grow, the desperation?

"Poor baby!" Boyd murmured, as though all too aware of her fears. He was suppressing urges so intense he didn't know how he was able to withstand them. "Come on." He used his normal persuasive voice. "Home." He bent to give her a leg up onto the Arabian mare, who was standing so quietly she might have been listening in on their conversation. Then, when Leona was in the saddle, he turned away to whistle up his bay, who was lightly grazing several feet away.

The secrets of the heart, he thought. It was time to bring a few of them out into the open. His feelings for Leona, the strong bond they had always shared, was stored in his blood.

CHAPTER THREE

"GOSH, THERE YOU ARE! I've been searching for you every-where." Robbie, looking almost distraught, rushed down the corridor of the west wing towards her. "Been riding?" He glanced down at her clothes.

"You know I love to ride," Leona answered, trying to gauge his mood. "What time did you get here?"

"Oh, about an hour ago," he said. "I had hoped we could have a game of tennis."

"I don't see why not." Leona lifted her wrist and glanced at her watch. It would be daylight for hours yet. Besides, physical exertion might dampen her flaming passions. "Is everything okay?" She stared directly into his dark eyes. Should she warn him that Boyd planned to have a little chat with him? Perhaps not yet.

"It is now." He shrugged cheerfully. "You know I'm lost at Brooklands without you."

"Even so, you seem off balance."

"I'm fine, Leo," he said, now faintly testy. "I had the great misfortune to run—literally—into Tonya. That woman is the very devil. Jinty is in wonderful spirits. She gave me a great big hug. If I didn't know better I'd have thought I was her favourite nephew. Rupe, needless to say, was overjoyed to see me again. Where's Boyd? Never sighted him."

"He came riding with me," Leona said, deliberately offhand though it took a huge effort. She continued on her way down the picture-lined gallery towards her room.

"Did he now!" Robbie exclaimed, following her up. "The relationship growing, is it?"

"Not that I'm aware of." She kept on walking.

"Despite the fact you're Boyd's marmalade kitten?"

She had to laugh at such a fanciful description. "I always thought of myself as the stray duckling."

"Ah, Leo, sweetie, you yearn for his good graces," Robbie said, loudly sighing. "So do I, for that matter. Black tie tonight?"

"You know it is."

"I bet you've brought something exquisite to wear." How beautiful Leo was, Robbie thought proudly. Glorious hair, glorious skin, glorious eyes—a romantic dream.

"Nothing else like it in the world," she joked. In fact she had brought two beautiful evening dresses with her. *You know who for.* "I tell you what. Let me have a quick shower after that gallop. Get into your gear and I'll meet you at the courts in around twenty minutes."

"You're an angel." He hugged her, an inbred Latin style in all his movements. "Shall I ask Simon and his girlfriend to join us? I think Simon is planning on announcing their engagement quite soon." Simon was one of the Blanchard cousins, also working for the firm.

"Good idea. Emma is so nice."

"And her family own a *nice* big sheep station," Robbie pointed out waspishly. "Let's not put that little fact aside."

"Ah, well, money usually marries money," Leona said.

"And power begets power. How enviable it all is! And a very good idea, I suppose. These days women get half of what a guy has if they split up, so why then shouldn't women bring a dowry with them like the old days? Rupe is madly pushing poor old Chloe at Boyd."

"Robbie," Leona reproved too sharply but she couldn't help herself.

"Leona," he responded heavily. "You have to remember there's always tremendous pressure on people with lots of money to keep up. They have *huge* overheads. Houses, cars, planes, yachts, skillions of employees. To old Rupe's eyes it would be utterly right to push Boyd and Chloe together. She's a nice girl. Bit dim but everyone likes her. Even me and I'm vaguely anti-women. After all, two fortunes are better than one. It's not marrying for money at all. It's plain common sense."

"Then maybe I shouldn't point out that Annalise quite likes you," she put in lightly. Annalise was one of the clan, an intelligent, graceful young woman, still at university.

"Does she really?" Robbie's lean cheeks flushed with colour.

Leona smiled at him.

"I'd never be allowed to court Annalise," he said gloomily. "I'm the peasant in your midst."

"Oh, don't start that phoney inferiority stuff again," she warned him. "It's all a pretence. Even I can see you're an attractive guy. There's no reason why you couldn't ask Annalise out. I'm sure she'd accept."

Robbie, for answer, suddenly vaulted effortlessly over an antique chair, one of several set along the wall. "Have you heard from the parents?" The acid was back in his tone. Leona's father and Delia were currently in London, a mix of business and pleasure. They weren't due back for another fortnight.

"I heard from Dad the other night," Leona volunteered, still concerned by how superficial that brief conversation had been. Her father might have been reading from a prepared script, though maybe he'd felt inhibited by Delia's presence most probably behind him.

Perhaps Leona's great likeness to her mother tied her poor father in knots. Instead of turning to her as all he had left of his beautiful young first wife, he had turned not away, but aside. Leona was certain that her father didn't love Delia. Never had. He had simply felt it necessary as a Blanchard, a man of consequence who moved in high society, to have a partner, a token wife. Delia, a career socialite, was glamorous enough. She could play her part. Without being in the same league as the main family, or occupying the same stage, her father was nonetheless a wealthy man. Delia would never have married a nobody, thus proving Robbie's sage theory.

"Mummy dearest was too busy to ring *me*," Robbie said, as though thrilled to bits that she hadn't.

"She didn't speak to me either, Robbie."

"We're like two lost children, aren't we, Leo? Makes us vulnerable, don't you think?"

A truth that couldn't be ignored. "Well, I don't intend to let it swamp me," she said. "Don't let it swamp you either. It's not easy being part and yet not a part of the mega-rich."

"Well, *you're* in," Robbie said. "You're part of the tribe. I never will be." They had arrived at her door.

"You've got lots going for you, Robbie. Now, go change. I'll meet you down on the courts. We'll beat those two."

"A piece of cake!" Robbie smiled, returned to good humour.

By the time they came back from their triumphant doubles match the house had its full complement of weekend guests. Pre-dinner drinks in the formal drawing room. Dinner at eight. Leona loved these occasions. She loved seeing the men in black tie. She loved being given the opportunity to dress up. She knew Jinty and the highly ambitious Tonya would be looking their most glamorous. The sisters bore a close family resemblance, both blond and blue-eyed, but whereas Jinty made the most of her eye-catching full figure, Tonya had elected to go for skin and bone. For that matter Leona couldn't actually remember ever seeing Tonya eat anything.

She had wondered why Chloe Compton wasn't among the guests until Geraldine had informed her that Chloe was attending the wedding of an old school friend in Auckland, New Zealand.

"Chloe won't go away. Dearie me, no!" Geraldine offered, somewhat darkly.

"Go away?" What was Gerri going on about?

"Don't be dense, child." Geraldine had actually pinched her. "It doesn't suit you. Every last member of the Compton tribe is campaigning for Chloe to become Mrs. Boyd Blanchard."

"But I thought you *all* were!" Leona answered in amazement. "Let's face it. It's Rupert's dearest wish."

"Bugger Rupert!" said Geraldine.

Bathed, make-up and hair done, Leona looked down at the two evening dresses spread out on her Versailles-style bed. One was a beautifully draped emerald-green georgette silk with a *faux* diamond brooch detail at the waist. Green, after all, was her colour and the dress was definitely sexy. Maybe too sexy. The other was chiffon of a colour that defied description. Neither pink nor apricot but a marvellous blend of the two. Bea had actually picked it out for her.

"This colour was made for you, Leona, my dear, with that magnificent mane of hair. Not many can get away with the ethereal style either, but you can. Take it. It's a gift!"

Closely fitted to the hip, embroidered to one side with

matching flowers and leaves, the neckline plunged, as was the fashion, the skirt flowed gracefully to the floor. No doubt about it, it was exquisite. And it looked even better on.

What kind of statement did she wanted to make? The *femme fatale* or the springtime nymph? In the end she opted for the ethereal, romantic look. No getting away from it, it did suit her style of looks and she was rather worried about pushing her sexuality. She couldn't afford to be too obvious about it. *Sweet little Leona* to Rupert—that was the way he would want her to remain. Rupert wouldn't hear of any other woman for his son but Chloe Compton. She understood that fully. And Rupert had long since developed the habit of getting everything he wanted.

But then—Boyd had kissed her. If he never kissed her again, she would remember it for her whole life. And, remembering, live off it. Wasn't there a law that said one was only allowed one great love in life? She hoped not.

When she walked into the drawing room in her high heeled evening sandals, her chiffon skirt floating around her, everyone with one notable exception, looked at her with open pleasure, Peter Blanchard, one of the cousins, with open adoration. She had known Peter all of her life. He had been her escort on many, many occasions and she was very fond of him. He was good-looking, clever and charming in his way. He had a number of university degrees under his belt, one from Harvard Business School. Like most of the clan, he worked for Blanchards.

Unfortunately, he couldn't hold a candle to Boyd, who was staring across the room at her, blue eyes glittering. She started to breathe deeply. That was right. In and out. She had the sudden delirious notion that her dress had turned transparent. Her glance shot away to Rupert, who was smiling his approval. Rupert was standing with his son in front of the fireplace, with its white marble surround and magnificent eighteenth century English mirror. Both men were of a height, both possessed of a charisma that commanded attention.

The fireplace when not in use in spring and summer was generally occupied by a large Chinese fish bowl filled with masses and masses of flowers and greenery. Tonight the big blue and white bowl held a profusion of pink Oriental lilies, with twisting dried branches, spear grasses and a fan of palms. Leona noticed abstractedly that the lilies matched the colours of her dress—pink with speckled golden-apricot throats.

Geraldine, seated on one of the damask upholstered sofas in conversation with one of the Blanchard wives, waved her over. She presented a vision of striking eccentricity in her favourite imperial purple with diamond and amethyst earrings as big as chandeliers swinging from her ears. Tonya was half turned away, as though Leona's entrance had been staged and in any case was of no interest to her. Champagne glass in hand, she looked very glamorous in a short evening gown of a deep glowing shade of fuchsia. All the women had made a real effort to sparkle and glow. Simon's serene Emma wore blue to match her eyes. It was a comparatively modest gown given the evening wear around her, but she wore it with unselfconscious ease, certain of her place in the scheme of things.

And here was Jinty, the hostess with the mostest. That certainly applied tonight. No one, but no one could hope to outshine Jinty, Leona thought as Jinty flowed towards her. She had gone all out tonight. Money simply wasn't an issue. She wore a couture black satin strapless gown, above which her creamy bosom swelled proudly. Her thick blonde hair was coiffed to perfection, swept up and back. She would have a hairdresser in residence. But everything was simply a backdrop to showcase the "Blanchard Diamonds".

They were so glorious that the owner of the most magnificent collection of jewels in the world, the Queen of England might have envied them. The suite comprised three pieces— necklace, pendant earrings and bracelet. All white diamonds, they were colourless and flawless. A double row of pear-shaped diamonds encircled Jinty's neck. Appended to the bottom row was a large square-shaped diamond enhancer enclosing a huge canary diamond that Leona knew weighed in at over thirty carats. The earrings alone featured two nine carat drops that flashed and scintillated with Jinty's every movement. Everyone in the family knew the suite had been acquired at the turn of the twentieth century from a famous South African billionaire who had plenty more where they'd come from. The diamonds had been mined at De Beers, Cecil Rhodes' first diamond mine. So the suite had a history.

The last time Leona had seen the whole suite Aunt Alexa had been wearing it at a grand state ball. Jinty often wore the superb earrings. Sometimes the bracelet. But so far the necklace hadn't had an outing. Tradition had it that the suite was to be handed down through the generations for the use of the current wife of the head of the Blanchard family. Which made Jinty merely a custodian, which was a blessing. If Rupert and Jinty ever split up, her share would be in multiples of millions, but she would never get away with the "Blanchard Diamonds".

"Jinty, you look simply marvelous!" Leona said, because she *did*.

"Why, thank you, dear!" Jinty responded brightly. "The diamonds make me feel like a goddess."

"They look wonderful on you. They really do." And she meant it.

"And you look perfectly beautiful as usual," Jinty responded graciously. "Where did you get that dress? The colour is extraordinary. Especially with your hair."

"Bea picked it out," Leona said.

Jinty gave a faint shudder. "Can't stand the woman, though I know she's a genius of sorts. Ugly though, don't you think? Rupert won't hear a word against her. Now, I must get you a glass of champagne." She turned away in time to see Boyd approaching. "Ah, here's Boyd with one," she said brightly.

Boyd stopped in front of them, handing a glass of champagne to Leona. "No need to tell you you look ravishing, Leona," he said, an unmistakably caressing intonation in his voice.

"That she does," Jinty seconded rather abruptly. "Where's that stepbrother of yours, Leo? We can't go into dinner without him."

"There's plenty of time," Boyd murmured, looking towards the entrance hall. The circular library table that stood in the middle of the spacious hall, which was paved in a diamond pattern of marble and stone, was the perfect spot for another stunning flower arrangement, this time a profusion of roses, gerberas, lisianthus and leaves. "Here he is now," Boyd said as Robbie suddenly hove into view.

"Slowcoach!" Jinty spoke crisply, a little afraid of Robbie's satirical tongue. She didn't linger, but moved off as though her husband had beckoned. He hadn't.

Leona stood with the fragile crystal wineglass in her hand.

"Come and sit down," Boyd said.

"Geraldine was looking out for me."

"Geraldine can have her moment later. You're mine now." His hand slipped beneath her elbow. Maybe she was becoming paranoid, but she had a sense that the whole room had snapped to attention. Tonya of the high slanting cheekbones was looking daggers at her. Tonya was having a lot of difficulty accepting Boyd was as good as spoken for. Ignoring the competition, especially in the form of Chloe Compton, was a heroic effort or a piece of madness on Tonya's part so far as Leona was concerned, but Tonya had thrown herself wholeheartedly into the hunt.

Maybe all we women are delusional, Leona thought. Seeing signs and intentions where there were none.

Robbie, looking gratifyingly handsome and very Italian in his formal gear, which any discerning eye could see *was* Italian and a perfect fit, met up with them in the centre of the drawing room with its apple-green and gold upholstery and curtains and a splendid duck-egg blue, white and gold plated ceiling.

"Sorry I'm late," he apologised. "Usually I don't have a problem, but I had trouble with my tie. You look wonderful, Leo." His dark eyes moved over her with pride and admiration. "Doesn't she, Boyd?" he queried, not so artlessly.

Boyd just smiled. "I don't know if wonderful quite says it, Robbie. Magical comes to mind."

Robbie suddenly caught sight of Jinty. "Good grief!" he breathed. "What's she got on, the Crown Jewels?"

"Those, my man, are the Blanchard Diamonds," Boyd corrected him. "Not the same thing."

"You've seen the earrings before," Leona reminded him. "Jinty often wears them."

"But the necklace!" Robbie was looking dazzled. "I've an overwhelming desire to go over and take a closer look, but I don't know what would happen. Our Jinty has a mean streak. She might punch me in the nose. I have to say those diamonds look great on her, but think what they would look like on *you*, Leo!" He turned to her.

"No, no, no!" Leona shook her head vigorously, making the deep waves and curls dance. The Blanchard Diamonds were destined for Boyd's *wife*. She wasn't wearing a necklace anyway. She had nothing that could remotely match the jewellery around her in any case. But she was wearing her mother's lovely earrings, a daisy wheel of pink sapphires and tiny diamonds with a silver baroque pearl appended from each.

"A Midsummer Night's Dream!" Boyd suggested. "You don't need diamonds, Leo. A crown of flowers on your head would be perfect."

Robbie stared up at the taller man. "That's it *exactly*. God, you're a romantic guy, Boyd. No wonder the women love you. You say really romantic things."

"To Leona, I think you mean?" Boyd's voice was vaguely self-mocking.

Robbie was still staring back at Boyd thoughtfully. "Come to think of it, yes. To Leona." He made a sudden move. "Listen, I'm going to grab a Martini."

"As long as you don't make it bath-sized," Boyd warned. Some time tomorrow morning he intended to have his little talk with Robbie. He would not be allowed to continue on the path he'd been taking.

By eight o'clock everyone was seated at the long mahogany table. Twenty-four in all, looking as though they belonged perfectly in such a grand room. It was Jinty's job to keep an excellent table. Rupert expected it of her, so she had made it her business to employ the best people. Older members of the clan, however, had privately expressed the opinion that occasionally Jinty's food was too exotic for their taste.

Leona had been placed beside Peter, a little right of centre table. Robbie was opposite her. Geraldine was to her brother's right. Boyd was seated to Jinty's right with Tonya all but opposite him. Everyone was arranged according to the pecking order.

"Some artistic genius has arranged the flowers," Leona remarked to Peter, touching a gentle finger to a rose petal.

"Can't be Jinty." He bent closer to whisper in her ear. "Some of darling Jinty's early floral arrangements went spectacularly wrong."

Strangely, it was true. Leona had previously thought one could scarcely go wrong with beautiful flowers but obviously there were many routes to getting things right. There was definitely an art to mixing colours. Tonight, tall glass cylinder vases wrapped in ivy, equally spaced down the table, held an exquisite mix of yellow and cream roses and buttercup-coloured day lilies. No doubt the flowers had been chosen to complement the cream damask cloth, the gold and white plates and the gold napkin rings. It all looked very lovely.

The first course was served. Superb large white scallops on an Asian risotto cake with fresh pesto and lime slices. That went down well. Sipping at her crisp white wine, which had a tang of citrus to it, Leona caught Boyd's eye. Instantly she experienced an electric touch to her mind, heart and body. How easy it was to become lost in that profoundly blue gaze.

Peter was saying something to her, but she barely heard.

"Are you listening to me?" Peter tapped the knuckles of her hand for attention.

"Of course I am." She had to gather herself. "You were talking about your trip to Antarctica. How it changed you for ever."

Peter smiled, pleased she had been paying attention. The whole family knew he had a real thing for Leona. It was as though he couldn't get past her. "It's an amazing place. A world of blinding white ice. It might sound strange, but there's only one other place in the world where I've been so overwhelmed."

"Our Outback," Leona guessed. "The vastness, the mystical quality, the extraordinary isolation?"

"Very good." Peter tapped her hand again. "Both places

have had a powerful effect on me. Sometimes I think I would have liked to be an adventurer," he confided, giving her his endearing smile.

"Instead you're inordinately clever at handling a great deal of money, Peter."

"Well, there's something in that. Can't wait for the polo match tomorrow afternoon. That's what I need, a damned good gallop. You're going to be on the sidelines cheering me on?"

"Wouldn't miss it for the world," she said, smiling.

The main course arrived. Nothing too complicated, more a classic. Racks of spring lamb with a buttery, crisp green herb crust served with a medley of vegetables including freshly baked young courgettes stuffed with peas and spring onions.

Conversation around the table flourished. These country weekends had become something of a ritual. Down the opposite end of the table, their hostess, Jinty, kept talking to Boyd, obviously captivated by his conversation. It was obvious to them all that she was fascinated by her stepson and oblivious to the building tension in her sister, Tonya. Looking at Tonya's strained, impatient face, Leona could feel the turbulent current from where she was sitting. Robbie, across the table, kept catching her eye, his dark eyes glistening with malicious humour. She could read what he was telling her. What did Rupe think about his wife paying so much attention to his son? Rupert, as sharp as they came, would have been observing what was going on. An intolerant man at the best of times, Rupert might have a few words to say to Jinty when the evening was over. He would know Boyd was simply being Boyd, a brilliant conversationalist who, without any effort on his part, became the object of women's fantasies.

* * *

Desserts arrived. A choice between a bitter chocolate mousse tart and Rupert's great favourite, a richly flavoured deep-dish apple pie served with double cream.

"I hope Rupert doesn't make a habit of ordering up that apple pie," Peter murmured. "There has to be an incredible number of calories in it and just look at how much extra cream he's putting on!"

"Don't worry, Rupert will live for ever," Leona murmured back, thinking mournfully that only the good died young.

After a lingering coffee and liqueurs everyone adjourned to the drawing room, where Jinty was to entertain them. Jinty was quite an accomplished *chanteuse*, using her mellow *mezzo* to sing everlasting blues favourites made famous by the likes of Ella Fitzgerald and Peggy Lee. To top it off, she accompanied herself on the big Steinway concert grand.

"Don't clap too much," Peter, who wasn't a music lover, warned Leona in a quick aside, "or we might be here until four in the morning."

As it was, Jinty knew the perfect moment to stop. The entertainment had gone on for the best part of an hour. Now a genuine round of applause broke out when she rose, tall and voluptuous from the piano seat, her somewhat haughty face softened by such appreciation. She gave a little bow, the lights from the four matching giltwood chandeliers as nothing compared to the dazzling white flashes given off by the "Blanchard Diamonds".

"I'd give my soul for the earrings alone," one of the Blanchard wives was heard to whisper to her husband, perhaps as an incentive for him to work harder.

Leona felt she knew better than that. The soul was sacred. Bad enough to give your heart away.

Boyd was much in demand. So much so it was difficult to

get near him. Even Tonya's all out efforts at seduction were being sabotaged. One of the great-uncles, a distinguished High Court judge had detained Peter who, though desperate to get back to Leona's side, was compelled to pay his respects.

It was a beautiful evening, the great coffered dome of the sky awesome with stars. Some of the guests had begun to step outside for a breath of garden-fragrant air and to cool the overflow of emotions induced by Jinty's scintillating performance. Turning her head, Leona just chanced to see Jinty quietly remove her diamond pendant earrings—which must have been quite heavy—and slip them into a Limoges ormolu mounted covered bowl, one of a collection on a small circular table that was supported by two gilded swans, their long elegant necks bent.

Now that was careless. Reckless, even. It would be a disaster if any part of the suite went missing. Clearly Jinty trusted everyone, guests and servants alike. Not that Leona didn't, but still… She couldn't in a million years have done it, was amazed that Jinty had. She couldn't begin to imagine Rupert's wrath if the earrings disappeared. Not that anyone foolish enough to attempt such a criminal act could hope to sell them on the open market. In their own way, the "Blanchard Diamonds" were famous.

Right away she headed towards Jinty to what…remonstrate with her hostess…issue a warning? Jinty wouldn't take kindly to that; married to Rupert Blanchard, she was queen of all she surveyed. Nonetheless Leona was halfway across the room, chiffon skirt flowing, a springtime nymph in flight, when a black-jacketed arm reached for her.

"What's the hurry?"

Excitement surged. She spun to face him. "I was just going to…going to…"

"Get it out, Flower Face," he urged.

What could she possibly say? Jinty has taken off the diamond earrings and left them in a Limoges porcelain bowl back there. Surely an unsafe place? It struck her forcibly that Jinty wouldn't want Boyd to know that. The diamond suite, after all, would one day be handed down to Boyd's wife.

"I was just going for a breath of air," she managed, realising that Jinty needed protection.

"You mean you were going into hiding from Peter," Boyd suggested dryly. "You really should put poor old Pete out of his misery."

"I've never put him *in* his misery," she said sharply. "I can't help it if Peter's got a bit of a crush on me."

"Bit old for a crush, isn't he?" Boyd offered in a sardonic tone of voice. "Peter must be twenty-eight."

"So?" She stared defiantly into his brilliant eyes. "Haven't you heard of men having crushes in their eighties? There was Goethe for one. Tolstoy, I'm sure. Great-Uncle William fell for that twenty-year-old ballet dancer, remember? People in their nineties find their one true love in nursing homes. There must be plenty of others."

"Please, that's more than enough," Boyd said, drawing her to his side. "Don't let's have a brawl here. I've been praying we'd get a moment alone."

"Praying?" The familiar banter had resumed. "I didn't think you liked me all that much."

"But I do enjoy kissing you," he said, sweeping her out onto the terrace. "Where did you learn to be so darn good, by the way?"

"It's called doing what comes naturally." Leona smiled and waggled her fingers at Geraldine, who was standing with a little group of her closest family allies. Geraldine waggled her fingers back, her grey eyes sparking with interest.

"Then you were born an expert."

"So were you." There wasn't time to add anything further.

"Quick, over here," Boyd said, almost lifting her off her feet.

"Whoa!" She blinked, wondering what had happened, then it clicked. "Ah, you've spotted Tonya." She didn't bother to stifle her impish glee. "Or could it have been Jinty. She's *awfully* fond of you."

He was steering her down a camellia-lined path, walking fast. "I wish she'd remember she's a happily married woman," he said, as though it bothered him.

"That doesn't make her immune to your appeal," she mocked. "And *is* she so happy?"

They were sliding like shadows away from the broad circle of exterior lights and into the mysterious glimmering light beneath the canopy of trees. "Jinty treasures money," he said.

"So do most people," Leona added dryly. "They say they don't, but they do."

"Only Dad is in a position to be far more generous than most men. Money matters a great deal to women like Jinty."

"So when Rupert says *jump,* Jinty has to jump." Leona didn't like the idea of jumping on demand.

"I guess that was the deal," Boyd said, his tone dry as ash.

"Does it always have to be deals where there's money?" she asked. "Shouldn't love be stronger than any deal?"

"I'd like to think so," Boyd said.

"Good thing you're your own man then," she mocked him. "Rupert has Chloe lined up for you."

"Think I need you to tell me that?" He glanced down at her, this ravishing young creature who lived to cross swords with him. "This time Dad's wishes and his judgement are way off kilter. I like Chloe. That's a long way from falling in love."

"My thoughts entirely. But she *loves* you," Leona felt

obliged to point out. "Listen, can you slow down? Those long legs of yours!"

"Sure," he responded immediately. "Leo, I'm not about to offer Chloe Compton an engagement ring, if that's what you're thinking."

"It surely doesn't matter what *I* think," she said. "I'm only your cousin. Of sorts. Way down the pecking order. About three would you say on a scale of one to ten? If you did want to please your dad and offer Chloe an engagement ring, Tonya might well have a nervous breakdown. It wouldn't be a pretty sight. Not to mention all your exes. Thought of that?"

"I'd be so pleased if you didn't mention my exes," he said. "Which does not include Tonya, by the way. Dad invites her just to annoy me."

"I'm so glad you see that," she said cheerfully. "But you have established quite a reputation as a ladies' man."

He brought them to a halt. "Stop, Leo," he said. "I thought this afternoon might have been lesson enough for you."

She turned up an innocent face. "This afternoon? I don't recall."

"Then let's give you a reminder."

In the second or so it took him to pull her into his arms Leona felt such a concentration of sensation—excitement, rippling desire, a meltdown in her limbs—it was almost terror. Boyd had the power to turn her inside out. Should she trust such power? Should any woman trust such power? And it wasn't just blind sexual yearning. It was much, much more. Like salvation. Or finding her true home.

His soul. Her soul. One and the same. Or had they in kissing opened a door that should never have been opened? Only time would tell.

His hand was lightly around her throat, his thumb gently stroking her chin up to him.

"I want you," he said, scarcely above a murmur.

She tried to speak and found she couldn't. Instead, she gave a convulsive shudder. Fear or longing or a mixture of both? Common sense told her she should pull away. This was Boyd, the Blanchard heir. Out of her league.

"This is madness!"

"Then I've been mad a long time," he said, his mouth trailing kisses all over her face.

Such an admission from Boyd made her forget everything. All sense of caution was in shreds.

His hand moved to her breast, trapped a nipple that had already blossomed.

It took time for cold reason to kick in. *Want?* It had all shades of meaning. Did Boyd want an affair? Did he want to solve the mystery he thought she was? It was a huge open question.

"Boyd, we must stop. This isn't possible…" she gasped.

His voice sounded fathoms deep in languor. "I don't think you really mean that. Anyway, it's happening." Very slowly, as though savouring the ecstasy of the moment, his mouth made its sure return to hers.

Her defences crumbled. Desire over reason. She couldn't resist it. He kissed her and kissed her. And she let him.

She was his. How could she now be deprived of him?

CHAPTER FOUR

TONYA DISCOVERED THEM returning to the house. "Where have you two been?" she called, her tone shrill and demanding.

Boyd laughed. "Tonya, what does it have to do with you?"

The darkness hid Tonya's flush. Even she couldn't miss the lick of sarcasm. "For heaven's sake, Boyd, everyone was wondering where you were, that's all."

"I have enough of the family on my back when I'm at work," Boyd responded, the arm Leona was holding tensing to steel.

"The fact remains that everyone wants to say goodnight." Tonya aimed a glance so fierce at Leona that her eyes glowed in the semi-dark. "Peter has been looking for you everywhere."

"Come on, Tonya," Boyd intervened. "Leona and Peter aren't a couple."

"You'd better tell *him* that," Tonya retorted with a knowing laugh.

"Tonya, why is it you get such an amazing number of things wrong?" Boyd wasn't trying to hide his irritation.

Instinctively Leona pressed her fingers into his jacketed arm, trying to soak up some of his flaring temper. Was Tonya a complete fool?

"I have the evidence of my own eyes." Foolishly, Tonya failed to see what was so obvious to Leona. She was making him angry.

"Then make a wish for a pair of glasses," he retorted curtly.

"Look, why don't we continue on to the house?" Leona made the hasty suggestion, wondering if she had a skerrick of lipstick left. Tonya would fasten onto that in a flash. God knew what questions would be asked then. Tonya obviously needed no encouragement to interfere in other people's business.

"If you were a good sister you would have seen to your brother," she said, rounding on Leona as if she were a recalci- trant schoolgirl. "He says the most impertinent things." Tonya's voice was filled with resentment. "It's difficult to stand there and take it."

"Robbie is given to speaking plainly," Boyd said. "One wonders why you wanted to come this weekend." His voice had taken on a note that would have alerted the thickest skinned woman.

Leona couldn't bear to see Tonya crushed, no matter how well merited the put-down. "Excuse me, won't you?" She broke away. She felt she had little option. They had nearly reached the terrace, which was now almost deserted. If Tonya contin- ued in a similar vein she would surely come to grief. Why was Tonya investing all her energies into trying to attract Boyd? Maybe she was mad after all.

"Where did you get to?" Peter was hovering just inside the French windows, obviously on the lookout for her.

"Were you worried?" Leona asked. Perhaps she should have filled out a logbook. Once she had said her goodnights to a downcast Peter and the rest of the party, Robbie moved swiftly towards her. For a handsome young man he looked ghastly. He was very pale beneath his suntanned skin, his lustrous dark eyes glittering like coals. Obviously he'd had too much to drink. Robbie always did go over the top.

"Where did you go?"

Leona had to fight for control. "You're the third person to ask me that. Or, in Tonya's case, *demanded* to know." Because she loved her stepbrother, she weakened, linking her arm through his, urging him towards the staircase.

"God, she's a stupid woman!" Robbie cursed. "Sometimes I find it hard to believe she and Jinty are sisters. At least Jinty had the brains and the cunning to land old Rupe. So where *did* you disappear to?"

"Boyd and I went for a stroll."

Robbie gave a low whistle, pregnant with meaning. "No wonder Tonya tore after you."

"Why is that exactly?" she asked, feigning ignorance.

"Sweetie, there's no way you can fool me. You've loved Boyd since you were a little girl. Now you're a beautiful woman. Boyd has made it pretty clear he can see that."

"And it will come to nothing," Leona said fatalistically.

"I don't agree with that at all." Robbie cut any further protests short. "You're special. Think Boyd doesn't know that? Just don't let him share your bed until you're well and truly married. I know plenty of girls who have blown their chances."

"I'll keep that in mind, Robbie," Leona said, thumping her hand on his arm.

They had reached the gallery by the time Leona stopped to take a really good look at him. He had a decided pallor. "What's wrong?" she asked worriedly. "You're deathly pale. You simply can't drink too much, Robbie."

Robbie shut his eyes. "Robbie?" She shook his arm.

"God, hell, no!" he replied. It wasn't blasphemy. It sounded more like a plea for forgiveness.

"Oh, Robbie, what's happened? You're in trouble, aren't you? I just knew it." Her green eyes darkened with anxiety.

"Talk to me, please." If Robbie couldn't pull himself together he had an uncertain future. That was the very last thing she wanted for him. "Here, come into the bedroom." She all but pulled him through her bedroom door.

"Don't leave the door open," Robbie warned, slumping into an ornate Louis chair. "Jinty's efforts at redecorating are atrocious," he moaned. "That bed, for one, is utterly ridiculous." He lowered his head into his hands.

"Forget the bed. What's wrong with you? Is there anything I can get you?"

"I'm not drunk, Leo. I know better than to break Rupe's house rules," he said, then broke into a wild laugh that had nothing to do with humour.

"Oh, Robbie, you're breaking my heart. What is it?" Leona went to him, laying her hand gently on his head. "Whatever it is, you can tell me. We'll face it together."

"I don't think even *you* will forgive me this, Leo," Robbie said, looking soulfully up at her. "I'll never forgive myself. I must be bad. And mad. Carlo, after all, was a scoundrel."

"Carlo wasn't a scoundrel." Leona surprised herself by coming to Carlo's defence. "I've always had the feeling that your father was badly maligned by Delia," she said. "She found it useful to denigrate him so she could get sympathy from the family. If I were you I'd look him up. I don't believe Carlo was anywhere near as bad as your mother makes out. She's a very devious and manipulative woman."

"And you're not exaggerating," Robbie moaned. "But I do carry some Mafia genes." He reached inside his breast pocket and, to Leona's horror and amazement, withdrew Jinty's diamond earrings.

Leona was so shocked she said absolutely nothing. Then, after a moment, she gave a little sobbing gasp, bending over and clutching her breast as though she had taken a bullet right to the heart. "Robbie…Robbie…Robbie! What were you thinking? You're going to have to explain. Have you completely lost your mind?"

"Possibly temporary insanity," Robbie groaned, feeling a tidal wave of guilt and remorse. "I live among all these filthy rich people and I can't change places with a one of them. Money corrupts, Leo. It seduces. It leads you into temptation. And finally sin."

Leona stared down at him, her blood running icy-cold. "We have to get them back," she said decisively. "You saw Jinty put them into the Limoges bowl?"

"An incredibly stupid thing to do," Robbie muttered, as though Jinty's stupidity lessened his own crime.

"Nowhere near as stupid as your lifting them," she said. "What did you think you were going to do with them? The Blanchard Diamonds are famous."

Robbie slumped even further. "I told you I went cuckoo. It's a bloody nightmare. It didn't take me a moment more to come to my senses, I swear. I was desperate to find you, only you'd disappeared."

"And what was I supposed to do, put them back?" Leona asked incredulously. "I've spoilt you rotten, Robbie. I'm your sister. I've always tried to be there for you, and you go and do a thing like that to the Blanchards—Rupert will have you hanged."

"Good thing they don't hang people any more." Robbie gave a hollow laugh. "Forgive me, Leo. It was a mad moment over which I had no control. I wanted to get back at them. Most of them treat me like I'm dirt beneath their feet."

"Oh, stop feeling sorry for yourself," Leona flashed, then she went to him and took the earrings out of his clenched hand. "I have to get these back. And I have to do it right away."

Instantly Robbie rose to his feet, his face ashen. "I can't let you do that, Leo. It's time to be a man. I'll find Boyd. I'll explain what happened. He'll tell me what a bloody fool I am—tear strips off me—but he'll work it out."

"Not Boyd," Leona said. "We can't involve Boyd in this. I'll do it. They've all retired for the night."

"What if Jinty has already gone to collect the earrings and found them missing?" Robbie spoke with quiet horror, scratching a sharp finger down his cheek and leaving a trail of blood.

"She hasn't checked," Leona said. "She can't have. If she had, the whole house would be in an uproar."

"Hammerings on the door. The oldest rellie turfed out of bed. The likes of me strip-searched." Robbie brightened just faintly. "Let me do it."

"And what if you're caught out? No, leave it to me."

No one in the long gallery of the west wing, though the faces in the paintings stared very hard at her.

No one coming up or going down the grand staircase, unless they were the ghosts of Blanchards past. No sound of voices or footsteps either. It was as though the night had swallowed everyone up.

Leona had never felt so terrified in her life. The diamonds were freezing, like chunks of ice in her hand. The big chandeliers were off but there were still a number of lamps and sconces burning. She pressed on stealthily, quiet as a mouse, if ever a mouse would have been allowed to take up residence in such a house.

What if she met up with someone—Rupert? She didn't think she could deal with that. Rupert was famous for appearing when least wanted or expected. What excuse would she have for coming downstairs again? A book from the library, perhaps?

Who would possibly swallow that? Maybe an insomniac who read until sunrise? Could she say she had lost one of her own earrings? Danger in that. She was wearing them, for one thing, and the very mention of earrings would be sure to alert Rupert, who was equally famous for his sweeping powers of deduction.

God, she felt sick. Sick and shuddering with nerves. For a moment, she stood outside the drawing room, trying to sense if anyone was inside. Not that they would be in there singing songs. She glanced in quickly, then out again. How could Robbie have done such a lunatic thing? It was wrong, wrong, wrong and he would have been made to pay for it. Rupert, beneath the cultivated veneer, was a hard man. Maybe cruel. He certainly hadn't made Aunt Alexa happy.

By now she was convinced there was no one in the drawing room. A few lamps had been left on in there as well. But everything was very still. So still. Distressed, worried sick for Robbie, sick for herself, she moved into the beautiful quiet room like a girl with wings. She had taken the precaution of removing her high heeled evening sandals, replacing them with a pair of ballet-style flats. Now her footsteps on the carpet were soundless.

So far, so good!

Yet she felt like a thief, guilty as sin. Her heart was pounding so hard it had all but jumped into her throat. At any moment she expected Rupert or Jinty to materialise like a couple of sleuths hard on her tracks. She had to move faster. Finally she reached the little gilded table, putting out a trembling hand… *Please, God, help me do this.* But would or should God extricate her from sin?

"Leo?" a voice that surely wasn't God's said from behind her, making her jump. "What are you doing downstairs? Couldn't you sleep?"

Tears pulsed in her eyes. She couldn't seem to breathe as the anguish and humiliation rolled over her. The game was up.

"Leo?" Boyd said again. "Are you okay?"

He sounded very concerned. What should she say? No, I'm not okay. And I never will be again. Should she spin around, hold the diamonds out to him with a jaunty, I couldn't resist taking them. Now I'm trying to put them back. The family might destroy Robbie but Boyd would never destroy her. He most certainly would be shocked and appalled, but she knew he wouldn't turn her in. Boyd wasn't Rupert. He had a huge reservoir of heart.

At this point, perplexed and intrigued, Boyd, who had come downstairs to turn off lights, moved purposefully towards her. His strong hands descended on her delicate shoulders, bare except for plaited wisps of chiffon that served as straps. Slowly he turned her to face him, conscious that she was scarcely breathing. "Tell me what's the matter." Urgently he searched her face.

"Nothing," she whispered, averting her red-gold head.

"There must be something. What have you got in your hand?"

"Nothing."

He looked at her in disbelief. "Of course you have." He reached down to take hold of her hand and, as he did so, it went nerveless and the diamond earrings rolled out of her grasp and onto the exquisite Savonnerie rug, the diamonds all the while shooting out brilliant white lights.

"This isn't possible!" Boyd groaned, bending to retrieve them.

"I don't know what came over me." Her voice shook. She was shaking all over.

"Well, I do." Boyd began to ease her backwards into an armchair. "What the hell is going on here? Robbie's in trouble. Surely to God he didn't think stealing the earrings was a way out?"

This was horrible. He suspected Robbie already. "It had nothing to do with Robbie," she said, vehemently shaking her head.

"So you stole them, did you?" he asked, his voice full of disbelief and disgust.

"It was a moment of madness, Boyd. I wanted to try them on. I *knew* I had to return them. That's what I was trying to do. You mustn't have noticed, but Jinty took them off towards the end of the evening and put them in the Limoges bowl."

"Ah!" He considered that for a moment. "So recount your movements for me, if you would. At what late point of the evening did you make your move? Let's see, you were in the garden with me, getting kissed senseless. Then you said your goodnights and went up to bed. I saw you and Robbie going up the stairs together. Robbie, your 'kid brother'."

"I'm telling you the truth, Boyd." She looked up at him, looming so tall above her, with huge anguished eyes.

"No, Leona, you're telling me one big fat lie. Why didn't you just come to me? Then you wouldn't had to do this. Why didn't Robbie have the guts to come to me and confess?"

"Robbie had nothing to do with it," she repeated. She stood a better chance than Robbie.

"Oh, stop it!" Boyd said, as though he'd totally run out of patience. How formidable he looked! How handsome! He had taken off his jacket but he was still in his evening clothes, the collar of his white shirt undone, his black dress tie hanging loose.

"Someone's coming!" Leona gave a terrified gasp, starting up in alarm. She looked towards the entrance hall.

Boyd didn't reply. He grabbed her as if she were a doll, hauling her back against the green and gold curtains. "Kiss me," he ordered bluntly. "Kiss me and make it good!"

She did exactly as he told her, a captive in his powerful

embrace. Their mouths locked in a kiss that, strategy or not, deepened and deepened until her brain turned to mush and she was moaning his name.

"Well, this *is* a surprise!" Jinty stalked into the room like a goddess of the hunt who had caught up with her prey.

Leona couldn't speak for the life of her. It was left to Boyd to query smoothly, "Surprise? It can't be that big a surprise, Jinty. I've always had deep feelings for Leona and she for me."

Jinty's determined jaw set in unflattering lines. "If I recall correctly, you and Chloe Compton are to make a match of it." She sounded chilly and utterly shocked.

"That might be *Dad's* plan," Boyd said, "but not mine. I make my own decisions, Jinty. I thought you knew that. I'm no more in love with Chloe than—who shall I say?—I'm in love with your sister, Tonya. Oh, by the way—" Boyd keeping one arm around the deeply trembling Leona, dug the other hand into his trouser pocket "—you really shouldn't leave extremely valuable heirloom jewellery lying around. Is that why you came downstairs?"

Jinty's skin flushed as if she were in disgrace. "You have my earrings?"

"I have the *family* earrings, Jinty," Boyd said pointedly, swiftly seizing the advantage. "They will eventually come to my wife. It's a good thing I happened to notice where you put them." He held the earrings out to her and Jinty moved forward to take them, her features sharply honed with all manner of emotions.

"I'd appreciate it if you didn't say anything to your father," she said stiffly.

"Jinty, I wouldn't dream of telling him. Just be a little more careful with them in future."

Jinty, diamonds in hand, turned to go. "I may be a little

slow," she said, "but I had no idea what was going on with you and Leona."

"But nothing *has* been going on, as you put it," Boyd assured her. "Not until this weekend. I was giving Leo a little time, that's all. She's been enjoying her career. I'm sure we're all very proud of her, but now I've decided we have to get on with the rest of our lives."

"Does your father know any of this?" Jinty asked through clenched teeth. It was obvious she had difficulty speaking she was so clearly stunned.

"Not as yet. He's been too busy trying to push Chloe at me. I'll tell him when I'm ready. Leona will make the most beautiful bride."

Jinty couldn't get out of the drawing room fast enough.

"Has everyone taken leave of their senses?" Leona asked when she was quite sure that Jinty had gone up the staircase.

"Well, I'm certainly in possession of mine," Boyd said. "We'd better get you upstairs before you collapse. And you could tell that cowardly little brother of yours—"

"He's not a coward," she said loyally. "He wanted to return the earrings to the Limoges bowl."

Boyd ignored her. "You know another thing about Robbie? He's well over his ears in debt."

"Is he?" She moaned as if it was all too much for her.

"You *don't* know?"

Her green eyes were dark with dismay. "Well…he tells me everything, but…"

Boyd cut her off. "He's got himself mixed up with people who are little more than thugs. The kind who target young idiots like Robbie, a rich kid, an easy mark."

"Dear God!" Leona let her head fall into her hands. "I blame myself."

"Well, you would, wouldn't you?" Boyd returned very crisply. "You've been covering for Robbie for years. Where is he now? And don't, I beg of you, Leona, lie."

"He's in my room."

"What, hiding under the bed?"

"You know why he gets into trouble, don't you?" Leona made a passionate effort to try to absolve Robbie from some of the blame.

"He has an identity crisis?" Boyd asked, unbearably suave.

"Yes, he does. His father deserted him. Dad doesn't know what to make of him. For heaven's sake, he doesn't know what to make of *me*. The proverbial cat would make a better mother than Delia. Robbie has suffered."

"Don't be absurd!" Boyd cut her short. "Robbie wallows in his suffering when he's being looked after very well," he told her grimly. "He has a more than adequate allowance. He buys the best of everything from Blanchards, then forgets to pay off his account. He's at university. He's a fine athlete, good-looking and clever. My heart bleeds for him."

"So what are you going to do?" she whispered.

"Oh, give me a break! I'm going to knock him senseless."

Leona winced. "You wouldn't do that." Was it possible?

"What good would that do?" Boyd shrugged. "You tell Robbie I want to meet him ten o'clock sharp tomorrow morning in the hall. We'll go for a nice long walk together."

"Oh, thank you, Boyd. Thank you." She felt like falling to her knees and kissing his hand.

"Alas, not the end of the story, Leona," he said tersely. "I meant what I said. That wasn't a bit of play-acting for Jinty's benefit. You *will* make a beautiful bride. *My* bride. You belong to me. No one else. Consider that *our* deal. Robbie gets thrown a lifeline. But if there's a next time when he gets himself into a really bad situation, he can drown. But for now, *you* marry *me*. You're the only one who can give me what I want."

The more she scanned his dynamic face, the angrier she became. So angry she started to stutter. "So…can…you t-tell me exactly *why* you want me?" Her green eyes flashed and rosy colour swept into her face. She was maddened by his easy arrogant assumption that she would go along with his grand plan. Robbie or no Robbie, she wasn't going to accept this sort of proposal when it was clearly as he said, a *deal*.

"Is it because you think you *own* me? Or think you can. Is that it?"

For answer, he knotted his fingers through her rose-gold hair, drawing her mutinous face closer. Then he brought his masterful mouth down on hers, almost bruising in its intensity, leaving his indelible mark. "That's it," he said. "That's it exactly."

"But that's blackmail!" Her legs were buckling. The fine flavour of him was on her lips and her tongue. No matter what heart, body and spirit craved, it would be spineless to give in to him without a fight.

"You have the choice, Leona," he told her. "It's over for Robbie or we start a new life together."

It was near impossible to calm herself. "What if your father decides it simply won't do?" She knew that was bound to happen.

His expression hardened. "My private life is a no-go area where my father is concerned, Leona. *I* pick my wife, Leona. I choose *you*. I've known you since you were a child. I understand you better than anyone else. For your sake I'll make sure Robbie gets pulled very firmly into line. And it will go no further. In my view, Robbie is more pampered than suffering and it has to stop." He sounded so incredibly stern she could have wept.

"How long have you been thinking about this?" she asked, considering with a rush of horror that it might be one way of getting rid of *all* the women who were chasing him.

"Does it make a difference?" he asked suavely. "Let's just say tonight has brought things to a head. No need for you to say anything to anyone. Not just now, anyway. I'll handle all the preliminaries."

"Preliminaries? What the heck does that mean?" she asked fiercely, her redhead's temper coming to the fore. "And what if I don't go along with it all? You'll throw Robbie to the lions?"

"I should have threatened to throw him to the lions sooner," Boyd answered very crisply. "But you *will* go along with it, so we no longer have to consider it. I'll speak to my father some time this weekend."

"Not frightened of anyone, are you?" she said caustically. "Well, *I* am. Please wait until I make my getaway before you speak to Rupert. He'll be furious."

"Are you sure you've got that right?" He was staring down at her with his bluer than blue eyes.

"Of course I've got it right," she retorted, frowning at the question. "Little Leo stealing his precious son away?" She was trying very hard to stare him down, but she couldn't.

"Why are you trying so hard to throw up excuses?" A vertical line appeared between his black brows. "You're beautiful. You're clever. You can be a handful, like now. But, that aside, you're a real asset to the family. Any family. So why are you so incredibly insecure?"

She flushed with anger. "Maybe it's an age thing," she threw back with intense emotion. "You've got problems too, though

God knows you've got the capacity to go about solving them. I'm twenty-four. You're thirty. One can gain a lot of experience in six years."

"You're suggesting I wait until you're thirty?"

"Thirty is fine for you."

"I want you *now*, Leo," he said. "You're off your head if you think I'm going to give you even another year. Make it six months."

That nearly knocked her out. "You sound absolutely mad."

He sighed deeply. "No one but no one can make me as mad as you."

"Yet you're talking about marrying me. Let's make it clear. Do we live together or do we retain separate apartments?"

"Well, it's an idea," he said, then began to laugh. "Don't you think I can make you happy, Flower Face?"

She looked away from him, fighting tears. "The thing is, Boyd, you can overlook the need for *love*. Okay, I know we've got an emotionally charged relationship. You say you want me. I'm frightened to admit that I want you too. But you're not the first man to tell me he wanted me. I don't want to boast, but I hear it all the time. But *want*? What does that mean? Does it mean simply assuaging a sensual appetite?"

"It certainly does," he said, his voice deep and sexy. "How can it not?"

"Don't you dare laugh," she said. "You're always laughing at me. I need someone to *love* me. Really love me." She was so overwrought she was almost shouting. "Why *don't* you, Boyd?" she cried in a fresh upsurge of anguish. "There, you can't give me an answer." She totally ignored the fact that she had scarcely given him time to open his mouth. Instead, she spun like a ballet dancer, heading for the entrance hall.

"Leona!" he called after her.

His voice begged her to stop but she wasn't having a bar of it. She was a woman for whom love was all important. Boyd's love. She wasn't a commodity to be bought on the open market-place, she thought furiously. It was hellish to love someone the way she loved Boyd.

When she arrived back at her room she found Robbie pacing the carpet like a panther caught in a cage. "Well?" He turned to her with anguished eyes, no colour whatever in his cheeks.

Leona crossed the room to fall back on the bed. Her head was whirling with chaotic thoughts. She had to close her eyes and count to ten. After she did that, she said, "You're off the hook."

Robbie raised his eyes to the heavens. "Thanks be to God," he said piously. "I think I'll go back to church. You were able to put the earrings back?"

"Almost." She sat up, feeling dizzy, looking more delicately lovely than ever, her chiffon skirt spread out on either side of her.

Robbie's expression turned to one of dread. "You were caught?"

She nodded. "It happens, Robbie," she said sombrely, at the same time wanting to put him out of his misery. "Boyd chose that very moment to come downstairs to turn off the lights. He saw me in the drawing room."

"Holy Mother!" Robbie was so overtaken by weakness he had to slump down on the opulent day bed. "You must have been terrified."

Even now she couldn't suppress her feelings of panic. "Of course I was, but I felt enormous relief that it was Boyd. What if it had been Rupert?"

Robbie gave an agitated laugh. "True, we'd have had to emigrate to Antarctica. So what happened?"

"That's for *you* to find out," she said, feeling unable to

explain much further. She had to sleep on Boyd's extraordinary proposal. She was already well into convincing herself that it smacked of a convenient way out for him. When they weren't striking sparks off one another, they did get along extremely well. Naturally she would in time be expected to produce an heir or heiress, so it was really a marriage of convenience. A lot of people settled for that. Rich people more than most.

"Listen, Robbie. Boyd wants you to meet him in the hall at ten o'clock sharp," she said, forcing herself upright. "The two of you are going for a little walk. You wouldn't want him swearing at you in the house."

Robbie began madly slicking his dark hair back. "Boyd doesn't swear even when he's angry. The most I've heard is the odd bloody. So you told him? Why not? I *am* to blame. I should never have let you."

"You'll be pleased to hear I didn't tell him, Robbie," Leona said. "But Boyd knows me too well. He knows I wouldn't have taken the earrings. He guessed you had. He knows all about the bad people you're involved with."

Robbie remained very still. "So what's he going to do?" He looked straight at her, awaiting her response much as a man in the dock would await a jury's verdict.

"I've told you, Robbie. Boyd sees you as being cushioned by wealth. Now that I've been forced to think about it, you *are*. Look at that suit. It must have cost a couple of thousand. Dad gives you a comfortable allowance. You'll get your degree and, if you want it, you'll be given a good position within Blanchards. I'm very sympathetic towards your personal problems. Why wouldn't I be? I have them as well. It's the old story of an unstable childhood, but we've survived and we have so much else, after all. You have to liberate yourself, Robbie. Not keep drinking from the poisoned well. Find your father.

Confront him. You could go in the summer vacation. For all you know, Carlo might be thrilled out of his mind to see you."

Robbie gave a bitter laugh. "I'll ask him why he never invited me. But the big question is—am I going to be *free* to travel? It was a very bad thing I did, taking the earrings."

"The only thing worse would've been for you to try to *wear* them," Leona said, trying for some light relief. "It *was* a bad thing, Robbie. An insane thing for someone so bright. But you didn't go through with it. That's in your favour. It was a moment of madness." Always protective towards him, Leona slid off the bed to give him a reassuring hug. "We both know Boyd is going to read you the riot act tomorrow."

"That's what I need." Robbie's voice was filled with self-disgust.

"Well, you're going to get it and it won't be pleasant. Take it on the chin. Boyd has assured me the matter will go no further."

"He'd do anything for you," Robbie said, then looked her in the eyes. "It's all about you. Did you ask him?"

Leona hesitated for only a few seconds. "Actually, he asked me to marry him." She didn't say that he had more like *informed* her they were to be married. Not the same thing at all.

Robbie's woebegone face lit up as his fears virtually disappeared. He put his hands around Leona's narrow waist and began to swing her around like a child. "But that's marvellous. Bloody marvellous! I couldn't think of anyone in the world who would be more perfect for you!"

"No thoughts there might be plenty of girls more perfect for him?" Leona asked breathlessly when he set her down again.

"No way!" Robbie exclaimed, breaking into another delighted laugh. "You two are made for each other. Actually, I was starting to think that Boyd was taking his time."

"Wh-a-t!" Leona stared back at him, flooded with astonishment.

"Gosh, Leo, you *radiate* off one another. I'm not the only person to see it, you know."

"So who's the *other*?" she asked in amazement.

"Lots probably." Robbie shrugged. "But good old Geraldine, for one. She's a sharp old bird."

"No sharper than her brother, Rupert," Leona said. "I'd hate to see his face when he hears."

"But Rupe is very fond of you." Robbie frowned.

"Maybe he is in a way. But *not* as a match for his son."

"Sweetheart," Robbie spoke very tenderly, trying to buck her up, "if Boyd wants you, he'll have you. No one will stand in his way. Boyd's well on the way to becoming more powerful than his dear old dad. And a damn sight nicer person."

"And that wouldn't be hard."

CHAPTER FIVE

WHEN ROBBIE ARRIVED back at the house around midday he looked numb.

"Are you all right?" Concerned, Leona took him by the hand, much as she had done since he was a little boy. For a brief moment he took comfort from her presence, then he drew a deep breath, steadying himself.

"I'm fine."

"Then I'd hate to see you when you aren't." Quickly, she led him by the quietest route through the house into the garden, bypassing the terrace with its outdoor sofas, armchairs and tables where some of the family had congregated, enjoying the sunshine. A buffet lunch would be served from noon until the main event of the day, the fastest field sport in the world.

Robbie, an excellent horseman, was on Boyd's team, as was Peter and Peter's first cousin, James, through his mother's side of the family. The opposing team was made up of fine New South Wales players. But Leona was far from sure that Robbie should now play. Many polo players, like Boyd, found the element of danger alluring—as did Robbie, for that matter, but he looked as though all the stuffing had been knocked out of him. Predictably, the over-protective Leona felt upset for him, perversely blaming Boyd for having come on too strong. There was no logic to it, but Robbie brought out her protective instincts. Boyd, on the other hand, could look after himself.

When they were a distance from the house she drew him down a long pergola that had been mounted on splendid Doric stone pillars. Long tresses of the wisteria floribunda "Alba" cascaded from on high, softening the grandeur of the pillars. There was a little white trelliswork pavilion at the end of the walk, Mughal in style and embellished with a beautiful old-fashioned deep pink rose that clung to the abundant light green foliage. Here they could talk in privacy.

Robbie sat down beside her, then put his dark head into faintly trembling hands. "Thank God that's over!" Gratefully he breathed in the calming scent of the roses.

Long entrenched in the business of looking after him, Leona burst out, "Boyd must have been very tough on you."

"No more than I deserved!" Robbie sat bolt upright, half turning to face her. "Hey, don't go blaming Boyd for anything," he exclaimed, obviously surprised and concerned that she had.

"How can I not?" she said, distressed by his appearance. "It's obvious he's knocked you for six. How can you play this afternoon? Polo is a dangerous, demanding game. You have to have all your wits about you."

"Listen, Leo, I'm playing," Robbie answered emphatically. "I wouldn't miss it for the world. I just have to regain my balance. A good lunch will help. Actually, I feel better than I have in ages. Can't you understand that? It's like going to confession and receiving absolution. Boyd was much too generous. I don't deserve it. He'll get the bad guys off my back. He said a lot has been invested in me to succeed. He also said I have your love and loyalty—hell, he reduced me to tears about that. Anyway, I swear to you, Leo, I'm going to mend my ways. I'm going to turn over a new leaf. I'm going to make you and Boyd proud of me. I know I've caused you a lot of anxiety and I've leant on you terribly. That has to stop. *Both* of us have to stop seeing me as your 'kid brother'."

"Boyd said that, did he?" She bit her lip.

"It's true, isn't it?" Robbie appealed to her. "Why are you trying to find fault with Boyd in this? He's my saviour. I thought you loved him. You told me you were getting married." He took hold of her arm. "Hell, *I* didn't have anything to do with this sudden decision, did I?"

"Of course you didn't." Leona stopped that idea in its tracks. "It's just that I see Boyd as invincible."

"We all die, Leo," Robbie said gently.

She shivered in the golden heat. "Don't talk about dying!" For Boyd to die would destroy her. "It's just I've spent so many years—"

"Putting up a front with Boyd?" Robbie suggested. "In some ways I think you find loving him the way you do terrifying," he added very perceptively.

"Isn't love terrifying?" she asked. "Love also sets one up for loss. The bliss of my childhood was shattered by the loss of my mother. Dad turned into another person. I think he forced himself to remarry. You know, the couples thing."

"He could have done better than Mother," said Delia's only child, betraying the full extent of his emotional dislocation.

"Did Boyd say anything to you about—" she stumbled over the word "—*us?*"

"He said you'd agreed he'd make the announcement after he'd spoken to his father."

"Who won't be at all happy," Leona repeated, showing her anxiety. The last thing she wanted to do was cause big trouble. For one thing, it might rebound on her own father, who held a high position in the firm. Rupert was not a man to be crossed.

Sharp-eyed Robbie inspected his stepsister's lovely distressed face. "Why, Leo, sweetie, Boyd won't give a damn about that. I keep telling you. He loves you. You're the only woman in the world for him. Hell, I just hope I can find a woman I can love like Boyd loves you. Don't you know how lucky you are?"

"Did he *say* he loved me?" Leona asked, so very uncertain of Boyd's true motives.

"Leo, he doesn't have to," Robbie said. "When have *you* ever put into words your true feelings for Boyd? You've spent your time throwing dust in his eyes. I'd say Boyd has acted admirably. He's given you an opportunity to grow up, stand on your own two feet, carve out a career. He's very proud of you. We all are. Who cares about old Rupe? To be honest, I don't think Boyd cares a lot about him either. Well, he *is* his father, but I have the feeling Boyd has never forgiven Rupe for the hard time he gave his mother. I do remember Aunt Alexa as being the loveliest lady and so kind to me. Then old Rupe ups and marries that gold-digger, Jinty. How he could after losing a woman like Alexa, I'll never know."

Leona didn't know either. "For someone who is only twenty, you're very perceptive, Robbie," she said.

"That's true." He took the compliment for a statement of fact. "How did beautiful Alexa marry that wicked man? It couldn't have been the money. Alexa's family is old money, establishment."

"In case you haven't noticed, Rupert is still a handsome, virile man," Leona said wryly. "If Jinty left him tomorrow—"

"That will *never* happen," Robbie assured her. "Being Mrs Rupert Blanchard counts for everything in Jinty's world. I bet she's cursing the day Oz cut away from the Queen's Honours system. She could have been Lady Blanchard. Now, wouldn't that be something?"

"Actually, there is a Lady Blanchard," Leona said, referring to the English side of the family. "But my point is that Rupert could have his pick of goodness knows how many women. Some as young as me."

"Then it's really a form of prostitution, isn't it?" Robbie opined. "Selling yourself for money."

Leona swallowed. "Well, I suppose that's one way to put it."

"It could never be you." Robbie turned to her with his flashing white smile. "You and Boyd are not like them. You're marrying for love. Hell, I feel like dancing!" He jumped up and held out his hand. "Come on. Let's go back to the house. I'm starving."

The three polo fields received constant year round attention from Rupert's groundsmen to keep the surfaces in fine playing condition. With the more than welcome spring rains, Polo One, with perhaps the most spectacular setting, surrounded by rolling hills and magnificent shady trees was looking in great shape. A crowd of spectators from near and far was seated on rugs, collapsible chairs, bonnets, boots of cars, cushions and so on, right around the field. Those who weren't early enough to find the choicest spots beneath the trees made sure they brought big beach umbrellas to ward off the brilliant sun.

Each team was made up of four players, wearing a different coloured jersey, bearing the number of the position they were playing. Robbie, who had made a lightning recovery, was wearing a green Number 1 jersey, which meant he was the most offensive player. Peter Blanchard was Number 4, primarily responsible for defending his team's goal. Peter's cousin, James, was at Number 2. James was more experienced than either Robbie or Peter. Boyd, as team captain, wore a deep red jersey that for some reason made his eyes look bluer than ever.

Boyd, with an impressive armoury of strokes, was the highest rated player so he had the pivotal position of Number 3.

Leona, pre-match, moved freely about the gathering, greeting and being greeted by the familiar polo crowd. All four men on the Blanchard team looked stunningly handsome in their gear, a thought she was not alone in having; the tight-fitting white trousers, coloured jerseys, high boots, knee guards and helmets gave them the glamour of men in uniform. The opposing team looked pretty dashing too. To make it even better for the young female spectators, six of the eight players were bachelors.

In a cordoned off area beneath the deep shade of the trees were the polo ponies. A great polo pony was essential to a fine player's performance and proficiency. The Blanchard team was superbly mounted. There were twenty-four ponies in all, mostly mares, that had to be made available during a match, due to the extreme demands put on a pony during the six period chukkas. Four minute breaks were taken to enable the players to change ponies.

Polo, one of the fastest, roughest, most dangerous games in the world of sport, was thus a rich man's game. The upkeep of the teams of ponies alone was sufficient to keep it that way.

Leona was nervous. Nervous and excited too. She loved the game—the speed and athleticism of horse and rider, the strategies the brilliant pivotal players, like Boyd, came up with to clinch a game. But she had two men in her life to worry about. Boyd and Robbie. Dangerous collisions could and did happen even with the "right of way" rule. Robbie, though a fine player, was known on occasion to be downright reckless. Boyd, an even better rider, the far more experienced, subtle and considered player, was nonetheless given to spectacular displays especially on his number one polo pony, the beautiful mare, Andromeda, in play today. Robbie's opposite number was a player Leona had watched many times before. Without question an experienced player with a big range of shots, he wasn't above a bit of barging, hooking and blocking his opposite number to slow him down. Mostly it worked. So there was a duel on there. Even Boyd, who relied on thought, action and fantastic speed as opposed to dirty tactics, which actually made him the superior opponent, when the chips were down played his team to win.

Leona was wearing white—always good in the heat—a pin-striped fine cotton shirt with matching crisp white trousers, an eye-catching navy and white leather belt looped through the waistband. To complete the look she had brushed her hair high off her forehead, then caught it into an updated French pleat. She looked, as she always did, very chic. It was, after all, part of her job and so far as the family was concerned that was the way they wanted and expected to see her. Rupert had already complimented her on her appearance and kissed her on both cheeks. Obviously his son and heir hadn't got around to having that heart-to-heart talk. Well, she *had* told Boyd she wanted to be well clear of Brooklands when that happened.

Jinty had had the good sense to keep a still tongue in her head, not wanting to fall out with the Heir. Tonya, though, as always, had a jibe to share. "Don't you find white a problem?" she smirked, inspecting Leona from head to toe, immensely jealous and agitated by the way Leona's slender figure and glowing head was soaking up all the sunlight.

"I'm not going to dig the garden beds, Tonya," was Leona's reply, her tone pleasant. Keeping one's cool in the face of Tonya's contrived insults and barbs only served to irritate Tonya the more. Tonya herself was looking bone thin but very stylish in a deceptively simple shift dress, its colour almost a match with Boyd's red jersey.

Robbie, then Peter, came up to Leona, expecting and getting good luck and best wishes for a win. Peter put his arm tightly around her in some sort of claim, before his kiss landed on the side of her mouth, despite her best attempt to dodge it.

Nevertheless she knew the clinch would set off a chain of gossip. She remembered how one elderly member of the family had had a girl pregnant from a single kiss she'd caught one of the cousins exchanging with his then girlfriend. "Such things do happen!" was the dire warning.

"That boy's in love with you," Geraldine now told her, shaking her arm as if to put her on the alert.

"What a lot of rot, Gerri!" Leona tried to answer carelessly.

"Not rot, my dear," Geraldine corrected her firmly. "Just be sure to tell him you're spoken for."

Spoken for? Leona felt the hot wave of colour stain her cheeks. "Are you going to tell me how you heard that?" Boyd was very close to his aunt. He must have told her.

"I've heard nothing. So far," Geraldine maintained, adjusting the brim of her straw hat to a snappier angle. "I have *eyes*."

Leona fell into the deckchair beside her, urgently taking Geraldine's hand. "So what exactly is it you think you've seen? And with whom?"

Geraldine patted the small fine-boned hand that held hers. Then her shrewd grey eyes went past Leona's lovely, imploring face. "He's coming over right now. Don't look so worried, child. I've had my suspicions for quite a while."

"Oh, my goodness!" Leona jumped up, stopping only to whisper in Geraldine's ear, "Gerri, I swear I'm frightened of you."

"Don't be frightened, child," Geraldine looked up with a reassuring smile. "Everything will be fine."

All it would need was a miracle.

"Flower Face, still running away?" Boyd swiftly caught

up with her as she dodged through the trees, catching hold of her hand.

"I have to, Boyd. I'm feeling absolutely stretched." Indeed she was. She rounded to stare up into his sapphire eyes, gem-like against his bronzed skin.

"You want us to have a nice quiet game?" he asked with such a beguiling half smile.

"Damn it! The game's only half of it," she said spiritedly. "I am nervous for you and Robbie. I couldn't bear it if either of you were injured."

"For heaven's sake, I thought all your thoughts were with Peter!" he scoffed. "Where does he get off, hugging you like that? I was gratified to see you turn your head away. He was most certainly aiming for an off-to-the-wars type kiss."

"Well, he didn't get it!" Leona said in a tart voice. "Have you said anything at all to Gerri about…about…us?"

"One would have to get up very early in the morning to take Gerri by surprise," Boyd said. "Gerri's a mind-reader. Why, has she said something?"

Leona bit her lip. "She said everything will be fine."

"And so it will," he said. "So, are you going to wish me luck?" Those blue eyes sparkled a challenge at her.

"Think you're clever, don't you?" she muttered. On impulse, she reached up and pulled his shining blue-black head down to her. "Good luck, *darling* Boyd," she crooned in a sweet seductive voice, her green eyes alight with malice. With infinite gentleness she cupped his dynamic face in her hands, then she kissed him squarely on his sardonic mouth.

There! Served him right! She never could resist his dares.

On her way back to her chair, Leona ignored the expressions on the faces all around her. Some were soft with astonishment, others hard with calculation. The family was already divided in its opinion of Leona and Boyd as a couple.

"Think you're a siren, don't you?" Tonya, frowning fiercely in the grip of jealousy, hissed at her as Leona passed close by. "Don't get your hopes up. You'll never lure Boyd."

"Still, he's just *wonderful* to kiss," Leona pretended to gush, hastening to take her place beside Gerri. The match was due to start.

Robbie, nicely set up by his captain, scored the first two goals.

"Oh, jolly well played!" Geraldine clapped enthusiastically. "Of course it was Boyd, the tactician, who turned the play to offence, but I must say Roberto responded brilliantly. I'm just loving this. Rupert was a darn fine player. But you wouldn't remember all that well, would you, dear?"

"Of course I do," Leona said. Rupert, approaching sixty, had been warned off the game by his doctor after a number of bone shattering "bumps" and one crashing fall in his late forties.

"Didn't have Boyd's finesse, though," Geraldine further commented.

As the match progressed it became apparent that it was a duel of wits between Boyd, captain of the Red Team, and Bart Ellory, captain of the Blue Team, the two most experienced players on the field. From time to time Leona found herself with a clenched fist to her mouth, while Geraldine persisted in jumping to her feet at her nephew's heroic deeds. The crowd was getting a superlative display of horsemanship and polo sense. Given yet another opportunity for scoring by his captain, Robbie got set for a full free swing, his team mate Peter wisely giving him plenty of room. A few seconds more and Robbie put the ball across the goal line, bringing the crowd to its feet.

At half-time the score was six-three for the home team. The second half promised to be a cliff-hanger.

"I don't know that my heart can take it!" Leona said, accepting the cold glass of sparkling lime and lemon that was handed to her. What a day! Just how many people had seen her kiss Boyd? How many more had heard about it since? Rupert was sitting with his cronies some small distance away. Eventually, Leona supposed, it would get to him.

What form would his outrage take? Leona was forced to ask herself the question.

Just minutes before full-time, facing a two-pronged attack, a member of the Blue Team frustrated by Boyd's superior speedier game, suddenly created a hazardous situation when he crossed the line setting up an inevitable collision and a certain foul that would result in a penalty. Leona didn't want to look but she couldn't turn away either. Her heart had jumped into her mouth and a wave of sickness welled up from the pit of her stomach. Even Geraldine gasped in fright and began to wipe away the perspiration that broke out on her face with a lace trimmed handkerchief.

Boyd's control of himself and his mount was nothing short of superhuman. Somehow, he managed to pull out of what looked like an imminent spill.

"You can breathe again, lovey," Geraldine instructed Leona, still gasping from the near miss.

Is anyone I love safe? Leona asked herself. Only that day she had called Boyd invincible. Well, she had been made to suffer for it. Boyd was the heart of her. The meaning of everything.

The silent crowd broke out into such applause that it bounced off the hills as the whistle blew, announcing a win for the Red Team. Now for the lavish afternoon tea with all the trimmings. It was Leona's experience that most people ate everything on offer.

Her own stomach was so upset she didn't think she could touch even a cupcake. A cup of coffee, however, would go down well.

By sundown just about everyone had headed off home, the outside spectators as well as family.

"What about lunch soon?" Robbie asked as they walked to his car.

"What, egg and lettuce sandwiches on a park bench?" she joked.

"The Harbour Master?" Robbie suggested.

"Fine!" She nodded abstractedly.

"So you've decided to tough it out?" Robbie studied her face. She looked very pale but resolute.

"Well, I've never thought of myself as a coward, Robbie. If Boyd is going to tell his father, I feel I should be here. If he doesn't want me by his side, at least I can be outside the study door."

"Leo, sweetie, this isn't a tragedy!" Robbie tried to comfort her. He had never seen Leo like this before and it bothered him. "I mean, you haven't been knocked up or anything. Have you?"

She shook her head in utter disbelief. "I'll pretend you never said that, Robbie."

"Sorry, sorry," he apologised. "I know that was totally out of line. I'm only trying to say…"

She cut him off mid-sentence. "I know what you're trying to say."

"Then don't look so sad. Boyd chose *you*. That says it all, don't you think? Rupe, wicked old tyrant that he is, won't be able to sway him. You *know* Boyd. He's his own man. Why, any other girl would be over the moon."

"Why wouldn't they be?" Leona smiled wanly. So why did she feel as if she had stepped into a minefield?

* * *

Boyd was actively searching for her by the time she made her way back into the house.

"Where have you been?" He moved swiftly towards her, blue eyes searing her to the spot so she couldn't run off. "You wouldn't have gone without saying goodbye to me, would you?" he asked.

"I'm not going anywhere," she said, straightening her delicate shoulders to confront him. "If you're going to speak to your father, I feel I should be here."

His expression lightened, like the sun coming out from behind clouds. "Leo, my love, you're made of the right stuff." He bent his dark head to kiss her cheek. Just a kiss on the cheek induced delicious shudders. "But you don't have to do this. Not yet. This is my father's house. I have to remember that. We both know he's always refused to countenance any change to his plans."

"I'm the very last daughter-in-law Rupert will want or expect." Even Boyd couldn't deny it.

Boyd, perhaps fearing they might be overheard, suddenly bundled her into the drawing room. "We've been through this before, Leo, and I don't want to go through it again. It's *you* I want. End of story. We had a deal, remember?"

"An indecent deal, some might say," she said, puffing a few tendrils of hair off her heated forehead.

Boyd muffled an exasperated oath beneath his breath. "So you want to back out?"

"Then I suppose you'll have Robbie detained before he's halfway home?" she flared.

"A deal is a deal," Boyd reminded her, looking every inch the acting CEO of Blanchards. "I don't want a life without you. If you're honest with yourself, *you* don't want a life without *me*."

He was exactly right but, before Leona could say so, they

were interrupted. They both spun as Jinty, her sister at her shoulder, sailed into the room. "Tonya is off," she said, as though Tonya was their very favourite person.

But Tonya was staring at them both as though they were aliens. "What's going on here?"

"Honestly, Tonya, have you never considered a career in the police force?" Boyd asked.

Tonya's sharp-featured face clouded over as she studied the striking tableau before her.

"Tonya!" Jinty, who was teetering between anger and embarrassment, cast her socially inept sister a warning glance.

Tonya either missed it or elected to take no notice. "Isn't this just too thrilling! It *is* true, isn't it?"

"I'm afraid so," Boyd said in mock sympathy.

Tonya stepped around her more substantial sister, who was trying to block her way. "She's pregnant, is she? I mean, that would be the only way."

Jinty snorted loudly, wondering what further damage her sister could inflict, but Boyd's handsome face darkened and his voice, though he didn't raise it, sounded like a call to war. "Jinty, would you please take your appalling sister out of this house? She could be in some danger."

Jinty didn't hesitate. She grabbed Tonya's arm, applying considerable pressure. "Out we go, Tonya. Out, out, I say! But, before we go, I expect you to apologise for that unforgivable remark."

"The hell I will!" a distraught, bitterly angry Tonya ranted. "All this time Rupert's sweet little Leo with her red-gold curls and her big green eyes has had her eye on the pot of gold."

"Pot of gold! Is that what I am?" Boyd asked and gave an ironic laugh. "Try to get control of yourself, Tonya. Make the effort."

"I said come with me, Tonya." Jinty's voice rose, near to a

screech. "I've been praying for years and years you'd learn how to keep your stupid mouth shut, but it has all been for nothing."

"But you've said yourself—" Tonya started to protest, but Jinty gave her a furious push ahead.

"Unbelievable!" Boyd muttered as they moved out of the door, Tonya dissolving into wails.

And that wasn't the end of it.

Rupert suddenly appeared, looking deeply irritated—something he did very well. "What on earth's going on?" he asked, staring towards the front door. "Was that my wife I heard screeching? Or was it one of the peacocks?" Peacocks did, in fact, roam the estate.

"It was Jinty," Boyd confirmed. "Tonya put her in a very bad mood." When his father didn't respond, Boyd asked, "It was you who dumped Tonya on us?"

"You can't dictate to me, Boyd. This is my house, might I remind you?" Rupert returned with supreme arrogance.

"The house *is* yours as the current custodian," Boyd flashed back. "The house then passes to me. I've told you before, Tonya is a born trouble-maker. One wonders why you choose to ignore it."

"Oh, she's harmless." Rupert threw up his hands. "Besides, Jinty likes her here," he said with dizzying untruth.

"Jinty is as unhappy to see Tonya as the rest of us," Boyd flatly contradicted. "If you have the time, Leona and I would like to speak to you."

"Certainly, certainly." Rupert was now at his most affable. "Come back to the study. What's it about? Leo has already had a big promotion. One step at a time now, Leo." He wagged a finger at her. "You're only twenty-three, aren't you?"

"Twenty-four, Rupert," Leona said, marvelling that her voice sounded so composed.

"You're not going to tell me you're thinking of getting engaged?" He swung round to beam at her. "Young Peter, is it?" he asked conspiratorially.

"Young Boyd," Boyd corrected very dryly, making the position manifestly clear.

Rupert stopped dead, just outside the open study door. "Is this some sort of joke?" His black brows rose and before Leona's very eyes he turned into Geraldine's tyrannosaurus.

"Why don't we go inside?" Boyd suggested, clearly unimpressed by his father's shape shifting. But the strain was showing on Leona. She was trembling. Rupert broke people. He was ruthless when crossed. Everyone in and outside the business world knew that. What about her father's job? Rupert could sack her father on some pretext. Being a billionaire with vast holdings both at home and abroad would give any human being way too much power.

In brooding silence Rupert took a seat behind his massive partner's desk. He kept his handsome head down. He didn't look up. His blood pressure must have shot up because his face was very flushed.

Boyd saw Leona seated in a leather armchair, then he took the one beside her. "I can't believe it's such a shock to you, Dad. You don't miss much. I know you and the Comptons have foolishly set your hearts on an alliance between our families, the thinking being that one family fortune is great, two is even better. Just like the Middle Ages. Chloe is a nice girl. I'm fond of her. She'll make someone an excellent wife, but that someone surely isn't *me*."

That statement appeared to anger Rupert beyond words. He stuck out his bottom lip with the utmost belligerence. "What are you telling me?" He stared balefully at his son.

"It would be better for all if you could learn to accept that I make my own decisions, Dad," Boyd said quietly. "Leona is the woman for me."

Rupert stared back almost wildly. "She's not a woman. She's a girl. She's your cousin. She's family. I tell you, I simply won't have it."

"Rupert, please!" Leona's voice begged for calm.

"You stay out of this, Leo," Rupert thundered, shooting an intimidating glance at her.

"I was only going to say you shouldn't allow yourself to get so angry," Leona spoke up bravely. "You've gone very red in the face."

"It's a wonder I'm not purple!" Rupert bellowed. "I thought you were different, but you're like every other god-dammed female."

"That's enough, Dad," Boyd said, rising to his feet. "I consider myself honoured that Leona has consented to marry me. And, I have to tell you, she needed persuading."

Rupert swore violently.

"Okay, that's it! We're done here!" Boyd put out a hand to Leona. "Come on, sweetheart, we're going."

She took Boyd's hand. "What have you got against me, Rupert?" she asked as Boyd started to draw her away. "Is there something I should know about? You may be disappointed that Boyd won't fall in with your plans, but you're much *more* than disappointed, aren't you? You find the idea *intolerable*. What is the real reason you're so angry? There has to be one."

"Don't do it," Rupert said, looking fiercely into her eyes. "And that's an order." His voice was harsh with authority. "If you know what's good for you, your father and that upstart Robbie, you'll do as I say." As he spoke the blood was draining from his face, leaving a marked pallor. He looked far from a well man. Indeed, he looked as if he was suffering a psychotic episode.

"What the hell's going on here?" Boyd demanded, brilliant blue eyes narrowing to slits.

For answer, Rupert lifted his heavy head, laughing darkly. "You'll be waiting a long time before you'll take the reins from me, my son!"

Arrogance, but the arrogance of achievement, settled on Boyd like a cloak. "I've as good as taken over the reins now, might I remind you, Dad? How could you threaten Leo and her family in such a way? I can tell you now you'll have me to deal with if you try to hurt them in any way. You may be put out by our decision—you've spent a lifetime imposing your will on us all—but this time you won't get anyone to back you. The family is very happy with me in the driver's seat. So are the shareholders. So were you, for that matter. Leona is, by anyone's standards, a beautiful, gifted, cultivated young woman. You've always treated her most kindly. What's the huge problem now?"

"It's not a good thing for you two to marry," Rupert said rigidly, adopting his familiar autocratic tone.

Boyd tightened his hold on Leona's trembling hand. "Stop talking rubbish. You know what you're saying is ridiculous. There's no impediment whatever—legally, morally or socially—to Leona and me marrying. We're not even full second cousins. You'll have to do better than that."

Leona, mind racing, broke in, her green eyes fixed on Rupert's face. "If you think there is some impediment, Rupert, you should speak out." She could hear the fear in her own voice. Rupert's violent reaction could be carrying them into dangerous waters.

There was a long silence, during which Rupert's eyes

drifted to the picture of Serena, which had hung on his wall since her death.

Leona heard the mounting anger and the challenge in Boyd's voice. "So what are you going to come up with now, Dad?" he asked with icy contempt. "Guess what, Leo's your half-sister? I wouldn't put anything past you. You'd defame Leo's dead mother. You'd defame my own beautiful mother, who had to tolerate so much from you. Only it won't wash. There *was* no affair between you and Serena, if that's what you're trying to suggest. God, you disgust me!"

Abruptly, life for Leona had moved beyond challenging. Her breath was locked in her chest. "This isn't happening, is it?" She looked to Boyd for confirmation. It came to her that he appeared much the more formidable of the two men.

"Sit down again, Leo," Boyd said, putting gentle pressure on her shoulder and easing her into her chair. "Don't let this upset you. This is only Dad playing his rotten games. He *wanted* Serena. My mother knew that. She told me years later that Dad had developed a real yen for Serena—the unobtainable—but Serena was an innocent. She didn't even know about your secret infatuation, did she, Dad? She was a young wife and mother and she and my mother were very close. Serena would never have betrayed her husband, her child or her close friend even if she had known of your aberrant feelings."

Leona's voice was little above a whisper. "No, she wouldn't have," she said. She might have been only eight, but she remembered her mother vividly—her vital presence, her wonderful sense of fun, her endless grace, her capacity for loving, their secure family unit. These attributes had informed her life. "Is that why you've been so kind to me all these years, Rupert? Because I remind you of my mother?"

"The one woman he couldn't have," Boyd said, with no

sympathy at all for his father. In fact, he was staring at him with open disgust on his face. "It follows, as it does with men like Dad who spend their lives in competition with their sons, I couldn't be allowed to have you. My father is paranoid about losing. He lost my mother's love very early on. Didn't you, Dad? It took a while but then she began to see through you."

"Shut up, Boyd!" Rupert gritted, his handsome features cold and set.

"Is *that* it, Rupert?" Leona appealed to Boyd's father, sounding desolate. "You wanted to deny your own son?"

Difficult as it was to comprehend, there was a great ambivalence in Rupert Blanchard's complex nature. Existing simultaneously with a great love and pride in his son and heir was a tremendous level of competition and rivalry. That conflict had found its most powerful expression right here and now. Boyd had to be denied Leona as he had been denied Serena. Not that Serena had been aware of his illicit feelings or the conflicts within him. Rupert couldn't attempt to explain it. It just *was*.

Rupert had passed to a stage where he no longer tried to formulate answers. All his life he'd been under tremendous stress. People imagined that being a scion of the very rich was fortunate indeed. He'd had no real choices in life. His father had made it very clear to him that he was to take over Blanchards, run it with the same hard-headed skills and determination as the men of his family did. His sisters were permitted to do as they liked. Gerri had followed an academic career, while Josephine, who kept well clear of the limelight, had married her medical scientist, had four children and led a happy, fulfilled life. Not him. His beautiful Alexa had escaped him. In spirit at least. Serena had been a mid-life aberration. It could never have come to anything. But he had not forgotten. He had given Serena's daughter, Leona, her mirror image, every advantage.

She was a lovely young woman in her own right. Now he was finding it unbearable for his son and Leona to be looking at him in the way that they were.

Rupert groaned aloud, then buried his face in his hands. He had always thought that he knew Alexa well, yet he had never known that she had discovered his secret infatuation. Not only that, Alexa had confided his secret to their son. Why not? Mother and son had always been very close.

The humiliation was not to be borne. Neither was it to be permitted. Rupert Blanchard reached out for a small trophy that sat on his desk, then crushed it in his bare hand.

CHAPTER SIX

AS THEY CAME out of the study and walked quickly towards the entrance hall, they saw Jinty poised in an attitude of listening at the bottom of the staircase. Obviously she was wondering what was going on, so she had taken the opportunity to eavesdrop. What they didn't know was that Jinty was also taking a near primitive satisfaction in the fact that Tonya, her own sister, had missed out. Not that she had ever had a chance, but then Tonya had never really caught on to the hard realities of life.

"Is everything all right?" she asked, adopting an expression of concern. Impossible not to notice the look of strain on their faces.

"Not exactly," Boyd said, his tone almost breezy. "Dad isn't best pleased by our news."

"Did you think he would be?" Jinty asked, throwing out her hands, palms up. "He was sure you'd go for Chloe."

"Maybe not. But did he—or anyone else for that matter— *really* think I was going to go along with his plans?" Boyd gave a slight grimace. "If he's so very fond of Chloe he should divorce you, then ask Chloe to marry him. There's every chance she'll say yes."

Jinty wondered if he weren't spot on. "Actually, I rather liked Chloe," she said. "A thoroughly nice, malleable young woman, but clearly she's no match for Leo, who has so many things going for her." The merest flicker of malice. "Should I go to him?" Jinty looked from one to the other. "Be supportive?"

"Of what, Jinty?" Boyd asked, very direct. "You're going to back us, then?"

"Why, certainly!" Jinty said without a blink. "Somehow I'll make your father understand that Leo is *your* choice. Heavens, the whole time we've been married, Rupert has doted on Leo. Occasionally it has made me quite jealous. God knows it's no secret that Rupert doesn't love *me*. We rub along well together, that's all. I do have the certainty I'll be a rich woman for life but there's little in it for me of the heart. Shall I go to him?"

"Only if you want your head bitten off," Boyd replied. "Dad could do that quite easily. Incidentally, has he seen Drew Morse lately? I think he should have a check-up; his colour didn't look too good. The thing is there's no crossing Dad. He can't deal with it."

"Well, that's nothing new to me," Jinty said and briefly shut her eyes. "Rupert expects everyone to obey his every whim. Anyway, I must apologise for Tonya."

"Oh, gosh, whatever for?" Boyd asked sardonically.

"Poor Tonya never mastered the social niceties, which is one reason why she's still unmarried."

"Perhaps she should enrol in a personal development course," Boyd suggested.

Jinty blinked, then reassumed her practised smile. "Be that as it may, I do sincerely wish you and Leo the very best, Boyd. Rupert can't dictate everyone's life."

"Certainly not mine," Boyd clipped off. "Now I'm driving Leo back to Sydney. No way do I want her driving herself after an upset like that. Ask Eddie to drive her car to her apartment some time tomorrow. I'll organise someone to drive him back." He glanced down at the silent Leo, who was looking and feeling shell-shocked. "We'll collect our luggage and be off. Where shall we leave Leo's keys, Jinty?"

"On the console table, please," Jinty said, gesturing. She was already starting to walk down the corridor that led to her husband's inner sanctum. "I have my own fears for Rupert's health," she paused to confide. "He drinks far more than is good for him and I can't get him off his infernal cigars."

"Picked up the habit from his own father and his father before him," Boyd said, still scanning Leona's pale face. "Let's collect the luggage." He spoke to her quietly. "I can't wait to get out of this place."

"Where are we going?" They were driving into Sydney before Leona came out of her reverie—a long internal dialogue that had never stopped.

Boyd was staring straight ahead. He too had been very quiet on the trip, which seemed to have taken record time.

"My place," he said briefly.

For once Leona didn't argue.

Fifteen minutes later they slid into the underground car park of Boyd's grand old apartment building, which had undergone mammoth restoration only a few years before. Boyd had the penthouse, which was actually two units that had been turned into a very spacious unified whole. She had never been to the penthouse on her own but she had been invited many times to his dinner parties.

In silence they took the lift to the top, Leona not even knowing what she was doing. She felt so dazed and astounded by both Boyd's and Rupert's disclosures that she had difficulty taking it all in. It seemed to her like something out of a block-buster novel filled with family secrets, money, sex and complex people with passionate unfulfilled yearnings. Or did novels only mirror real life? She had always known that Alexa's marriage had been unhappy, but never in a million years would she have suspected that Rupert had fallen blindly in love, however briefly, with her own mother, Serena. Yet Boyd had known and he had never said a word.

Until tonight.

No wonder he felt so connected.

To *her*.

They were inside. Leona waited. She didn't move.

"You're in shock, aren't you?" Boyd asked, closing thumb and finger around her chin, lifting it. He stared down into her face in concern.

"You know I am." She turned her eyes away from his searching regard, staring at without really seeing a large, light-filled Australian bush landscape that hung above the modern console in the entrance hall.

"I don't blame you." He dropped his hand, then took her gently by the arm. "Do you feel like something to eat? We could eat here or we could go out. I know an excellent Italian restaurant within walking distance."

She allowed him to lead her into the living room, with its double height coffered ceiling and contemporary architect-designed furniture. The total effect was one of supremely elegant individualism. Masculine, most certainly, modernistic, but welcoming to women. She knew Boyd had bought the place because of its history. This was one of Sydney's grand old dowager buildings with stunning night-time views of the city skyline. As well there were those soaring ceilings and the classic architectural elements which included marvellous fluted columns that divided the open-plan living-dining area. Architects and decorators had worked around the clock before Boyd had moved in.

"Well?" he prompted, steering her towards a custom built sofa.

"I'm not hungry."

"All the same, you should eat something. My father is a very devious complex character, but you can't let him get to you. I for one am starving. I always have a very light lunch before a match—God, it seems like years ago instead of this afternoon—nothing at all at afternoon tea, there were so many people wanting to talk to me. I need to feel *human* again."

"It was wrong of you not to tell me," she said, clutching a striped silk cushion to her breast like some kind of defence.

He sat down beside her, intensity in his blue eyes. He was wearing a plain white T-shirt and navy jeans and even then he was handsome enough to take a woman's breath away. "Tell you what?" he asked. "That my father was infatuated with your mother, who had *no* idea at all, for a brief period in their lives? What good would that have done?"

She turned on him fiercely, tears standing in her eyes. "It would have explained Rupert's attitude towards me. He's never seen me as a person in my own right. When he looks at me he sees my mother."

"We all do, Leo," Boyd pointed out gently. "For that matter, I couldn't count the number of people who've remarked on the colour and shape of *my* eyes. Everyone in the family knows I inherited my eyes from my mother."

"So some part of them does remain?" she asked more calmly.

"Definitely. Turn your head and the family see Serena. Turn your head and you'll see Blanchards, dead or alive. Every family has its own genetic blueprint."

She couldn't be consoled. "It was sick, Rupert lusting after my mother. I can't use any other word. She was a happily married woman. Besides, he had a most beautiful wife—your mother. I always knew Aunt Alexa had suffered."

"Most of us get to do our share of suffering, Leo," he said in a taut voice, taking the cushion from her and throwing it onto an armchair. "Falling in love isn't all that rational, is it? It blindsides us. Dad didn't do anything *too* terrible. He didn't go after Serena like he goes after everything he wants. He didn't break up his marriage, which evolved into little more than shadow play, or hers. My mother stayed for *me*. Much as I'm not in a mood to say it, I have to consider Dad as a victim. Falling in love with the wrong woman could be a very special hell."

"You think so?"

"I've waited a hell of a long time for you."

That filled her with real shock, then a wave of elation that quickly gave way to suspicion. "So I was being seriously considered from early on?" She didn't wait for an answer but swept on. "At some level you hate your father, don't you?"

His handsome features tightened. "No, I don't hate him, Leo," he said, putting his hand over hers. "How can I? I don't want to hate anyone. It does no good at all and he *is* my father. He's always backed me."

"Not in this!" Her breath fluttered and she drew her hand away from the surge in her blood. "Is that why you're doing it?"

He trapped her hand again, his blue eyes burning into her. "I'll forget you said that."

"*Is* it?" she persisted with a rush of emotion. "All of us can see there's great rivalry between you."

"The hell you can!" he bit off. "The rivalry is all on my father's side. I've tried as hard as I know how to be a good son, a good heir. I know Dad had a very tough time with my grandfather. There was always the constant pressure on him to measure up. I feel pressure too, but not in the same way. I'm not at war with my heritage, which I've often felt Dad was. Rich kids, like Dad was, can suffer extreme emotional deprivation, Leo. You should know a bit about that."

"Oh, I do," she confessed, "and I wasn't even a rich kid."

"But you *are* part of the family."

"Well, being taken under the wing of a rich kid like you was riches enough for me," she said ironically. "And there's the fact that my surname *is* Blanchard."

"And it's going to remain that way," he assured her, a naturally dominant man.

She wanted nothing more in the world than to slump against him, have him gather her up. Didn't he know she basked in his strength? Love for him was beating painfully in her throat. Even then she found herself unable to break free of the cycle of confrontation. "Because you say so?" she flashed.

"Because I say so," he answered quietly.

"So it's a kind of duty to marry you, is it?" It was stupid but she couldn't seem to get control. "A bit like royalty? At least Leo knows how things work! She's not likely to rock the boat. Once the family is over the initial shock, they'll start to philosophise—well, it's not *all* that bad, is it? Tailormade in a way. Leo is, after all, one of us. She *has* shown she knows how to conduct herself. No wild card there." She broke off the perfect mimicking. "I tell you, Boyd, this whole thing has spooked me."

"Is it any wonder?" His eyes were on the pulse that beat frantically in the hollow of her throat.

"And it can only get worse." She had seen the harshness, the massive affront in Rupert's face, and he was a man one crossed at one's peril.

"My father isn't going to fight me on this," Boyd said, sounding utterly self-assured. "But, should he try, he'll find for the first time in his life he won't win."

"*Second* time," she corrected and gave a broken laugh. "He lost out on my mother."

His eyes held an electric blue flame. "Please forget that, Leo. It was nothing more than a fantasy. What's real is this—I'm not going to lose out on *you*. I wouldn't consider it for all the money in the world."

"Nice to know then you're not going to lose any," she mocked. "I can't pretend I'm overjoyed by your very pragmatic proposal. *Deal*, I suppose we should call it. I want to keep my dignity and my sense of self intact. It's hard when I have to keep reminding myself I had to buy your silence to protect Robbie."

"Is it?" Boyd gave a brief laugh, then rose to his six foot plus. "God, I'd almost forgotten Robbie, though he did precipitate matters. Our defining moment came when I caught you red-handed with the Blanchard Diamonds."

"I gave them back, didn't I?" She still felt the panic.

"Ridiculous! You didn't take them in the first place. You love your kid brother so much you would even have taken the rap. Well, it's time for a fresh start, Leona. For you and for Robbie. He has to quit the unloved boy act and his multiple addictions. The way you always cover for him is actually hindering his self-development. I'm telling you now. I've already told him. One more foolish move from him and he's out on his ear. If I were Dad, he'd be as good as a dead man. Now, I think we should eat. You look as ravishing as ever, though a mite pale. I'll change out of this T-shirt and jeans. Give me a few minutes. We can walk to the restaurant."

They went out into the balmy night. A high sky awash with stars. They bloomed over the Harbour, as they always did over water, extravagantly beautiful diamond daisies. It seemed as if everyone in the world was in love as they made their way to the restaurant. Comfortably married couples, leaning in towards each other, strolled along the street or dipped into arcades, admiring the brightly lit, expensive speciality shops that included a society florist who charged an arm and a leg for a sheaf of long-stemmed roses. Music spilled out from somewhere. A very old favourite, but with a modern twist. Young lovers, interested only in one another, appeared unable to untwine their limbs. A family was coming at them four abreast, the youngsters clearly enjoying themselves and their night out on the town. The party split in two and fell to either side of Boyd and Leona, who smiled and thanked them.

Car lights threw streams of silver foil down the ebony surface of the road. Tail-lights glowed red; a kaleidoscope of colours from neon signs on the buildings. Traffic lights flashed red, amber, green. Busy cosmopolitan Sydney with such general goodwill in the air, Leona thought. They were looking towards Sydney Tower, one of the tallest buildings south of the equator. She had dined countless times at the Tower's revolving restaurants, which afforded arguably the most splendid panoramic view in the world. Sparkling Sydney Harbour in all its magnificence: the Harbour Bridge, the iconic Opera House with its glistening white sails, surrounded on three sides by deep blue water, the city buildings and, beyond the city central, its famous blue and gold beaches. One could see clear out to the Pacific Ocean on the one side, the mountains of the Great Dividing Range to the other. Loving her home town the way she did, Leona felt a surge of pleasure.

Delicious Italian food further soothed her. Diners sat deep in conversation, some flushed with sexual invitation, reaching across to hold hands. She finished two glasses of an excellent red, then took the unprecedented action of asking Boyd to pour her another. She did enjoy a glass of wine, especially champagne, but she was no drinker. Rather she was discovering the numbing effects the fruity wine was having on her distress. She didn't have to drive home—*was* she going to get home? They had finished one bottle. Now they were onto another. Boyd, as ever, looked perfectly sober. She imagined she did too. But mightn't he be over the limit to drive? It didn't take much. Blanchards shunned bad publicity and Boyd was ultra responsible. Maybe he planned on sending her home in a taxi, which perversely aggrieved her. There were plenty whizzing up and down outside.

The small, beautifully shaped trees that lined this exclusive little enclave were twined with sparkling white lights. That lifted her spirits as well. She had never been to this restaurant before. She liked it. Trust Boyd to find it. The staff were unobtrusive but she realised they were being waited on hand and foot. No doubt Boyd always left a large tip.

"Feeling better?" Boyd asked. She was aware that he had been studying her right throughout the meal.

"How could I not be? This is a seriously good restaurant."

"Our secret," he said, giving her a smile that made her shiver.

She leaned forward to whisper, "It doesn't just cater to *you*, Boyd Blanchard. I'm going to bring friends here. They ought to be famous."

"Your friends?" He lifted a black brow, pleased to see she was looking happier.

"No, the chefs at this restaurant. How precisely am I getting home? Or are you going to suggest I walk?"

"I bet you could do it too." He finished his short black coffee, then lifted a hand for the bill. "How is it you look like an ethereal dream when you're so athletic?" He slanted her a mocking smile.

"I aim to be strong," she said. "I work out." She watched him add a substantial tip to the bill before handing the plate along with his platinum credit card, back to the waiter, who had appeared like a genie from a bottle.

Back out on the pavement, a good-looking young busker was moving around, violin tucked into his neck, playing the most romantic of solos. He had to be one of the Conservatorium's best students, Leona thought, because his playing was absolutely top class, thrilling really. One reason perhaps why he hadn't been moved on. A small crowd was sitting listening, and there were intermittent bursts of applause, while others continued strolling. The scintillating environment drew the crowds, day or night.

"Leave him something," Leona prompted, in the next breath realising that Boyd had no need of a prompt.

"I usually do," Boyd told her dryly. "I'm a very generous man. Haven't you noticed?"

Once she was accidentally bumped by a slightly manic young man wearing huge yellow sunglasses, no matter it was night-time, obviously showing off to his giggling girlfriend. Boyd quickly tucked Leona in to his side. "Real catch, isn't he?"

"They're probably both at school. So do we shout for a taxi here?" She tried hard to sound composed, but she wondered if he could feel her trembling.

"My thoughts were that you should stay the night," he said.

In an instant her blood changed course. It began to whoosh madly up against her artery walls. She didn't know what was going to happen next.

"Don't have visions of my trying to seduce you," Boyd told her smoothly. "It's not going to happen. I'd just feel a lot happier if I had you in plain sight."

She felt so foolish, standing there, bereft of words. "I'm not suicidal," she managed at long last. Not suicidal, just wired inside. *Stay the night!* He wouldn't have to try a centimetre to sweep away her every last inhibition. She thought of him, pulling her to him, his hands on her, his mouth on her... Oh, God! Even the godless prayed when they were in trouble, she thought. Not that she was godless. She was definitely a believer. This was the *worst* thing and the best thing that could happen to her. She should agree right away.

"Staying over is out of the question!" she said, swallowing hard. Another minute and she would lose touch with all reality. It was a huge problem being in love with someone—at the same time making sure they didn't know it. Soul-destroying really to have to hide one's feelings from the person you loved most in all the world. But how could she make a clean breast of it when he couldn't—or wouldn't—or worst of all, didn't feel the same as she did. Love was terrible, terrible, terrible and there were many degrees of it.

"How you do go on, Leo," Boyd gently mocked her. "It seems like a very good idea to me. You've had a huge upset. Dad really can be the most callous of men."

"I have to say he is. There's such an emptiness in him. And, behind the powerful persona, a strange neediness. Jinty, on her own admission, can't fulfil his emotional requirements. Probably after we left a huge fight broke out."

Boyd gave an ironic laugh. "Jinty would have backed down fast. She surprised me when she said she had concerns about Dad's health. She's never mentioned it before."

They had paused at the junction, the traffic humming around them, predominantly luxury cars, waiting for the green light. "I thought Rupert saw Dr Morse on a regular basis?" she queried. She had a mental vision of Rupert's dusky-cheeked glare. And, behind it, to her mind, a kind of raw, unresolved grief. Rupert at the best of times wasn't a barrel of laughs, but that didn't prevent her from feeling compassion for him.

Boyd looked down at her. Her beautiful skin was lustrous as a pearl in the city's glow, her wind-tossed hair a glittering aureole around her small fine-boned face. She didn't know how beautiful she was. Her beauty, like her musical speaking voice, was simply a part of her.

"I know Dad has been taking blood pressure medication for years now," he said. "He's drinking too much these days, which would probably reduce or wipe out the effect of the medication." The light changed and they moved off as a couple, her arm linked through his. "People have stopped smoking in droves, yet Dad still goes for the Cuban cigars. I've said as much as I can say to him. He doesn't listen anyway."

"So how would you feel if he suddenly had a heart attack, God forbid?" Leona asked, feeling wretched. "Why don't you just call this whole business off? At least for now. Let him come to terms with the unacceptable, if that's at all possible. Besides, don't a lot of men think one girl is as good as the next?"

Boyd's laugh was without humour. "I'm definitely not one of them. I *won't* call it off, Leo, because it suits me very well. What's more, I refuse to talk about it further. You'll just have to be good and slip into the role of being my fiancée. It won't be difficult for a clever young woman like you. In a few months' time, we'll have the wedding. You can name the day. What about it?"

Her hand shot up as a gust of wind blew a thick skein of hair across her face. "Boyd, I can't!"

"Why not?" he asked very reasonably, helping her tuck the long lock behind her ear.

"Because…because…" Red wine soothed. It also excited the blood.

"You don't really know why not, do you?" he said.

"I do know you've set us on a very dangerous course. Your father was obviously intended by nature to be a tyrant. Maybe you will turn into a tyrant at some stage."

"It can't happen if I have you," he retorted and pulled her closer. "I can always rely on you to pull me into line. Besides, do you know anyone better you'd like to marry?" he asked, dodging an elderly man who appeared to be either dead set on walking into them or simply didn't see them.

"I haven't been thinking of marriage at all," Leona lied. "I'm more into a career, or haven't you noticed?"

A smile brushed his handsome mouth. "Leo, I know your job means a lot to you. You do it extremely well. Your job is safe. Bea has been known to frighten assistants to death but the two of you get on very well."

"Well, I'm used to frightening people."

"Tell me about it," he groaned.

They were back inside the apartment, which was more like a house. She went about switching on lights that were grouped on slim, elegant power boards. "This is some pad! We could be high up on a mountain. Far away from the world."

"Is that how you feel?" he asked in a voice that made her pulses drum.

"Leading question." She continued wandering about as though new to the penthouse when she knew it well. "It all turned out very well, didn't it? It's sort of sculptural in a way. Masculine, but female friendly."

"And it suits the purpose." He followed her, keeping a few paces away. "Personal space, business space. I can switch on or I can switch off completely."

"What are you now?" She didn't dare turn to look at him, instead running her hand over a small bronze sculpture of a horse—Tang dynasty, she knew. Both she and Boyd loved the arts of Asia.

"Bordering on the disturbed," he confessed quite unexpectedly.

She spun in shock, meeting his brilliant blue gaze. "Isn't that the way we usually are when we're together?"

He acknowledged her point with a dry smile, beginning to shrug out of his light beige cotton jacket, worn over a blue open-necked cotton shirt. It came to her that manufacturers didn't make women's shirts in that beautiful shade of blue. She would talk to Bea about it. "Are you going to sit down?" Boyd asked.

"No, I'm going to wander," she said, moving about as though she couldn't contain her restless excitement. "You and the architect and designers worked well together. The interiors are great, both the informal and the formal. It's a reflection of you. Boyd Blanchard. Literally the Man at the Top. This has to be four or five times the size of my apartment."

Boyd settled himself into a plush sofa, spreading both arms along the back. "It's big because it has to be, Leo."

"I know that. Anyway, I love my apartment. Chloe been here? Stayed overnight?" She gave him a swift challenging glance.

"Who's Chloe? I've never heard of her!"

"I hate to say this, but *I* have. Lots of people are going to be upset if you push through with this."

"Why don't you let me worry about that?" he said. "Since you mention her, I should tell you I've said nothing whatever to Chloe that would—"

"I thought you didn't remember her?"

He ignored the jibe. "That would give her to understand that I hoped to marry her. We've known one another since we were kids."

"So in the end she was just one of the girlfriends?"

His eyes narrowed. "If I didn't know better, I'd think you were jealous."

"No way!" She shook her head emphatically, though her heart felt heavy in her breast. "Really, when I think about it, it might be best if I go on home."

"But it's pouring outside and you have no umbrella," he joked.

"Then how come I can see the stars shining?"

"Here, come and sit beside me." He patted the sofa. "We'll just talk. It's me, Boyd, remember? You're acting like you expect me to launch into wild erotic games."

"Perish the thought!" A kiss—kisses, maybe. Madness. She knew neither of them could stick to kisses. Whatever flaws there were in his grand plan, they had well and truly discovered they had chemistry to burn.

"So you can't have a worry." His manner was utterly relaxed. She drew a slow breath. Didn't he know she was vibrating with nerves? Too much was happening to her, way too fast. The idea of their being a couple—an engaged couple—struck awe into her. She couldn't bear to think of Rupert's fantasies involving her innocent mother. That would have to keep until later. It seemed as if Rupert had longed all his life for what he couldn't have.

"Trouble is, I'm a working girl, Boyd," she explained briskly. "I need to go home. Organise what I'm wearing tomorrow. I can't go to work, in any old thing. Bea expects me to look great at all times. It's part of the job."

"And you're known for it. Don't worry, I'll wake you early," he promised. "I have a board meeting at eight-thirty."

She shook out her glittering cloud of hair—red, gold, copper lights. "If I could only work out what you *really* want of me," she said with perplexity. "Okay, I recognise some things—"

"Tell me *what* things," he challenged.

She sheered away from that. She had the unnerving feeling that she must look as if she urgently needed to be touched. It was taking every ounce of her self-control to deny him, deny herself. Nonetheless, she found the backbone to say, "Thank you, but no. I'd like you to call me a cab."

He didn't argue. He stood up. "All right, if that's the way you want it. But I won't let you go home alone. I'll come with you and take the trip back."

"It's not necessary." She was so strung up her blood was bubbling away like streams of lava.

"I'll do it, all the same," Boyd said, every bit as determined as she.

She began to walk rather frantically towards the entrance hall, but in the end she couldn't stand it any more. She spun round quickly, unaware that Boyd was so close behind her. He loomed above her, trapping her in his blue gaze.

"Boyd!" She came close to breaking down, only her lungs were out of air.

He took hold of her as if he owned her. As if she were the very image of his every desire. "God, Leona," he muttered, breathing her in. "I just can't…can't…be without you any more."

At his words, her mouth opened like a rose. She didn't want to think. She only wanted to *feel*. She had been waiting for this since for ever, suppressing every natural instinct. Now all she wanted was to let go. There was only his breath mingling with hers, his mouth, their burning need, the swift slide into the most passionate rapture that had at its centre an element of melancholy.

Love was ecstasy. It was also a force that made intolerable demands. It stripped away pretence. It stripped away all defences. She stood with her arms locked around his waist. He was cupping her face in his hands, holding it up to him.

Whatever words or lack of them were between them, their physical intimacy had developed at breathtaking speed. Now it had a life and a will of its own, saturating them both in its heat.

Boyd's hand moved slowly, voluptuously, languorously, down the silky column of her neck, over the slope of her shoulder to her breast. She moved even closer to him, crushing her body against him, willing his seeking hand to find the tight little bud that was her nipple. He had such beautiful hands. Thrillingly, one cupped her small high breast. She shuddered as his thumb began to move with exquisite eroticism over the aroused peak.

Excitement was soaring, beat by beat. This was to die for. This never to be borne, piercing sweetness. Sweetness the love poets spoke of so eloquently. The overwhelming flood of feeling she was experiencing was so matchless it was allowing her to dream dreams where Boyd was with her always.

Moving with ravishing slowness, he lifted her, understanding her want was as great as his. They were in the master bedroom. She was lying on the huge bed, on top of the luxurious quilted pearl-grey silk cover. He stood at the side of the bed, his lean body poised over her. "I want you here like this always," he murmured, bringing down his arms so that his palms lay flat on the bed on either side of her. "Sleep with me?"

"And let you take my soul?" He already had her body. She stared up into his sapphire eyes. This was Boyd, the man she had known and loved since she was a child. Wasn't it likely she had been programmed by the stars to fall in love with him? The splendid room seemed to be fading in and out. The high ceiling was swooping...there was only him. And her. Everyone else was far away. Her rapt state had little to do with the wine she had drunk at dinner. It had much more to do with being drunk on love. A love so powerful it could be regarded in some lights as entrapment.

"Does a woman lose her value once she sleeps with a man?" she asked very quietly.

He gave a twisted little smile. "How can you of all people ask me such a question?"

"No, Boyd. *Listen* to me." She half raised herself off the bed, clutching at his shirt front. Her beautiful eyes were filling with tears. "If we do this, there can be no going back."

His expression turned tender. He lowered himself onto the bed beside her, gathering both her hands in his. "My darling Leo, the last thing I want in this world is to go back. We go forward. Everything I have. Everything I am. Everything I hope to be. I'm handing it all over to you."

The way he was looking at her, the sound of his voice, gentle and low… Not only her heart, but her whole life was in his hands.

"You belong to me, Leo," he said. " I belong to you. You never fail me."

Could he bestow a greater compliment? He looked utterly sincere. She lay back again against the pile of silk cushions, throwing her arms above her head in a pose that was unconsciously erotic.

His hand fell to stroking her beautiful hair. "Don't fight me," he begged. "Don't fight us. Not now."

She gave a little wince of regret. "I only fight you because I think I can't let you get the best of me."

He bent his head to kiss her trembling mouth. "Leo, I'll take anything you can throw at me to get the best of you. Besides, our little spats were only a distraction, weren't they? I suppose they served a purpose while you were growing up. But not now. God, what a day!" He sighed, throwing back his dark head and momentarily closing his eyes. "I was totally incapable of sending you home. I want you here with me. *Finally.*" He glanced down at her willowy body. "I want to undress you. I want to do it right now." He spoke in such a deeply caressing voice it seemed to her she could refuse him nothing. "Is it a safe time for you?" He leant forward to search her eyes.

She felt her whole body flush, her answering, "Yes," barely above her breath.

Immediately he dipped his mouth to hers, gathering her into his arms so hungrily that every last barrier might have been removed.

"Do you realise how frightened I am?" His ardour was so lushly powerful her very flesh seemed to be melting. Could she really give him what he wanted? He was a deeply passionate man. Could she satisfy him as she so desperately wanted to? Could she satisfy the desire that glittered in his eyes?

There was an exquisite gentleness and understanding in his downbent gaze, as if he read her mind. "Sweetheart, you're safer with me, more free with me, than you could be with any other man. Your well-being is more important to me than my own. My only concern is to make love to you like you deserve. So, my love, where do we start?" He reached down a hand. "With the shirt, I think. I hate these little buttons."

Her voice trembled as she tried to make a joke. "You can't rip them. This outfit was very expensive."

"And it looks it too. I love the way you dress, Leo. I love all the different ways you do your hair. I love your voice. I'm in constant awe of your charm."

It was dizzying to hear such things, although Boyd had always complimented her on her appearance—really *looked* at her. She didn't mean to say it, but somehow it came out. Part of her insecurities? "How many women have you slept with?"

His glance licked across her like a blue flame. "Suddenly I forget." Very smoothly he removed her fine cotton shirt, tossing it onto an armchair, exposing her stretch-silk bra.

"Pretty," he said, trailing a finger into her creamy cleavage. "Cheeky even, Ms Blanchard! I bet the briefs match."

"I love good lingerie." She gave a fluttery breath, passing rapidly to a rapturous excitement. Beneath his moving fingers lay her heart. It belonged as much to him as her.

"I should tell you I slept with Mark Tyler." Get it over, she thought. Create trust?

He frowned slightly. "I know."

Mortification brought the blood to her face. "You know everything, don't you?"

"Yes."

It had been her first time—she had thought long and hard about it—Mark was a tender, caring person, but in the end it had been a mistake. Afterwards she couldn't begin to imagine why people raved about sex. Her experience with Mark had been a case of reversed stereotypes. Mark had been the one in tears while she had passed very quickly to wanting him to get dressed and go on home.

But then her heart belonged elsewhere. Little detours, she had found to her cost, served no good purpose. She wanted and wanted…and the only one who could satisfy that want was Boyd.

"I once had the misfortune to be caught in a bar with poor old Mark," Boyd was saying. "I had to sit through a maudlin two hours while he mourned your split. He adored you."

"Adored me?" she gasped as he caressed her body. "Didn't take him long to get engaged. You had your affairs. By the time I was twenty I thought it high time I had mine. My two, that is. Neither of them worked. You were a curse laid on me in childhood."

He broke off his exquisite ministrations to place a silencing finger against her lips. "Leo, don't say that!"

A silent tear rolled down her cheek. "I'm sorry. I meant

blessing. I really shouldn't be saying any of it. I'm no match for you, Boyd."

"Sweetheart!" There was a look of the utmost concern on his striking face. "You more than match me. I'm *mad* to make love to you, but if you don't wish it…"

Now she couldn't suppress her urgency. "Kiss me," she said, reaching up to clasp a hand around his handsome head. "Kiss me." At that moment she felt proud and strong. Maybe even a little bit in charge.

Boyd's laugh was exultant, coming from deep in his throat. "I'm going to cover you in kisses, starting at your toes. But first I think I'll finish taking off your clothes."

CHAPTER SEVEN

LEONA MADE IT TO THE office on time. She was in such a state of euphoria she had to resort to autopilot. It would take her days, weeks, years to fall back to earth. She wouldn't have been surprised if someone had stopped to tell her the jacket of her Gucci suit was on inside out. But no one mentioned it as she entered the lift, or as she walked through the office, although she wasn't actually walking, more like floating on air. She supposed she smiled and waved, offered little pleasantries like she always did when she came into work.

Sally, her much valued assistant finally got through to her. "Oh, good, you're here, Leo. Bea said she wanted to see you in her office the *instant* you arrive." Known for her unflappable temperament, Sally sounded fevered. Bea did tend to have that effect on people.

"Did she say what for?" Leona put her bag down on the desk.

Sally snorted. "God, Leo, Bea doesn't confide in the likes of me." Bea could, on occasions, be excruciatingly rude. "But she looked kind…kinda…" Sally tipped her nut-brown head to the side, searching for the right word.

"She looked what?" Leona put something away in a drawer, and straightened up.

"Sort of worried, unhappy, can you believe? Bea always behaves like God."

"I'll go to her," Leona said. "Do I look okay?" she asked, as Sally was still watching her.

"You look *wonderful*." Sally responded with utter sincerity, thinking that dressing was an art form that for all her efforts had somehow escaped her. Leo had such style, mixing up this and that, colours, belts, scarves, what have you, always individualising everything. She wouldn't have the courage. "All lit up from inside," she concluded.

Leona gave her the loveliest smile. "Thanks, Sal. I can't think how I got dressed this morning."

"Big night?" Sally asked, rolling her eyes.

"Something like that." The best night of her life. She'd lost count of how many times they had made love, their wants and needs had been so great. She felt she had taken Boyd in through her every pore. The more she got, the more she wanted. No sensation in the world could surpass the feeling of having him deep inside her, then coming, and coming again. This was what the great novelists wrote about and even then it was so much more.

She had desperately wanted to *feel* love, fearing it at the same time. What she'd got was the answer to every woman's prayers. But the fervour of it all had somehow weakened her knees. What she wanted was maybe a few hours' sleep...then to be awakened by Boyd, finding her reflection in his sapphire eyes.

"Sit down, Leo," Bea said, sounding oddly as if she was coming down with a cold. She was frowning too and her frown grew deeper by the minute.

"Do we have a problem?" Leona asked, intuition working overtime. She had taken to heart what Rupert had said. But surely he couldn't have made a move on her this quickly?

Bea's laugh was as brittle as cracked glass. "I've known for donkey's years you're in love with Boyd."

Leona blinked. "Can you say that again? No, never mind. How do you know—do I have a sign on my forehead?"

"Why wouldn't you be in love with Boyd?" Bea stared back at her intently. "God, come to think of it, I'm in love with him myself. We *all* are. I've never met anyone like him for all my world travels."

"So what's the matter, then? You look upset, Bea."

Bea pulled a mirror from a top drawer, held it at arm's length, then closer. "Dear God, just as I expected! My worst fears confirmed. I swear it gets harder and harder to look presentable. Sometimes I remind myself of a garden gnome wearing haute couture. We've really bonded, haven't we, Leo?"

"We're soul mates, Bea," Leona said. "I love and admire you."

"Oh, dear!" Long regarded by everyone in the business as hard as nails, Bea made a wry little face. "Don't make me cry. No use beating about the bush, Leo. Our Lord and Master rang me last night."

"What time?"

"Does it matter?" Bea's painted eyebrows rose.

"I suppose not. Rupert wastes no time getting cracking. He wants you to give me the boot, right?"

For answer, Bea picked up a ballpoint pen and hurled it across the room. "Probably unlawful. Unfair dismissal. No, he wants me to give you a promotion."

Leona sat bolt upright. "I know! He's going to open a Blanchard flagship boutique in Outer Mongolia?"

"Close. No, he wants you to take over from Rosie Quentin at the Perth store. Rosie isn't young any more; we'd been thinking of replacing her, as it happens. Of course with a sizeable golden handshake. Rosie wouldn't go quietly into the night."

"And sending me across to the other side of the continent is Rupert's way of weaning me off Boyd. Is that it?"

"Truly you're a smart girl," Bea said, smoothing a hand over her newly pewtered bob. It would be fair to say the colour didn't suit Bea at all. Bea's former colour had been close to ebony—more in keeping with her long heavy-lidded ebony eyes—she called them currants in a doughnut, but one had to tread very carefully with Bea. "Rupert might be my boss but, just between the two of us, the man's flawed. He wants you away!" Bea threw out her short arms. "And that's an order!"

Leona gave a hollow laugh. "I couldn't care less what Rupert wants," she said and meant it. "Boyd has assured me my job is safe. *You* still want me, don't you, Bea?"

Bea frowned so fiercely her eyebrows made a straight line. "Dearest girl, surely you know I'm grooming you to take over from me. Why else have I put in all this effort?"

"And, hey, I appreciate it," Leona said. "There's no one in the business to touch you."

"Oh, a couple have tried." Bea waved the contenders away. "The truth is I'm a genius."

"No one else like you," Leona confirmed. "Let me talk to Boyd about this, Bea."

Bea gawped at her. "Dearest girl, you're not going to come between father and son? Rupert could go into cardiac arrest if he's crossed."

"And there's *my* father," Leona said.

"Good God, so there is!" Bea reeled back. She knew Rupert Blanchard and his capacity for punishing anyone who hindered him. "You need to get your defences ready, my girl—speak to Boyd," she advised.

* * *

Leona had to wait until the Board Meeting was over. She knew from Boyd that Rupert wouldn't be in attendance. Rupert was at Brooklands. She made her way to the top floor of the Blanchard Building, the nerve centre, where she never normally went, whiling away the time by looking down on the city through the tall plate glass window while Boyd finished off a conversation with two of his father's most powerful allies, one of them Jack Compton, Chloe's father.

"Why, it's Leona!" Stewart Murray, the merchant banker who lived like a prince, still very dashing in his sixties, and with a prodigious liking for good-looking women, greeted her with open pleasure. "How are things with you, my dear?" He beamed, kissing her on both cheeks. "You look lovely. A really, really lovely girl. There's something absolutely delicious about a redhead."

"Why, thank you, Mr Murray—" Leona smiled "—I'm very well." She turned her attention to Jack Compton who, she noticed, had gone very grey and was set to go snow white. "How are you, Mr Compton?"

"Fine, Leona," he huffed, as if Leona didn't happen to be one of his favourites. "I was just telling Boyd that Chloe will be home on Monday. We've missed her. We should all go out to dinner some time."

"That would be lovely, Mr Compton," Leona said, knowing it would never happen. Lord knew how Jack Compton would react when he learnt she had snatched his beloved daughter's intended bridegroom.

Boyd was waiting for her outside his office door. She drank him in—all the marvellous details. He was wearing an expensive suit, tailored to fit like a glove. He was so tall and lean and he carried himself so well, their top male model, internationally in demand, couldn't do better. His brilliant eyes sparkled, his whole image dynamic, glowing with health and energy in a very sensual way.

"You look beautiful," he said, his eyes moving caressingly over her. "I have to agree with Stewart. Redheads are absolutely delicious. Come into the office." He asked over his shoulder, "Everything okay? Not that I'm not thrilled to see you here."

"Listen, I have to talk to you," Leona began, shutting the door. "It's urgent!"

He was instantly alert. "I won't let you change your mind, Leo," he warned.

"It's not that."

"Then nothing else matters," Boyd said, attempting to draw her into his arms.

"No, Boyd!" She drew back. "You've got to hear this. I'm very worried that Rupert might take his anger out on Dad. Dad could lose his job or get shifted, even demoted." Her father was still relatively young, he could find another job, but none she was sure, to measure up with the pay and prestige of Blanchards.

Boyd made a little clicking sound of impatience. "I thought we'd agreed I'd handle this."

"Yes, but Bea spoke to me this morning. Rupert rang her last night. Rosie Quentin—she's in charge of Fashion in Perth—is due for the chop. Rupert wants me to take over."

"Have you gone mad?" Boyd locked his hands around her willowy waist, drawing her to him and not letting her get away.

"It's not me!" she protested. "It's your father. I mean, Perth's a great city. I love Western Australia—"

Boyd silenced her with a kiss. She returned it. How could she not? She could have kissed him for ever. "I'll speak to Dad," he said.

She put her hands on his shoulders, staring into his beautiful eyes. "Chloe's father suggested we should all go out to dinner. Can you believe it? They'll be totally unprepared."

"How could they be totally unprepared?" he said crisply. "I've told you—"

"I know what you told me. I believe you."

"Why, thank you." He gave a wry smile.

"But people can and do believe their fondest hopes will be achieved. Instead of bolstering the Compton hopes, Rupert should have been shooting them down."

Boyd's laugh was a shade impatient. "Odd, that! Dad does get a great kick out of raising people's hopes, *then* shooting them down. Leave it to me, Leo."

What else could she do?

It turned out to be a hectic day. Bea couldn't see a thing right with the glossies from the latest fashion shoot. She swished the photographs—excellent really—off the table in a fit of frustration. The models, male and female, the glorious North Queensland tropical location, the clothes they were wearing—everything met with scathing contempt. Bea had conveniently forgotten she had hand picked the lot.

"I've got it!" Leona found herself interceding at one point, just about ready to try anything. Shots in the local cemetery? Maybe the fire station? Would that capture Bea's attention? "Take them all out on location to Uluru. The contrast between the beautiful sophisticated clothes and the savagely beautiful Outback environment could be brilliant."

Lights flicked on behind Bea's dark obsidian eyes. "Now why on earth didn't *I* think of that?" Suddenly she was happy. "Well, well, what are you waiting for?" She clapped her hands together, then waved Leona off. "Go and find me Daniel."

Later on Leona rang Robbie to check that he would still be

going with her to the airport to meet their parents, who were due in from Hong King early the following morning.

"I don't understand why you want me," Robbie said, genuinely puzzled. "Your dad has only said half a dozen sentences to me in all the time he and Mother have been married."

"Well, it's not as if he's excessively jolly with me," Leona reminded him. "Anyway, saves me hanging around by myself. So set your alarm."

"Actually, I might stay up all night instead of going to bed," Robbie suggested.

"Not if you want to look your best. Besides, I've got something to tell you."

"Something good, I hope." There was a sudden note of anxiety in Robbie's bantering tone.

"Might as well tell you now. Rupert wants to call a halt to any wedding plans. He and Boyd had *words*."

"Fantastic!" Robbie's voice carolled loudly down the wires. "Wish I'd been there. Don't worry about old Rupe, Leo. Boyd is already long strides ahead of him. If I were you, I'd start planning my wedding gown. Something utterly exquisite and a veil with a long train. Two little flower girls, maybe a pageboy, if the kids will consent to do it these days. After all, the whole continent will be watching. It's actually thrilling and of course I'll be a groomsman." A reflective pause. "You're not thinking of breaking my heart, are you?"

"Never!" Leona said stoutly.

"A true blue Blanchard can be best man," Robbie said generously. "I'll be for ever in Boyd's debt. Honestly, he deserves some kind of medal. He's got those thugs off my back. Unbelievable, I'm *safe*! I can come out of hiding!"

"Make sure it stays that way," Leona warned with enough firmness to register.

Robbie's answer rang with sincerity. "I swear to you, Leo, I'll never place another bet. I've learned my lesson. I could have ended up in a police line-up—probably their best-looking ever suspect—instead I received mercy and a second chance. All I want to do now is earn the respect and trust of the people who love me—you and Boyd. Well, you, anyway. Boyd might learn to love me as I make a clean sweep of all my bad habits. After all, I'm going to be godfather to your first child. Or one of the godfathers. I could live with that. And there's another thing," he confided. "I plan on visiting Italy in the summer vacation. It's just possible I might get to see my dad."

In a nerve-racking day Leona found herself smiling with satisfaction. "You've made the right decision, Robbie," she said. It could well be that Delia had been holding back on her son for many long years. Delia was like a lot of other women who fancied themselves wronged, and may well have had her revenge on the wrong male.

Although her father and Delia knew they were being met, their faces registered neither pleasure nor appreciation.

"Surely you have morning lectures, Roberto." Delia lost no time getting underway, her voice set at that familiar grinding edge.

"Not until eleven, Mother!" Robbie retaliated by giving his mother a great big bear hug.

"Oh—oh, be careful!" Delia cried, wrenching herself away. Robbie had come perilously close to messing her hair, a glamorous cast-iron coiffure regularly tinted a champagne-blonde. It was a style she hadn't changed in years.

"You needn't have bothered, Leona," her father was saying, accepting her kiss on his cheek with no visible sign of emotion. "We could have caught a taxi home."

"No bother, Dad." Leona kept her smile in place when she felt like seizing her father by the arms and shaking some life into him. Her father, though a handsome, quietly distinguished-looking man, bore little resemblance to the happy, loving father she remembered from her early childhood. It was as though the real Paul Blanchard had died with her mother. Emotionally speaking, he gave every appearance of a man who had lost all feeling. "Marital frostbite", Robbie called it. "Mother does a super job of that!"

"Goodness, we might have to hire an extra car for all the luggage," Robbie observed as they jostled with the crowd at the baggage carousel. Delia was busy pointing out a number of pieces of designer luggage as they came tumbling through the shute. "I expect you've brought lots home for me and Leo, eh, Mother? Clothes, leather goods, Swiss watches."

"Oh, do stop, Roberto," Delia chastised him. "I mean, what *else* could you possibly want?"

"What about a return ticket to Rome?"

Delia turned on him in what looked like shock. "Why Rome?"

"Why not?" He leaned forward to grab yet another bag. "I think it's high time I met my dad. Remember him, Mother? Carlo D'Angelo. The last time I saw him, he was making a run out of our house with you chucking things at him, missing every time."

"Shut up about that, Robbie, right now!" Delia said angrily "Your father was a sorry specimen of humanity. He left us both." All of a sudden Delia, normally a picture of health, was looking quite sickly.

"Shall we go?" Paul Blanchard actually took action. He seized hold of his wife's arm. "People are looking, Delia," he said in a warning undertone. "We can't have that. If Robbie wants to meet up with his father again, neither of us have the right to stop him."

Robbie looked momentarily gobsmacked, then he indulged in a triumphant high-fisted salute picked up from the local champion tennis player. Delia could rage non-stop for seven days and seven nights but she wouldn't stop her son from making that trip, Leona thought. Carlo D'Angelo may have bolted from his first marriage but there remained the distinct possibility that he hadn't forgotten his first-born child.

"Would you like me to make tea or coffee?" Leona asked some ten or fifteen minutes after they had arrived at her father's and Delia's house. Large, modern, architect-designed, it was impressive with a great location, but mercifully not overly pretentious.

Robbie had already left. "I'm outta here!" he'd told Leona in a quick aside. Even so, he was looking happier and more in charge of himself than she had ever seen him.

"God, no!" Delia responded graciously. "I want my bed. I detest that last leg of the flight home."

Leona looked to her father. "I wonder if I might have a word, Dad?"

Delia laughed as though Leona had said something utterly unreasonable. "Not *now*, Leona. Your father is as jet lagged as I am. I would have thought that was obvious."

"Actually, I feel perfectly well," Paul Blanchard answered in his usual courteous manner. "What is it you want to speak to me about, Leona?"

"It's private, Dad," she said. The last person she needed was Delia right under her nose.

"Really?" Delia gave a vehement shake of her head. So

lavishly had it been sprayed, not a single hair moved. "Does that mean you don't want me?"

"I wouldn't keep you from your bed, Delia," Leona said very sweetly. "You do look a little peaky. Would *you* like some tea, Dad?"

"I suppose I would." He suddenly gave her a smile—that rare smile that caught at her heartstrings. "You look very beautiful, Leona. What's been happening to you?"

"Why don't we go into the kitchen?" Leona said and moved to take her father's arm. "I'll make the tea and I can tell you then."

But there was worse to come.

"You and Boyd?" Paul Blanchard sat at the long bench in the very sleek contemporary kitchen, eyeing his daughter with genuine shock.

Not a good sign, but Leona felt she had to meet the challenge.

"Yes, Dad. Me and Boyd," she confirmed quietly. "He wants to marry me, even though it appears it's come as a tremendous shock to you."

Paul Blanchard was driven to resting his dark head with its silver wings in his two hands. "But Leona, we all know Rupert's plans." He lifted his head again. "The Compton girl. It's almost a business deal. That's the way Rupert's mind works. Unite two dynasties. Rupert and Compton have been waiting for the relationship to deepen. I thought you understood that."

"I did," Leona answered, frowning. "But you can't seriously believe Boyd is going to allow his father to pick his bride for him. You *know* Boyd. It's preposterous. He's his own man."

"Leona, I'm well aware of that." Paul Blanchard sighed deeply. "I think the world of Boyd. We all do. It's not a question of Boyd having to measure up to his father like Rupert had to measure up to his, and incidentally never did, which I believe seriously affected Rupert's character. The Old Man watched Rupert's every step like a hawk. He even had his spies. On the whole, Rupert had a rough time. But, that aside, Boyd is ready right now to take over Blanchards. What's more, the majority of the Board will back him. It's another case of the King and the Crown Prince. I can almost feel sorry for Rupert. His resentments remain deeply entrenched. This news of yours will precipitate a huge rift between father and son. It will affect Blanchards, the whole family. That's what you're telling me isn't it? Rupert is totally against you and Boyd."

Leona studied the leaves at the bottom of her teacup as though they held the answer. "I think you could say that. Rupert is used to riding roughshod over everyone. He's trying it out on his own son. It won't work."

"No, it won't," Paul Blanchard agreed. "But the more Rupert thinks about it, the worse things will get. The man's a tyrant. My dear, even *you* have no idea. Rupert has become more and more power drunk as the years have gone on. He could hurt me, you know, not that I wouldn't survive. So don't worry about that. But we're *all* vulnerable where Rupert is concerned."

"Do you think Rupert would actually stoop to manoeuvring you out?" she asked worriedly.

"In the blink of an eye," Paul Blanchard confirmed, mercifully not sounding all that worried about the prospect "The man is heartless. I know in one way he is enormously proud of Boyd, but in another he recognises his son has qualities he never had. Rupert is into power for power's sake. Boyd isn't like that. He's a very different human being. That's his mother in him. Wonderful woman, Alexa. She made a terrible mistake marrying Rupert, but then again they were manipulated by the Old Man. To be very, very rich, Leona, is something to be avoided. Great wealth ironically doesn't bring happiness. It brings terrible risks. You might remember that. If you marry Boyd, your whole life will change. You're my daughter. I love you. I'm afraid for you."

Leona could see her father was deeply serious. "Don't be afraid, Dad," she said. "I know I can trust Boyd with my life. There is something I would like to ask you. Did you ever feel at any time that Rupert was a bit too fond of Mummy?"

Her father turned to look at her as though she had said something utterly crazy. "What in the world put that idea into your head?"

She gave him an imploring look from her beautiful green eyes. "Just something Rupert himself said. I mean, I was as shocked as you, but lots of people have something to hide, Dad. I think Rupert's secret was that at some stage he became infatuated with my mother." Tears sprang unbidden into her eyes.

"Darling girl," Paul Blanchard groaned as he reached to put a hand on her shoulder. "If Rupert, the old bastard, was ever infatuated with my beloved Serena he forgot to tell *us* about it. I never saw anything of the kind. And I can put your mind entirely at rest regarding your mother. She had absolutely no idea. Why, Serena and Alexa were great friends! They loved one another. Your mother loved me. I never did know *why* she did, but she did. We were wonderfully happy, the three of us. Either Rupert is a total liar, delusional, or he managed to keep this perverted infatuation very well hidden. The thing is, Leona, *everyone* loved your mother. She was immensely lovable. My love for her has never faded. Only a small part of me is still alive. I know you can see that. The best of me went with your mother."

Leona took her father's hand and held it. "Do you see too much of her in me?" she asked sadly. "Do you, Dad? Please tell me."

Now tears stood in her father's eyes. "I've hurt you a lot, Leo. I beg your understanding and forgiveness. But you're right.

You're so like your mother, a lot of the time the pain becomes unbearable. It's what's known as good old-fashioned despair."

"Yet you married Delia?"

Paul Blanchard's broad brow wrinkled. "I married Delia because I thought she would have the generosity of spirit to become a surrogate mother to you. I saw things in her that apparently weren't there. My own fault. I wasn't seeing straight at the time. I was like a man in a coma. I should have known, just seeing how Delia was with her own little son. Roberto has suffered as well and he didn't deserve it any more than you."

"I'm afraid that's true, Dad. But surely it can all change; it's not too late, even for you. Robbie told you he wants to go in search of his father."

"Then I'll give him all the help he needs. It's possible he might find out a great deal that his mother has never wanted him to know. Delia became very warped after Carlo left her. I know Carlo loved his boy. I do know that. Roberto is the very image of him. Part of Delia's policy was to keep Carlo out of his son's life. It's an alarming thought, but Delia could easily have kept so much from Roberto."

"I've been thinking along those lines myself," Leona admitted. "Do you feel you and Delia should stay together, Dad?" she asked after a minute. It was her fervent belief that her father and Delia would be better apart.

Paul Blanchard gave his daughter a twisted smile. "I can't find it in my heart to talk to her about a divorce."

"Maybe it's what you both need," Leona said. "At the very least, you can bring things out into the open."

"You mean a kind of purge? It would be pretty awful to divorce Delia, Leo."

"She deserves a good shake up," Leona said.

Her father gave a sad laugh. "I have to agree with that. But it's not us I'm worried about at the moment. It's you and Boyd. Rupert can be a very menacing man. He thinks nothing of hurting people. He'd better make sure he does nothing to hurt you, my darling, or he might get what he thoroughly deserves."

The *my darling* from a father not given to endearments nearly brought Leona to tears.

CHAPTER EIGHT

LEONA WAS WALKING briskly to her car in the basement car park, humming a little melody she had made up on the spot. Something romantic. She had a flair for such things. She was having dinner with Boyd that night and the familiar excitement had started up in her blood. For the first time she allowed herself to believe he might *truly* love her as a man loved the woman he wanted to marry. What had happened with Robbie had nothing to do with anything. The incident with the earrings had merely been an excuse, a blind, Boyd loved her, she knew it. Maybe she had always known it. The thought exhilarated her right down to her toes.

"Leona!" a peremptory voice called. "Don't drive away. I want to speak to you."

Leona spun round, infuriated by the tone of voice and the presence in the basement of its owner. "Well, I don't want to speak to you, Tonya," she said sharply. "What on earth are you doing here? I have to be somewhere else. Boyd and I are going out to dinner."

Tonya's rather spindly legs covered the short distance between them in record time. Strangely, she kept shaking her left foot as though a pebble had lodged in her high heeled sandal.

"Why do you think he's decided to marry you and not Chloe?"

It was spoken with such extraordinary venom that Leona drew back a pace. "Jinty been speaking to you, has she?" Well why not? They were sisters. Even so she was surprised at Jinty's lack of discretion.

"Not Jinty, no." Tonya's sharp features tightened. "The fact is my sister and I have had a huge falling out."

"I'm not surprised. You have all the tact of a blunderbuss."

Tonya drew her mouth inwards. "Don't worry about me, thank you very much. I'm fine. It's you who should be worrying. Never mind who told me, but I *know*."

"So you want to offer congratulations?" Leona spoke very dryly.

"He doesn't love gorgeous little you," Tonya fired up. "He's *fond* of you. We all know that. But fondness is quite a different thing. You're family. He's known you since you were a little kid. But he doesn't love you as a man should love the woman he's going to marry. I mean you're not on equal terms, if you know what I mean."

"And you've figured that out all by yourself, have you?" Leona forced herself to remain calm when she was feeling under siege.

Tonya gave a bitter smile. "I've had inside help," she confided. "Not for the first time either. Every family has a gossip and I've learned a hell of a lot from her. Let's face it, you're suitable enough, presentable, you know the score. Rupert wants Chloe, of course, but quite a few of the family have grown tired of Rupert and his wants. They're looking to Boyd to head up the family and Blanchards. Boyd has chosen you for what I'm sure are excellent reasons by his light. I've already suggested a couple. Boyd really thinks things through. Chloe can't hold a candle to you in looks and Boyd appreciates beautiful women. It wouldn't be a huge problem taking you to bed. Best of all, you're young enough for him to mould any way he wants. What amazes me is how you can't see any of this."

Leona took her car keys out of her handbag, then zapped the remote. "Have you quite finished?" she asked coldly. She really detested Tonya.

Tonya clicked her tongue. "I know it's absurd. After all, I don't like you, but in a way I'm disappointed in you, Leona. I thought you had more backbone. But you're utterly spineless. You're being manipulated. Can't you see that? Boyd may be everything a woman wants—I mean even *I* wasn't immune to his appeal—but I wouldn't trust him any more than I would trust his old man. It might well be you're simply a pawn in the father-son power play. Plenty of precedence for that. And there's that other business."

It was a clever trick and Leona fell for it. "What other business?" she asked in a disgusted voice.

"God, so uppity already!" Tonya crowed. "You're not Mrs Boyd Blanchard yet, pet. And it might never happen so don't get too carried away. I'm talking about your dear sweet mother, the lovely Serena."

For a non-violent person, Leona felt a surprising amount of anger starting to roar inside her. It burned, then singed. She wanted nothing more than to smack Tonya across her sneering mouth. "I'd stop now if I were you," she warned, her emerald eyes lit by little flames.

But Tonya was never one to heed a warning. "Rupert had the hots for her, I've been told," she continued blithely on, eaten up by malice.

Be careful, the voice inside Leona's head strenuously urged. *Keep in control. Control is always rewarded.* She was a Blanchard. She couldn't afford to get into a cat fight.

"The same source?" she managed crisply. "A woman as malicious as you? I think I know who it is, but Rupert won't thank either of you for putting that one about."

Tonya shrugged. "What could he do? It's the truth."

Leona by this time was feeling ill. "You have a nasty tongue, Tonya. You relish spreading disharmony."

"What if it was Geraldine who told me? Geraldine, Rupert's own sister?" Tonya's thin face took on a truly foxy expression. *The one thing you can't do is lose it! Get in the car. Drive away.*

To hide her feelings of immense shock, Leona averted her head, leaning forward to open the car door.

"People love to gossip, Leona," Tonya taunted her, absolutely brazen in her stance. "Even that arrogant old bitch, Geraldine."

Leona was severely tempted to send Tonya sprawling. Instead, she turned back to confront the bitter, hostile woman. "Geraldine would never betray the family," she said with absolute certainty. "And Geraldine would never, under *any* circumstances, confide in *you*, Tonya. You see, people don't like you. They don't trust you. And with good reason. They know just how much damage you like to inflict."

"Such loyalty!" Tonya hissed. "But Geraldine *did* speak to me. Why don't you ask her? She'll deny it, of course, but I had to get it from *somewhere*. Think now. Isn't Geraldine the most likely person? I dare you to ask her."

"I wouldn't dream of upsetting her," Leona replied, very forcefully for her. "You really are a horrible woman."

Tonya laughed, as though she thought Leona incredibly naïve. "Have it your own way, you poor deluded girl. No skin off my nose. Boyd will gobble you up, but one day he'll spit you out."

The moment she arrived home, agitated and upset, she called Boyd. He hadn't arrived home but she left a message claiming she had a headache and could they please postpone dinner?

Fifteen minutes later he called her. "I'm coming over right away," he said, firmness and authority vibrating down the line. "I know you too well, Leo. You may have a headache—I'm sorry for that—but my guess is you've come into contact with someone out to hurt you."

"That's not it at all!" Hurriedly, she tried to deny it. "There's no need to come."

"I'm leaving now," Boyd said, his tone implying that he was wise in the way of women.

In her bedroom she changed quickly from her work clothes into a loose yellow dress. Boyd always did see through her excuses. So what was she going to tell him? The last thing she wanted to do was cause more trouble. But trouble was coming. She could smell it. She could even put a name to it. *Crisis.*

I won't marry you. I can't.

He wouldn't listen to that. Protests were in vain. Never mind the fact that losing him would kill her. Was that just another underlying fear? That one day he might abandon her, just as Tonya had prophesied? It would be bliss to live without fear, but fear was part of being human. It wasn't easy either accepting the fact that ultimately she stood alone. Inside her own skin. She wasn't by nature a clinger. She couldn't cling to Boyd.

What else might she say to him?

Tonya claims—she waylaid me in the car park—she and Gerri had a conversation regarding Rupert and his infatuation with my mother.

He would be as sceptical as she was. They both knew that Gerri had repeatedly dismissed Tonya as a foolish malicious woman, which she undoubtedly was—Geraldine seldom got anything wrong.

What about the power play between you and Rupert?

Hadn't she, herself, suggested to Boyd that he might be using her as a pawn? Hadn't he stated his position?

Was that the real motivating factor? Was Boyd's main focus wresting Blanchards from his father? Boyd was extremely ambitious, with all that went with it. Choosing the right wife was a serious business. Chloe, Rupert's favourite, didn't suit. But Leona, now, was suitable to take on as a wife. It was simply an extension of their early days. He had always taken care of her. She was part of his world. Moreover, he now had the knowledge that they were sexually compatible.

Venom, once injected into the system, was hard to fight off. People like Tonya didn't live by the rules of common decency. She was a sick woman who went around trying to spoil things for others. The realisation came to Leona—Tonya had a festering envy for all the Blanchards. It could be a very corrupting thing to be drawn into the world of the very rich, not being able to keep up with the pace and, as a consequence, becoming deeply resentful of the perceived inequities in life.

Boyd made no attempt at small talk. "What's wrong?" he asked, so attuned to her that he was instantly alert. "Come and sit down." He drew her into the living room, settling them on a sofa.

Then he waited.

"Well?" He took hold of her hand, studying her porcelain profile, so strikingly offset by her flame of hair. She was wearing yellow, a sun colour that he loved on her. "Nothing is so bad you can't tell me," he said. "Nothing is so bad I can't fix it for you."

Leona couldn't look at him. To look at him was to lose herself. Extreme as it might sound, it was the truth. At odd times over the last six or seven years she had dreamed of him falling in love with her. But it had been a fantasy, her *dream*. Now he had actually asked her to marry him. The dream had come true, but with all the capacity for conflict that entailed. There was an entire family, a business empire involved here.

"Leo, I can't force it out of you," he said gently. "Tell me."

She turned her pretty hands palms up. They were almost imperceptibly trembling. "Where do I start?"

"Why not with the name of the person you bumped into today? I didn't say this was going to be easy, Leo. Dad has always tried to run people's lives. He's tried to threaten us but it won't work. I've reached the stage where I have my own power base. I won't give you up."

She turned to him with a faintly melancholy look on her face. There were so few people who experienced a grand passion in life. So *few* people. Surely she had been blessed? But wasn't Boyd talking more like a man ready to seize power and assume the throne than a man deeply in love? He was used to power. It fitted him like a glove.

"Why not?" she asked plaintively.

He lifted her hand, then kissed her fingertips one by one. "Because you utterly enchant me."

"You don't seek to own me?" She was on the verge of tears. Boyd wanting to marry her, and marry her very soon, would be dizzying for any girl. Hadn't she believed, along with just about everyone else, that he and Chloe Compton would eventually make a match of it? Still, people talked a lot. Often they got it wrong. Geraldine definitely hadn't believed it. Geraldine was much older, far wiser, than she was. Geraldine was very perceptive.

"That works both ways," Boyd was saying, holding back a long curling swathe of her hair. "I own you. You own me. You're mine. I'm yours. I wouldn't knock it if I were you. The way we mesh is the stuff of fiction. The two of us together will be right at the heart of the family. If life is a journey, then I've chosen you as my life's partner every inch of the way."

"You don't see me as a blank canvas?" She wished she could stop these pathetic questions, but she couldn't. Was she, as Tonya had suggested, a young woman he thought he could mould as he wished? Ordinarily, she was far from being a pushover but there was no question who of the two of them was the dominant personality. Boyd knew it. She knew it.

"To be painted in at will? Don't be ridiculous, Leo," he scoffed. "You don't need *me* to tell you how gifted you are. You're so clear-sighted about so many things, yet you constantly question yourself. Or, more to the point, me!" He caught her chin, turned her face, kissed her mouth. There was something vaguely punishing in it, yet it had the power to reverberate deep within her. It was a mind-bending feeling to love someone so much that it was almost a grief.

Closing her eyes, she asked, "Do you think that under any circumstances Gerri would speak to another member of the family about Rupert's infatuation with my mother?"

She got an answer immediately. "Leo, look at me."

It was an order and she obeyed, meeting the full force of his hot blue gaze. "She's spoken to *me* about it," he said. "Geraldine is my aunt, a big part of my life. She knew I would find out at some stage. What she didn't know was my mother had already told me. One or two of the older members of the family might have had an idea. But it's not a topic for discussion, as you can well imagine. Everyone was a lot closer in those days. People have eyes. Anyway, it's all in the past, Leo."

"But the past is never past, is it? It never really goes away. It has a habit of resurfacing when we least expect it. It affects our behaviour. It makes us feel good about ourselves, or it can make us feel worthless. Why do you think I've always been so supportive of Robbie? He desperately needed help with a mother like Delia."

"And you gave it to him."

"And he gave you *me,* didn't he? Isn't this what it's all about?"

"A form of blackmail?" He cocked an eyebrow at her, almost amused. "You can't *really* believe that. You're just tormenting yourself. Robbie's stupidity just brought things to a head. I was sick of the games we played, Leo. It's just as I told you. I wanted to move forward. As for Dad! Is it a crime to fall in love with someone at any age, even if that love is unrequited? I've thought so much about this over the years. You're right. The past is never over. Incidentally, there have been quite a few sexual infidelities in our holier than holy family, as far as that goes. I used to be very angry with my father, mostly on account of my mother. Now I believe that so far as Serena was concerned, Dad didn't do anything that wrong. When Cupid aims his arrows, there's not much anyone can do about it. Dad couldn't help his feelings. He's always been a soul in torment. Maybe it was part of a mid-life crisis. It's a well documented phenomenon. The point is, ultimately he didn't act on it. Feelings are one thing. We can't help them. Actions another. Actions we *can* prevent. So what are you sitting there mulling over, Leona? Obviously something has badly distressed you and I very much want to know what it is."

She was having a lot of trouble telling him. Why? Because he didn't say, *I love you...love you...love you...*

He *did* love her. She knew that. But perhaps not in the way she desperately wanted.

Maybe the fault lay in her. Was she expecting too much? The truth was that she wanted him to love her to bits. Why didn't she say, for that matter: *You're everything I want and love. I adore you!* She'd had so little affection after her mother had died. Her father, so remote. Delia, appallingly stingy with even a kind word. Children from dysfunctional homes carried a lot of baggage into adult life. It seemed she was one of them.

Neither of them, for that matter, was using the L word. It was killing her.

"It wasn't that muckraker, Tonya, was it, by any chance?" Boyd was questioning with quick impatience. "Now there's a woman who should see a good psychiatrist. She's eaten up with envy of her sister. Of anyone, in fact, who has something she so desperately desires. Was it Tonya who was lying in wait for you? That's her style."

Leona drew a deep breath. Should she relieve her own stress and, as a consequence, make more trouble? She didn't think so. Tonya was such a fool she didn't know what she was getting into if she made an enemy of Boyd.

"So she was," he said flatly, so attuned to her he was reading her body language.

"I don't believe I said that." She was hopeless. A bundle of nerves.

"I can read your mind."

"The blank canvas?"

"I told you to stop that."

A head rush of excitement as Boyd, with a desire so fierce and palpable she couldn't miss it, pulled her across his knees, a featherweight in a soft as silk yellow dress that left her throat and arms bare and rode up over her knees to her satin thighs. "I won't have you trying to put distance between us, Leo," he said, pressing her head back over his arm. "I won't let you. Gerri would never confide family matters to Tonya."

"I know, I know." Her voice sounded small and contrite. "I'm sorry." A pause, then, with a flash of spirit, "What am I sorry for?"

"I can't think of a damned thing." Boyd laughed, a flash of white against bronzed skin. It totally obliterated the daunting expression that had darkened his face. "You're so beautiful." His hands were moving compulsively over her, the magic of it penetrating her slender, streamlined body. One hand palmed her breast, registering her rapid heartbeat. "I want to make love to you until you don't care about anyone or anything but me. You're mine, Leo, but you have to trust me. That's an order. So obey!"

Who could argue? Certainly not with desire. Who could stand fast when it swept all before it?

When his mouth came down on hers it opened like a poppy to the sun. Her breath fluttered, joined with his. To be with him was like a waking dream. A delirium of the senses. A rapture that lifted her so high she might have had wings.

They were lying in some blissful fugue state, locked in each other's arms, Leona crushed to his body with one strong arm. Their lovemaking had been gloriously passionate, both of them losing themselves in a storm of emotion. Yet it had all been soundless, save for the moans of pleasure that the flesh of one gave the other. Whatever might befall them, their coupling had the perfection one could only dream of. Was everything else just a waste of words? Leona wondered as she lay in the tender aftermath of their passion. Surely it had been ordained they should share a destiny? Where else could she find a man to love like she loved Boyd? She had to let malice and Rupert's machinations bounce off her. She had to be strong and capable. Put away her fears. Show courage. Tackle life head on. If she lost Boyd, for whatever reason, she would have to live with terrible regret for the rest of her life.

The shrilling of the bedside phone brought them swiftly

back to earth. *Go away,* Leona wanted to cry to the real world but the real world surely wouldn't.

"Don't answer it," Boyd echoed her thoughts, as instinctively she turned away.

"It's all right. Whoever it is, I'll cut it short." She swung her slender legs off the bed, then picked up the handset. "Hello?" She groped behind her for the sheet, but Boyd pulled it gently away, spreading his hand over the naked curve of her back.

"Leo, is that you?"

Oh, my God! Here it comes. How many times in life was happiness overtaken by unforeseen disaster?

Beset by premonition, Leo turned her head to Boyd, one hand covering the mouthpiece. "It's Jinty!" she whispered, the pupils of her green eyes dilated with anxiety.

Boyd sat up immediately, revealing his splendid naked torso, the white bed sheet wrapped around his long legs, black brows knotting.

"Yes, Jinty," Leona spoke into the phone. "Is everything all right?" *It can't be.* Jinty rarely rang her.

"Far from it." Jinty's voice was so taut it had to be stretched to its limits. "Is Boyd with you? It's Boyd I want."

It's Boyd I want. Obviously in the scheme of things she didn't count.

Boyd, who was pressed up close to Leona so he could clearly hear Jinty's voice, put out his hand for the phone. "It's Boyd, Jinty," he said in a strong, rather clipped tone after Leona passed it over. "What's happened?"

Swiftly Leona rose from the bed to slip into her robe, fastening the sash. She didn't need anyone to tell her something was really wrong. It could only be Rupert. Was he dying—dead? There were always consequences for one's actions. For a moment she thought she might faint.

"And where is Dad?" Boyd was asking. His tone was grave, but calm. That put the strength back into Leona's limbs.

"Come home, Boyd," was Jinty's reply.

"Well?" Leona asked after Boyd put down the phone.

"Dad has had a bad turn," he said, "or so Jinty tells me. Dr Morse is with him."

"Is he going to be hospitalised?" Leona put a hand to her throat, wondering if it was all her fault.

Boyd had no difficulty reading her transparent expression. "Don't go feeling guilty, Leo," he cautioned. "Dad's not going to die. If there were something really wrong Drew would have admitted him to hospital like a shot. What Dad wants to do is block us any way he can. I *know* him. The worst part of it is he's prepared to drag you into it, despite the fact that he gave every appearance of loving you right up until now."

"You're saying it's a ploy?" she asked incredulously. "Surely he wouldn't do that. It's so—"

"*Unfair* is the kindest word at my disposal. *Despicable* might be closer. *Pitiful* closer yet. Nevertheless, he is my father and Jinty has asked me to go to Brooklands right away."

"She sounded so strange…frightened," Leona said, ever ready to show compassion.

Boyd gave a cynical half smile. "The only thing Jinty would be frightened about is losing her position in life. She worked flat out to bag Dad, the billionaire. She got him and she's paid a price. They're not close, Leo. You know that. Even if Jinty had been a lovely woman—lovely inside and out, like my mother—Dad wouldn't have let her in. That's the way he is. He doesn't love anyone. He doesn't trust anyone. It must be like being in prison."

Leona shook her head in negation. "He loves *you*, Boyd."

"Only as an extension of himself," Boyd said, harshness in his voice. "And maybe only until I'd reached full maturity and shown I wasn't prepared to act on his every command. There's such a duality in him and there are many degrees of loving."

"Well, he doesn't want a bar of *me*," she whispered. "Not now!"

Boyd went to her, gathering her to his powerful lean frame. "Because at heart he's so deeply envious, Leona, and he can't combat that terrible feeling. It's the cause of the schism between us. You don't have to be a genius to figure that out. Dad has come to believe he missed out on everything he wanted. He hinted at it repeatedly, yet he hides his insecurities behind aggression. He can't bear to think *I* might get to know all that love is, when *he* missed out. Dad is not a paradigm of the virtues, I'm afraid. Dad's a tyrant; he's spent a lifetime threatening people. He must have decided early that was the way to go. He would have been happy enough to see me marry a woman I didn't love rather than let me have you."

He kissed the top of her head, then dropped his hands to her shoulders. "Come, let's take a shower together. Then we'll drive to Brooklands. It won't take long. No, Leo, don't back away. Brooklands is my home as much as his. You're with me. That's the way it's going to be. I won't have you pushed aside. Actually, I thought we might get married on your birthday, which will make you a beautiful Easter bride. What more could a man want? There's not a lot of time, but time enough to make all our plans."

Moments before they left her apartment, Boyd put a staying hand on her shoulder. "Here, I want you to wear this." From his tone he might have been suggesting she don a cardigan against the cool evening air.

"What is it? I'm warm enough. I'm—" She didn't finish. How was it possible for her to find words? Boyd had taken a ring from the inside breast pocket of his jacket.

And such a ring!

The central stone was a magnificent emerald, the colour of such extraordinary intensity it had to be Colombian. The emerald was flanked by a blaze of diamonds that continued around the band.

"Come here to me." He swept her into his arms, showing both strength and tenderness. "If you don't like it, we'll change it."

She went to speak but her voice had disappeared. She was stunned. At the same time her sense of alarm persisted, Rupert at the heart of it. Yet Boyd was her rock. It would be Rupert who would back down. Rupert who would need to change his stance.

"I thought it had to be an emerald with your eyes," Boyd was saying, cupping her cheek in the palm of his hand. "Don't be afraid to trust me, Leo," he said in a deeply moving voice. "Don't be afraid to love me. I'm here to help you stretch your wings. Give me your hand, sweetheart. They're the prettiest hands I've ever seen." He bent and very gently kissed the sweet curves of her mouth.

"How long have you had this?" she whispered as he slipped the exquisite engagement ring down over her finger. The fit was perfect.

"Oh, I've been keeping it safe," he assured her, giving her his beautiful white smile. "Safe for *you*. Now we'd better get going. I need to talk to Drew Morse before he leaves. If Dad has had a real turn it might galvanise him into changing his lifestyle. He can't continue to disregard his health any longer."

When they arrived a couple of hours later the huge house was ablaze with lights, which Boyd found excessive. "So much for global warming," he said tersely, pulling in alongside Drew Morse's car, then switching off the ignition. "It can't be all that bad with Dad," he said. "Drew is still here, but he wouldn't leave until I arrived."

"Do you think I should stay in the car?" Leona suggested. She wasn't one to willingly cause pain. "If Rupert really isn't well, mightn't the mere sight of me exacerbate his condition?"

"You're not forgetting you're my fiancée, are you?" Boyd stared across at her. "No, you're not staying in the car. You're coming into the house with me. A house that one day will be yours. I know your tender heart, Leo, but believe me when I say Dad has planned this. It's simply a case of Rupert Blanchard pursuing his strategies. At the very least he'll think he brought a stay of action. Come along, Flower Face. We're in this together."

Jinty was waiting for them, dressed in a floor-length glamorous house gown, with a fantastic print. Her dismayed expression—she didn't have time to hide it—gave them a clear indication that she hadn't been expecting Leona. Just Boyd.

"Thank God you're here!" she cried, reaching out to grab hold of Boyd's arm. "I've nearly been out of my mind with worry."

Boyd looked at her, handsome face impassive. "Dad's upstairs?" he asked.

"Yes, his bedroom." Jinty gestured with her hand. "Drew is with him."

"So Drew saw no necessity to have Dad airlifted to hospital?" Boyd asked, still looking Jinty in the eye.

"Well…well…he was just waiting to see."

"See what, Jinty? This is me you're talking to. I don't like to sound unsympathetic, but we both know it's much more a case of Dad cracking the whip than anything else. We'll go up."

Jinty looked alarmed. "Surely it would be better if Leona

stayed downstairs with me?" she asked sharply. "Rupert has been extremely upset. This might make him worse."

Boyd's frown deepened.

"Really I think you should go up on your own, Boyd," Leona advised, laying her hand on his arm. "Make sure first what condition your father is in. I'll stay with Jinty for now."

"If Dad's okay he can say hello to my fiancée," Boyd announced crisply, his blue eyes on fire.

"Check on him first," Leona cautioned. "Do it for me."

He paused, looking down at her. "Okay," he said gently.

"Come into the drawing room." Jinty drew Leona hastily away as Boyd mounted the staircase. "My goodness, I must say Boyd works fast. That's quite an engagement ring you're wearing. May I see it?"

Leona felt strangely reluctant to show her. Jinty had never demonstrated any genuine friendship towards her. She held her hand out briefly, the lights from the chandeliers flashing off the brilliant stones.

"Heavens, it's glorious!" Jinty said. "That emerald has to be—"

"Green for my eyes," Leona supplied, chopping off Jinty's estimate of how many carats there were in the large emerald and surrounding diamonds.

"May I try it on?" Jinty asked, not even bothering to fight off her lust for magnificent jewellery.

Leona found that distasteful, even shocking. So much for Jinty's being out of her mind with worry. She was still staring bug-eyed at the ring.

"It wouldn't fit you, Jinty," Leona said, gently shaking her head. "Could you please tell me exactly what *is* wrong with Rupert? As you pointed out, he's not looking after himself."

There was a hard glint in Jinty's eyes. "True, but my dear, I thought you knew what's really wrong with him. Rupert is very much against this engagement. Given that, as his wife, I don't feel I can stand against him on this. Or even remain neutral."

"So you've changed your tune?" Leona asked with remarkable composure. Jinty was having a hard time hiding her jealousy. "There've been many times you've disagreed with Rupert. I have no wish to be unpleasant, Jinty, but let's face it, it's really none of your business. Even Rupert goes way too far thinking he can dictate to Boyd. He certainly can't choose his bride. Boyd has chosen me. End of story. It would be a very good idea if you would show your usual good sense and accept that. We thought you had. Or that's what you gave us to understand. By the way, I had a run in with your sister today. She really should see a psychiatrist. It's fashionable these days."

Jinty's good-looking face registered both shock and anger. "I told that stupid creature to keep well away."

"Now that was always a tall order. Tonya doesn't listen to anyone. Do you happen to know the name of the mole in the family? There is one."

Jinty eyed her with marked dislike. "I'm sure I don't know what you mean," she said, oozing self-righteousness.

"The insider Tonya has sought information from?" Leona prompted. "I'm not suggesting it was you. Someone not averse to letting the family skeletons out of the cupboard and so forth?"

Jinty's eyes flashed with sudden recognition.

"You've thought of someone?" Was she now going to deny it?

"What do you want to know for, Leo?"

"I want to stop that person from doing any more talking," Leona said, realising that was exactly what she intended to do. "Rather I do it than Boyd. I know you're finding it hard to deal with—I know you've got a soft spot for Boyd—who could blame you?—but I'm not the pushover you think, Jinty."

"No, you're not," Jinty agreed wearily, as if unwilling to carry the discussion any further. "I never thought you were. Young maybe, but highly intelligent and often very kind. The informer in the family would have to be Frances Blanchard. She's as sharp as a tack and a great gossip. I used to see Frances and Tonya with their heads together. My bet is Frances. When women aren't loved they tend to grow bitter."

Upstairs in the master bedroom suite, Boyd shook hands with his father's long time physician and friend, then approached the bed. "I see you've been giving yourself hell, Dad." Boyd turned his dark head. "What do you reckon is the matter with him, Drew?" he asked.

Drew Morse discarded the last remnants of misplaced loyalty to his patient. "I won't pretend with you, Boyd. You're far too clever. Rupert here is very much against your marrying Leona. God knows why. I think she has to be one of the most delightful young women on the planet. He's been working himself up into what one would diagnose in a child as a major tantrum. I've told him that. Spot of tachycardia. I've taken care of that. Rupert hasn't been looking after himself properly for years. The cigars have to go. Less of the fine food and drink. The after dinner brandies. A bit more exercise is in order, the usual thing. Your father is fit enough, even though he's been disregarding my best advice for years. He can do it no longer. I've told him if he doesn't he's a prime candidate for a heart attack or a stroke."

Boyd turned back to his strangely silent father, taking the hand that lay on the coverlet. "Do you hear that, Dad?"

A black shadow crossed Rupert Blanchard's heavy handsome face. He shook off Boyd's hand, then pointed a finger at Drew Morse, much in the manner of pointing a gun.

"Thanks a lot, Drew. For everything. You can go now. That's my formal dismissal. Don't come back."

"Very well, Rupert," Drew Morse responded, picking up his bag. He had served Rupert Blanchard faithfully for many long years but he had always known it would come to this.

Boyd stood up for a moment. "If you wouldn't mind waiting downstairs for me, Drew," he said with quick empathy for the older man's feelings, "I'd like to have a word with you. I know you've been devoted to my father's best interests in all these long years."

Drew Morse gave a faint smile. "I'll wait if you want me to, Boyd."

"Now isn't that too touching," Rupert Blanchard sneered as the doctor closed the bedroom door quietly behind him. "Sure he gave me his best attention and he got well paid for it. I'd say attending to me alone bought him the fancy car he has outside. I hope you've come by yourself." He shot his son an intent, piercing glance.

Boyd remained standing. "Leona, my fiancée, is downstairs."

For a moment Boyd thought his father was about to spring out of the bed. "Don't do this, Dad," he warned. "It needn't be this way. Think of your own health if you can think of nothing else. The last thing I want is for you to drive yourself into a heart attack."

Rupert Blanchard shot his son a malignant look. "Sure about that?"

"Absolutely!" Boyd said in a voice charged with pity for his father but dismay for his father's mind set.

"Could I see Leona for a few minutes?" Rupert abruptly changed tack. His voice, big and blustery a moment before, went whispery with sudden weakness.

"Certainly!" Boyd agreed, his own tone softening. "As long as you give me your word you'll say nothing to upset her. She certainly won't be wanting to upset you. Leona, as we both know, has a tender loving heart."

"I know that. Just bring her up." Rupert waved a listless hand. "You have my promise. Then you can go away. I need to speak to Leona privately."

Three heads turned towards Boyd as he walked into the drawing room. Drew Morse was sitting with the women and went to stand up at Boyd's approach. Boyd waved him back into his armchair. "That's fine, Drew. I won't be long." He spoke directly to Leona. "Dad wants to have a word with you, Leo. He's promised he'll say nothing to upset you but, Dad being Dad, I don't trust him."

Leona went quickly towards him, embracing him. Behind the composure she could see the high level of strain. "I can handle it, Boyd. Is he all right? Dr Morse says he is." Relief had settled on her lovely young face.

Boyd found he couldn't answer. "I don't want you to see him on your own," he said doggedly.

Jinty broke in. "For God's sake, Boyd, what could he do? You and Leona are engaged. Like it or not, Rupert will have to accept that. He's far from being a fool. Perhaps he's already accepted it and wants to tell Leona so."

"I'll go up." Leona made the swift decision. "Rupert used to have a lot of affection for me. Perhaps some of it has returned."

"As you wish—" Boyd sighed "—but I'll wait right outside."

"You surely can't think Rupert would harm Leona?" Jinty asked in amazement.

"He'd better not try." Boyd's answer was taut enough to cut rope.

Drew Morse shook his head. "I've given him a sedative, Boyd. That's keeping him quiet."

Boyd sat in one of the antique chairs that were dotted along the wide corridor. His body, Leona could see, was on high alert. "I'll get this over quickly," Leona said, dropping a kiss on his cheek. "I'm not a little girl, Boyd. I can look after myself."

"The slightest sign of trouble and you get out of there," Boyd said. "I'm right outside the door. You tell him that."

When she thought about it afterwards, Leona wondered how it hadn't occurred to her before.

"Please shut the door after you," Rupert requested, quietly lying back against the pillows. He looked pallid and drawn and she knew a sharp pang of pity.

"How are you feeling, Rupert?" She approached the bed and took the chair beside it.

"Groggy," he said, his eyes lingering on her though not really seeing *her* at all. "I don't think there's been a single day I haven't thought about your mother," he suddenly confessed. "The way her life ended here on Brooklands. I often go to the place. I loved Alexa passionately when I married her, but I lost her early. She quickly came to see behind the façade, to see the real me. That was the problem. She saw me for what I am. Serena didn't. She was such a lovely innocent young creature. You could be her double. All I know is in my mid-forties I fell madly in love with her. I wasn't receiving any love from my wife. I wasn't giving any either. I knew it was insane but I couldn't prevent it. I was like a raw teenager in romantic agony. God knows what would have happened, only she was killed."

"Nothing would have happened, Rupert," Leona assured him. "My mother was unaware of your feelings. She loved my father.

She loved me. She loved Alexa, your wife. You did nothing wrong. Try to set your mind at rest instead of tormenting yourself with what would never have been. People constantly fall in love with the wrong person. It happens every day and every day it brings pain. Love is a mystery, isn't it? It's granted to some. Not to others. I'm so sorry your life got so twisted."

"My life—or much of it—has been utterly barren," Rupert maintained, appearing to grow angry.

"You might blame yourself, Rupert," Leona bravely suggested. "You should have cast off your bitterness, been more expansive, opened yourself up to others. You have a splendid son. That in itself is a wonderful thing. The promise of grandchildren. Instead, you've nurtured your torment. You've lived on the dark side."

He gave a grunt of bitter laughter. "Are you saying I don't have a chance at redemption?"

Leona shook her head. "I'm not saying that at all. You have every chance if you want it. We all want it for you."

Rupert stared deeply into her eyes. Not *her* eyes. Leona was painfully aware of it. Rupert had never seen her for herself.

"I'm no saint," he told her harshly.

"No, you're not," she agreed. "Neither am I. I try to do my best."

Rupert didn't hesitate. "How much would it take for you to go away? To break off this engagement? You can give Boyd some cock and bull sob story. You don't think you can live the lifestyle. He knows exactly how difficult it is. But I've been thinking. Everyone wants money. I'm prepared to give you a lot."

Leona felt any residual feeling she had for Rupert sink into the mud. "Wouldn't I be getting a lot as Boyd's wife?" she asked, assuming a Jinty inspired world-weary tone.

For a moment Rupert looked bitterly disappointed in her, then he said, "Is that why you're marrying him?"

"Of course." She nodded her red-gold head. How long she could sustain this act she didn't know.

Rupert sat up in the bed. "What a wonderful actress you are," he rasped with massive contempt. "Perfect performances. So go on then, name a figure. Might as well. My son won't be ousting me just yet, my girl. I'm good for another fifteen to twenty years. I'll do the right things and I'll have the best of care. So how much will it take to make you happy?"

Leona lifted her left hand to stare down at her glorious ring. "How many stars do you suppose are in the Milky Way, Rupert?" she asked. "I read once it was around one hundred thousand million, same number as our brain cells, though you appear to have lost a few million of those." Abruptly she stood up. "Boyd, very sadly, is quite right. Incredible as it may seem, you want to deny him happiness. You know he'll find it with me. I adore him. I always did. First love. Last love. Only love."

"Bitch! You bitch!" Rupert cried out, falling back against the pillows.

Leona walked very calmly to the door. "Goodnight, Rupert," was all she said.

CHAPTER NINE

TALK OF THE RIFT between father and son spread like a summer bush fire. Everyone in the two Sydney stores got together in groups, wondering and whispering about what might happen. Through all the years Rupert Blanchard had been the bogeyman, the boss who struck terror into the staff. Some of them had dreadful memories of him stripping pieces off them. Boyd, thank the Lord, was entirely different. The new wave Blanchard, enormously popular with the staff. They were behind him to a man. He already had the female vote. Leona was easily accepted as a great, if surprising choice. No one had picked up on the big romance. The two of them had been extremely quiet about it.

Leona openly wore her ring, accepting a never-ending flow of good wishes from near and far, which for the most part were utterly sincere.

Robbie had been exuberant with joy. "You're really, really meant for each other."

Geraldine had put it a little differently. "About time!"

"Gosh!" Sally sighed when Leona showed her the ring. "You have to be the luckiest girl in the whole wide world!"

"And Boyd is the luckiest man!" Leona retorted, then they both broke into laughter.

"Seriously, you're the perfect couple!" Sally pronounced when she sobered. "Bea says she knew it was going to happen from way back. Yet she never said a word."

"Pays not to," Leona warned.

Two days after Chloe Compton arrived home from New Zealand, she rang Leona asking her if they could meet for coffee. Chloe had received phone calls when she was in Auckland, telling her to come back as soon as she could—something was wrong. The one thing Chloe hadn't counted on was losing Boyd to his cousin—or cousin of sorts—Leona Blanchard. Everything she had seen had given her to understand the two were antagonistic. Well, not exactly *antagonistic,* but that was as far as she could get. They were always sparring anyway.

Leona's first instinct had been to drop the phone, instead she thought furiously as Chloe was speaking. Meeting Chloe didn't seem like a good idea, especially as Chloe couldn't manage her best wishes or at a pinch congratulations when everyone else around Leona was doing so. She didn't think she could bear Chloe telling her how broken-hearted she was, drowning them both in misery. In the end she told Chloe she was all booked up for at least a fortnight.

"Maybe I could come to your apartment one evening after work," Chloe suggested. "I promise I won't keep you long."

"You know where I live?" Leona asked in surprise. With her Blanchard name, she liked to keep as anonymous as possible—even her telephone number was ex-directory.

"Of course," Chloe responded, uncharacteristically sharp. "Boyd pointed out the building to me one evening when we were driving home from dinner. From recollection, I think he said, 'That's where my little cousin lives'."

Leona found that impossible to believe. Apart from anything else, Boyd would have to have gone right out of his way to drive past the building. "Maybe you're mistaken about that, Chloe," she said, maintaining a friendly voice. "Boyd has never referred to me as his little cousin, even when I *was* little. Can you tell me over the phone what this is all about? I can understand and I sympathise if you got it wrong about Boyd's feelings for you. Probably we can't be friends right now, Chloe, but in time?"

Chloe hung up on her.

Chloe announced herself at the apartment the very same evening. Obviously she knew Boyd was in Melbourne for a few days.

"Could I come up, Leona?" she asked, standing squarely in front of the video screen so Leona could see her.

How could she refuse? Chloe was a respectable young woman from an establishment family. It seemed very unkind, even unmannerly to refuse her entry. Not without misgivings, Leona pushed the button to release the security door. Why was Chloe so desperate to see her? Was she about to tell her she and Boyd had actually talked marriage?

That couldn't be. Just *couldn't*. So many things were happening in her life, she felt pounded to a pulp.

Chloe duly arrived at her door, a tall angular young woman, attractive without being eye-catching, good dark hair, chocolate-brown eyes, always beautifully dressed. Her fine skin was blotched with colour. "I'm sorry about this, Leona," she apologised, "but I have to talk to you." She stepped into the apartment before Leona could even move away from the front door.

"Well, come in," Leona invited wryly. "Can I offer you something—tea, coffee, a stiff drink?" Actually she didn't have any stiff drinks on hand. Some white wine and beer in the fridge was probably the best she could do.

"White wine, if you have it," Chloe said, slumping onto one of the living room sofas. "This is such a mess!"

"I hope you don't mean the apartment." Leona tried for a little lightness.

"God, no, it's lovely. Just like you." Chloe's voice was faintly trembling. "I mean what's happened."

Leona stood there, facing the other young woman. "You surely can't mean our engagement?"

Chloe began to cry.

"Oh, please don't cry, Chloe," Leona begged. "Here, I'll get you something to drink."

Swiftly she retreated to the galley kitchen to pour them both a glass of wine. *A mess? Okay, let's think.* The worst possible scenario—and it *did* happen frequently in real life—was Chloe about to confound her by telling her she was pregnant with Boyd's child?

Get a grip. Boyd had told her to trust him. Trust him she would.

Chloe left off drying her eyes. She accepted her drink, then took a hearty gulp. "Are you really certain Boyd is the right man for you, Leona?" she questioned.

Leona bit her tongue against a sharp answer. "I couldn't be happier, Chloe." Calmly she took a seat on the sofa opposite.

Chloe placed her hands on her hot cheeks. "Why wouldn't you be?" she moaned. "You've landed a great prize. It's the very opposite for me. The parents, especially my father, are in a terrible state. It's like a bomb has been dropped on them."

"That seems very extreme," Leona said. "I know all the talk was of an alliance between you and Boyd, an arranged marriage in the good old tradition, but that's what it was, Chloe. *Talk.* Misinformation put about by Boyd's father and your father. We both know they're the kind of men who love running their children's lives."

"Fathers!" Chloe said bitterly, downing what little was left of her wine. Leona thought it inadvisable to offer her another.

"Do you know, for the first time in my life Daddy was actually paying me some attention," she said, earning a big twinge of sympathy from Leona. "He'd hoped for a son and he got me. If I'd been a fish he would have thrown me back. I've been miserably conscious I'm a nothing person since I was a child. Do you understand that, Leona?" She shot Leona an appealing agonised glance.

"I do and I'm *so* sorry, Chloe." Leona felt genuine pity for the other woman.

"My big chance was to land Boyd," Chloe confided. "That would have made me really someone in Daddy's eyes."

"Maybe you and Daddy set your sights too high?" Leona suggested. "Women have been chasing Boyd since he left school."

Chloe was biting her lip with tension. "Why wouldn't they?" she said. "He's a man to take a woman's breath away. I love Boyd. We've known one another since we were children. I was pretty sure he was falling in love with me."

Leona had been prepared for this so it didn't come as the blow that perhaps was intended. "Could you swear to that, Chloe?" she asked. "I know Boyd, the man. I'm certain he wouldn't have given you false hope."

"We went lots of places together." Chloe lifted her chin. "Daddy thought it was a very good sign. Rupert always made a fuss of me, singled me out. You must know you're currently in high disfavour? Rupert is absolutely furious with Boyd."

"None of which will do you any good, Chloe." Leona was becoming tired of this whole conversation. She glanced at her wrist watch, giving a little start. "I don't like to hurry you, but I'm dining out this evening." She had no difficulty telling the white lie.

"But Boyd's in Melbourne!" Chloe huffed, as though that was the first step in Leona's journey to becoming unfaithful.

"I do have friends, Chloe," Leona answered mildly enough. "Now, if there's nothing else I can help you with?"

Chloe stood up, squaring her shoulders and gathering her very expensive designer bag. "Daddy will never forgive me for losing out on Boyd," she said. "It was my one opportunity in life to gain his approval."

"I'm sure there will be others," Leona replied gently. "Why don't you try to make a life for yourself, Chloe? Moving out of your parents' home would be a start."

Chloe looked back at Leona with startled eyes. "And lose out on my inheritance?" she cried. "Sorry, that's just not on!"

So much for independence!

After Chloe left Leona was overtaken by a strange loneliness. Women in love were so terribly vulnerable. What she desperately needed was Boyd's reassuring presence.

At nine-thirty the phone rang.

She flew to it. "Hi, Flower Face. I've been tied up in meetings all day. Couldn't wait to ring you…"

In an instant all Leona's doubts and fears were blown away.

They were back in place the following day. Immediately she caught sight of Boyd's face Leona knew something had gone terribly wrong. He had arrived back from Melbourne mid-afternoon. They had dinner planned for this evening. Now he had arrived at the apartment, looking so blazingly handsome, so formidable, the sheer *maleness* of him made her reel. It was almost as if a big argument was on simmer, waiting to boil.

"Is something wrong?" she asked, eyeing him tentatively. He hadn't kissed her. Was it any wonder she felt a black cloud descending?

"Why didn't you tell me Dad offered you money to break

off the engagement, leave town, go overseas?" he asked, a muscle working along the clean-cut line of his jaw.

She stared back at him, speechless.

"No answer?" he asked, his blue eyes brilliant with high mettle.

Was she going to have to live with this for ever?

"Who told you?" she countered. She had never said a word to Boyd about her last conversation with his father. It was too demeaning, not to her but to Rupert. Loving Boyd like she did, she wasn't about to offer him further upset. Now it seemed that had been a tactical error. The Blanchards dealt in tactics, didn't they?

"Okay, so it's true." He pulled her to him, locking an arm around her. "What was the final figure?"

She leaned back against his arm. Fiery sparks of electricity. "What did Rupert tell you?" Because she was so stung, she spoke in a provocative manner quite unlike her.

"Ten million." His tone was tight with disgust.

She broke away with a brittle laugh, moving into the living room. "Pretty cheap, I'd say. You're worth far more than that, Boyd." Her tone was unmistakably contemptuous. "I'm holding out for more."

He came after her, fighting down his explosive mood. He'd had a tough agenda and he was nearly dead on his feet. "You won't get it or anything like it," he said. "I don't believe a bloody word of it anyway. Why didn't you tell me? Why *won't* you trust me, Leo? What can I offer you that will make you love me?"

She spun so quickly the skirt of her lovely sea-green dress swirled about her legs. "I do love you!" She was swept by passionate revolt. "But you're a dreadful lot, you Blanchards. You're famous for being dreadful. There should be warning placards saying: Don't get mixed up with this lot! You want to know what's going on? I'll tell you. Chloe Compton arrived on my doorstep yesterday, desperate to unburden herself."

Boyd groaned aloud. "You didn't tell me that either."

"I didn't want to upset you," she answered hotly. "Now I simply don't care. Your horrible father did offer to buy me off. I didn't tell you because I thought it too demeaning to Rupert. Shows what I know about how low Rupert can stoop. As for Chloe, she accepts you don't love her—"

"Love her? God!" Boyd's expression indicated the level of his disgust was sky-high. "Go on. She told you we were lovers. We were trying to have a child together. I'm prepared to believe anything." He threw his tall elegant body into an armchair.

"She didn't go that far," Leona told him coldly. "Poor Chloe considers herself a nothing person. Landing you would have been the defining moment of her life. Her father would have been proud of her for the very first time."

"Being proud of his only daughter—his only child—is a problem for Compton," Boyd said, gritting his fine teeth. "Why doesn't Chloe have the guts to get out and make a life of her own? Anyway, forget Chloe. Sad for her, she *is* forgettable."

"I think even she realises that. Anyway, I think Chloe believes—maybe a lot of people do—you and Rupert are fighting a duel with me in the middle."

Boyd groaned, thrusting a frustrated hand through his crow-black hair. "That's probably true. We *are* fighting a duel. But it's not one *I* brought on. I'm content to succeed my father in due course. This isn't about me or you, Leo. It's about Dad. It's about how life has warped him."

"So it's a fight to the finish?" she asked, breathing fast. There was so much emotion in the room it was draining the air out.

"I won't give you up, Leo," he said. "Not for Dad. Not for Blanchards. Not even for *you*. Are we going out to dinner, or are we just going to go to bed?" he asked, an unbearably cynical note in his voice.

At his tone Leona angrily pulled the pins out of her beautiful hair and shook it free of its arrangement. "Neither, as it turns out," she said in the manner of a young woman who had had enough. "I don't give a damn about going to bed. This has gone right beyond sex. I won't be used as a pawn, Boyd. I'm a *woman!*"

"My God, aren't you!" he said, getting up and coming towards her. He didn't want half measures. His whole being was crying out for her.

"Don't you dare kiss me!" she threatened, tears standing in her eyes. "You didn't kiss me when you arrived!" she accused him, every word ringing with intense disappointment.

Boyd took her face between his hands, bringing it closer to his. "Well, I'm kissing you now." He bent his head and began to kiss her passionately, like a drowning man clinging to his one hope in life.

"Come to bed with me, Leo," he whispered between the most ardent of kisses.

"I won't. I mean it," she cried, her small fists clenched hard. It suddenly seemed immensely important to stand firm. She fought off the familiar waves of desire that were flooding her body. Besides, there was this strange exhilaration in defying him. No matter how much pain she was giving herself, she had her pride. Did he love her or lust for her? Was she the silly sacrificial lamb?

"Okay!" Abruptly, Boyd threw up his arms in an exaggerated movement of surrender. "I don't know what else I have to do, Leo. Right now, I'm so bloody tired, I'm fresh out of ideas. I want you so badly I can hardly think of anything else. But I'm not going to tolerate your switching on and off. I'm not going to tolerate your keeping things from me. I understand your motives, but I think you would know I can handle any amount of upset. It's the keeping things from me I don't like. I've asked you to share my life. Doesn't that say it all? You're not some bimbo I lust after. Give me a break. Either we're together or we're *not* together. It's up to you."

The ultimatum delivered, Boyd turned on his heel and strode to the door.

Within seconds her hot raging blood ran cold in her veins. She had to fight the powerful urge to run after him, but her thoughts were all over the place. In the end she let him go, even though he was an inseparable part of her. She had to think this whole thing through. Not only Rupert was trying to drive them apart. It took her a while to realise she was crying silently, the tears sliding down her cheeks. Boyd was prepared to stand up to his father, the most ruthless of men. Rupert couldn't control their lives. Why was she so afraid? Even her father wasn't afraid that Rupert might ruin his career with Blanchards. He was prepared to move on. Possibly without Delia at his side.

What, then, should *she* do? She sat down on the sofa with a box of tissues, folding her legs under her. The surest way to wreck her life was to lose Boyd. He was so much stronger than she was. More equipped by nature and long experience to cope with all this fallout. What she had to do was face up to the demanding job of becoming his wife. Probably if she were a few years older she might be able to cope better. It hadn't been easy being part of the Blanchard family. But she did owe them a lot. Most of them, as she had so recently found out, were right on side with her. All except the most powerful Blanchard of them all.

Either we're together or we're not!

Boyd had challenged her and with good reason. She had to let go of her fears. It wasn't Rupert who could destroy her dreams.

She realised with a sense of shock it was *her own self.*

* * *

An hour later she rang Boyd at his apartment, judging he would have had ample time to arrive home. She was all ready with her apologies, desperate to make up. What woman in her right mind would risk losing such an extraordinary man? She wasn't going to have to walk through life alone. She had Boyd.

The phone rang out and his answering service picked up. He hadn't gone home.

She did her best not to break down. She left her message. *"It's me. I'm so sorry for tonight. I don't know what gets into me at times. Speak to you tomorrow."*

It was as much as she could manage without dissolving into a flood of tears.

Leona was not to know it, but Boyd had gone over to his aunt Geraldine, his long time confidante and supporter, to talk through the dark situation his father—her brother—had mired them in. They talked until so late that Geraldine suggested he stay the night, which he did and not for the first time. Geraldine now knew the full story but she would never say a word. Nevertheless she had been ready with plenty of advice.

"Nothing wrong with a man speaking his mind," she said. "But you have to remember Leo's age and her tender heart. Then there's the fact she's being beset on all sides. Drat that Chloe. She needs to get herself sorted. Rupert has been responsible for such a lot of hurt. No need to tell you that. You'll be seeing Leo today, of course."

"Of course." Boyd bent to kiss his aunt's cheek.

As it happened Boyd had outside appointments for most of the morning so Leona wasn't able to get through to him.

"I'll tell him you called the moment he arrives, Miss Blanchard," said Vera Matthews, his secretary. Although Leona had often invited Vera to call her Leona, Vera, a woman of the old school, immensely capable and loyal, stuck to the more formal Miss Blanchard.

She still hadn't heard from Boyd by lunchtime so she went off in search of a solitary coffee. She had asked Sally to join her but she was so snowed under she said she would have a bite to eat at her desk.

It was as Leona was returning to the office just under an hour later that she saw Rupert and one of the Blanchard Board members in intense discussion outside Stewart Murray's merchant bank. She couldn't do as she wished and cross the street to avoid them. She couldn't get caught jaywalking on top of everything else.

It was Bob Martin who first spotted her, smiling and tipping the brim of his hat. Bob was a nice man. Rupert was at work again; no doubt he would be looking to ensure Bob's support if any battle was to take place in future. She smiled back, pointing to her watch and quickening her step, miming that she was late back for work. She could have gone over but she couldn't bring herself to do it. She was disgusted with Rupert. She was trying very hard not to be frightened. Rupert was such an intimidating man. Yet men like Rupert had an absolute certainty that they were always in the right.

The pavements were thronged with people, workers coming off or going on their lunch break, tourists, shoppers clutching lots of bags. She wasn't aware of Rupert until he spoke from directly behind her. "You know exactly what you want, don't you, my dear?" His tone was deliberately low but she heard every grim word with unnatural clarity.

"Yes, I do, Rupert," she said quietly with clear-headed courage. Her strength had returned. She turned to face him as he came alongside her, a big handsome man, faultlessly groomed, with a palpable aura of power and, it had to be admitted, on this day of days, a frightening aura of violence. "I want your son. I want Boyd. He knows exactly what he wants too. The best thing for us all, Rupert, is to be family. The worst thing would be for you to enter into a losing battle with Boyd. He doesn't want that. Neither do I."

Rupert's eyes narrowed to slits and his cheeks flushed red. "Such insolence!" He gave a harsh laugh.

"Please, Rupert," she begged, feeling sadness for the man he had become. The worst part was that it seemed impossible for him to change.

They were now close to the junction, facing Blanchards' main store, hemmed in by the lunchtime crowd. Leona had never felt so uneasy in her life. Yet her own personal safety wasn't on her mind. The opposing traffic was given the green light at the precise moment that a brutally strong hand moved to shove her in the middle of the back. She let out a cry, closing her eyes as her willowy body, unprepared for the onslaught, bowed forward. She lost balance in her high heels and stumbled onto the road.

People nearby reacted in an instant, filled with alarm, but frozen in position. It was all happening so fast. Others hurrying to catch the lights wondered what was going on. The young woman with the beautiful mane of red-gold hair appeared to have catapulted from the pavement into the direct path of the oncoming cars. One skidded around a corner, avoiding certain trouble. The following car, an SUV unaware of the woman in the road came on. No city driver dared to hold up the steady stream of traffic. A woman with her small daughter standing to the left of where Leona had been standing cried out, terrified.

Leona herself scarcely had time to panic, though she expected to be run over in the next moment. Only Rupert galvanised himself. He scooped her up from behind, all but flinging her slender body back into the crowd without thought for himself and the dangerous proximity of the oncoming SUV. The driver, however, was swiftly to realise in horror that he was going to hit a pedestrian. No comfort at all in the fact that the pedestrian shouldn't have been on the road with the lights against him.

Rupert's tall heavy body was picked up and flung down on the road as if he were no weight at all.

The whole world seemed to grind to a stop and Leona fainted for the first time in her life.

The six o'clock news started with a bulletin: Rupert Blanchard dead—although the shocking news had already broken on the street and on the Internet. With sombre faces and subdued voices, anchor men on different television channels relayed the account of how the retail giant, billionaire and philanthropist, one of the richest men in the country, had bravely put his own life on the line to save that of his future daughter-in-law, Leona Blanchard, who had recently become engaged to the Blanchard heir, Boyd Blanchard. Rupert Blanchard had been swiftly transferred from the accident scene to the nearest hospital but tragically he had died en route from a fatal head injury.

Leona, still in shock and detained at the hospital, almost believed it. Rupert had given his life to save her? Let everyone believe it. At the end he did. The rest was best left unsaid. She had given a statement to the police. She had told them she felt dizzy and had stumbled in her high heels. Rupert had been there when he was desperately needed. The tragedy was that he had been unable to save himself. She would never forget his sacrifice.

That would be the family line. She *was* family. Boyd was now at its head. Responsibility had already fallen heavily on her shoulders. She could bear it. Rupert had punished himself in his own way.

"A terrible, terrible thing!" the young nurse in her room said, tears standing in her eyes, her voice very gentle. "He must have loved you a great deal."

It had taken hours for Boyd to take charge of what was now a tremendous crisis for Blanchards. More was expected of him than most other people. He had grown up with that. Staff all over the building were crying, a sure indication that great wealth alone was enough to bring forth tears, he thought with faint bitterness. His father had not been loved.

Boyd had spoken to everyone he wanted to speak to, needed to speak to. He had given endless instructions thanking God for his personal staff's cool, calm efficiency in the midst of chaos. All he wanted was to get to the hospital to pick up his beloved Leona and bring her home. He had talked to a doctor—somebody—who had assured him she wasn't in any way hurt, only in shock, as was to be expected. Much as he longed for it, there was no way he could get to her until he had taken care of everything that needed to be taken care of, which was a great deal. He had heard the story, had spoken to the police, had seen the television news.

Something was being hidden here. His instincts over many long years had been honed razor sharp. He turned the whole thing over and over in his mind. He wouldn't believe a single thing until he had Leona where she needed to be—safe in his arms. From now on he wouldn't let her out of his sight.

He parked outside the hospital in a doctor's reserved spot, not caring. He didn't pause at reception. He swept on to the room where he knew Leona had been taken. She wasn't on the bed. She was sitting on a chair, fully dressed, her beautiful hair cascading over her shoulders. It was the only thing that looked vital about her. She was white as milk, fragile as spun glass.

His heart melted with love. "Leo, sweetheart, I came as quickly as I could." He went to her, raising her with exquisite gentleness to her feet, keeping his arms protectively around her.

She smiled at him. He had never seen a sweeter, more poignant smile in his life.

"Boyd," she said very quietly, reaching up to stroke his cheek. "I'm *so* sorry."

"I know." He bent his head to kiss her. It was a kiss that was more a solemn vow—an affirmation that she was his woman, the woman he was to marry. She was looking so traumatised it cut him to the heart. "Are you ready to go home?" he asked. "The car is just outside." He was desperate to hold her. Comfort her. Help her over her shocking experience. He knew he wouldn't be able to get over it.

"I go where you go," she said, raising her eyes to his. "I love you with all my heart. I'll love you until my last breath. What if I never had the chance to tell you properly?" She was suddenly frantic, feeling once more Rupert's strong ruthless hand at her back. "I can't possibly imagine life without you. You know that?"

"I do. I do. Hush now," he soothed. "You've had a terrible shock. I'm here. We're together. I'll never leave you. We're an invincible team, you and I. Now, let's get you out of here. We won't talk about anything until you feel you're ready."

The knowledge that he had guessed what might have happened flashed through her. How could she keep anything from Boyd? He always saw through to the truth. He saw behind the smokescreen, even as part of him mourned the manner of his father's passing.

"He did save me in the end," she said sadly. "No secrets between us, Boyd?"

"No secrets," he confirmed, hugging her to him, trying his hardest to crush the horror he felt at what his father had seriously contemplated in a moment of madness, like some wicked god who demanded sacrifice. It didn't bear thinking about. Not now, though it would be with him all the days of his life. His whole being was committed to comforting his love, his only love—Leona.

"Only the two of us will ever know," she whispered.

He turned her to him. Kissed her. Their first public kiss. More loving kisses would be recorded by the media over the many long years of their public life. Indeed it was to become near impossible for the public to imagine one without the other. They were the Blanchards, not only a symbol of wealth and power, but wonderful humanitarianism and family love.

That early evening, with a momentous day drawing to its close, Boyd and Leona walked arm in arm down the long corridor, each gathering strength from the other. Those of the hospital staff who were about at the time smiled gently, compassionately at them. All were sensible to the fact that they were looking at two young people deeply in love. The *real* thing was lovely, impossible to miss.

Rupert Blanchard's unhappy life was over. Theirs had just begun.

EPILOGUE

TIDINGS OF JOY! RARE OLD TIMES!
Daisy Driver.
Aurora Magazine.
Place: Brooklands, the fab Blanchard estate in the beautiful Hunter Valley.
Occasion: The thrillingly spectacular Blanchard wedding.

EXCITEMENT REACHED FEVER pitch at the wedding between the charismatic Boyd Blanchard and his utterly enchanting bride, Leona, who won't have to bother changing her surname. It was unquestionably the wedding—might I say celebration—of the year. Take it from one who gets invited to these things. The ceremony was held in the most romantic of venues, Brooklands' famous rose gardens brought to their peak for this wonderful occasion. A dream temple was erected for the moving ceremony—many a tear, me included, a virtual torrent of sobs from someone behind me. For my money, a union of *souls*—I've never been more sure of anything in my life—the open air temple filled with the bride's favourite flower, you guessed it, the rose in all its beauty and bewitching scent.

The cream of society came from all over the country. Dressed to kill. Lashings of bling. A whole contingent from overseas. The tab, I understand, was picked up by the groom. Generous man!

The bride's dress made by our leading fashion designer, Liz Campbell, also the bride's friend, was so ravishing I find it near impossible to describe and I'm not one, as most of you will know, who is usually lost for words. But, for our avid readers, I'll have a go. Take it for granted it was gorgeous as one would expect with such a gorgeous bride. Oh, that magnificent mane of red-gold hair and the luminous skin! Forgive me, I digress. The gown was strapless, moulded skin tight to the body, dipping into the cleavage, a lustrous silk taffeta the colour of the eye-popping South Sea island pearls around the bride's throat, hand embroidered with ivory roses, as was a wide band of the marvellously billowing skirt that showcased the bride's tiny waist. One had to see the exquisite fit, the detailing, that bell of a skirt that became a short train to fully appreciate the effect. An elbow-length tulle veil was held in place by an exquisite head-piece crafted with ivory rose bouquets, decorated with shimmering crystals and tiny pearls, the leaves quivering on tiny gold wires. Swinging from the bride's ears—wait for it—were the fabulous Blanchard Diamond earrings, part of a suite I was told was acquired way back from a South African billionaire. What a family heirloom! As the light hit them the female guests gave a collective gasp. It took quite a while for me to lose the retinal after-burn. Honestly, girls, there's *nothing* like an enormous diamond and when they weigh in at heaven knows how many carats it's a sight your reporter will never forget.

Our beautiful bride had six bridesmaids in all, all stunning, all sliver-thin so they could get into the form-fitting long strapless gowns that echoed the lovely shades of the roses—porcelain pink, blush pink, gold, soft yellow and an exceptionally beautiful apricot. Such a colour palette perfectly complemented the bride's radiant colouring. Four little flower girls from the Blanchard family, impossibly pretty, in tulle and taffeta pale gold dresses with satin ribbons for headdresses with long flowing back bows attended the bride, along with two little pageboys, twins of the Blanchard clan, who behaved remarkably well considering what six-year-old tots can be like.

The groom looked absolutely splendid, girls. A fairy tale prince. Alas, now taken! Seriously, why can't we all have a prince? His attendants had to be a line-up of some of the handsomest and most eligible bachelors in the country. I don't like to single one out—they all looked terrific—but the bride's stepbrother, Roberto, who flew home especially from his gap year stay with close relatives in Italy, is going to be a man to look out for. Remember, I was the first to tell you!

The reception was held in Brooklands' magnificent ballroom. Out of this world! Some of you will recall the groom's beautiful mother Alexa, holding her famous charity functions there. Maybe we'll see the like again? Here's hoping! Anyway, the food and drink—a bubbling fountain of French champagne—were sumptuous. I actually got to dance with man about town, Peter Blanchard, who said nice things to me, and when prompted, about my column. I think he took a fancy to me because I made him laugh.

Back in Sydney again and at my desk trying to calm down after a magnificent over-abundance of everything.

Of course one of these days I'm going to get married too. No register office for me, girls, but a big, BIG, wedding, just like the Blanchards.

How rare and beautiful was that! I seriously doubt if I'll ever cover such a sublimely romantic wedding again.

MANHATTAN BOSS, DIAMOND PROPOSAL

TRISH WYLIE

Trish Wylie tried various careers before eventually fulfilling her dream of writing. Years spent working in the music industry, in promotions, and teaching little kids about ponies gave her plenty of opportunity to study life and the people around her. Which, in Trish's opinion, is a pretty good study course for writing! Living in Ireland, Trish balances her time between writing and horses. If you get to spend your days doing things you love, then she thinks that's not doing too badly. You can contact Trish at www.trishwylie.com.

For Marilyn, the kind of reader who makes me
remember why I write, even on the days
words are hard to find...

And for John—the best tour guide
in New York City.

PROLOGUE

'HE'S NOT COMING.'

'What do you mean he's not coming?'

Clare O'Connor turned away from the floor-length mirror, her chin lifting so she could search his eyes. Not that she knew him well enough to be able to read anything there. Tall, dark and brooding she'd named him after their first meeting. And despite the fact she'd since had glimpses of a wicked sense of humour, when he chose to use it, she still thought her initial impression was on the money.

She shook her head. 'What do you mean he's not coming? Did something happen to him?'

A muscle jumped in his jaw. And it was the first indication she had that he was telling the truth. She shook her head again, nervous laughter escaping her parted lips. No way. There was no way Jamie had done this to her. Not now.

'I'm sorry, Clare.'

When one long arm lifted towards her she stepped back, the world tilting a little beneath her feet. 'Where is he?'

'He's gone.'

'Gone?'

Gone where? Why? What had happened? This kind of thing didn't happen in real life! She tried to form a coherent thought rather than parroting everything she was told. Why now? Why not yesterday or the day before that or the day before that? When there'd been time to cancel everything and let everyone know. Why let her follow him all the way across the Atlantic if—?

'He didn't have the guts to face you.'

Clare laughed a little more manically. 'So he sent *you* to tell me?' Of all the people Jamie knew he had felt *this guy* was the one to send? It was almost funny. 'No phone call? No note? Is this a joke?'

'No joke. He's gone and he's not coming back.'

The determined tone to his voice made the edges of her vision go dark. When she felt herself swaying, two large hands grasped her elbows to steady her while she blinked furiously.

'You need to sit down.'

Clare yanked her arms free, her gaze focusing on a smudge of dirt on his jacket before sliding over the dark material and noticing several other smudges along the way. But she wasn't interested in how they'd got there, she just needed to think. She needed to—

When her chin jerked towards the door and her eyes widened with horror, his husky voice sounded above her head. 'I'll go.'

Dear God. All the people beyond that door, waiting for *her*—how was she supposed to face them? But she couldn't let him go out there and do her dirty work for her. Not that the offer wasn't tempting, but they were waiting for *her.* And some of them had flown thousands of miles—*for her.* So it was her responsibility to tell them...

Swallowing down a wave of nausea, she reached for his arm. 'Wait. Just give me a second here.'

Taking several deep breaths of cool air, she tightened her fingers around his forearm, as if the part of her that was drowning naturally sought out something solid to keep her from going under.

From somewhere she found the strength to keep her voice calm. 'Did he leave with her?'

'Clare—'

She flexed her fingers as she looked up. 'Did he? I want to know.'

'How long have you known?'

Up until he'd asked that question she'd never really known for sure. But she had her answer now, didn't she? So much for telling herself it was paranoia...

Letting go of his arm, she nodded firmly while biting down on her lower lip to stop it from trembling. If the price of naïveté was the death of the starry-eyed dreamer then the job was done. And she was about to receive her punishment on a grand scale, wasn't she?

'I'll tell them. It's because of me they're out there in the first place.'

'You don't have to.'

'Yes, I do.' An inward breath caught on a hint of a sob so she closed her eyes and willed it away, promising it: *later.* Later when no one could see. 'Jamie might not care about them but I do. They'll hear it from me.'

When she opened her eyes and glanced up, she saw what looked like respect in his eyes. And for some unfathomable reason she felt laughter bubbling up in her chest again—hysteria, probably. Possibly a hint of irony that it took something so completely degrading to earn respect from the man who had never approved of her in the first place.

When she lifted the front of her long skirt in both hands, he stepped back and opened the door for her, towering over her as she took a deep breath and hovered in the gap.

'I'm here if you need me.'

She smiled at him through shimmering eyes and then stepped forwards, her gaze focused on the flower-decked arch at the top of the room instead of the sea of faces turning her way.

It was the most humiliating day of her life.

'I'm afraid there won't be a wedding today…'

CHAPTER ONE

'I'LL CALL YOU.'

'*Do.*'

Quinn opened his office door and looked up from the file he'd been reading, not entirely sure if it was the tail-end of the conversation or the sight of his personal assistant being hugged so tightly by some guy he'd never set eyes on before that brought a frown to his face. He should be aware of everything that happened in his own offices after all, shouldn't he? And he had the distinct niggling feeling he was being left out of the loop somehow—something he never, *ever* let happen.

Leaning his shoulder against the doorjamb, he watched with narrowed eyes until the stranger cut her loose.

'New boyfriend?'

The familiar lustrous sparkle of emerald eyes locked with his as the main door closed behind her mystery man. 'And when exactly do I have time for a boyfriend?'

'You know what they say about all work and no play.'

With a shake of her head, Clare bent to retrieve a

sheet of paper off her desk. So Quinn allowed his gaze to make a cursory slide over her tailored cream blouse and simple linen trousers, watching the subtle grace of her movement. If he'd been a romantic of any kind he'd have said Clare moved like a ballerina. She certainly had a ballerina's body: fine-boned and slender—a few more curves maybe, not that she ever dressed to flaunt them or that Quinn had ever looked closely enough to confirm their presence.

But since Quinn Cassidy had graduated with honours from the school of hard knocks he was somewhat lacking in anything remotely resembling romance. So if forced to use a word to describe the way she moved it would quite simply be feminine.

One of the things he'd liked right from the start was the fact she never felt the need to do anything to bring that femininity to a man's attention. It was also one of the many reasons she'd survived so long working as his PA. The one before her had barely had time to take off her jacket before she'd started leaning her cleavage towards him. It had been like sharing an office with a bar-racuda.

He shuddered inwardly at the memory.

'Speaking of work—' she calmly handed him a sheet of paper when he nudged off the doorjamb and took a step forwards '—here's a list of all the places you have to be today and when. Try and make a few of the appointments on time if you can—for a wee change.'

When she accompanied the words with a sideways tilt of her head and a small smirk that crinkled the bridge of her nose, Quinn couldn't help smiling, even though technically he was being told off. In fairness he didn't think his timekeeping had ever been bad, but in the year since Clare had come to work for him she'd been determined he should be at everything at least ten minutes early. He reckoned, however, that if he was early for every single meeting, and had to twiddle his thumbs while he waited for people to turn up, it would add up to a whole heap of wasted time in the long term.

So he rebelled regularly on principle.

He glanced over the neatly typed list before lifting his chin in time to watch Clare perch on the edge of her desk, a thoughtful expression on her face while she swung her feet back and forth. So he waited…

Eventually she spoke in the softly lilting Irish accent she hadn't lost since she'd come to New York. 'On the subject of *play*—it's been a while since I had to make a trip to Tiffany's…'

Quinn cocked a brow. 'And?'

She shrugged one shoulder. 'I just wanted to make sure I wasn't falling behind. Up till recently I'd been considering keeping a stock of those wee blue boxes here to save me some time.'

He watched as out of the corner of her eye she caught sight of an errant pen lying on the edge of the desk, giving it a brief frown before she dropped it into a nearby container with a satisfied smile. It never ceased to amaze him, the amount of pleasure she derived from the simplest of things.

'You're just missing your trips to Tiffany's.' He shook his head and looked her straight in the eye. 'I can't run all over Manhattan breaking hearts just so you can while away a few more hours down at your favourite store, now, can I?'

'Never stopped you before.' She thrust out her bottom lip and batted long lashes at him comically.

True. But he wasn't about to get drawn into another debate about his love life when he was suddenly much more interested in hers. 'So who was the Wall Street type?'

'Why?'

'Maybe I need to ask him what his intentions are towards my favourite employee…'

'So you get to vet all my boyfriends now, do you?'

Quinn folded his arms across his chest, allowing the corner of the sheet of paper to swing casually between his thumb and forefinger. 'You said he wasn't your boyfriend.'

Another shrug. 'He's not.'

She lifted her delicate chin and rose off the desk to walk round to her swivel chair, swinging forwards before informing him 'He's a client.'

Quinn knew what she was getting at, even if it apparently meant her part-time hobby had morphed into something bigger when he wasn't looking. 'This matchmaking game of yours is a business now, is it?'

'Maybe.' She drummed her neat fingernails on the sheaf of papers in front of her. 'Problem?'

Two could play at that game—she should know that by now—and her poker face wasn't worth squat, so Quinn continued looking her straight in the eye. 'Maybe.'

'Because it's during working hours or because you still think the whole thing is a great big joke? I'm not falling behind with my work, am I?'

The thought had never crossed his mind. Thanks to Clare, his working life ran like a well-oiled machine. Not that he hadn't managed to get things done before, but with her around everything was definitely less stressful than it had been before. There'd once been a time when he'd thrived on the adrenaline of being under pressure, but he'd outgrown those days. And, frankly, the matchmaking thing was starting to grate on him.

'I'd have thought you of all people would under-stand the danger of matching starry-eyed people with someone who might break their heart.'

It was a sucker punch, considering her history. But he knew Clare pretty well. If dozens of people came back to cry on her shoulder in a few months' time she'd feel responsible, and she'd silently tear herself up about it. She was digging her own grave. Quinn simply felt it was his responsibility to take the shovel out of her hand.

'C'mon, if they're so desperate they can't find a date without your help, then—'

Disbelief formed in her eyes. 'Is it so very difficult for you to believe that some people might simply be sick to death of trawling the usual singles scene? Not everyone has the—' she made speech marks with crooked fingers '—*success* you have with women…'

Quinn ignored the jibe. 'I s'pose that means I should expect to find long lines of Ugly Bettys and guys who still live with their mothers arriving in here every five minutes from here on in?'

If she thought for a single second he was going to be happy about that she could think again. He hadn't batted an eyelid when she'd matched up friends of mutual friends outside of work, but the line had to be drawn somewhere. And he was about to tell her as much when she pushed the chair back from her desk and walked to the filing cabinets.

'Don't worry, Quinn. If word keeps spreading as fast as it has these last few months, then pretty soon I'll be making enough money to be able to afford my own office. And then it won't be your problem any more, will it?'

'You're quitting on me now?'

The thought of the endurance test involved with breaking in another PA made him frown harder. Prior to Clare he'd gone through six in almost as many months.

'If you needed a raise all you had to do was say so…'

Clare continued searching the drawer. 'It's got nothing to do with getting a raise. It's a chance to build something on my own. And if I can help make a few people happy along the way, then all the better.'

Okay, so he could understand her feeling the need to stand on her own two feet. That part he got. But he'd been pretty sure the arrangement they had had been working for both of them. Why rock the boat?

Stepping over to the desk, he turned on his heel and sat down on the exact same spot Clare had, schooling his features and deliberately keeping his voice nonchalant.

'You've obviously been thinking about this for a while. So how come I'm only hearing about it now?'

'Maybe because you've never asked…'

'I'm asking now.'

It couldn't possibly be taking so long to find whatever it was she was looking for. Not with her hyperefficient filing system. Half the time he only had to think about information he needed and the next thing he knew, it was in front of him. She was avoiding looking at him, wasn't she?

'O'Connor—'

'You know, if you'd bothered reading the schedule I just gave you you'd see you have a meeting in less than twenty minutes…'

Nice try. Setting the schedule down, Quinn pushed upright and took the two strides necessary to bring him close enough to place his hands on her slight shoulders, firmly turning her to face him. When her long lashes lifted, her eyes searching each of his in turn, he did the same back before smiling lazily.

'Working for me proved too tough in the end, did it? If you recall, I warned you at the start I was no walk in the park.'

Clare's full mouth quirked at the edges—they both knew she dealt with him just fine, even on the days every other person on the planet would have avoided him.

'Well, I won't say there aren't days I have to bite my tongue pretty hard. But it's got nothing to do with the work—it's something I need to do for me. If I can make it here, I can make it anywhere.' Her smile grew. 'That's how the song goes, right?'

Quinn fought off another frown. 'So how much notice are you giving me?'

'Oh, I'm not handing in my notice just yet.'

But it was coming, wasn't it? She was serious. And her job had long since exceeded the usual remit of personal assistant. She was his girl Friday—co-ordinating the Clubs, making sure staffing levels were sufficient, putting together promotions, booking live acts, filling in when someone was sick even if it meant working for fifteen hours straight…

Everyone who worked for him had even taken to *calling* her 'Friday', and she always smiled when they did, so Quinn had assumed she was happy in the role she'd taken on. The thought that she *wasn't* happy irritated him no end. He should have known if she wasn't.

And how exactly was he supposed to list all she did for him in a Help Wanted ad if she *did* quit?

Realising his hands had slid downwards, his thumbs smoothing up and down on her upper arms while he thought, Quinn released her and stepped back. 'You'd miss all the craziness here, you know.'

Her voice softened. 'I will. I've loved it here.'

Despite the fact she'd just allayed one fear, it was the fact she hadn't used 'I would' or 'I might' but *'I will'*, that got to him most.

But he hid behind humour. 'I'd better think about making a trip to Tiffany's on my own to get one of those blue boxes for you, then, hadn't I?'

The smile lit up her face, making the room immediately brighter than it already was, with the summer sun filtering in between the Manhattan high-rises to stream through the large windows lining one wall.

'You should probably know I have a wish list…'

'And I'll just bet there's a diamond or two on it.'

She nodded firmly. 'Diamonds are a girl's best friend, they say. But don't go overboard.' She patted his upper arm. 'I haven't had to suffer my way through the usual broken heart required to get a blue box from you.'

Files in hand, she walked back to her desk, silently dismissing him even before she lifted an arm to check her wristwatch. 'Twelve minutes now—and counting.'

He stepped over to retrieve the schedule, and his gaze fell on the bright daisies she had in a vase on her desk. Like a trail of breadcrumbs, they were everywhere she spent any time—the simple flowers almost a reflection of her bright personality. Anywhere he saw daisies they reminded him of Clare.

When he didn't move she looked up at him with an amused smile. 'What now?'

'I can't stand in my own reception area for five minutes if I feel like it?'

'No—you can't. I have work to do. And my boss will give me hell if it isn't done.'

Another frown appeared on his face while he went into his office to retrieve the jacket he'd left lying over a chair, remaining in place until he stopped at the glass doors etched with his company's name.

'We're still going to Giovanni's later, right?'

Clare's head lifted and there was a brief moment of hesitation while she studied his face, confusion crossing her luminous eyes.

'Of course we are. Why?'

'Want me to come back for you?'

'*No-o.* I think I can manage to make it back to Brooklyn on my own—always have before.' She dropped her head towards one shoulder, still examining his face. 'Did you get out of some poor woman's bed on the wrong side this morning? You're being weird.'

'That's what I get for trying to be thoughtful? No wonder I don't do it that often…'

Clare lifted her arms and tapped the face of her watch with her forefinger, silently mouthing the words, *Ten minutes…*

'You see, now—*that* I won't miss when you're gone.'

She smiled a smile that lifted the frown off his face. 'I'm not leaving the country, Quinn. You'll still see me. And we'll always have Giovanni's on a Wednesday night—it's set in stone now.'

When he stayed in the open doorway for another thirty seconds she laughed softly, the shake of her head dislodging a strand of bright auburn hair from the loose knot tied at the nape of her neck. 'Would you go away? I have just as much to do as you do. And I'll have even more to do if I have to answer phone calls all day from people wondering why you're late—which you already are cos there's no way you're making it to that meeting in eight minutes.'

'Wanna bet?'

She rolled her eyes. 'Five bucks says you don't.'

'Aw, c'mon—it's hardly worth my while stepping through this door for five measly bucks.'

'If you don't step through that door it'll cost you that much in cab fare to the nearest hospital.'

He fought off a chuckle of laughter at the empty threat. 'Loser picks up the tab for dinner.'

'You're on. Now, go away. Shoo.' She waved the back of her hand at him.

Reaching for his cellphone as he headed for the elevators, Quinn realized he'd miss their daily wagers. He liked things the way they were. Why did he have to have his life knocked off balance again? Hadn't he spent half of it on an uneven enough keel already? And it wasn't that he didn't understand her need to build something, but the dumb matchmaking thing wasn't the way to go. Not for Clare. Not in his opinion.

'Mitch—Quinn Cassidy—I'm on a tight schedule today, can you meet me halfway?'

See—sometimes in order to win a bet a guy had to bend the rules a little—play dirty if necessary. Occasionally he even had to get creative. And Quinn liked to think he was a fairly creative kind of guy when the need arose. Plenty of women had benefited from that creativity and none of them had ever complained…

He'd find a way to make Clare see sense about the matchmaking—he just needed the right opening, and it was for her own good after all. She'd thank him in the long run.

What were friends for?

CHAPTER TWO

'YOU KNOW, I THINK I'LL have dessert.' Quinn patted his washboard-flat stomach as he came back to the table, smiling wickedly in Clare's direction.

'You *cheated.*'

'You said I'd be late—I wasn't—*I won.*'

Clare couldn't hold back the laughter that had been brewing inside her all evening, thanks to his ridiculous level of gloating. But then he'd always been able to draw laughter out of her, even when he was being so completely shameless.

'I need someone else to hang out with twelve hours a day.' She glanced around to see if any of their friends, seated round the table, would take up her offer. 'Anyone?'

'Nah, I'm irreplaceable.' Turning his chair with one large hand, he sat down, forearms resting on the carved wooden back while he dangled the neck of his beer bottle between long fingers with his palm facing upwards.

'She tell you she quit her job today?' The bottle swayed back and forth while startlingly blue eyes examined each of their faces in turn; a smile flirting with the corners of his mouth.

'Don't listen to him.'

Erin smiled. 'Oh, honey, we never do.'

There was group laughter before Quinn continued in the rumbling, husky-edged voice that made most women smile dumbly at him. 'Yup, she's dumping me to go help the sad and the lonely.'

'Leaving *you* sad and lonely?'

Clare laughed softly when Evan took her side with his usual deadpan expression. 'He'd never admit it out loud but he'd miss me, you know…'

'Rob and Casey got engaged.' Madison smiled an impishly dimpled smile when Clare's face lit up. 'That's three now, isn't it?'

'Four.' Clare almost sighed with the deep sense of satisfaction it gave her. 'And I've had ten referrals in as many days.'

'You're charging the new fee you talked about?'

She nodded. 'And I talked to a website designer yesterday. He reckons we can have a site put together in a month or so—soon as I'm ready.'

'Make sure there's a disclaimer somewhere.' Quinn rumbled in a flat tone.

Clare scowled at him. 'Just because you don't believe in love in the twenty-first century doesn't mean other people don't.'

His dark brows quirked just the once, his gaze absent-mindedly sweeping the room. 'Never said I don't believe in it.'

Clare snorted in disbelief. 'Since when?'

Attention slid back to her and he held her questioning gaze with a silent intensity that sent an unfamiliar shiver up her spine.

'So if I'm not married by thirty-four it automatically means I don't believe in it, does it?'

'You only believe in it for *other people...*'

And, come on, he couldn't even say the word out loud, could he? Not that she doubted he felt it for family and friends, but when it came to Quinn and *women...* well...they probably cited him in the dictionary under 'love 'em and leave 'em'.

Without breaking his gaze, he lifted a hand to signal a waitress—as if he had some kind of inner radar that told him where she was without him having to look. Or more likely because he knew waitresses in restaurants had a habit of watching him wherever he went. They were women after all,

'I could throw that one right back at you.'

It was just as well he was sitting out of smacking distance, because he knew why she wasn't as starry-eyed about love as she'd once been. Not that she didn't believe she might love again one day. She'd just be more sensible about it next time. It was why the method she used for matchmaking made such sense to her. Didn't mean his words didn't sting, though...

And now he was putting her back up. 'If you believe in it, then how come you have such a problem with me doing what I do?'

Quinn broke the visual deadlock to order dessert with a smile that made the young waitress blush, and then attempted to drum up support. 'C'mon, guys—tell her I'm right. People will blame her when they don't end up riding off into the sunset on a white horse.'

Clare dipped her head towards one shoulder, a strand of hair whispering against her cheek while she blinked innocently. 'Aren't you always right? I thought that was the general impression you liked people to have.'

There was chuckling around the table, but Quinn's

expression remained calm, inky-black lashes brushing lazily against his tanned skin. 'I'm right about *this*.'

'You're a cynic.'

'I'm a *realist*.'

'You don't have a romantic bone in your body.'

A dangerously sexy smile made its way onto his mouth, light dancing in his eyes. 'I have a few dozen women you can call who'd disagree with that.'

Clare rolled her eyes while the male contingent at the table laughed louder and the women groaned. 'Whatever miracle it is you pull with women it has nothing to do with romance—it's got more to do with your *availability*.'

'I keep telling you I'm available, but do you take advantage of me? Oh no…'

It was impossible not to react. And since it was either gape or laugh, she went with the latter. Quinn could say the most outrageous things, smile that wicked smile of his, and he *always* got away with it. He was that guy a girl's mother warned her about: the devil in disguise.

Clare could hardly be blamed for having had the odd moment of weakness when she'd wondered what it would be like to flirt a little with someone like him. Thankfully, with age came the wisdom of experience. And she'd been burned by a devil in disguise once already, hadn't she?

She smiled sweetly. 'You see, I *would*, but I hate queues.'

'I'd let you jump the line, seeing we're friends…'

'Gee, thanks.'

'You believe in love at first sight now as well, I s'pose?' Erin leaned her elbows on the chequered table-cloth and challenged Quinn.

'Nope.' He shook his head and lifted his hand to draw a mouthful of liquid from the moisture-beaded bottle. 'Lust at first sight? That's a different story.'

He clinked his bottle with Evan's in a display of male bonding that made Clare roll her eyes again.

'And we wonder why you three are still single.'

Quinn's face remained impassive. 'I still maintain you can't use the 'finding soulmates' tag line on business cards. It's false advertising…'

'Soulmates *exist*—you ask anyone.' She reached for her wine glass while Erin and Rachel agreed with her.

Quinn nodded. 'Yep, right up there with chubby cherubs carrying bows and arrows. They had a real problem with one of them stopping traffic on East Thirtieth a while back—it was on CNN…'

Morgan almost choked on a mouthful of beer.

Taking a sip of wine and swirling the remaining liquid in her glass while she formulated a reply, Clare waited until Quinn had thanked the waitress for his slice of pie.

And then, despite deeply resenting the fact that she felt the need to justify her fledgling business, she kept her tone purposefully determined. 'Soulmates are simply people who are the right fit for each other. That means finding someone with common goals and needs, someone who wants what you want out of life and is prepared to stick with you for the long haul, even when things get tough—'

'You go, girl!'

Madison winked while Clare kept her gaze fixed on Quinn, watching him stare back with a blank expression so she couldn't tell what he thought of her mission statement.

She persisted. 'What I do is put a person looking for commitment with someone who feels the same way they do about life. That's all. Whether or not it works is up to them. I'm the middle man in a business deal, if you want to put it in terms you'll understand.'

Quinn's eyes narrowed a barely perceptible amount. 'And now who's the cynic?'

She set her glass down on the table and leaned forwards. 'If I was a cynic would I even bother in the first place? People need other people, Quinn; it's a fact of life.'

'And meeting the right guy's not easy—you ask any girl in New York.'

Erin's words raised a small smile from Clare. 'No, it's not. But men in the city find it just as tough as the women, especially when they *both* have busy careers.'

Quinn set his bottle lightly on the table, lifting a fork. 'You don't feel the need to go out and date any, though, do you? Hardly a good ad for your business: the matchmaker who can't find a match…I think this is your way of avoiding getting back in the game when everybody at this table thinks it's about time you did.'

Clare gritted her teeth. He could be *so* annoying when he put his mind to it.

'Clare will date when she's ready to—won't you, hon?' Madison smiled a smile that managed to translate as sympathy into Clare's eyes.

But Clare didn't need any help when it came to dealing with Quinn. She'd been doing it long enough not to be fazed. 'It's not that I'm not ready, it's—'

'Jamie wasn't a good example of American guys, O'Connor—you need to get back out there.'

The words drew her gaze swiftly back to his face, and her answer was laced with rising anger. 'And how am I supposed to find the time to date anyone when I spend so much time with *you*?'

It stunned the table into an uneasy silence; all eyes focused on Quinn as he frowned in response. 'So I'm your cover now, am I?'

She opened her mouth, but he'd already shrugged and returned his attention to his plate, digging forcefully with the edge of his fork. 'Funny how it hasn't stopped *me* finding time to date in the last year.'

Now, *there* was the understatement of the century! Without looking round the table to confirm it, Clare felt five pairs of eyes focusing on her. Waiting…

She damped her lips before answering. 'So long as the relationship doesn't last more than five or six weeks, right?'

The eyes focused on Quinn, who shrugged again. 'You know by then if there's any point wasting your time or theirs.'

'And you're too busy to waste any time, right?' Which kind of proved her point.

'Still made the time to begin with, didn't I?'

Okay, he had her on that one. But before she could get herself out of the hole she'd apparently just dug for herself, he added, 'Maybe I should just save myself some of that precious time by getting you to find my 'soulmate' for me. Then I can settle down to producing another generation of heartbreakers and you can stop using me as a stand-in husband.'

Clare inhaled sharply, her lips moving to form the name for him that had immediately jumped into the front of her brain.

But Erin was already jumping to her defence. 'That was uncalled-for, Quinn.'

'Yet apparently overdue.' The fork clattered onto the side of his plate before he leaned back, lifting his arms and arching his back in a lazy stretch. 'Can't fix a problem if I don't know it exists in the first place, can I?'

He said it calmly, but Clare knew he wasn't happy. So she made an attempt at humour to defuse the situation before it got out of hand. 'And why bother finding a wife when I fill eight out of ten criteria for the job every day, right?' She added a small smile so he'd know she was kidding. 'Maybe I'm *your* cover?'

The corners of his mouth twitched. 'Okay, then, since we're in such an unhealthy relationship—you find my mythical soulmate and I'll not only get out of your way, I'll get off your case about the matchmaking too.'

Evan's deep voice broke the sudden stunned silence with words that would seal her fate: 'She'll never in a million years find someone for *you* to settle down with.'

And that did it—Clare had had enough of her fledgling business being the butt of the guys' jokes. So it was a knee-jerk reaction.

'Wanna bet?' She folded her arms across her breasts and lifted a brow at Evan. But when Evan held his hands up in surrender, she looked back at Quinn. To find him smiling the merest hint of a smile back at her, as if he'd just won some kind of victory.

So she lifted her chin higher, to let him know he hadn't won a darn thing. 'Well?'

'You win, you can do matchmaker nights at the clubs and I'll split the door with you.'

What? Her heart raced at the very idea, a world of

possibilities growing so fast in her mind that she skimmed over the fact that the offer had been made so quickly. Almost as if he'd planned what to wager before the bet had been made. But she wasn't blinded enough by the business potential not to ask the obvious. 'And if I lose?'

Quinn cocked his head. 'Having doubts about your capabilities already, O'Connor?'

'Simply making the terms clear in front of witnesses. And if you're trying to claim you've only been playing the field all these years because you haven't met the right girl, then I guarantee you—I'll find you a girl who can last way longer than six weeks…'

'Wanna bet?' The smile grew.

Which only egged her on even more. 'I think we've already established that.'

Though she couldn't help silently admitting her unknown forfeit was scaring her a little. She'd call the whole thing off if her payoff wasn't so huge, and if he just didn't have that look in his eyes that said he had her right where he wanted her…

'I'm starting a pool—who's in?' There were several mumbled answers to Morgan's question.

None of which Clare caught because she was too busy silently squaring off with Quinn, neither of them breaking the locked gazes that signalled a familiar battle of wills. Well, she was no push-over these days, so if he thought she was backing down now they'd gone this far in front of an audience he was sorely mistaken.

'If you lose…'

She held her breath.

'It's a blind forfeit.'

Meaning he could chose anything he wanted when

it was done? *Anything?* He had to be kidding! She could end up cleaning his house for months, or wearing clown shoes to work, or—well, the list was endless, wasn't it?

He continued looking at her with hooded eyes, thick lashes blinking lazily and silent confidence oozing from every pore of his rangy body. And then he smiled.

Damping her dry lips, she looked round at the familiar faces, searching each one for a hint of any sign they'd see what was happening as a joke and let it slide so she could get out of trouble.

No such luck.

'You could just admit I'm right about this business idea of yours and let it go. Keep it as a hobby if you must. That'd give you more time for dating, right?'

With a deep breath she stepped over the edge of what felt distinctly like a precipice. 'No limit on the number of dates. And once you hit the six weeks without a Tiffany's box I automatically win.'

'Fine, but if I say it's not working with one we move on. I'll give you…' his gaze rose to a point on the ceiling, locking with hers again when he had an answer '…three months to find Little Miss Perfect.'

'Six.'

'Four.'

'Five.'

'Four from the first date…'

It was the best she was going to get and she knew it. *'Done.'*

There was a flurry of activity as their friends sought out a pen, and Morgan used the back of a napkin to place their bets. And in the meantime Quinn had Clare's undivided attention while he slowly made his way round to her, hunkering down and examining her eyes before extending one large hand, his husky-edged voice low and disturbingly intimate.

'Shake on it, then.'

Clare turned in her seat and looked at his out-stretched hand, her pulse fluttering. She damped her lips again, and took another deep breath, before lifting her palm and setting it into his. Her voice was equally low when she looked up into his eyes.

'Cheat this time and you're a dead man.'

A larger smile slid skilfully into place a split second before his incredible eyes darkened a shade, and long fingers curled until her smaller hand was engulfed in the heat of his. But instead of shaking it up and down to seal the deal he simply held on, rubbing his thumb almost unconsciously across the ridges of her knuckles. Then his voice dropped enough to merit her leaning closer to hear him, and the combined scent of clean laundry and pure Quinn overwhelmed her,

'Don't have to. Cos either way I win—*don't I?*'

CHAPTER THREE

QUINN SINCERELY DOUBTED he'd be asked as many questions if he applied to join the CIA. Who knew proving his point was going to involve so much darn paperwork? It was a deep and abiding hatred of paperwork that had merited a PA in the first place...

Swinging his office chair back and forth while he read through the rest of Clare's questionnaire, he wondered why she couldn't just have answered the majority of them herself. Because if working together and spending time together socially wasn't enough, then the fact she'd lived in the basement apartment of his Brooklyn Heights brownstone for the last eleven months should have given her more than enough information.

She knew him as well as anyone he hadn't grown up with ever had; it was a proximity thing.

Lifting the folder off his desk, he challenged gravity by leaning further back in his chair, twirling his pen in and out of his fingers and laughing out loud when he discovered: *How important is sex in a relationship?*

It even came with a rating system. Unfortunately he didn't think the rating went high enough for most men.

'It's not supposed to be funny.'

Rocking the chair forwards, he swung round to face the door where Clare was standing with her arms folded. In fairness he thought she'd done well to stay away for as long as she had. He'd had the questionnaire for a whole ten minutes already.

'Aw, c'mon, O'Connor. Not only is it funny, you gotta admit some of it's pretty darn pointless too.'

'Like what, exactly?'

With a challenging cock of his head he wet his thumb and forefinger and loudly flicked back two pages, looking down to quote. '"Do you feel it's important that the man earns more money than the woman"?'

When he looked up Clare was scowling. 'Some people think that's important—you'd be surprised how many men feel emasculated if the woman earns more than they do.'

He nodded sagely. 'You know the *pathetic* rating on all your male clients just went up a couple dozen notches right there, don't you?'

'Spoken by the man who sends a gift from Tiffany's as a goodbye. Money is hardly an issue for you, is it?'

'I never felt like less of a man when I didn't have any. Money's not what makes a man a man. Women who think that aren't interested in who he really is.' He looked down and flicked over another page. 'And another one of my personal favourites: "Do you feel pets can act as a substitute family?"' Lifting his chin, he added, 'Shouldn't you ask about dressing them up in dumb outfits and carrying them around in matching bags?'

'Not everyone wants children.'

'Why don't you just *ask that*, then?'

Swiftly unfolding her arms, she marched across the room and reached for the edge of the questionnaire. 'It's on page five. I knew you weren't taking this seriously. You've no notion of finding the right girl.'

Quinn held the questionnaire out of her reach behind his head, fighting off the need to chuckle. 'I'm taking this very seriously. You just might want to think about tailoring the questions differently for men and women—no self-respecting guy is gonna read this without tossing it in the nearest wastepaper basket.'

Clare stood to her full five-seven, the look of consternation written all over her face making him feel the need to laugh again. But somehow he doubted she'd appreciate it, so he cleared his throat.

'I'm just giving you my professional opinion. You do questionnaires for the clubs' clientele all the time and none of them are ever this bad.'

'They have to be the same questions so I can put like-minded people together.'

'What happened to opposites attracting?'

'The things that matter have to match.' She folded her arms again. 'You can back out of this any time you want you know—just say the word and we can go back to the way we were before.'

Nice try. But it was attempting to get back to the way they were that had given him the dumb idea in the first place. It was the very opening he'd been looking for. There was no way he was letting her out of this one. And she was no more likely to find him a soulmate through a questionnaire than he was to start dressing pets in clothes. Not that he had time for pets right this minute but there was a dog somewhere in his future—a large dog—one docile enough to make a loyal friend for kids to climb all over.

He lowered his arm and flicked through the pages to see if he could find a question that asked about pets *and* kids. Every kid should have a dog, he felt—and, not having had one when he was a kid, Quinn had no intention of his own kids missing out. And, yes, he *would* be ticking the kids question on page five—he came from a large family—there had just better be a box that said 'some day'.

'If you're going to treat this like a big joke it'll never work. You have to give it a chance.'

'I already told you I'm taking it seriously.'

When she didn't say anything he looked up, momentarily caught off-guard by the cloud in her usually bright eyes. 'What?'

Clare pursed her lips and let them go with a hint of a *pop*, shifting her weight before her brows lowered and she finally asked, 'You're *genuinely* interested in meeting someone you can make an *actual* commitment to?'

What was that supposed to mean? He had a suspicion he wasn't going to like the way she was thinking. 'You don't think I'm capable of making an *actual* commitment?'

'I didn't say that.'

It was what she'd meant, though. And he'd been right. He didn't like what she thought one little bit. 'I'm financially secure, own my own home—in one of the highest-priced real estate areas outside of Manhattan, I might add—and I've already done more than my share of playing the field. Why wouldn't I want to make a commitment at some point?'

And now she was frowning in confusion, as if none of that had ever occurred to her before.

Quinn happened to think he was an all-round pretty great guy if you discounted his earlier years. The vast majority of women seemed to agree. And surely the very fact he'd resisted the kind of trouble that could have led him into a rapid downward spiral in his teens was testimony to his determination to make a better life for himself—and anyone who might end up sharing it.

Okay, so he wasn't a saint. Who was? But what had he done to rate so low in Clare's opinion?

Clenching his jaw, he turned his chair back to the long desk lining one wall, tossing the questionnaire down. 'I'll throw this your way before I go. And then we'll see if there's anyone out there prepared to take on this bad boy.'

'Quinn—'

'Send in the monthly accounts and get Pauley on the line for me.'

In all the time she'd worked for him he'd never once dismissed her the way he just had. But he'd be damned if he'd feel guilty about it after *that*.

The accounts were set gently in front of him.

'Thanks.'

'Pauley's on line two.'

He lifted the receiver, his hand hovering over the flashing light when she spoke, her lilting accent soft with sincerity. 'It's not that I think you *can't* make a commitment, Quinn. I just didn't realize you felt you were ready to. I'm sorry.'

Taking a deep breath of air-conditioned air, he set the receiver down and turned in his chair to look up at her. And the gentle smile he found there had him smiling back in a single heartbeat. But then she'd been able to do that ever since he'd got to know her better.

Sanding off the edges of a rough mood with her natural softness…

He could really have done with her being around for the decade of his life when he'd been angry every hour of every day, if she had that effect on him every time.

'We've never talked about any of this, that's all. And we're still pretty new to this friends thing, if you think about it.'

Clare nodded, her chin dropping so she could study the fingers she had laced together in front of her body before she looked at him from beneath long lashes. 'It's not felt that way in a long time.'

'I know.'

There was an awkwardness lying between them that hadn't been there in a long time either. Quinn felt the loss of their usual ease with each other, but he couldn't see how to fix it without continuing on the path he'd already taken.

'What happens after the questionnaire?'

Lowering his gaze, he caught sight of her mouth twitching before she lifted her chin. 'We have a sit down interview.'

His eyes narrowed. 'About what?'

'Dating etiquette…'

His eyes widened. She had to be yanking his chain. 'You think I don't know how to behave on a date?'

'It's *how* you behave we need to discuss.' And now she was fighting off laughter, wasn't she? He could see it in her eyes. 'Men and women can have very different expectations of dating.'

Quinn was at a loss for words. Now he wasn't just commitment-phobic, he didn't know how to treat a woman either? She probably thought he kicked kittens too.

'A lot of men expect a first date to end with—'

He held up a palm. 'That debate can wait.'

When her mouth opened, he pointed a long finger towards the door. 'Work now—deep water later. I don't pay Pauley to hang on the phone all day.'

Waiting until the door clicked shut behind her, he stared at the wood, and then ran a palm down over his face. If she thought he was discussing his sex life with her in that little sit-down interview of hers then she could think again. And if she was going to delve into his private life on any level beyond the one he'd given her access to, then she'd better be prepared for the turn-about is fair play rule. In fact she could go first. His mom had raised all the Cassidy boys to be mannerly— no matter how much they'd protested.

Actually, now he had time to think about it, getting to know her better appealed to him. There were plenty of things he'd like to know that he'd never asked because it felt as if he'd be crossing some kind of in-visible chalk line. If he delved beneath the surface a little he could find out if she was hiding behind the matchmaking. And if she was?

Well. He could use that.

Not to mention the point he now had to make regard-ing his eligibility as potential long-term partner mate-rial, should he ever decide to settle down—which, in fairness, wasn't going to be any time soon.

But it was a matter of pride now...

All right, so she'd never believed her questionnaires were all that amusing until she started reading Quinn's that evening at home. It turned out knowing someone beforehand shed a whole new light on the answers—

some of them so blatantly Quinn they made her laugh out loud.

But then there were the other ones…

Ones that made her wonder if she knew him anywhere near as well as she'd thought she did, or if she'd ever made as much of an effort *trying* to get to know him as she should have. Thanks to the questionnaire, she wanted to know everything. Everything she might have missed or misconstrued. Even if she discovered along the way that the friend she had was an illusion she'd conjured up in her head. Like an invisible friend a small child needed after they'd gone through an emotional trauma they couldn't deal with alone.

On paper Quinn was quite the package: stupidly rich, scarily successful at everything he did, liked pets, wanted kids one day, supportive of a woman's need for a career as well as a family. Add all that to how he looked and it was a wonder he'd managed to stay single as long as he had…

It certainly wasn't for the lack of women trying to hunt him down.

Ever since she'd first been introduced to Quinn he'd been either in the company of or photographed with stunningly beautiful women. None of them she now knew, as his PA, lasted beyond the maximum six-week cut-off point before he backed off and Clare was told to send a little blue box. And miraculously, barring the few weeping females she'd had to lend a sympathetic ear to, Clare was unaware of any of them stalking him. But surely one of them would have been worth hanging on to?

Thing was, if he genuinely was ready to make a commitment to someone then she was going to have to take their bet more seriously.

When the phone beside her sofa rang she picked it up without checking the caller ID. 'Hello?'

'What you doing?'

For some completely unfathomable reason her pulse skipped at the sound of his familiar rough-edged voice. 'Talking to you on the phone. Why?'

It wasn't as if she could confess to committing all his questionnaire answers to memory, was it?

'Thought I'd come down for my interview.'

Now? Clare dropped her chin, her eyes widening at the sight of the minute cotton shorts and cropped vest she'd thrown on after her shower, *sans* underwear. Not that she'd ever felt the need to dress up to see him, but what she was wearing wasn't designed for *anyone's* eyes—not even her own in a mirror. It was a 'not going anywhere on a hot, humid summer's night' outfit.

'Are you home?' The slightly breathless edge to her voice made her groan inwardly.

'Yup, I'll bring down a bottle of something.'

'Erm…I'm not exactly dressed for company… You need to give me a minute.'

There was a pause.

Then, 'And now you know I need to know, right?'

The way his voice had lowered an octave did something weird to her stomach. And her lack of a reply gave him reason enough to ask the obvious: 'You *are* dressed right?'

'Stop that.'

'Well, at least I didn't use the tell me what you're wearing line.'

'You may as well have.' Feeling confident he wouldn't appear while he was upstairs on the phone, she curled her legs underneath her and settled back, wriggling deeper into the massive cushions as she smiled at the all-too-familiar banter. '*Friends* don't do that kind of phone call.'

After a heartbeat of a pause he came back with another rumbling reply, adding an intimacy to the conversation that unsettled her all over again. 'I'd consider it, with that lilting accent of yours. We could do one as part of the date training I'm apparently in need of.'

She shook her head against the edge of the sofa and sighed. 'I give up.'

''Bout time too. So tell me what you're wearing that's such a big problem.'

When a burst of throaty laughter made its way out of her mouth she clamped a hand over it to make sure nothing else escaped.

'C'mon…it can't be that bad. It's sweats two sizes too big, isn't it?'

She frowned, blinking at a random point on the wall over her mantel. Because, actually, she didn't think she wanted one of the most eligible bachelors in New York thinking she couldn't wear something sexy if she felt like it. Not that she was looking for a blue box of her own at any stage.

Widening her fingers enough to speak, she felt an inner mischievous imp take over. 'How do you know I'm not wearing something sexy I don't want you to see?'

When there was silence on the other end of the line she contemplated jumping off the Brooklyn Bridge out of embarrassment. And then, above the sound of her heart thundering in her ears, she heard an answer so low it was practically in the territory of pillow talk. 'Are you flirting with me? Cos if you *are*…'

If she was—*what*? She swallowed hard and summoned up the control to keep her voice calm as she risked removing her hand from her mouth. 'You're the one who said he wanted it to be a training call.'

Another long pause. 'A training call before a training date is a bit of a leap, don't you think?'

'I didn't start this.'

Terrific. Now she was an eight-year-old.

'I'd argue that, but let's just give this another try. What exactly is it you're wearing that means I can't come down there right this second?'

'You don't think I even *own* anything sexy, do you? When you think of me down here you automatically assume I'm dressed like a slob.'

'Can't say I've ever wondered what you were wearing down there before this phone call.'

The Brooklyn Bridge was getting more tempting by the second.

Then he made her stomach do the weird thing again by adding 'Always gonna wonder after this though. And any inappropriate thoughts I have will be entirely *your* fault. You're the girl next door—I'm never s'posed to think of you as anything but cute.'

'I'm the girl *downstairs*. And for your information I'm wearing something entirely too sexy to be considered cute.' She almost added a *so there*.

'Liar.' She could hear him smiling down the line. 'And don't pout. With those braids in it makes you look about sixteen.'

Clare shot upright and looked out of the French windows leading to their small garden. To find Quinn sitting on the stone steps, long legs spread wide and a bottle of wine tucked under one arm while two glasses dangled from his fingers as he grinned at her. She didn't even need to be closer to see the sparks of devilment dancing in the blue of his eyes. *The rat.*

He jerked his head. 'C'mon out. It's cooler now.'

'I don't drink wine with peeping Toms.' She smirked.

'I'm in my own backyard looking into an apartment *I own* and if you'd been naked I like to think you'd have had the sense to pull the drapes.'

She dropped her chin and looked down again.

There was another rumbling chuckle of laughter. 'I promise not to make a pass at you. We haven't even been on a training date yet.'

'That's not how it works.'

'No?'

Clare scowled at him. '*No*. It's a *discussion* about dating—not a dress rehearsal.'

'If you plan on winning this bet you might have to treat me as a special case.' He even had the gall to waggle his dark brows at her before jerking his head again. 'Come on.'

'I'm staying where I am—it's your dime.'

Quinn shrugged. 'Okay, then.'

Clare sighed heavily while he lodged the receiver between his ear and his shoulder. Tugging the loosened cork free from the bottle, he set the glasses down before lifting them one by one to pour the deep red liquid. Then he set the bottle at the bottom of the steps before leaning forwards to place a glass by the door.

Lifting the other glass, he pointed a long finger. 'That one's yours.'

'Can't reach it from here…'

'You'll have to come get it, then, won't you?'

'I'm good, thanks.'

'I'm not actually so desperate—'

'Thanks for that.' And, ridiculously, it hurt that he'd said it. 'A little tip for you, Romeo: don't use that line on any of the dates I send you on.'

'I was going to say, not so desperate I have to force myself on a woman. You really think I'm slime, don't you? When did that happen?'

Heat rising on her cheeks, she mumbled back, 'I don't think you're slime.'

'Good. Cos I was starting to wonder…'

Unable to hold his gaze for long, even from a distance, Clare frowned at the music she had playing in the background. It had been fine listening to the sultry tones when she'd been on her own, reading his questionnaire, but she really didn't need a romantic ambience now he was there in person—especially when she was feeling so irrational with him close by. So she lifted the control, aiming it at the CD player.

'No—leave it. I gave you that album for Christmas. Hardly likely to give you something I wouldn't like listening to, was I?'

Clare had discovered a lot of the music she loved thanks to Quinn's massive collection upstairs. When she'd first moved in she would hear it drifting downwards on the night air, and for weeks every morning conversation had started with 'What were you playing last night?'

Sometimes she'd even wondered if, after a while, he'd chosen something different every night just to keep her listening. It had become a bit of a Cassidy-O'Connor game.

'So, how'd I score on my questionnaire?'

The hand holding the controls dropped heavily to her

side. He really didn't miss a thing, did he? And there was no point trying to deny she'd been reading it when she still had it on her lap.

'It's not a *test*. Did you tell the truth all the way through it?'

'The whole truth and nothing but; didn't take the Fifth on a single one. Why?'

Clare shrugged, risking another look at him. 'There was some stuff I didn't know, that's all.'

The familiar lazy smile crept across his mouth, and his voice dropped again. 'Ahh, I see. Surprised you, did I?'

'Maybe a little…' She felt the beginnings of an answering smile twitching the edges of her mouth.

'I did say we were still pretty new to this friendship thing.'

'Yes, you did, but I really thought I knew you better. Now I feel like I wasn't paying enough attention.' When the confession slipped free of its own accord, her heart twisted a little in her chest, and her voice was lower as she followed the old adage of 'in for a penny'. 'And I'm sorry about that, Quinn—I really am. I should have been a better friend. You helped me out when I needed help most, when I was broke and jobless and about to become homeless. If you hadn't been there…'

Quinn's reply was equally low, and so gentle it made her heart ache. 'Don't do that.'

'But—'

'But nothing.' She heard him take a breath. 'I needed a PA; you needed a job. I had an empty apartment; you needed a place to live. It was good timing. And you were right to stay when you did. Don't second-guess that—it took guts to stay.'

Great, now she had a lump in her throat. She even had to look away long enough to blink her vision back into focus. What was with her tonight? She hadn't felt so vulnerable in a long, long while.

'Do you miss home, O'Connor?'

'I *am* home.' Clare frowned down at her knees when she realized how the statement could be misconstrued. After all, she couldn't keep living in Quinn's basement for ever any more than she could keep relying on the job he'd given her. It was well past the point where she should have been able to step out from underneath his protective wing.

'New York is home now.' She made an attempt at lightening the mood. 'And when I have lots of successful matchmaking nights at your clubs and half the door I can afford an apartment of my own, can't I?'

The teasing smile she shot his way was met with one of his patented unreadable expressions. 'Can't get away from me fast enough, can you?'

'I'm not trying to get away from you.'

'Looks that way…' He twisted the stem of the wine glass between his thumb and forefinger, dropping his gaze to study the contents. 'You need to be careful there, O'Connor. You might hurt my feelings…'

He threw her a grin, but Clare's heart twisted at the very thought of hurting him even the littlest bit. Not that she thought she ever could. It took a lot to get through Quinn's outer shell—ninety-nine point nine percent of things were water off a duck's back.

Without thinking, she swung her legs out over the edge of the sofa, looking straight into the dark pools of his eyes so he knew she was sincere—because she *was*.

'Why would I want to lose one of the best friends I've had since I moved here?' She smiled a little shyly at him. 'And anyway—you'll have met the woman of your dreams pretty soon and, hard as it is to believe, she might actually want you to herself. Though I'm sure that'll wear off with time. And when it does you can both have me over for dinner—I'll even bring the wine...'

Somehow she managed to hold her smile, but it hadn't been easy. Because she knew the relationship they had would change if they both had partners. What she hadn't known was how much the idea of it would hurt. They'd never be the same again, would they?

A part of her wanted things to stay the same.

Quinn continued staring at her across the divide. 'She's gonna have to be something pretty darn special to pin me down. You know that, don't you?'

'I wouldn't let you settle for anything else, would I?' She lifted her brows in question.

'Not even to win the bet?'

'Not even to win the bet.'

'Promise?'

It was the huskier-than-usual edge to his rough voice that did it. Clare's subconscious was taking it as a sign of vulnerability. And in a man like Quinn it was so potent she felt herself drawn to her feet and tugged towards the windows—the need to reassure him was as vital as the need for air. When she was standing on the other side of the glass she smiled, hoping he understood how much she wanted to see him happy.

'Cross my heart.'

When she lifted a hand to back up the pledge she knew she'd made a mistake. Because with the open invitation he immediately lowered his gaze to her breasts, where it lingered long enough for her to feel as if she'd been touched. She watched the rise and fall of his chest change rhythm, her own breathing matching the faster pace. And then she saw his gaze slide lower still: over her bare midriff, down the legs she'd always thought were too skinny and all the way to the tips of her toes— the toes it took every ounce of control she possessed to stop from curling into the wooden floor.

With a sharp upward jerk of his chin his gaze tangled with hers, making her irresponsible heart kick up against her ribcage before he frowned—as if he wasn't any happier with what he'd just done than she was that she'd invited it to happen.

'Should have pulled the drapes...'

'I wasn't expecting company.' Clare dug her finger-nails into the soft flesh of her palm to stop any attempt at covering up when the damage was already done. 'Just as well it's only you, really...'

'Many things I may be. Blind isn't one of them.'

Her jaw dropped.

But before she could think of anything coherent to say Quinn pushed to his feet and turned away, looking over his shoulder to add, 'We'll have the dating talk in the office.'

'Okay.'

'And pull the drapes.'

Her hands lifted to do as she was bid while she watched him make short work of the steps with his long legs. And when the curtains were closed she kept her hands gripped tight to the edges, while she took long, deep breaths to bring her heart-rate back into a normal rhythm. She felt as if she'd just run a marathon.

And he'd done that just by looking at her? No wonder women fell all over him!

It was because it was the first time he'd ever looked at her the way a man looked at a woman, that was all. Up till then she'd been—well—she'd just *been there* as far as he was concerned.

Thing was, she wasn't entirely sure she wanted to be in the background to him. Not that she wanted anything more, but she didn't want to be invisible either. There were times when it was all too easy to feel that way in a city the size of New York—especially for someone who came from a tiny village in the west of Ireland where everyone knew everyone.

If a connoisseur of women like Quinn Cassidy couldn't see her then what hope did she have of not disappearing into the crowd? And she *wanted* to be seen. The thought surprised her, but it shouldn't have. Not really. It was time. She was long since over the mistake she'd made; it was time to move on—to get back in the game as Quinn had said. And if he was ready to make a commitment to someone then surely she could give love another try too? She'd just have to make sure she didn't pick someone who was a womanizer this time round—been there, done that. If she hadn't, then she might have been tempted to try some of that flirting with Quinn she'd wondered about. And that?

Well, that was a disaster waiting to happen.

CHAPTER FOUR

'HAS O'CONNOR TALKED to Madison about any plans she's been making?' Quinn casually bounced the basketball from one hand to the other, bending at the knee and raising an arm above his head before gauging the distance, pushing off the balls of his feet, and sinking it through the hoop.

He'd been sinking hoops with Morgan and Evan at the court a couple of blocks from where he now lived since they'd been tall enough to stand a chance of scoring points. And while he was avoiding Clare's dumb talk on dating etiquette he'd felt the need for some male bonding—even if it meant broaching the subject of her in front of the new guy who had joined their team.

Jamie had been the original fourth member of their crew, but after his run-in with Quinn there was no question of him ever returning without a replay of their last talk. It didn't stop Quinn's resentment of anyone new taking his place though...

'The matchmaking thing, you mean?' Morgan got the ball before it hit the ground. 'How's that panning out for you? You registered for a dinner service yet?'

'Funny.'

'You better win this one.' Evan slapped Quinn's back hard enough to rock him forwards. 'My money's on you—don't let me down.'

'There's no way she's pinning me down—I'd have found the right woman on my own by now if she existed—it's a percentages thing.' It wasn't his fault he'd never met a woman he wanted to keep around for long. And anyway, he was a busy man—women had a tendency to expect a guy to commit to more time at a certain point in the relationship.

If Clare left he'd be even busier. Not to mention on edge and tense in a way he hadn't been in two years. With her there he'd been calmer, more relaxed, less likely to suffer an ulcer by pushing himself too hard when there wasn't as much of a need to succeed as there had once been. Going back to the kind of life he'd had before Clare was less and less appealing the more time he had to think about it...

He set his hands on his hips, watching for an opportunity to steal the basketball back. 'I take it she hasn't talked about quitting work and moving out, then?'

The bouncing stopped and a huddle formed around him. Morgan was the first to ask 'Since when?'

Evan followed, in the traditional pecking order. 'She heading back to Ireland?'

'O'Connor? That's the cute redhead, right?'

Quinn glared at the new guy as he dared to join the conversation. Since when did he think he had the right to join a discussion on Quinn's private life? But Morgan was already getting down to details.

'What makes you think she's leaving?'

After another five seconds of glaring to make his

point, Quinn turned his attention to Morgan. 'Maybe when she said so. I'm intuitive that way.'

'Oh, this is really bugging you, isn't it?'

Quinn shrugged, lifting his forearm to swipe it across his damp forehead while he fought off another wave of anger for coming on to her the way he had. 'I thought she might have said something to one of the other girls.'

Evan's dark eyes sparkled in a knowing way that merited a *don't go there* glare from Quinn, to which he responded with his trademark surrender hands.

'I'm just saying—'

'Well, don't.'

The new guy tried again. 'I didn't know you two were a couple.'

Morgan smiled. 'Oh, they're not a couple in the traditional sense of the word…'

Quinn snatched the ball out from under his elbow. 'I can afford to go join a country club somewhere, you know. I don't have to mess about on this court with you losers any more.'

'Yeah, but this is *our* court. You don't ever forget where you came from—remember?'

Evan nodded. 'Nowhere's better than Brooklyn.'

When they high fived each other while still looking at him, Quinn shook his head. An investment consultant, a cop-turned-security-specialist and a big-shot club owner, they'd all come a long way from their early days. But when they got together with any shape of a ball they still had an innate ability to act like teenagers. There was probably a reason women believed men never grew up. What they didn't get was that the responsibilities that came with age and hard-earned money meant there was an even greater need for time spent messing around with a ball.

But it wasn't helping Quinn.

If Clare had been talking to the other women about her plans to go it alone then he'd know she was further down the line. If she hadn't then he'd know it was a new idea, which meant he had time to—

Well, he'd get to that part when he had the information he needed. All he knew was that it wasn't just about work any more. Her running hotfoot out of every corner of his life felt distinctly *personal*.

So he asked the one question that had been eating at him most. 'Does she know about Jamie?'

'You have another girl?'

Quinn's head turned so fast towards the new guy he heard the bones in his neck crack. 'Look—I know you're just here to shoot hoops, and I'm sure deep down you're a great guy, but take five, would you? Go get some iced water or something…'

The commanding tone to his voice was all it took.

When the younger man shrugged and turned away, Morgan lifted and dropped an arm. 'Is there any chance of you not scaring off another one? I'm running out of second cousins.'

Quinn pushed again. 'Does she know?'

'I don't see why you don't just tell her. You stood up for her when you barely knew her—she was nothing to you back then.' He threw in a smile of encouragement. 'She might be grateful you did it.'

'Before or after she works out I made things worse?' Morgan grimaced.

And Quinn had his answer. 'So she doesn't know.'

'The only way she'd know was if one of us told her.'

Evan placed a hand on his shoulder, squeezing hard before he let go. 'It's always been your call.'

Quinn nodded brusquely, turning his head and letting his gaze travel to the wire surrounding the court and the traffic beyond as a walking tour made its way past, a guide's voice telling loud tales of the Brooklyn they'd all known most of their lives—even if Quinn had arrived a little later than the others.

'If she was planning on going home to Ireland we'd all have heard about it by now,' Morgan added.

Quinn mumbled the words 'This is her home now. She belongs here.'

There was a long enough silence to draw his attention back to their faces, each of them studying him closely enough to make him feel like a bug under a microscope. 'What?'

'Nothing…'

'Nope. Me either.'

'Well, let's finish the game, then—I'm at the Manhattan Club in a couple of hours.' This was his last respite before he had to take his genius plan to stage two—the plan that had seemed like such a great idea before he'd taken a good long look at Clare in what had barely made it past the quota of material needed for a swimsuit.

For coming up on eighteen months he'd managed to avoid looking at her that closely. *Eighteen months.* And now it was indelibly burned into his brain so he knew he'd never be able to look at her without seeing her as more than Clare who lived downstairs and worked for him.

Tearing up the court like a man possessed, he threw all his anger and frustration into the physicality of the game, ignoring the heavy heat magnified several degrees by a concrete cocoon of tall buildings around him and under his feet.

Why couldn't she have been wearing sweats two sizes too big? He didn't want to see her as a woman. The second he started looking at her that way it changed things. And he knew himself. If she didn't see him as a man in return it would become some kind of challenge to him, wouldn't it?

And then she'd be in *real* trouble.

Clare stared with wide eyes at her own reflection.

'You look amazing, Friday.'

Not the word she'd have used. 'It's too short.'

When she tugged on the hem in a vain attempt to make it longer the younger woman laughed, meeting her gaze in the mirror. 'Not with those supermodel legs it's not. Hostesses represent that kind of glamour, even if we're just glorified waitresses. We're the first thing people see when they walk in the VIP lounge. Think of us as business class air stewardesses, or Miss United States contestants. You could do this job, you know, when you get bored looking at the boss every day…'

Looking at him? Oh, chance would be a fine thing. He'd been the Scarlet Pimpernel for the last forty-eight hours and she'd sought him here and sought him there while he'd deftly managed to find one reason after another to stay out of the office.

She tugged on the hem of the shimmering black dress again, trying to convince herself it was only her toothpick legs on show and that in the modern age legs weren't anywhere near scandalous. It could have been much worse, all things considered. But she wouldn't have done this kind of job unless they were really, *really* stuck—cute wasn't anywhere in the same region as glamorous, was it?

Her gaze lifted to her tumble of red curls framing a face so unfamiliar to her, with huge, darkly made up eyes designed to look sultry and full lips shining a bright enough dusky rose to make it look as if she was permanently ready to be kissed.

Well, she'd wanted people to see her, hadn't she?

'Come on, I'll show you the basics and we'll practise the patented smile and walking in those heels.'

Clare grimaced. 'Terrific.'

'You'll be great, Friday—you always are—it's why we all love you so much: you're a trooper.'

Yup, everyone who worked for Quinn Cassidy adored her—barring the man himself, who apparently couldn't bear to stand in the same room as her. If he wanted out of the stupid bet then all he had to do was say so. She didn't have a problem with that.

What she *did* have a problem with was how much she'd missed having him around. She'd missed his gruff voice, his lazy smile, the way he had of occupying her time with attempting to keep him in line work-wise, the number of times in a day he made her laugh…Not that she was likely to tell him any of that when he already had an ego the size of Manhattan.

But it didn't bode well for the long term if she missed him before their relationship had been changed with the arrival of new partners…

Well, maybe she wasn't as independent as she'd thought she was. It was a depressing thought.

By the time Quinn had showered, changed, and made it back into the city, the club had filled to capacity with members from their exclusive guest list. So he checked there hadn't been any major hiccups anywhere before stepping into his usual role. It was a few hours in, when he was halfway round the VIP lounge making sure the more famous of the faces were being pandered to, that he did a double take.

A blinding rage swiftly followed.

With a forced smile for the A-List actor who'd had his arm around Clare's waist, he closed his fingers firmly round her elbow and guided her forcefully through the crowd into a deserted hallway, where the music was lower.

'What do you think you're doing?'

Clare twisted her elbow free, rubbing at it while she frowned up at him. 'I'm sorry—it's been so long since I last saw you I didn't recognize you in there.'

'I could say the same—why are you wearing that?' To his complete and utter fury he let his gaze slide over her again, what he could see making him stifle a groan of frustration. It was like some kind of test. He'd meant it when he'd told her he wasn't *blind*!

It wasn't as if he didn't see at least a dozen women wearing short dresses coated in overlapping onyx discs a minimum of three nights a week. He'd seen so many he barely looked any more—but then none of those women had been Clare, had they?

Clare wearing one was something entirely different.

What was with his obsession with her legs all of a sudden anyway? He'd seen them hundreds of times. Granted, it had never been when they were encased in sheer black stockings with their shape enhanced the way only dangerously high heels could.

His gaze rose.

The hair and make-up were something new too— new and completely unnecessary. Clare didn't need that much stuff on her face, or her hair curled. He'd always liked the way her hair framed her face in soft waves and the fresh, natural—

He gritted his teeth. *'Go home, Clare.'*

Moist lips parted in surprise a split second before he saw fire spark in her eyes. 'I'm not being sent home like some kind of rebellious teenager. We're three down with flu on a night this place is packed to the gills. What is your *problem*?'

'You don't belong in here!'

Raising his voice proved a bad move on his behalf, simply fuelling the fire. 'I've worked behind the bar here at least a half dozen times!'

'*Behind* the bar! Not on the main floor with Hollywood actors coming on to you and trying to get your phone number.'

'Well, *excuse me*, but who was it told me to *get back in the game*? You can't have it both ways—make up your mind, Quinn.' She shook her head, curls bobbing against her bare shoulders. 'I'm going back to work.'

'This isn't your job.' He blocked her escape, anger still bubbling inside him like boiling water. And he couldn't remember the last time he'd been so angry.

That was a lie—he could remember the exact time and place—and the fact that it had indirectly involved her that time too.

'I'm not kidding—you're not going back in there. Get changed and go home. I'll get one of the limo drivers to take you.'

For a heartbeat he thought he'd got through to her. But then she took two steps back and lifted her chin, her eyes sparkling as she held her arms out to her sides. And when she spoke her voice was thready with what he assumed was suppressed anger.

'If you think I'm not up to the glamorous standard you expect in the VIP room then just say so, because—'

She thought she wasn't gorgeous enough to work alongside the other girls? It was precisely *because* she was gorgeous that he didn't want her there. It was the very fact his eyes had been all too recently opened to how sexy she could look in or out of that short, little dress.

With considerable effort he managed to stop himself swearing. 'It's got nothing to do with how you look. You don't work in there.'

'I work for *you*!' She dropped her hands to her hips and scowled hard. 'And working for you means filling in wherever we're short—you know that—so why is it suddenly such a big deal this time?'

Because it was. That was why. But it was hardly the most mature answer. And, yes, he knew he was being unreasonable—date/don't date—keep working for him even if he had to trick her into it/don't let her do the job she'd always done…

She was making him crazy.

'If I have to carry you out of here over my shoulder you know I'll do it.'

Clare chewed on her lower lip, then damped it with the rosy tip of her tongue, drawing his gaze and increasing his frown. Then she took a deep breath and focused on his jawline.

'If you want me to leave you'll have to fire me. I don't think I want to work for you any more anyway. Not when you're being like this.'

When her lower lip trembled before she caught it between her teeth Quinn dropped his chin to his chest and took several calming breaths, puffing his cheeks out as he exhaled while his heart thundered as hard as it had during his session on the basketball court. And naturally Clare chose that moment to step in close enough for the light scent of springtime flowers to tease his nostrils.

Closing his eyes for a brief moment, he breathed deep and then looked up without lifting his chin. 'I'm not firing you. I just need you to go home. Please.'

Please had to help, right? Desperate times and all that—and it was for her own good. If she kept wandering under his nose pointing out how sexy she could be then there was going to come a time when he wouldn't be held responsible for his own actions.

She shook her head, her eyes shimmering as she asked in a tremulous voice, 'What's happened to us lately?'

Now, there was a question. One he wished he had an answer for. Because *something* had changed. The equilibrium was gone—and whatever it was had him in the kind of free fall he had absolutely no experience of.

Until he'd sorted through just what was making him act the way he was, he couldn't keep taking it out on Clare, could he?

He lifted his head. 'You don't belong somewhere partygoers might paw you after a few drinks. The girls who work that room know how to deal with them—they're tough cookies.'

'You still see me as some pathetic female in need of rescuing? Great—it's good to know I've come so far in the last year.'

'You're not a pathetic female.'

'You're treating me like I am.'

'No, what I'm doing is looking out for you. I'm told it's what friends do.'

She tilted her chin up the way she always did when

she was drawing on her inner strength. 'I'm not your responsibility, Quinn.'

'In here you are—my club, my rules. And if I say you're going home, then you're going home.'

For a second she gaped at him. Then her hands rose to her hips again. Her head was cocked at an angle, and sparks danced in her eyes just before they narrowed...

Heaven help him—he'd never been so tempted to kiss an unreceptive woman in all his born days.

But before he did something incredibly stupid, and before she let loose, he lowered his voice to the deathly calm, deliberately slow tone that signalled he'd reached the end of his rope.

'Walking out or being carried out?'

'You wouldn't *dare*—'

'Your choice.' He bent over at the waist, grabbed her hand in a vice-like grip—and tossed her over his shoulder, turning swiftly on his heel.

'Quinn Cassidy, you put me down this minute or—'

When she struggled he lifted his free hand and reached for a hold to steady her, his fingers curling above her knee. She gasped, stilled, and Quinn felt the impact of what he'd done clean to the soles of his feet.

The silken material of her stockings seemed to crackle against the tips of his fingers. And he couldn't stop it happening, errant fingers sampling the softness of the material and the heated skin underneath. Would her skin be as soft if he touched it without the minute covering, or even softer? There had always been something incredibly enticing about the sensitive skin behind a woman's knees, or inside her elbows, or in the hollow where her neck met her shoulders, or on her inside leg further up—

Quinn's stride faltered as he felt the most basic of male responses slamming into him uninvited. And as a result he had to grit his teeth so hard to regain some semblance of control that his jaw ached from the effort.

'If that hand goes so much as one millimetre higher I'm going to scream harassment so loud your mother will hear me in Brooklyn.'

'What hand?' He lengthened his stride.

Clare grasped hold of fistfuls of his jacket as he jogged down the stairs. 'And if people can see my underwear—'

Glancing sideways, he scowled at the lacy upper edge of stocking he could see, swearing beneath his breath.

'I told you to leave. *You* wouldn't listen.'

'You are the most ill-tempered, unreasonable, stubborn—'

'I've been called worse than that in my time, sweetheart—trust me.' Kicking the toe of his shoe on the bottom of the front doors he dumped her on her feet in front of one of the club's massive security guards. 'Get Clare a limo. She's going home.'

'Feel sick, Friday?'

Clare lifted her hands to push her curls off her flushed cheeks, grumbling beneath her breath. 'To the pit of my stomach, Leroy.'

When he went to call a limo forward Quinn spread his feet and crossed his arms, forming a human barrier over the swinging doors. He watched while Clare tugged angrily on the hem of her skirt.

'I hate you when you get like this.'

'I said please.'

'You said please as a last-ditch effort and we both

know it.' She blew an angry puff of air at a curl of hair, folding her arms to match his. 'You are *not* a nice person.'

Quinn shrugged. 'Never claimed to be.'

'Has it ever occurred to you the reason you have so few friends is because you can be like this?'

It was out of his mouth before he knew his brain had formed the words: 'Has it ever occurred to you I have so few friends because I like it that way?'

When the obvious questions formed in her eyes he turned his profile to her. May as well just throw his entire life story at her and have done. It was cheaper than therapy, right?

'Why?' Her voice had changed.

From his peripheral vision he saw her take a step forward, his spine immediately straightened in response. Enough was enough. 'I'll bring your things back with me. Just go home, Clare. I don't want you in there dressed like that. End of story.' He turned his head and fixed her gaze with a steady stare. 'Just this one time do me a favour—and don't push me.'

When he saw the limo pull up behind her he jerked his chin at it. 'Go.'

He turned and had his palm on the door when he heard her low voice behind him. The emotion he could hear crushed the air from his chest.

'I don't want to go back to the way we were before we became friends…'

Quinn felt the same way—but rather than saying so he pushed the door open and walked away. If she'd been anyone else—*anyone*—he'd have acted on how she was making him feel. He'd have found an outlet for all his frustration. But she was Clare. She was *Clare*, damn it—and she mattered to him. The fact he'd reached out a helping hand when she needed it in the past may have been partly because he felt bad about the tangled web of lies woven around her not long after she came to the States. But she mattered to him now.

Maybe more than she should.

CHAPTER FIVE

'CAN WE TRY AGAIN?'

Clare didn't get it. This was the third woman in a row Quinn hadn't got past a first date with. What the heck was he doing wrong? Because if he was doing it on purpose...

She tried to get to the root of the problem. 'Can I ask exactly what it was that put you off going on a second date with him?'

It was the kind of question she always asked so she could build up a better profile of her clients. Maybe a little more than professional curiosity on this occasion, but still...

'It'll help me with your next match if I know...'

There was a pause. 'Don't get me wrong—I mean, he was charming and attentive and all that. And there's no doubting he's incredibly good looking. But...'

'But?'

'Well, it took me a while to figure it out, cos he was clever about letting me talk about myself. And, let's face it, we like it when they're interested in what we have to say. But when I tried getting to know *him*...'

Ahhh—now, *that* she got. It had taken spending practically every hour of every day with Quinn before Clare had had a chance to get to know him better. Prior to that he'd been a constant brooding presence in the background. Everyone else had made her feel welcome from the day she'd arrived, but Quinn…

'Thanks for telling me, Jayne. I'll call you in a few days, when I've had a chance to look through your match list again.'

'Actually I was wondering about maybe seeing Adam again…'

Clare smiled. 'I think Adam would like that. I'll talk to him and get back to you.'

Her gaze slid to the glass doors as she hung up. Quinn's dark head was bowed as he flipped through the mail.

'Congratulations. You're three for three.'

'Hmmm?' He didn't lift his head.

'That was Jayne. You want to tell me what was wrong with this one?'

When he glanced briefly her way she smiled, ignoring the way her pulse skipped out of its regular rhythm. Not that she wanted to put it down to nervousness, but things had been different since the night he'd carried her out of the club. And she knew she couldn't blame it all on the fact that they'd argued either…

She had watched him that night. It wasn't as if she hadn't seen him working the floor on the odd nights she'd stood in, but she'd never paid as much attention before. And in the VIP lounge, between all the smiling and accepting tips from customers, she'd been more than a little impressed by what she'd seen.

She'd always assumed he'd gone into the club business because he loved the constant party atmosphere—and there was certainly no disputing that he'd laughed loud and often. But he hadn't partied alongside the guests, hadn't touched a single drop of alcohol, and he'd had a quiet hold on the room that had been positively palpable. He'd noticed everything—down to the tiniest, seemingly insignificant detail; the merest hint of a voice rising and he had been there to defuse the problem with a hundred-watt smile and a good dose of patented Cassidy wit. He'd greeted everyone, no matter how internationally famous or infamous, as if they had been long-lost family members, nearly all of them returning the courtesy by making sure they'd seen him to shake his hand or kiss his cheek before they left...

And in a dark designer label suit he hadn't been just sexy as all get out, he'd been imposingly in charge. It was *business* to him—and a firm reminder to Clare never to make assumptions about him ever again.

'She was high maintainence.'

When he headed for his office, Clare pushed her chair back and followed him. 'In what way?'

Tossing the mail on his desk, he shrugged his shoulders out of his jacket, hanging it on a rack in the corner before glancing at her. 'In every way. Did nothing but talk about herself all night, for starters...'

Clare quirked a brow. 'Really? That's funny—she says you encouraged her to do that to avoid answering questions about yourself.'

When he began to roll up the sleeves of his pale blue shirt, Clare's gaze dropped to watch the movement of his long fingers. A flex of his forearm muscle and the stilling of his hand jerked her gaze back up.

He was studying her with hooded eyes and lazy blinks of thick lashes. He looked away and swapped arms. 'She picked at every course, complained four times to the waiter, name-dropped for all she was worth and spent a half-hour talking to me about the best beauty treatments in her favourite spa—*high maintainence.*'

Clare leaned her shoulder against the doorjamb. 'The last one was no good because "she barely talked, ate too much and dressed like a Quaker." Quote, unquote.'

'And?'

When he smoothed his hand up to push the folded sleeve into place she found her gaze dropping again, convinced she could hear the sound of his skin brushing over the light dusting of hair on his forearm.

'*O'Connor?*' The edge to his gravelly voice brought her gaze back up again. 'Could we get to the point?'

Impatient. He'd been that way more and more of late. And he'd just seen her watching him, hadn't he? There was no way he hadn't. Judging by the tic that had developed on one side of his strong jaw, he wasn't best pleased about it either.

It was the third time he'd made her shrivel up inside with embarrassment. First when she'd inadvertently invited him to look at her semi-naked body, then when he'd made it plain she wasn't up to the standard expected of hostesses in the VIP room, and now because she'd just given away the fact that she was noticing him physically.

But then the latter had been creeping up on her of late; she still hadn't quite got round to hiding it. It was because she was matchmaking for him, at least she hoped it was—couldn't be anything more. She wouldn't *let it* be anything more.

Slowly damping her lower lip, she smoothed both

lips together, as if evening out lipstick, before lifting her chin. 'If you're going to dismiss all of them after one date, maybe I should just let you see some of the files before I set up any more.'

That was something she never did normally, because allowing someone to judge someone else on looks alone was one of the major mistakes people all made before they came to her. Something she'd once done herself.

He took a breath that widened his broad chest and it took every ounce of self-control she had not to drop her gaze again to watch the movement.

Quinn shrugged. 'It might speed things up some.'

Silently she vowed she was never matchmaking for someone close to her again. It took too much out of her. Though she somehow doubted she'd have fretted as much if it had been Morgan or Evan.

The silent confession made her frown.

Quinn lifted an arm and checked his heavy watch. 'Bring 'em in now, if you like. I have ten minutes.'

Ten minutes to select someone he might end up spending the rest of his life with?

She turned on her heel and marched to her desk, muttering below her breath. 'Taking this seriously, my eye. He spends more time selecting people for his flipping VIP list than he does with someone he might wake up with every morning. God help her. She'll be wielding an axe after less than six months—'

He called after her from the other room. 'You need to speak up if I'm s'posed to hear that.'

Clare closed her eyes and quietly called him a name.

When she dumped all his matches on the desk in front of him he rolled back his chair and reached out a long leg to toe another chair forward.

'Sit.'

Her brows rose; the vaguest hint of a smile toyed with the corners of Quinn's mouth before he turned his attention to the first file.

'Nope.'

Clare reluctantly sat down as he lifted another file and began reading. And since she had nothing better to do she decided to study his profile to see what else she might have missed.

Her examination started with his close-cropped midnight-black hair, down over the equally dark brows folded downwards as he concentrated on the file. It lingered on the flicker of thick lashes framing his amazingly blue eyes, and then she smiled at the way his nose twitched the tiniest amount a second before he glanced her way. Almost as if he could sniff out her unusual levels of curiosity.

'How long are you gonna stay annoyed about what happened at the club?' He tossed the file.

Clare rolled her chair closer, glancing down at the photograph on the next file before he discarded it. 'Who says I'm still annoyed? And what was wrong with that one, exactly?'

'Dated her last year.' He studied the fourth one with a little more interest. 'And you're still annoyed—I could cut the atmosphere in this office with a knife.'

'Oh, and that's entirely my fault, is it? What's wrong with *her*?'

'Dated that one too. I'm just trying to remember what it was that bugged me about her.'

He nodded, tossing it to one side with the others. 'Now I remember. Has a million cats.'

Clare rolled closer still, his scent wrapping around her like a blanket. '*Three* cats.'

'In a tiny one-bedroom apartment. And they slept on the bed.'

Yes, obviously he'd know that, wouldn't he? She took a deep breath of his scent and rolled back a little when she realized he was about to discard the next one. She'd forgotten she'd offered to find matches for a few girls after tearful post-Tiffany-box phone calls, but she remembered the one he was looking at now.

'Go ahead and lose that one too. She spent a half hour calling you names when you dumped her.'

'Built your business on my cast-offs, did you?'

No. She could probably double her client list if she did. 'I knew I shouldn't have let you skip the dating talk.'

'So why did you?'

Because having felt his hands on her when he'd carried her, she hadn't wanted to chance getting details to go with the images born of her furtive imagination, that was why.

She sighed heavily when another file bit the dust. 'What's wrong with that one? She's stunning.'

'Redhead.'

Clare fought the urge to tuck a strand of red hair behind her ear, her voice sharp. 'Maybe you should just tell me what it is you're looking for.'

'Maybe you should tell me why it is you're still so mad about that night at the club.'

'The fact that you hauled me out of there, tossed me over your shoulder and sent me home with my tail between my legs isn't enough?' To say nothing of the fact she'd made an idiot of herself by saying what she had before he'd walked away. Would it have killed him to say something in reply?

'I said please.'

'Yes, I remember. But I never really had a choice, did I? And I hate to tell you, but these bullying tactics of yours need to stop. They're not remotely attractive in my opinion.'

His hand hovered over the next file and then dropped while he slowly turned his chair towards her. 'So what *is*, then—in your opinion?'

He wanted a list? She was supposed to just sit there, with his knee scant inches from hers and the vivid blue of his sensational eyes studying her face so intently, and tell him what she found attractive about him? Had the air conditioning gone down? Lord, it was warm.

She fought the need to flap a hand in front of her face. The cotton of her blouse was sticking to her back so she was forced to lean forwards, away from the heated leather of the chair.

Which Quinn apparently took as an invitation to lean forwards too, so that when Clare's gaze lifted his face was a little too close for comfort.

Her breath hitched.

And Quinn's washed over the tip of her nose as he spoke. 'Go on, then. I'm all ears.'

Clare tried to find general answers to his question rather than personal ones. Not an easy task with her brain wrapped in cotton wool. And when the portion of it still working was finding so many of the answers straight in front of her eyes: the sinful sweep of that mouth, the one narrow lock of short hair just long enough to brush against his forehead. How could she possibly be attracted to him *now*, when he was being a jerk? Instead of before, when he'd made her smile every day and she'd loved spending time with him?

Her tongue stuck to the roof of her mouth.

Quinn's gaze shifted, the blue of his eyes darkening a shade while he examined a wave of hair framing one side of her face. And when Clare saw his fingers flex against the files she wondered if he'd considered brushing it back for her. A part of her ached when he didn't...

'Well?'

'It's...well...it's subjective, isn't it?'

'All right.' His gaze locked with hers again. 'Tell me what it was you found so attractive about Jamie, then.'

Clare's eyes widened. No way was she having that discussion with Quinn. *No way.*

Apparently he knew her well enough to see that, because he nodded brusquely and changed tactic. 'You still hung up on him? Is that why you're not dating?'

Where on earth had *that* come from? Surely he knew the answer? There were days when she couldn't even remember what it was that had made her throw caution to the wind in the first place, defying good advice from family and friends who'd worried that if she got into trouble so far from home they wouldn't be close enough to help. Justifiably worried, as it had turned out in the end...

But it had taken the all-consuming misery of complete humiliation for her to know she'd probably never loved Jamie the way she should have. She'd just been swept away by the romance and the adventure of it all. And it hadn't been enough. If he'd been right for her she would never have felt the niggling doubt in the back of her head that had been there even when she'd said yes to his proposal...

So she could answer Quinn's question with complete conviction. 'No, he has nothing to do with it.'

'Do I remind you of him?'

Clare gaped at him. *What?* But she could tell from the determined fix of his jaw that Quinn wasn't messing with her; he needed to know. Though why he would even think it in the first place astounded her.

'You're nothing like him.'

All right that wasn't a completely honest answer, and judging by the look on Quinn's face he knew it too, so she silently cleared her throat to say the rest more firmly. 'You use the same phrases sometimes and you have the same accent—but so do Evan and Morgan. The only reason you're like that is because you all grew up together.'

'And that's it?'

His voice was even rougher than usual, and a harsh cramp crushed the air out of her chest so that she exhaled her answer. 'Yes.'

And, with her all too recent revelations on the subject of how little she really knew him, it was reassuring to know there were still some things she knew with her whole heart. Quinn might be a serial-dater but at least he was open about it. He didn't pretend to be someone he wasn't. Forewarned was forearmed. And any woman who fell for him fell for him faults and all. He would never let her be made a fool of the way Jamie had.

Quinn Cassidy had an honourable streak a mile wide, despite the matching streak of wicked sensuality.

He studied her some more—as if he needed to find visual confirmation in her eyes. Then—Lord help her—his gaze dropped briefly to her mouth. And Clare couldn't even manage an inward breath to ease her aching chest until he looked back into her eyes.

'So you're not dating because you're afraid of getting hurt again? Is that it?'

'No. I'm not dating because I—'

'Don't have time?' His mouth twisted into a cruel impersonation of humour. 'Yes, you tried that one already. And it's part of the reason I'm putting a stop to all the extra shifts you put in at the clubs. I've told them you'll not be filling in any more.'

Clare opened her mouth.

But Quinn kept going. 'It's not like you're not being asked out on dates either, is it? Mitch has been flirting with you for months now.'

When he frowned, Clare's eyes widened in amazement, because for a second it almost looked as if he was—*jealous*? Was that why he hadn't wanted her in the club that night? Had the thought of men coming on to her bothered him?

As if able to read the thoughts in her eyes, Quinn frowned harder and turned towards his desk, leaving her looking at the tic that had returned to his jaw. 'Next time he asks you out you should say yes. You gotta start somewhere.'

So much for jealousy; a jealous man didn't send the woman he was interested in out on a date with another guy, did he?

'No one high maintainence, no cat ladies and *definitely* no exes from here on in.' Gathering the files into one pile again, he set them on the edge of his desk.

And if he was remotely interested in her as anything other than a friend he would hardly continue dating under her nose, would he? Clare reached for the files, angry with herself for momentarily feeling pleased he might have been jealous.

'Can she breathe in and out?'

'Take that as a prerequisite.'

'You know you can still back out of this any time you want.' Clare took a deep breath as she prepared to push to her feet. 'Just say the word and I'll start planning my matchmaking nights at your clubs.'

Reaching for a padded envelope on the top of the pile of mail, Quinn grumbled back, 'Would I still be wading my way through them if I wanted to quit?'

'So you're not messing up the dates on purpose?'

'Why would I do that?'

'You tell me.'

'I may twist the rules but I've never shied away from playing the game—have I?'

The phone began to ring on her desk, and Quinn glanced sideways at her when she didn't move. 'It's traditional to answer it when it makes that noise.'

Clare stared at him for a long moment. But she never could leave a phone ringing—even if it was a public phone box somewhere. So, pursing her lips in annoyance, she pushed to her feet and walked into the reception area, wracking her brain for reasons why she'd used to enjoy Quinn's company…

'Cassidy Group.'

'Hi, gorgeous. How you doing?'

'Mitch.' Clare smiled when she saw Quinn look towards the open doorway. 'All the better for hearing your voice—as always.'

He chuckled. 'Ready to go out with me yet?'

It was the same conversation they'd been having every week for months. But with Quinn frowning Clare smiled and changed her usual answer. *'I'd love to.'*

Quinn sharply pushed his chair back and took two

long strides forward to swing his door shut. It slammed. And Clare smiled all the more.

'So, where are you taking me?'

CHAPTER SIX

QUINN LEANED BACK IN his chair, dropping his hands below the table, where they formed fists against his thighs. It was as visceral a reaction as he'd ever experienced and, realistically, he had no one to blame but himself. But telling her to go out on a date was one thing. Listening to her accept Mitch over the phone was another. *Seeing them together...* Well...if he'd taken a second to think about how that might feel he might have been better prepared.

'Quinn?'

He forced a smile for the woman across the table from him. Under normal circumstances he'd have been pretty pleased with date number four. Blonde, gorgeous, bright, funny, easy-going... The kind of woman he'd have asked out if he'd met her on his own. But he'd known inside fifteen minutes that there was no spark.

His errant gaze sought Clare again as she walked through the room with that damned feminine grace of hers. No legs on display, but she was sensational regardless, the material of her long skirt flowing like liquid silk with each step. Had she known where he was taking his date for dinner? There was no way she could have. And

Mitch was obviously out to impress if he was paying for dinner in the Venetian Renaissance-style dining room at Daniel.

She had her hair up in one of those ultra-feminine styles that made a man's fingers itch to let it loose. And when she leaned her head to one side to listen to what Mitch said as he drew out her chair a long earring brushed against her neck. Her eyes sparkled, she laughed musically…

Quinn fought a deep-seated urge to storm over and remove her from the room the same way he had from his club.

'Is that Clare?'

He dragged his gaze away. 'Yes.'

Lorie's eyes lit up. 'Is that her boyfriend?'

A part of him wanted to yell *no* good and loud, but he swallowed the word. 'You work at the Natural History Museum? What do you do there?'

While Lorie talked he forced himself to stay focused on her. Being a course ahead of Clare and Mitch was a bonus—all he had to do was concentrate through dessert and they were out of there.

When the waiter laid the napkin across her lap Clare smiled up at him and accepted the menu. She knew Mitch was making a real effort and she appreciated that—she did. He was a genuinely nice guy. It was just a shame that every time she looked into his brown eyes she found herself wishing they were blue.

She lifted her water and took a sip, glancing over the rim at the other tables as she swallowed.

The water went down the wrong way.

Mitch chuckled as she grasped for her napkin, choking behind it as tears came to her eyes. 'You okay?'

'Mmm-hmm.' She managed to surface for a weak smile.

Someone, somewhere, really had it in for her, didn't they? She coughed again, waving a limp hand at him. 'Went down the wrong way.'

'I guessed.'

Her chest ached. And she could try telling herself it was due to the coughing, but that would be a big fat lie. Had Quinn known where Mitch was taking her for dinner? If he had she was going to kill him…

'This place is lovely,' she managed in a strangled voice she hoped Mitch would put down to the choking.

'It is, isn't it?'

Smoothing the napkin back into place on her lap, she lifted the menu and tried her best to study it. After three attempts she gave in and peeked over the edge to look across the room again. Well, at least it looked as if Quinn was getting on better with this date than he had on the others—that was something. She frowned.

Mitch smiled. 'Do you know what you want?'

Now, there was a question. Clare smiled back, and then forced her gaze to the menu. She could do this. She could pretend Quinn wasn't across the room from her—on a date she'd set up for him—she just needed to concentrate

'So, Mitch, have you always been a wine merchant?'

Lorie dropped out of Quinn's favour the second she decided to start eating off his plate. He hated women who did that. If they'd wanted what he was eating then they should have ordered it in the first place as far as he was concerned. And it didn't help that when he glanced at Clare she was feeding Mitch something off her fork, one hand cupped beneath it in case anything dropped while she watched him lean forward to accept the offering.

Quinn lifted his napkin and tossed it to one side of his plate while he fought the need to growl. Was she playing up to Mitch on purpose because she knew he was there?

Although she hadn't given any indication she'd even seen him, had she? Not that he knew for sure, when he was trying so hard not to look at her every five minutes.

Quinn had more respect for the woman he was on a date with—normally. And it wasn't Lorie's fault his head was so messed up—oh, no, he *knew* whose fault it was. And right that minute she was using a thumb to brush something off Mitch's chin while she laughed.

'You want coffee?' Quinn willed Lorie to say no.

'I'd love some.'

Clare laughed at Mitch's antics as he rolled his eyes and made exaggerated noises of pleasure. He really was a nice guy, but it was like being on a date with a sibling, and instinctively Clare knew they both felt that way. It was just one of those things—no chemistry. Mutual liking, yes, but no spark. They could be friends, though, she felt.

'Okay, your turn.' Mitch loaded a fork with some of his chanterelle-filled corn crêpes.

It had seemed like a nice thing to do when neither of them could decide what to have from the menu, but Clare suddenly felt a little self-conscious about leaning across the table to share. Especially if by some miracle Quinn happened to look her way. Not that he'd done anything but devote his attention to Lorie all flipping night long, but even so…

As a compromise, she reached out her hand and took the fork, rolling her eyes the same way Mitch had. 'Mmm.'

'Amazing, isn't it?'

'Mmm.' She nodded, handing him back his fork.

When she sent the seeking tip of her tongue out to catch any lingering hint of the flavours from her lips she looked across the room again—and her gaze clashed with Quinn's.

He didn't even flinch.

He remained unmoved while holding her gaze in silent siege across the room. *She* wasn't unmoved. She could feel her pulse beating a salsa, could feel heat curling in her abdomen, her breathing was laboured. But Quinn just stared.

He didn't even blink.

'Clare?' Concern sounded in Mitch's voice.

When it took another moment for her to break eye contact, Mitch turned and looked over his shoulder. Quinn at least did him the courtesy of nodding in his direction, which was more than he'd managed for Clare.

Mitch then studied her face, and the knowing look that appeared in his eyes made Clare want to crawl under the table. He smiled softly. 'Do you want to leave?'

She was officially the worst date in the world. How was she supposed to look people in the face and give them dating advice when she was so bad at it herself? Do as I say…*not as I do…*

'No.' She smiled back at him, equally as softly.

'It's awkward for you with the boss here.'

Clare wished it was that simple. But Quinn being her boss had nothing to do with it. So she took a deep breath and laid her hand on Mitch's, squeezing as she spoke. 'It's fine—honestly. And I'm having fun. Why wouldn't I? You're a great guy.'

'That's almost as bad as being told I'm *nice.*'

She laughed, sliding her hand back across the table. 'You're more than nice. Because you're going to swap desserts with me too, aren't you? And that's the mark of a *great* guy—trust me.'

Why, oh, why couldn't she be attracted to a great guy for once in her life, instead of the kind of man who would inevitably break her heart? Was it so much to ask?

Quinn's impatience grew after the silent stand-off with Clare. He wanted to be as far away from her as humanly possible, especially after she'd looked at him that way, leaving him with a dull ache in his chest and a heavy knot of anger in his stomach.

The distance between them suddenly felt like a gap the size of the Grand Canyon. He hated that. Perversely, he wanted to be the one sitting there while she smiled the soft smile she used to use to haul him out of a dark mood—the very smile she'd just given Mitch before setting her hand on his. He wanted to be able to laugh with her the way they used to. He wanted the familiarity of the back-and-forth teasing that had brightened his days since he'd got to know her better.

He missed her. It didn't make any sense to him, not when he saw her every day. But he missed her.

The next morning he threw on a faded Giants' T-shirt and sweats before allowing the sights to blur together around him as he ran his usual route round Brooklyn

Heights and along the promenade. He did his best thinking while running. Things became clearer.

Usually.

He stopped at the end of the promenade and grabbed hold of the railing, bending over as he evened out his breathing and frowned at the Statue of Liberty across the shimmering bay, his heart still pounding in his chest.

Nope, catching his breath didn't help either.

So he pushed upright, turning and running harder towards home until the aching in his lungs distracted him again. But when he got to his front door and looked up he frowned harder; nowhere to run, nowhere to hide…

Clare was sitting on his stoop.

When she lifted her chin and casually looked him over, Quinn's body responded. She really had no idea what she did to him.

It took considerable effort to force nonchalance into his voice. 'You're up early.'

'Always been a morning person.' She lifted a thin newspaper off the step beside her and waved it at him. 'I kept the sports section for you. And I brought you some of that juice you like.'

Quinn's eyes narrowed as he braved a step closer, taking the sports section from her before he sat one step down and accepted the proffered juice.

'Is it my birthday already?'

Clare shrugged and leaned back against the brownstone wall that lined the steps. 'If you don't want it, don't drink it.'

After drinking half of it, Quinn set it down and then shook the paper open before laying it out on his knees. If she had something she wanted to say he reckoned she'd get to it soon enough.

'So how was the date with Lorie?'

He feigned interest in the paper. 'There won't be a second one, if that's what you're asking.'

'Why?'

'She ate food off my plate.' He shrugged. 'It makes me crazy when someone does that.'

Exasperation sounded in her voice. '*That's* the reason you're dismissing her after *one date*?'

'Up till then she'd been doing fine.'

'Well, she obviously wasn't that distasteful to you— your car wasn't here when I got home last night.'

Quinn took a silent breath to keep his impatience in check. 'At what time?'

When she hesitated, he held the breath he'd taken— inwardly cursing himself for giving her a hint of how curious he was about *her* date.

Fortunately for him, she didn't seem to notice. 'Just before midnight.'

'Mitch turned into a pumpkin, did he?'

'Very funny. I thought I talked to you about sleeping with someone on the first date.'

The edge to her voice brought his chin up, his gaze searching her eyes until she turned her face away. 'You let me skip the dating etiquette talk, remember?'

Quinn studied her for a long moment, the instinctive need to reassure her surprising him. He lowered his voice. 'I didn't sleep with her, O'Connor.'

'You just talked all night, did you?'

'No-o…I dropped her home and went to the club for a while. This whole jumping to conclusions thing working out for you, is it?' He let a half-smile loose.

'Well, it's not like your track record helps any.'

'There you go with that low opinion of me again.

If you'd bothered having that etiquette talk with me you might've discovered I'm not completely lacking in morals.'

While she mulled that one over he turned his attention back to the paper, calmly turning the page to make it look as if he was actually reading it.

'Well, maybe we should have that talk. That's four for four now, so something's not right.'

'I should string them along some, should I?'

'I'm not suggesting that—'

'Good—cos I think you'll find I do the opposite of that in general.' He raised a brow as he turned the page again. 'So how was *your* date?'

'It was…' she hesitated again '…nice.'

Quinn grimaced. 'Ouch—poor guy—what'd he do to deserve that? I thought you liked Mitch.'

'I do like him. He's—'

'Nice?' He lifted his chin again and saw the colour rising on her cheeks. That was the thing with creamy clear skin like Clare's—the slightest rise in colour was a dead giveaway. 'Nice enough for a second date?'

Clare hesitated for a third time, and when he dropped his gaze he saw her worrying her lower lip, the sight forming an unwarranted wave of warmth in his chest.

She exhaled. 'Probably not.'

Quinn nodded, guessing that looking pleased wouldn't endear him to her. 'Best not to string him along, then…'

It took a second, but Clare sighed deeply. 'Fine, you've made your point. But at least I didn't dismiss him offhand over something trivial. He didn't do anything wrong—it was me.'

Quinn's interest was piqued all the more. 'What did *you* do wrong?'

She avoided his gaze again, the thinning of her lips letting him know what it was costing her to tell him. 'I'm just out of practice, I guess; I couldn't relax.'

It hadn't looked that way to Quinn—but telling her that would be admitting he'd been watching. So that option was out. Option two might be to tell her she should try again, but he didn't want her to try again. Not if there was even the vaguest chance she might do it under his nose a second time.

He thought of something. 'Have you ever filled one of those questionnaires in?'

'No, of course I haven't—'

The idea began to grow. 'Maybe you should. You might be surprised what you learn about yourself. And it might give you a better idea what to look for in the next guy, don't you think?'

Clare's mouth opened.

But Quinn kept going. 'Yankees or Mets?'

'What?'

'Are you a Yankees or Mets fan? Can't have a divided house when it comes to sports—what if the guy you fall for takes his sports seriously and you're on the wrong side?' He tutted at her. 'I did say a different questionnaire for men and women might be a better idea.'

'I hate to be the one to tell you, but sports isn't high on the list of things that make a relationship work.' She looked highly indignant that he might think it was. 'A glorified game of rounders is hardly that big a deal in the greater scheme of things.'

Quinn shot her a look of outrage. 'I'll have you know that's my country's national sport you're talking about there, babe. A little respect please.'

'Don't call me babe.' She lifted a hand and began counting off her fingers. 'Kids, careers, goals for the future, similar backgrounds, shared hobbies…'

When she ran out of digits she frowned down at her hand and lifted the other one to repeat the process. Quinn cleared his throat and interrupted her.

'All more important than sports—I agree.' He let a lazy smile loose on her when she looked up at him. 'Little things can matter too, though. They count.'

'I'm not saying they don't. I just—'

'Like, for instance, I know if anyone dares set a cup of something hot down without a coaster it makes you crazy.'

'It leaves a ring.'

'Yeah.' He found his gaze drawn to a wisp of her hair caught in the breeze that had picked up. 'You told me. And I know no amount of expensive flowers will ever be as big a deal to you as a bunch of daisies…'

Clare's voice lowered, her mouth sliding into a soft smile that drew his attention to her lips as she formed the words. 'They're smiley flowers.'

Quinn looked up into her eyes, his voice lower too. 'Must be. Always make *you* smile, don't they?'

She nodded, smiling. So he kept going.

'Horror movies give you nightmares. Girl movies that make you cry actually make you happy.' Which had been a source of great amusement to him for a long while, but she knew that. 'So even though a guy might not get what the deal is with that, he should keep it in mind on movie night. Knowing the little things matters…'

She took a somewhat shaky breath. 'I guess so.'

'As does knowing the little things that'll bug

someone—like a person who eats off your plate or talks too much, or would rather spend a day in a spa than go play touch football in the park with the rest of your friends.' Something *they'd* done together dozens of times. and she knew he'd never brought another woman to. 'You should fill in one of your own questionnaires, O'Connor.'

Clare looked defeated. 'Maybe we should just forget the whole thing. It's obviously not working.'

To his amazement Quinn disagreed. 'You're not quitting on me that easy. If you even think about it that blind forfeit is gonna be a doozy. Trust me.'

Suddenly a third option came to him…

When they'd spent time together before he hadn't been so aware of her, had he? Maybe what they needed was a little more familiarity rather than the cavernous gap between them. It was worth a try…

He set the paper to one side and folded his arms across his chest. 'What you need is a no-pressure date. And we could combine it with the dating etiquette talk before you set me up again—two birds, one stone kinda thing.'

Clare's eye's widened. 'I'm not going on a date with *you*, if that's what you're suggesting.'

'A *practice* date with me.'

'*Any* kind of a date with you.'

Clare could feel her palms going clammy with nervous anticipation. He couldn't be serious.

Quinn merely blinked at her. 'It would be a good chance for us to try and get past all this awkwardness since the night at the club too, don't you think? Friends can go out for a night.' He nodded in agreement with himself. 'And we already agreed back at the start that

I'm a special case matchmaking-wise. You gotta admit I'm being pretty magnanimous about giving you a chance of winning.'

'Yes and why exactly *is* that?' It made her suspicious that there was something she didn't know. 'You find a way to cheat on these things ninety percent of the time…'

'I don't cheat. I think outside the box. You should take a trip out here some time—you might be surprised how much you like it.'

Which was a third generation Irish-American way of telling her she was boring and predictable, wasn't it?

'Last time I took a trip outside the box it didn't turn out so great for me.' She smirked.

'Too chicken to try again?'

Clare swallowed hard as he studied her with one of the intense stares that had been making her so uneasy of late. Thing was, now she knew *why* they made her so uneasy she really couldn't take a chance on *him* finding out. How could she ever face him again if he knew?

'Quinn…' She closed her eyes in agony when his name came out with a tortured edge that hinted at her discomfort. He really had no idea what he did to her.

When she opened her eyes he was still studying her. Heat immediately built inside her and radiated out over every pore of her body until she could feel the flush deepening on her cheeks. He could turn her inside out when he looked at her that way.

The devil's own smile appeared, and his voice was temptation itself. 'I promise you'll enjoy whatever we do.'

A worrying thought on a whole new level.

He nodded again. 'Monday night's good for me.'

Clare sighed. 'It's this kind of railroad tactic that'll lose you the right girl somewhere along the way, you know.'

'I'd heard a rumour it was about taking the bad with the good. And when I put my mind to it I can be *incredibly good*.' He gathered up the paper and the juice. 'I'll take that as a yes, then.'

When he pushed to his feet and stepped over her, the smile on his face was so smug Clare dearly wanted to hit him.

But she could survive *one date*.

She *could*.

She was pretty sure she could…

CHAPTER SEVEN

'SO IS THIS ONE OF your usual date destinations?' Clare watched him lay out the contents of the large paper bags he'd made up at a deli on their way there.

'That's the conversation opener you'd go with on a real date.' Quinn shook his head. 'If we'd just met you wouldn't know I'd left a half million women sobbing all over Manhattan, would you?'

The simple answer to her question would have been no. He'd never brought a woman to the Monday night movie in Bryant Park. None of the women he'd dated would have appreciated it, whereas Clare's face had lit up the minute she'd known where they were going. And, yes, it could have been because it took some of the pressure off. But he knew Clare. Her enthusiasm had just as much to do with her love of the simple things in life. Quinn liked that about her, always had.

He also liked that she hadn't been to Manhattan's version of an open-air mass movie night before. It made paying someone to snag a space for them before the crowds descended worthwhile.

Clare curled her legs underneath her on the blanket, one fine-boned hand smoothing the pale green skirt of her summer dress before she folded her hands together in her lap. It was a dress he hadn't seen before, and Quinn liked that she might have bought it for their date. Elegantly simple, it flowed in around her legs to hint at their shape when she moved, subtle and sexy at the same time—Clare O'Connor in a nutshell.

When he'd seen her wearing it, it had made him think about the first time Jamie had brought her to meet everyone—when Quinn had wondered why someone as classy as her had fallen for Jamie. Jamie was a player—always had been, always would be. It hadn't affected his friendship with Quinn, though, even when they'd been rivals for the girls in high school. Not until Clare.

'What's the movie?'

'Casablanca.' He continued laying out the picnic, watching from the corner of his eye as she plucked a whispering strand of rich auburn hair from her cheek.

Amusement danced in her luminous eyes when she looked at him. 'Oh, you really pull out all the stops, don't you?'

'Unfortunately I don't have that much pull with the people who organize this. I should take the credit on a real date, though, shouldn't I?'

The recriminating frown was small and brief. 'Only if you make it clear you're not telling the truth.'

'Complete honesty from the start, huh?' He smiled. *'Man*, you're a tough date already.'

Smiling softly in return, she turned to observe the crowd, giving him a chance to study her profile.

'If you're honest from the get go there's less chance of trouble further down the line.'

Quinn knew her statement was a personal conviction. Having been sucked in by a pack of lies from Jamie, she wouldn't want to make the same mistake again. Trouble was, there were secrets he was keeping about what had happened with Jamie that landed Quinn squarely in the territory of trouble further down the line if she ever found out.

When her gaze swung back towards him he made himself smile. 'So when she asks if she looks fat in something…?'

A burst of musical laughter trickled through the air, and the lilt to her accent was more pronounced. 'Ah, now, that'd be different, that would.'

'Mmm. Thought it might…'

She shook her head. 'So, is this the kind of date you prefer? Not a fancy restaurant like Friday night?'

Digging out the bottle of sparkling water she'd chosen instead of wine, he shrugged his shoulders. 'Thought you'd enjoy this.'

He could still feel her gaze on him while he focused on filling plastic glasses. It was getting to the stage where he was completely aware of what she was doing at any given time, even without looking. And when he *was* looking it was becoming an obsession. If she brushed her hair back he would swear it sent a whisper of her scent towards him. If she breathed deep or sighed he could almost feel the air shift. And if she touched her hand to her face or her neck—or idly ran the tips of her fingers over her forearm while thinking—he would find himself mesmerized, wondering what it would feel like to touch her.

She was rapidly becoming addictive.

The thought made him frown, which Clare took as a need for reassurance. Her voice took on a soothingly soft tone that caressed his ears. 'I will. I've wanted to do this since I moved here…'

'Passed dating test number one, then, did I?'

'You did.'

When he looked up she turned away again, and Quinn felt the reappearance of the gap between them. He hated that gap—hated that its presence made him feel the need to reach out for her.

Instead he made an attempt at humour. 'And I haven't even got started yet…'

It didn't go down the way he'd hoped it would. Because instead of a smile he saw her throat convulse, her fingers clenching and releasing in her lap. 'You shouldn't try too hard on a first date; just be yourself and you'll do fine.'

She was handing him *advice* now?

'Thanks. I wouldn't have known that if you hadn't told me.' Quinn's tone was purposefully dry. It would be nice if she could place him somewhere between Casanova and a guy on his first prom date. She couldn't have it both ways.

She let the comment slide. 'So what do you normally do on a first date?'

'Depends…'

'On what?' Her gaze tangled with his again.

Quinn handed her a half-glass of chilled water, the accidental brushing of their fingers sending a jolt of awareness to his gut. 'On whether or not I'm trying to impress the woman I'm with.'

Long lashes flickered upwards. 'And you felt the need to impress *me*?'

He cocked a brow. 'After you stomped all over my male pride by suggesting I didn't know how to treat a woman on a date?'

'I didn't say that.'

'My ego heard it that way.'

Clare scowled. 'So in order to impress me you thought picnic and a movie, an apple pie kind of date. Whereas if I was one of your usual women I'd get the champagne and caviar date: expensive dinner, best seats at a sold out Broadway show, limo to drop me at my door. That's what you're saying?'

Not as it happened.

'Is that what you'd have preferred?' He managed to keep the frown off his face, but it took considerable effort. She made it sound as if he saw her as less somehow. When in actuality he'd spent more time thinking about where he'd take Clare than he'd ever thought about a date venue.

'Do you have some kind of sliding scale?'

'No, I don't have a sliding scale. And I think you should stop this line of questioning before we have an argument on our first date, don't you?'

'It's a *practice* date.'

'Then play the game. Make small talk like we've never met before.' Striving for patience, he stretched his legs out in front of him, leaned back, turned onto his side and then propped an elbow to rest his head on his palm. 'Tell me about Clare O'Connor...'

'You already know me inside out.'

No, she was becoming more of a mystery to him every day. How her mind worked, for instance. He hadn't a clue about *that*, and it might help if he did. 'Play nice, O'Connor. This is s'posed to be a practice run for you too, remember? Try entering into the spirit of things.'

Confusion flickered over the green of her eyes; there was a split second of indecision. Then her chin tilted to one side and a hint of a smile quirked the edges of her full mouth. The latter made Quinn suspicious—because unless he was very much mistaken the accompanying sparkling he could see in her eyes was *mischief.* What was she thinking *now*?

'Okay, then.' Setting her water down on the rug between them, she unfolded her legs, stretched them out in front of her as she turned onto her side. Then she casually propped one elbow so she could rest her head on her hand, a curtain of softly waving hair immediately covering it as she smiled a slow, mesmerizing smile.

'Hello, you…'

Quinn forgot to breathe. She was playing up to him. She was flirting with him as if they were on a real date.

Clare was smiling impishly. 'This is where you say hello to me. You could smile too—that would help.'

Okay. He'd play. His answering smile was deliberately slow. 'Hello, you.'

She chuckled throatily, the sound intensely sexual. 'Tell me about you and then I'll tell you about me.'

'I asked first.'

'Whatever happened to ladies first?'

'I'm *letting* the lady go first.' Quinn's smile grew— he couldn't have stopped it even if he'd wanted to. 'Tell me something I don't already know.'

Shaking her head against her hand, she sighed dramatically, rolling her eyes. And then, while raising her knees to get more comfortable on the blanket, she confessed, 'I can stick out my tongue and touch the end of my nose.'

A burst of deep laughter rumbled up out of his chest. 'No, you can't.'

'Oh, yes, I can.'

He jerked his chin at her. 'Go on, then.'

Rolling her narrow shoulders to limber up, she wiggled her nose, eyes shining when he laughed at her antics. And then she took a deep breath and calmly stuck her tongue out at him.

Lifting her free arm, she made a flourishing move of her hand, lifted her brows—and touched her forefinger to the end of her nose…

Making him laugh even more. 'You're a funny girl.'

She rewarded him with a full, engaging smile that lit up her face. 'Your turn.'

'I like to save my best moves for the end of the night.' He threw an exaggerated wink her way.

'And you're a funny guy.'

'My PA tells me that every day.'

'She must be a very patient woman.'

'Practically saint-like…' He nodded.

Clare made a sound that sounded distinctly like a snort. 'With a halo, no doubt.'

'Oh, I'd say she has her fair share of mischief tucked away somewhere. It just doesn't come out to play very often.' As it was now, for instance. And Quinn liked it. He liked it a whole lot. 'She should let her hair down every now and again.'

'You don't think she does?'

'No.' He shook his head, his gaze fixed steadily on hers as he purposefully lowered his voice. 'I think she's cautious about letting loose.'

'Do you, indeed?'

When he made an exaggerated nod she surprised him again. This time by leaning closer, her face a scant foot from his when she looked at him from beneath heavy lashes. 'Didn't anyone ever tell you you should never judge a book by its cover?'

And when she bit down on her lower lip to control her smile it was suddenly as plain as day to Quinn why Jamie had been so taken with her that he'd persuaded her to follow him across an ocean. He still didn't know why she'd followed. But what he *did know* was that now he'd got a glimpse of a different side of Clare he wanted more.

'And now I'm intrigued.'

When she lifted her head a little, and her hair fell into her eyes, he instinctively lifted a hand and brushed it back so he could see her, his fingertips lingering against her soft cheek for a brief second.

Clare's eyes widened in response, studying him with an open curiosity he'd never seen before. But instead of asking her about it, he smiled, letting his heavy hand drop as he pushed for more information.

'Were you a mischief-maker back in Ireland?'

It brought the impish smile back, her chin dropping as her hand rose to check he'd tucked the strand of hair away properly. 'I had my moments. Doesn't everyone in their teens?'

'What was it like growing up there?'

Clare searched his eyes, and then shifted her gaze to look at the people over his head. But he knew she wasn't seeing them. The wistfulness on her face told him she was across the Atlantic again, in the land his own ancestors had travelled from.

'I was happy—free—but kids who grow up on a farm have a lot of freedom. We ran riot in all weather, made secret huts, tried to catch wild rabbits so we could keep them as pets, searched for fairies in the woods...'

Quinn was spellbound. By her expression as she shared the memories as much as by the picture she'd painted. Why had he never noticed how beautiful she was? Had he ever looked at her properly? He'd always thought she was pretty, but now…

'Find any?'

'Rabbits or fairies?'

'Fairies.'

'Nah.' She gave him a sideways, twinkle-eyed glance, lowering her voice as if sharing a secret. 'They're slippery wee things are fairies.'

'I'd heard that…'

The fact he'd lowered his voice to a similar level seemed to make her eyelids heavy. 'We had a fairy ring in the woods. So when we were little we were convinced they couldn't be that far away. My mother encouraged us to search for them—I think it gave her peace for a few hours. Three kids under the age of ten can be tiring.'

'I know.' It had been the same with the four in the Cassidy household when Quinn had been growing up. 'You should try it with a house full of boys.'

Her lashes lowered, making Quinn feel the need to crook a finger under her chin so he could continue looking into her eyes. 'I'd love a house full of boys. They'd love me their whole lives. Whereas a girl will have to hate me for at least half her teenage years; it's traditional she'll think I'm ruining her life…'

Long lashes rose, oh, so slowly. And Quinn smiled. He'd never thought of Clare with kids and he had no idea why. She'd be a great mom some day. She'd make sure they were ten minutes early for every school activity, she'd paint pictures of daisies with little girls—

make sure boys knew all the right things to say to any girl they were thinking of dating...

'So you don't think pets can be a substitute for a family, then, I take it?'

She caught the reference and scowled playfully at him, dragging another chuckle of laughter free from deep inside his chest.

Which made her laugh softly in return. 'No, I don't. Pets *and* a family, that's the box I'd tick. Every kid should have a dog.'

Quinn's smile faltered. Had she got that off his questionnaire? He racked his brain to see if he could remember finding the question when he'd looked for it.

Clare shifted suddenly, pushing upwards and curling her legs back underneath her as she reached for some of the cheeses he'd set out. 'What were you like as a kid?'

A date with Clare was like riding a rollercoaster. Quinn shook his head as he pushed up into a similar position to hers, because his childhood couldn't have been more different from hers if it had tried.

'You want crackers with that?'

Oh, he was a clever one, wasn't he? Clare took a much needed inward breath as she realised what had just happened. He'd done exactly what match number three had said he'd done with her—steered the conversation onto her, so that she'd end up doing all the talking. Well, he needn't think he was getting away with it. A practice date he wanted; a practice date he'd get. And she might be a tad rusty but she was pretty sure it involved a two-way conversation...

Then she remembered something. 'You had a nickname, didn't you? I remember Evan and Morgan keeping you going about it. What was it again?'

A quick glance in his direction saw his wide chest rise and fall before his gravelly voice grumbled back the answer. 'Scrapper.'

Lifting her chin so she could look into his amazing eyes, she smiled to encourage him to keep going. 'How'd you get landed with that, then?'

Quinn cocked a brow at her.

She smiled all the more. 'Got into a few fights, did we?'

'More than a few.'

'How come?'

'Anger management issues.'

Watching while he loaded a cracker with cheese, Clare felt a dull ache forming in her chest. 'What were you angry about?'

'I was nine when I got that nickname. You don't know why you're angry back then; you just know you are.'

He'd been getting into regular fights at nine? How bad had they been? Why hadn't anyone done anything to stop it happening? Had he been bullied? The Quinn she knew was the most in control man she'd ever met. He could defuse a difficult situation with a single glare. Had he learned that at some point because he'd *had to*?

The ache became a bubble of emotion. 'But you know now, don't you?'

'Yup.' He popped an entire heavily laden cracker into his mouth, his gaze straying out over the crowd.

Another memory came to her: she'd tried talking to Quinn about his past before, hadn't she? Way back at the start, when Jamie had first introduced her to his friends. She'd tried making conversation on the usual subjects, family, work, the weather… And Quinn had been so unresponsive she'd simply assumed he didn't like her much, so she'd stopped trying. But add that to the recent information from his date with match number three and she suddenly had a different picture. So she waited.

Opening up wasn't something that came easily to him. She got that now.

Eventually Quinn looked at her from the corner of his eye as he slapped large palms on jean-clad hips to remove residual crumbs. When she continued waiting in silence, he shook his head and grumbled out another piece of the puzzle. 'I met Morgan, Jamie and Evan the day I got that nickname…'

The slant of wickedly sensual lips formed a thin line before he continued, his voice lacking in emotion. Not even a hint of sentiment at the memory of the first time he'd met the men who'd been his best friends ever since—well—two of them anyway…

'It was my first day at school after we moved to Brooklyn from Queens. Word had got around about my old man before I got there—parents gossiping, probably. And when some of the boys made comments I didn't take kindly to—I took them on.' He shrugged. 'The guys broke it up and walked me home. I was pretty banged up.'

Clare's brows wavered in question. 'How many did you take on?'

'Five.'

On his own? The odds alone told her what state of *banged up* he must have been in. She thought of a nine-year-old Quinn, all bloody and bruised, being walked home by his new protectors—more than likely determined not to shed a single tear in front of them—and it broke her heart. She knew his father had died. How could those kids have said dreadful things to him when he'd just lost his father?

The anguish she felt must have shown in her eyes, because the smile he gave her was dangerous—doubly so when it was Quinn wearing it. It was a side to him she'd never seen up close before.

'Don't worry—I learned my lesson that day, picked up a move or two after that. And a decade of scrapping made me one heck of a bouncer at the first club I worked.'

Despite his reaction to what he obviously considered pity, Clare couldn't help it. Her jaw dropped. *That* was where he'd started his career with clubs—breaking up fights? New York was the best city in the world, but for a while it had been rough in places. He could have been seriously hurt—and if anything had happened…

She might never have met him.

Quinn misinterpreted her reaction again. 'Guess I should skip this little talk on the first date? Knew there was a reason I hadn't done it before.'

'Did you get in any trouble?'

'No—but thanks for the vote of confidence. First time I dealt with a cop was the night I got offered the security gig.'

Again he'd misinterpreted her. Clare was frowning in annoyance as much as confusion, because he did that *a lot*. And he should know her better. 'That wasn't what I meant. A police officer offered you the job?'

'Me and the guys were heading home when a fight got started. Some guy hit a woman—so I put him down and kept him there till the cops arrived. That's when the club offered me the job.' He jerked his shoulders again.

'Apparently I did it faster and with less fuss than anyone they'd ever seen before. Practice makes perfect, they say. And I'd got to the point in my life where I believed the best offence was a good defence.'

Clare stared at him, which started the beginnings of another dark frown on his face. 'So I wasn't your first damsel in distress, then?'

The frown dissipated. 'Guess not.'

When he searched her eyes for the longest time, Clare's heart thudded hard against her breastbone—a thought making her breath catch. Had he thought telling her about his past would change how she saw him? Didn't he know the fact he'd not only stayed out of trouble but turned himself into a respected self-made millionaire before thirty only made her respect him *more*? He was living, breathing proof of the American dream.

She thought he was amazing.

Unable to hold his intense gaze any longer, she dropped her chin and played at putting cheese on a cracker—being particularly fussy about the angles until she got her emotions under control.

'That's why you ended up owning clubs in the end?'

'I own clubs because they make money.'

'And money is all that matters?'

'Matters when you don't have it.'

Her gaze rose again to find him studying her, then he took a breath and turned to study the large screen where the movie would play.

'There are worse ways of making money.' He smiled, glancing at her from the corner of his eye. 'Opening night for the Manhattan one was fun, though, wasn't it?'

Clare smiled at the shared memory. 'It was.'

As manically insane as it had been on the run-up, she knew it had been the kind of night she'd never forget. When Quinn had offered her a job he'd still been at the planning stages. But one by one and side by side they'd worked their way through the many lists Clare had made to keep everything on schedule until they had had the kind of opening that had been the talk of New York and beyond for weeks afterwards.

It had been the first time she'd really felt her decision to stay in New York had been the right one. She had felt she'd achieved something—helped build something—and in a small way she'd felt as if she'd repaid a few of the many favours she owed Quinn. Best of all, they'd become friends along the way…

Or she'd thought they had.

'How did you afford the first one?'

And just like that he was frowning again. She'd never known his moods to fluctuate as much as they had of late.

'What difference does it make?'

Clare kept her voice purposefully soft. 'None. I'd just like to know.'

'All that matters is the first one made enough for the second one and the second made triple what the first one did…Thanks to Morgan's investment advice and the thousands of dollars VIP members pay annually I don't lose any sleep when bills come in.'

He took another breath and looked over the crowd.

Except now Clare wanted to know even more than she had before. He had a lesson or two to learn about reverse psychology. 'I've just figured out why it is I don't know you as well as I thought I did.'

When he didn't say anything in reply she smiled at his profile. 'Don't you want to know what I figured?'

'I'm sure you'll tell me regardless.'

'I will.' She waited until he glanced at her again. 'It's because you don't want me to.'

Quinn looked confused by the reasoning. 'That's not true.'

'Isn't it?'

'Who I was back then isn't who I am now.'

'But it's *a part* of who you are now…'

'You're like a dog with a bone, you know that?' He shook his head, turning so he could study her eyes with open curiosity. 'You know me well enough, O'Connor— little bit more than most, as it happens. Even before that questionnaire of yours. Why does it suddenly matter now?'

That was the million-dollar question, really. But Clare simply studied him right on back. And when she smiled softly at him it took a moment, but soon enough the light reappeared in his eyes and his mouth slid into an answering smile. Making her smile all the more…

'Okay, then, how did you learn the least-fuss method for your good defence?'

He chuckled ruefully, letting her know she wasn't fooling him with her change of subject. 'I lived in the local boxing club—fought in the ring as a junior to deal with the anger management.'

'Really?'

'Really. Even broke my nose, *twice.*'

'There's nothing wrong with your nose.' She studied it just to be sure.

'Second time straightened it some.'

When she looked back into his eyes she saw the light twinkling, and her jaw dropped with a gasp of mock outrage.

'Fibber.'

Deep, rumbling laughter echoed up from his chest and Clare felt her heart expand. See, now, there he was. *That* was the Quinn she knew. She'd missed him so very much.

'Had you for a minute…'

'Did not.'

'Did so.'

She lifted a handful of crackers and flung them at his chest, laughing with him when he rocked backwards, scrambling to catch them only to have them disintegrate in his large hands, scattering crumbs everywhere.

'You're a dreadful date, Quinn Cassidy.'

'No, I'm not.' His vivid eyes danced with silent laughter. 'And the first date is a trial run. By date three I'd win you over.'

It was a theory he could have done with putting into practice on some of the dates she'd sent him on. Before she could point out there wouldn't be a second date, never mind a third, with her, the huge screen came to life and Clare exhaled.

Saved by Humphrey Bogart.

Probably just as well. Because the fact there wouldn't be other dates with him left Clare's heart heavy. And that really didn't bode well…

CHAPTER EIGHT

IT STARTED TO RAIN the second the credits rolled. But when Quinn raised a hand to hail a cab, Clare tugged on his sleeve.

'Can we take the subway? The novelty hasn't worn off for me yet.'

Quinn normally avoided the crowds and the stifling heat at all costs, especially in summer. But her enthusiasm for the simplest of things was infectious, so he gave in. They weren't the only ones with the same idea; people crowded down the stone steps to stand in the ridiculous heat of the platform at Forty-Second Street.

The wave of bodies moved forward *en masse* when the train arrived, leaving Quinn and Clare standing in the packed compartment, which for the life of him Quinn couldn't find a reason to be unhappy about. Especially with Clare close enough for him to catch the scent of springtime from her hair. So instead he leaned down and teased her with a grumble of mock complaint.

'Oh, yeah, this was a great idea—very romantic end to the evening.'

Clare wrapped her fingers around a metal pole,

smiling over her shoulder at him as the doors slid shut. 'Just think of the good impression you're making on your carbon footprint.'

'It's not my carbon footprint I was trying to impress…'

'If you really were trying to impress me then you did fine with the movie and the picnic. It's the kind of night a girl doesn't forget too fast.'

An outdoor movie and a picnic in the park were the way to a girl's heart? Who knew? But Quinn knew he wouldn't forget it either. And he wouldn't be able to take another woman to Bryant Park without thinking of his night there with Clare.

The train jolted to a halt at the next stop, rocking Clare back on her heels. Quinn automatically lifted an arm and snaked it around her narrow waist to steady her—drawing her close. For a moment she tensed, the way she had the night he'd carried her, glancing sharply over her shoulder. Then he felt her take a deep breath and her slight body relaxed into his, curves moulding into dips and planes as if she'd been there hundreds of times and knew exactly where she would fit.

As was now usual, Quinn's body reacted. Meaning he had to focus on a random point down the compartment to give him something else to think about. So much for his familiarity theory… and his control theory… and…

The doors slid open, letting in more hot air. People got out; people got in. Then the doors slid shut again and the train jumped forwards.

Clare shifted her weight from one foot to the other, her body sliding against his as if she was dancing to some kind of silently sensual melody. It made Quinn close his eyes, frowning as the need to harness his physical reaction like an adult was overridden by a sudden vision of dancing with her. On the back of his eyelids he could see the play-by-play movie of it. He was turning her around in his arms, placing her hands on the back of his neck one by one, and then drawing her close, her breasts pressed tight against his chest, her hips swaying from side to side…

He snapped his eyes open. Now he was being tugged into erotic fantasies. By *Clare*.

Then he made the mistake of glancing down over her shoulder—in time to see a tiny trickle of moisture run from her collarbone down into the dark valley between her breasts. He stifled a groan.

Never had he felt so cornered by a woman: trapped deep underground in a dark tunnel in a compartment packed with people he barely noticed—and Clare pressed close enough to feel what she was doing to him.

She turned a little, her chin lifting and long lashes rising until her darkened green gaze was impossibly tangled with his. She even damped her lips with the tempting tip of her tongue.

Now Quinn's chest ached with the need for oxygen—the need to kiss her was so primal that his head was lowering before he had time to think about the consequences…

The train jerked to a halt again, bringing him back to his senses. So when a woman seated next to them stood up, Quinn practically manhandled Clare into the space. There. That was better. Now maybe he could breathe.

Clare being Clare, she spotted an elderly man behind him and immediately stood up to offer him her seat.

Even more frustratingly she returned to where she'd been before—this time facing him while holding the metal bar, her eyes sparkling with what looked like comprehension. She knew, didn't she? Knew what she was doing to him and wasn't the least bit upset about it. Well, if that was the case and she played up to him again, then all bets were off—new rules, new game.

Quinn's blood rushed faster at the thought of it.

She smiled. 'I think I can manage not to fall over this time…'

Meaning she was amused at his concern for her, or meaning she'd known he was about to kiss her and was letting him off the hook?

Quinn bent his knees and ducked his head to look out of the windows. 'Couple more stops.'

When he risked another look at her she lifted her finely arched brows. 'Are you okay? You look flushed.'

Quinn cleared his throat, purposely keeping the sound low so she wouldn't hear. 'I'd forgotten how hot it is down here.'

When he frowned at the double entendre she smiled all the more. 'It has all day to build up. But yeah, it's hot…'

Then she upped the ante by lifting a hand to the front of her dress and flapping the material against her breasts—which automatically drew his gaze downwards. It would serve her right if he reached out and hauled her in to kiss her until she was as affected as he was by their 'pretend date'. Quinn was hanging by a thread.

But she obviously wasn't as caught up in the moment as he was. When the train stopped again and *he* was the one that rocked towards *her* she giggled girlishly at his expression. Then she had the unmitigated gall to smile at another man as he walked past her to get to the doors.

Right under Quinn's nose.

So that was how she was playing it. She was on a pretend date with her best buddy after all. Part of the genius idea had been to help her ease back into the dating game. She'd tell him that if he called her on it too, wouldn't she?

It was just a shame the idea of her flirting even casually with someone else irritated him so thoroughly. That a part of him was now determined to make it very clear who it was she was with. So when the random guy smiled at her again as he stepped off the train, Quinn stepped closer, glaring at the man. Who in turn had the good sense to leave while Quinn lifted his hands to Clare's shoulders to turn her round, hauling her firmly against his body for the second time.

'What are you doing?' She looked down at his arms as they both circled her waist and held her tight. 'I can—'

'Shh.' He placed his cheek next to her silky soft hair and grumbled into her ear. 'If we were on a date this is exactly what I'd be doing about now. Play by the rules, O'Connor…'

Play by the rules? It was the second time he'd said that. Hadn't she played by the rules all night long? Hadn't she forgotten it was a pretend date entirely too much for her own good? Hadn't she—for a brief moment of insanity—been completely overwhelmed by the hope he was going to kiss her?

And, heaven help her, it was the most wonderful case of insanity she'd ever experienced. Just as crazy as it was to feel so right being held by him, with her body pressed so tight against his and his arms wrapped so firmly around her waist. Oh, Lord but it felt good.

Quinn was hard and lean, coiled muscle and heated skin and warm breath against her cheek. And he smelled sensational. Clare had never felt so very alive.

When his thumbs absentmindedly brushed back and forth against the base of her ribs she closed her eyes and leaned her head back against his shoulder, surrendering to sensation. She could have stayed there a lot longer—except the train was already slowing down…

Quinn immediately released her, stunning her when he tangled his long fingers with hers, her downward glance simply met with a gruff 'C'mon.'

It was still raining outside. And with a sideways glance and a smile that made her smile ridiculously back at him he asked, 'Can you run?'

Clare lifted her chin. 'Can you keep up with me?'

It was an empty challenge for someone who ran for miles round Brooklyn every day regardless of the weather. But with another smile and a squeeze of his fingers he glanced down at her low heels and back up into her eyes.

'I'll give it a shot.'

So they ran. The warm summer rain had soaked them through to the skin by the time they arrived breathless and laughing at the brownstone and Quinn saw her all the way to her door, still holding her hand while she fitted her key in the lock.

Heart pounding from exertion and a rising sense of anticipation, Clare looked down at their hands, watching as raindrops trickled off his skin onto hers.

'I need—' When her voice sounded thready, even to

her own ears, she took a second to control her voice. 'I kind of need that hand. It's attached to the rest of me.'

Lifting her lashes, she found his head bowed, wet fingers sliding over wet fingers while he watched. And then his chin rose, his eyes dark pools in the dim light, his face filled with shadows. But she didn't need better light to see him—he was Quinn—she could see him with her eyes closed.

As if the thought was a suggestion, Clare felt her eyelids growing heavy.

'For future reference, where does kissing on the doorstep fall in the dating etiquette rules?'

'Erm…' Clare nodded, her voice thready again '…I'd say that was under optional…or…'

In the shadows of his face she saw a smile forming, the sight making her heart flip-flop almost painfully.

'Or?'

If he didn't kiss her she might have to kill him. 'Or…at your own discretion…'

'Good to know.'

Clare held her breath. Quinn squeezed her fingers. Then he loosened them, sliding them free so slowly she felt the loss all the way to the pit of her soul. When he spoke his voice was so low she had to strain to hear over the sound of raindrops on concrete, on the leaves of the trees lining the street, bouncing off cars…

'Night, O'Connor…'

What? He was leaving? He wasn't going to kiss her?

Of course he wasn't going to kiss her; Clare felt like a complete idiot. They were *friends*. She was the cute girl who lived downstairs. He could have any woman he wanted in the whole of New York…

She'd never felt so foolish—even when Jamie had

left her to face all those guests alone. No, not alone. He'd left her with the best man. *The best man*; it was so ironic Clare almost laughed.

Quinn hadn't moved. And neither had Clare; her laboured breathing was nothing to do with the run they'd made and everything to do with how much she ached for a kiss she shouldn't want so desperately.

From somewhere she found the power of speech again. 'Night, Quinn.'

But he still didn't move. Didn't he know she was slowly dying in front of him?

The air caught in her lungs when his large hands rose and turned—knuckles brushing wet tendrils of hair off her cheeks in heartbreakingly gentle sweeps. The simple touch closed her heavy eyelids while the air left her lungs in one endless breath. How could a man with his experience not know what he was doing to her? The Quinn she knew would never torture her so severely.

'You should go inside.' The rough timbre of his voice was the sexiest thing she had ever heard.

'I should.'

But not before he left. She doubted she could get her feet to move. Every shuddering breath she took added to the yearning that had developed inside her, a shaking starting at her knees and gradually making its way upwards. The word *please* hovered precariously on the tip of her tongue…

If he didn't leave soon then she was going to make such a complete and utter twit of herself.

'I'll see you tomorrow.' Quinn's hands turned over, the very tips of his fingers whispering the last strands of hair off her cheeks.

Somehow Clare forced her eyes open, her ears hearing her voice say 'You will' while her heart yelled, *Don't go.*

After what felt like an eternity, he took a deep breath. 'Couldn't you just run your dumb matchmaking thing from my offices?'

Clare blinked up at him. Huh? Had she just missed something in the haze? Not that it wasn't the kind of suggestion she mightn't have considered before they'd made the stupid bet, but—

She shook her head to make her brain work. 'If you still think it's dumb then why are you doing it?'

Quinn's fingers stilled. 'If you're like this on a date then how come you're still hiding?'

'I'm not hiding. I just haven't met anyone I wanted to date…' It took all her strength not to add *until now* to the end of the sentence. Hadn't it occurred to him she'd been the way she had on their pretend date because she was with someone she already cared about? Maybe a little too much for what was supposedly a platonic relationship.

Quinn's arms dropped to his sides. 'Think about the office share—we could move things around some.'

'I can't keep relying on you to help me out.'

'Yeah, you can.'

No, she couldn't. Not any more. What had been tentative plans a few weeks ago were going to have to become more solid. She knew he'd always be there if she needed him—as a friend. And she loved that. She did. But she knew the relationship they had couldn't stay the same any more. Not if she was falling for him…

Quinn tilted his head back, letting the rain wash over his face as he stepped away from her. He dropped his chin as he spoke. 'Just think about it, O'Connor.'

Then he turned. When he took the steps two at a time and was on the pavement, a lucid thought finally entered Clare's head.

'Quinn?' She stepped forward.

He stopped, the street lights making it easier for her to see his face. 'Yes?'

'Are you doing all this matchmaking stuff to try and stop me from leaving work? Is that what this is all about?' A glimmer of hope sparked in her chest. If he wanted to keep her close by then maybe he cared as much as she did. Maybe he would miss her. Maybe, just maybe, that was a place to start?

Quinn frowned, glancing down the street and back before he replied, 'How honest do you want me to be about that?'

'Completely—as always.' She smiled somewhat tremulously, even though she knew she shouldn't. If he'd thought the whole bet up as part of some devious plan to keep her working for him then she should at least be miffed. It just wasn't easy to feel that way under the current circumstances. 'Any kind of lie breaks trust, remember? So are you?'

'You see everything in black and white, don't you? None of the hundreds of shades of grey in between…'

She shook her head, unable to understand how they'd got to where they were when not five minutes ago—

'Straight answer to a straight question—I just think if more people thought that way there'd be less heart-ache in the world.'

He looked down the street again.

Clare watched him push his hands into the pockets of his jeans. 'You could have told me you wanted me to stay.'

When he clenched his jaw, Clare willed him to talk to her. She'd never felt so far away from him. And it hurt. If he just said he wanted her to stay they could at least forget the dumb bet—because she really, really didn't want to matchmake for him any more.

'Go in, Clare.'

When he turned she took another step forward. 'Try it: "Clare, I want you to stay."'

With his profile turned to her she could see the clench of his jaw more clearly. 'That's all it would take, is it? You'd be content working for me and living here and never wanting more than that?'

Now, there was a question. She'd been happy working for him and living in the basement apartment. But never wanting more than that? *From him?* If that was even what he'd meant. It could simply have been a reference to the fact he thought she was hiding away and avoiding dating by using him as some kind of sub-stitute boyfriend. If he'd meant the latter then her answer would certainly be less complicated. But if he'd meant the former—did she want more *from him*? Well, a little encouragement might help, a sign, a flicker of...*anything*...that might indicate *he* was interested in there being more...

Clare floundered in a sea of uncertainty.

And while she did Quinn walked away.

CHAPTER NINE

'YOU DID *WHAT*?'

'It was a practice date.'

Madison laughed incredulously. 'The king of dating needed practice? I'm not buying it. Sorry.'

Clare tucked the receiver firmly between her shoulder and her ear. 'It wasn't my idea.'

'But you agreed to it.'

'Have you ever tried changing Quinn's mind when he sets it on something?' She practically growled at the file of a woman who was a ninety-four percent match for Quinn, immediately setting it on a teetering pile of discarded files. 'It made sense because he wasn't getting past the first date with any of his matches. I needed to find out why...'

'What *did* you find out?' Madison sounded highly amused. 'Tell all. Don't skip a single detail.'

'He didn't do anything wrong. That's just it. This whole thing is making me crazy.' She sighed again, feeling distinctly as if she was carrying the weight of the world on her shoulders. Hence the phone call for moral support. 'How do I get out of this dumb bet?'

'Oh, like hell you're getting out of it. You should hear

the debates we've been having with Morgan and Evan—you know they hero worship Quinn because of his rep with women? They think Quinn settling down is the end of an era. We think they're scared silly cos Quinn settling down means they might be next.' She paused for a moment. 'Do you think he's serious about it?'

'About settling down? I don't know. All I know is we've done nothing but bicker since it started.'

There was a much longer pause, then, *'Okay.'*

'What does *that* mean?'

'Let me ask you this—how long since you took a trip to Tiffany's for one of those little blue boxes?'

'Too long.' And she missed it. Spending hours browsing around the serene calm of the iconic store had been one of her favourite things to do. She should make a trip in her lunch break to see if it helped; it would be nice to find some sense of inner peace *somewhere.* Then it hit her.

'You think it's a sign he's got sick of playing the field, don't you?'

'That didn't occur to you?'

Obviously not. A small part of her had really believed he was playing some kind of game with her, hadn't it? There had certainly been clues along the way: the look in his eyes when he'd made the bet to begin with, his irreverence with the questionnaire, the ridiculous excuses for the lack of second dates—and that had been before she'd thought he'd only agreed to it as a way of getting her to stay put.

But if the lack of need for Tiffany's gifts was a sign he really was ready to settle down, then…

'Well…that'll be me moving out sooner rather than

later, won't it?' She'd mumbled under her breath but her friend heard every word.

'You're seriously thinking about moving out?' Madison's voice was filled with incredulity. 'When Morgan asked me about it I thought he was insane. Do you know how many people would give their right arm for an apartment like yours in Brooklyn Heights? That house of Quinn's has to be worth millions now.'

'*Morgan* asked you about me moving out?' Clare shook her head, frowning in confusion. 'When did that happen?'

'Not long after the bet was made. He even made me double check with Erin; wouldn't get off my case till I did. Apparently Quinn said something about—'

'*Quinn* did?' He'd been talking to Morgan about her moving out? What was he doing—looking for potential replacements before she'd even packed a bag? She hadn't said she was planning on going anywhere that soon! Did he want her to go? Was *that* it? Yes, she wanted to be able to afford her own place one day, and, yes, she would have to move if Quinn settled down with someone—what new wife would want a female friend of her husband's living downstairs from them? But Clare hadn't planned on going anywhere for a good while yet and she loved that apartment. Leaving it would be—

'Morgan seemed to think Quinn wasn't too pleased about you going, if that helps any.'

It did help—some.

Taking a deep breath and puffing her cheeks out as she exhaled, she leaned her elbows on her desk while she added the new information to the myriad of confusion she was already struggling with. There was really only one way to get out of the mess. What she should have done to begin with, and then she could have avoided *all* of the confusion. Things could have stayed the way they were. When she'd been *happy*...

The choice was clear. She wasn't going to matchmake for him any more. She was done. Even if it meant wearing a T-shirt that said 'Loser' as her forfeit. He could go out and find someone to make a commitment to on his own. And while he did she was going to work night and day to get the matchmaking up and running as a viable business. Then she could quit working for him sooner rather than later. And she could afford a place of her own too.

If he *had* made the bet as an underhanded way to get her to stay, then it had just backfired. Because he hadn't been asking if she wanted more *from him*, had he? Oh, no. If Quinn Cassidy was the remotest little bit interested in her that way he'd have done something about it. It wasn't as if he was famous for being the least little bit behind the door when it came to women...

Clare wasn't confused any more. She knew exactly where she stood. Lord, but she needed ice cream. 'I've gotta go—I have a gazillion things to do this afternoon before we go to Giovanni's.'

'Is Quinn going?'

'Course he's going. Why wouldn't he?' Things had been complicated beyond belief for Clare before the phone call with Madison, but Quinn didn't know that. So why wouldn't life go on the way it always had as far as he was concerned?

'Because it's the scene of the crime and all that...' Madison joked.

Clare smiled half-heartedly. 'Not helping. Just be a good girl and help me have fun later, okay?'

'It's that bad?'

'It's that bad.'
'Then it's a deal.'

'What's the deal with you and Clare?'

Quinn shot a frown at Morgan. 'Meaning?'

Morgan glanced at the two girls at the bottom of the table to make sure they were distracted enough not to overhear their low-toned conversation. He turned his back on them just to be sure. 'She's acting weird.'

'Weird how?'

Quinn did his best not to look at her. He'd barely been able to keep his eyes off her all night as it was, but that was what he got for being out of the office so much in the last forty-eight hours. Apparently he was so addicted to her he physically ached when she wasn't nearby. He wasn't the least bit happy about that.

Morgan shrugged. 'She's too bright—she laughs just a little too loud—like she's forcing herself to have a good time but she's not, if you know what I mean. Have you two had a fight?'

'No.' When he focused his attention on the thumb nail he was using to pick at the label on his bottle he could feel Morgan's frown.

'Something's going on, though.'

'Leave it be, Morgan.'

Quinn leaned back in his chair and gave in to his need for a fix of Clare—his mood quickly darkening when he spotted her chatting to some guy he'd never set eyes on before. The guy was laughing with her—and leaning close to listen to what she was saying—

When he set a hand on the small of her back Quinn was on his feet before Morgan had finished asking 'What's wrong?'

He saw her eyes widen in question as he worked his way through the tables. But he simply smiled back, stepping past the shorter guy to stand at her side and dismissing him with a quick glance before he placed an arm around her waist.

'You want dessert?'

Clare gaped at him. 'Excuse me?'

'We were just thinking about ordering dessert, so I thought I'd see if you wanted anything.' He shot her new friend a calm glare. 'This guy bugging you?'

Aiming an embarrassed smile at her new friend while removing Quinn's arm, Clare took hold of his hand and started moving away. 'I'm glad it went well for you, Sam. Good to see you.'

'You too, Clare. Thanks again.'

She nodded, tightening her fingers around Quinn's and tugging harder. 'Bye, Sam.'

Two steps away, she smiled through gritted teeth. 'Now we're going outside, where you can tell me just what you think you're doing.'

A quick check across the room was enough to confirm the suspicion that four pairs of eyes were watching them, so Quinn smiled for their benefit as he pushed open the door. 'You like dessert.'

'*I* like ice cream—*you* like dessert. Where do you get off coming on all Neanderthal man in front of one of my clients?'

Another client? How many clients did she have? They were everywhere. But it wasn't the fact that he'd just made a fool of himself so much as the fact she'd let go of his hand as if it had burnt her the second the door closed that made Quinn frown at her the way he did.

'Hasn't he ever heard of *office hours*?'

'Last time a client visited me during office hours *you* didn't like it.' She marched down the street, stopping on the kerbside where she swung round, her arms lifting and dropping. 'I've had it. I swear. You're making me crazy. I can't keep smiling and pretending everything's fine when it's not. Tonight has been the worst night I've ever had out with the gang. They've done nothing but watch us the whole time. I feel like we're some kind of *sideshow*!'

'They're just curious about how the bet is going.'

At least he hoped that was all it was. Frankly he didn't need any outside pressure or, heaven forbid— because the thought alone made him shudder—*advice.* 'It was made here—it's only natural they're thinking about it when we're at the scene of the crime.'

Clare's eyes narrowed. 'What did you just call it?'

The deathly calm edge to her voice made him frown again. 'Scene of the crime. Why?'

'That's what Madison called it on the phone today.'

'It's a common phrase.'

Her hands rose to the curve of her hips. 'Have you been talking to them about this? Because if this is some big joke and you've all been making with the funnies behind my back—'

Quinn's brows quirked. 'Yeah, cos I'm famous for being a big one for talking about my private life, aren't I? You're overreacting just a tad here, don't you think?'

Clare took a minute to debate it in her head before taking a breath that lifted her small breasts beneath her sleeveless blouse. Then she looked away from him, focusing on the people milling along the street in the humid evening air while she blinked hard and worried on her lower lip.

When she spoke her voice was thready. 'I don't want to do this any more. You win the bet.'

'Why?'

Quinn held his breath while he watched her struggling with an answer, her hands lifting from her hips so she could fold her arms defensively across her breasts. 'Because I don't want to matchmake for you.'

'Why?' His feet carried him a step closer to her.

When her gaze met his again he could see the lights from restaurants and passing cars sparkle in the glittering tears in her eyes. She was genuinely upset. Even though his very bones ached with the need to do something to fix it, he stood his ground, clenching his hands into fists so he wouldn't reach for her. He just needed her to say the words—and then he'd know crossing the line wouldn't be a big mistake…

Silently he willed her to say them.

Instead she shrugged her shoulders all the way up to her ears. 'I just want to go back to the way we were before all this started.'

It hadn't been all that long ago he'd told himself he wanted the same thing, but now… 'Clare—'

'So I think we should just drop all this and give each other a little space, don't you?'

Panic billowed up inside him, and the appearance of outward calm was costing him. 'I don't need space.'

Quinn's chest cramped at the anguish he could see in her eyes. It brought him another step closer before she added, 'Well, it's not like we've been the same since we made the bet, is it? Some space might do us good.' Her throat convulsed. 'I have plenty of holiday time chalked up. I might take a break. I'd make sure everything was up to date, obviously…or you could hire a temp…'

Now he was crowding her? He forced his feet not to take him any closer while she looked so fragile. How was he crowding her? If anything hadn't he been giving her space already? Apart from on their night out that was, when they'd got on better than ever. Until the very end anyway.

He didn't want space, damn it. It was the very fact she'd been so keen to get away from him that had made him start to look at what he *did* want. He wanted *her.* The thought of losing her had made him open his eyes.

Finely arched brows disappeared under the waving curtains of her soft hair. 'Say something.'

Quinn frowned harder. What was he supposed to say? There was a danger if he pushed too hard too soon she might run. Maybe if he gave her some space she'd have a chance to miss him, absence and the heart and all that. But what if he'd already left it too late?

It was the most complicated relationship he'd ever been in. But then it was the first one he'd ever wanted to fight for, which was probably why he was behaving so out of character for him...

Clare searched his eyes, and when she spoke her voice was threaded with emotion. '*Please* say something.'

His heart beat erratically; the simple act of breathing in and out became difficult for him. It felt as if he was having his heart dug out of his chest. He couldn't imagine what it would be like not to see her every day. She was tangled up in his life in so many ways. He wanted to hear the soft lilt of her accent, wanted to see the smile that always made him smile back, wanted that hint of light springtime scent as she walked by. He wanted daisies in pots and pens in those holders with dumb pictures of fluffy animals on the front. He wanted to be told off for not being at meetings on time and to be teased when he rebelled.

He searched frantically for a way to tell her all that without backing her into a corner. But she was shaking her head and unfolding her arms...*and moving away from him.*

Quinn had had enough of being someone he wasn't.

One step forward was all it took, and then his fingers were thrusting into her hair, her face was caught between his large palms—and he was kissing her the way he'd wanted to kiss her at her front door. Except that the moment his mouth touched hers all the frustration he'd been feeling shook loose and the kiss became urgent, frenzied, almost desperate. As if he was trying to break through every obstruction that had been in his way to claim her somehow.

Clare rocked back onto her heels under the on-slaught, but it was the way she clung to his shoulders, the moans that she made deep in her throat and how she met him halfway with an equal amount of ferocity, that finally broke through the haze.

He moved one hand from her face, snaking his arm down and shifting back enough to allow it space to slide around her waist. Then he drew her in close to where her body fitted against his so perfectly. His fingers flexed against the back of her head, his thumb began a slow smoothing over the soft skin of her cheek. And the kiss changed, slowing by increments until he eventually found a gentleness completely at odds with the passion they'd just shared.

A smile formed on Quinn's lips when her moans became sighs and hums of pleasure that vibrated against his mouth. She had as much fire in her belly as he did, he knew that from the preceding maelstrom, but she was still sweet, gentle Clare. And he wanted to see her—to see how she looked after he'd kissed her.

So he dragged his mouth from hers and looked down into her heavy-lidded eyes. The green was so very dark, her pupils enlarged, and when his gaze dropped she ran the tip of her tongue over her swollen lips. She'd never looked more beautiful.

She would never know what it took to set her away from him. Or how much strength he needed to do what he was about to do.

He stepped back. 'I'll give you a week.'

Clare's eyes widened, her voice one decibel above a whisper. 'What?'

'You wanted space. I'll give you a week.'

She took a swaying step forward. 'Quinn—'

Saying his name so it sounded like a plea didn't help with his resolve, and his voice was terse as a result. 'One week, Clare. Think about what it is you want.' Taking a deep breath, he glanced to his side and then back, lowering and softening his voice so that she understood. 'If this happens there's no going back.'

Pushing. Yes, he knew he was—but he couldn't stop it happening. She needed to understand. He'd tried to fight but it was pointless. Especially after that kiss. If he was going to take his first ever steps out of the land of catch and release and into the unknown universe of catch and keep then she needed to be very sure of what she wanted. There *was* no going back.

Quinn would do everything in his power to make her as addicted to him as he was to her...

If Clare was the culmination of all the dating experiences that had come before her then she was going to reap the benefits of that experience. Quinn had learned who he was. He remembered the women he'd thrown back while waiting for the mythical *one* he'd questioned even existed. What it came down to was that the way Clare had made him feel since he'd opened his eyes had gradually impressed on him the need to keep this one. There had never been anyone like her in his life before and there might never be another. So he was going to fight to keep her.

He'd never been so damn scared in his entire life.

CHAPTER TEN

CLARE HAD NEVER BEEN so miserable in her entire life.

It was her own stupid fault—she shouldn't have let him walk away. He'd said he didn't want space from her but he'd given it to her in spades. He'd travelled all the way across the flipping country before she'd had time to catch her breath…

'I'm gonna go look at a few places for clubs on the West Coast,' he'd calmly informed her the next morning *over the phone.*

Clare knew he'd toyed with the idea of a place closer to where some of their A-list members lived, and that he'd planned a trip for later in the month. But she knew he'd moved it up. And she knew why. So she'd tried telling him over the phone that she didn't need a week, but he'd cut her off mid-sentence. Apparently since he was the one to set the deadline he was determined both of them would stick to it, whether she liked it or not.

How stupid was he? How could he kiss her like that and then leave? She'd come off the phone hating him. Distancing himself from her hadn't helped her confidence. Especially when he'd left her with the choice between being with him and possibly losing him or not being with him and losing him anyway. Because he was right; there was no going back—they would never be the same ever again.

Twenty-four hours later she'd descended into misery. She missed him so much she couldn't breathe properly. He felt so very far away—and not even in terms of mileage either. She'd never needed to be held so badly in all her life. His solid strength surrounding her—that fresh soap and pure Quinn scent, the feel of his warm breath against her hair and the gravelly edge of his voice sounding in her ears—and if she looked up she'd see the vivid blue of his eyes, and the sinful curve of his mouth would quirk as he tried to hold back a smile…

Another twenty-four hours and she was rapidly spiralling into the realms of tears. So she'd called the cavalry for an afternoon of retail therapy. It had seemed like a good idea at the time.

'Okay, spill.'

She blinked at Erin. 'Spill what?'

'What's going on with you and Quinn?'

Clare scanned the faces of the crowd in the Mexican place they'd found to have lunch off Fifth and Broadway, the fruits of their labours in at least a dozen bags spread at their feet. She didn't want to talk about it, as if part of Quinn's personality had rubbed off on her. She didn't want the whole thing debated, or differing opinions added to the myriad of emotions she was already experiencing. She just wanted him home.

'Can we skip it?'

Erin pushed the remains of her burrito to one side so she could rest her elbows on the table. 'Not when you look like someone just died, no.'

'I really don't want to talk about it.'

Her friends exchanged glances. 'The whole match-making thing opened your eyes, did it?'

'Possibly.' She smiled weakly at Madison, since Madison had asked the question. 'But I really don't want to talk about it.'

'How does he feel?'

Apparently not wanting to talk about it was getting her nowhere. Leaning back, she took a deep breath while she contemplated how Quinn would feel about her talking to the girls about him. Listening to the low mariachi music for a minute, she answered herself: he'd hate it. But desperate times and all that, so she leaned forward again.

'You've known Quinn a lot longer than me, right?'

'Not as long as Morgan and Evan. Why?' They all leaned closer together around the circular table.

'Do you know how he got started in business?'

It obviously wasn't the question they'd been expecting; a look of confusion was exchanged before Erin spoke. 'He already had two of the clubs when I started hanging around with them—I dated one of Morgan's cousins for a while back then...'

Madison shrugged. 'I don't know either...'

Clare frowned and shook her head. 'I swear, it's like some kind of state secret.'

'Does it matter?'

That had been Quinn's theory too, hadn't it? But Clare nodded, because it did; it was a prime example of the kind of things she didn't know about the man she was going to trust with her heart.

Madison continued, 'There's no point asking the guys either—they guard Quinn's privacy like Rottweilers. I don't think he lets that many people get close to him.

It's why everyone was so surprised when he ended up such good friends with you.'

Oh, great. Now she was getting weepy. She could feel her chest tightening, her throat was suddenly raw, and next her eyes would start stinging... The words were making her ache right down to her bones. It wasn't as if Quinn was uncomfortable with people or lacked confidence—in fact he could probably do with a little less of the latter—so why did he hold people at arm's length that way? And, more to the point, why was he still doing it with her?

It was only when a hand squeezed hers again that she realized she'd been staring into nowhere. Her gaze dropped and then followed the arm upwards until she met Erin's eyes.

'Everyone has always wondered what the deal was with you two. Haven't you noticed how many people treat you like a couple already?'

Actually, no, she hadn't. And the idea astounded her. 'Since when? We weren't a couple.'

Madison let the past tense slip by. 'Not in the traditional sense of the word, no. But there's always a fine line between friendship and something more. Didn't you see the way we all reacted the night of the bet? When you made that comment about being a wife in eight out of ten ways we all gasped. It was the first time either of you had ever confronted it. We've been wondering if it would make either of you look at each other differently...'

A little heads-up would have been nice.

'When you think about it, Quinn's been in a relationship with you longer than he's ever been with any other woman.'

Clare had never thought of it that way. It gave her hope, but, she said, 'Doesn't mean I'd make it past the six week cut-off point.'

Erin scowled at her. 'Hey—where's that famous Irish fighting spirit we all love you for, huh?'

Drowning under a quart of ice cream a night—that was where it was. She was going to weigh three hundred pounds by the time Quinn came home. Forcing a smile into place, she took a deep breath, lifted her shoulders and nodded firmly. 'You're right. Let's go and look in the windows at Tiffany's. I'm going to pick a parting gift so expensive it'll bankrupt him.'

They shook their heads in unison, joint smiles negating the admonishment Madison aimed her way. 'Stop that. If he breaks your heart he'll have us to deal with.'

A week was seven days too long for Quinn. He'd known there was no way he was sticking to it, so he'd put himself on a plane. Even if he hadn't been feeling the need to bang his head against a brick wall for that genius idea he couldn't have stayed away the full seven days. Not while he missed Clare the way he did...

By day three, having dutifully looked over all the potential real estate, he decided enough was enough.

Her time was up. So when another summer day had come and gone away in an eternally sunny Los Angeles he booked a flight home. It didn't matter what she'd decided, he was going home and he was going to launch a charm offensive. He liked that plan much better. It wasn't backing her into a corner. Not the way he had by giving her an ultimatum in the first place. Granted, it wasn't giving her the space she'd asked for either, but tough. By giving her space he'd taken a chance she might form a list of reasons not to get involved with him…

The thought made his need to get home more urgent than before. So by the time he got out of a yellow cab in front of his house—when he should have been bone tired after three nights without sleep and an eight hour flight—he was edgy, restless and frustrated beyond belief that he couldn't just go knock on her door. But it was late—he couldn't go and wake her up just so he could start seducing her, could he? Slow and steady won the race, they said. Whoever they might be…

One of the worst things Clare had endured since Quinn had left was insomnia. It was getting to the stage where she felt like the walking dead. So for the third night in a row she groaned loudly in frustration and threw the light covers off her body before swinging her legs over the edge of the bed and sitting up.

She glanced at the blue digital readout on her alarm clock—half past midnight—so that meant she'd been tossing and turning and feigning sleep for two hours. And she'd tried watching a movie, she'd tried reading a book—heck, she'd even tried some of the relaxation techniques she'd learnt in the handful of yoga classes she'd taken with Madison and Erin back in January, when they'd all said it was time to try something new.

But nothing had worked.

She made her way into the kitchen and poured a glass of water, then rinsed the glass, set it on the side and turned to open the French windows. It had been hor-rifically humid all day long, something the Irish girl in her still found it hard to adjust to. So when she stepped barefoot onto the lawn the fine mist of rain that appeared was almost a godsend.

Closing her eyes, she leaned back, lifting her arms wide and letting the lukewarm spray sprinkle down on her face. Then she turned slowly on her heels, feeling the grass between her toes and breathing a deep lungful of damp air. Actually, it felt quite good.

Now if the aching would just go away—if the part of her that felt as if it was missing could just be returned to her—if she just didn't hurt *so very much*... The next deep breath she took shuddered through her entire body; if he would just *come home*...

Then she could show him, literally, that space was the last thing she wanted.

Dumping his bags in the hall, Quinn walked through the darkness to the kitchen at the back of the house, not needing light to see where he was going. What he should do was go and run off the varying methods of seduction his imagination had decided to supply while repeating the words *slow and steady* until his body got the message.

The dim light from the house next door's motion-sensitive security lighting cast long shadows on the floor from the windows, where a fine mist of rain was frosting the glass. He'd gone running in worse. If he went running it would maybe help with the deep-seated need to go downstairs.

He hesitated in the middle of the room, unsure why he'd gone in there in the first place.

He wasn't going downstairs, but he wondered what she was doing. It was after midnight so she was probably asleep. Was she wearing what she'd been wearing the night he'd sat outside her window? Did she own any of the sexy things she'd talked about on the phone that night?

Okay—now he *really* needed to go for a run—and possibly a cold shower…

Yanking his jacket off, he stepped over to the French windows to throw it over the back of a chair. At first he had to blink a couple of times to be sure he was seeing what he was seeing. Once he'd convinced himself he wasn't seeing her simply because he wanted to see her so badly he smiled at what she was doing. What *was* she doing? Was she crazy? His heart didn't think it was crazy—his heart thought it was exactly the kind of unexpected and uniquely endearing thing Clare *would* do. Joy in the simple things, right?

Only Clare…only *his* Clare…

She focused hard on her breathing while she continued turning, forcing the need to cry—again—back down inside. It was all about control after all. And she really needed to get it under control before she saw Quinn again.

Tilting her outstretched arms from side to side like a child making impressions of an aeroplane, she leaned her head from shoulder to shoulder and smiled sadly at the sudden need for the comfort of childish games. She bent her knees, crossed one leg over the other and turned a little faster, resisting the urge to make aeroplane *noises* too—but only just. The buzzing when a child pressed its lips together to get the engine noise had always made her smile too.

When she tried the turn a second time she stumbled, arms dropping and eyes opening as she chuckled at her

own ridiculousness—she really was losing her mind—
and it was then she looked up and saw him standing on
the edge of the patio...

The world tilted beneath her feet. Quinn smiled the
most amazingly gorgeous, slow, sexy smile at her and
her heart flipped over in her chest in response.

He was *home*.

When he dropped his chin and his expression held a
hint of uncertainty, joy bubbled up inside her.

She breathed out the words. 'You're home.'

'I'm home,' the gruff-edged voice she loved so much
replied. 'Miss me?'

Clare felt her eyes welling up, her throat tight so the
most she could manage was to nod frantically.

She saw him exhale—as if he'd been holding his
breath until he got her reply—and his voice was even
gruffer than before. 'How much?'

When her heart stopped, her feet grew wings. She
was across the lawn and flinging herself into his waiting
arms before she'd allowed herself time to second-guess
what she was doing. Then, with her arms around the
thick column of his neck, her cheek against his, she
laughed joyously as he lifted her off her feet; groaning
against her ear. '*Good*—cos *I* missed *you*.'

She leaned back to look into his sensational eyes.
'How much?'

Quinn examined her eyes for a long moment before
informing her. 'Okay, you better know what it is you
want, O'Connor. This is your ten second warning.'

Clare smiled uncontrollably at him, wriggling her
toes in the air. 'My what?'

'Ten-second warning.' He nodded the tiniest amount,
his deep voice intimately low as it rumbled up from his

chest. The vibration filtered through their layers of clothing to tickle her overly sensitive breasts. 'In ten seconds I'm going to kiss you. So that's how long you have to stop me…'

Clare stared at him in wonder, sure that any minute she was going to awaken and end up miserable again because she'd dreamed what was happening.

His chest expanded. 'Ten…nine…eight…'

She ducked down and pressed her mouth to his.

His lips were warm and firm, and for a long moment he froze, allowing her to tentatively explore their shape. But when her lips parted and she added pressure he moved with her, the kiss soft and gentle and so very tender that it touched her soul. It felt as if the part of her that had been missing was being returned with each slide of his mouth over hers. She could kiss and be kissed by him for days on end. She really could.

Moving her hands, she let her fingertips brush against the short spikes of his cropped hair while she breathed his scent in deep. And then she caught his lower lip between her teeth in a light nip, and smiled against his mouth when he groaned low down in his chest, the sound more empowering than anything she'd ever experienced.

Letting her feet swing from side to side, her body brushing back and forth against his with the movement, she smiled all the more when the sound in his chest became a groan, his words vibrating against her lips. 'Are nice Irish girls supposed to kiss like this?'

Clare lifted her head enough to change angles. 'Maybe I'm not as nice as you like to think I am.'

'Hmmm.' The sound buzzed her sensitive lips in the exact way the aeroplane noise would have if she'd made it. The thought made laughter bubble effervescently inside her. 'I wasn't complaining…'

He moved one arm, keeping her suspended off the ground as if she weighed nothing while his free hand rose to thread long fingers into her hair. And then he cradled the back of her head in his palm and deepened the kiss—stealing the air from her lungs and making her feel vaguely light-headed.

Clare couldn't have said how long they kissed for; she didn't even realize he was gently swinging her from side to side until he began a slow circling to go with it. And it made her wonder how long he'd been standing watching her turning circles on the lawn—what he was doing was a more sensual version of what she'd been doing alone.

Using the hand in her hair to draw her back a little, so he could look at her when she finally lifted her heavy eyelids, his eyes glowed as Clare smiled drunkenly at him.

'Hello, you.'

Clare's heart swelled. 'Hello, you.'

She looked over her shoulder when he started carrying her across the patio and down the steps, turned to look at him again as they got close to her doors. The disappointment evident in her voice, she asked, 'Are we stopping kissing now?'

'Like hell we are.'

The firm reply made her wiggle her toes again while she openly studied his face.

'Forgot what I looked like, did you?'

'You were gone a very long time. I'm just checking nothing has changed.'

In front of her large sofa, he let her slide oh, so

slowly, down the length of his body, until her feet touched the floor. Then he sat down, tugging her onto his lap before leaning over until she was lying on her back looking up at him.

Quinn's hand rose, and he watched as his fingertips smoothed her hair back before beginning a slow exploration of her face, his gaze rising to tangle with hers while he traced her lips. 'Something has changed.'

She knew he didn't mean their faces. 'It did—a while back.'

He nodded, lowering his gaze to watch in wonder as he brushed his thumb back and forth over her lower lip. 'One step at a time, okay?'

'Okay.' She lifted a hand and framed the side of his face, the small sigh and the lowering of his thick lashes to half-mast telling her everything she needed to know for now. 'I need you to talk to me, though, Quinn.'

He took a deeper breath. 'You might need to work with me on that. It's new ground.'

'I know.' Smiling softly, she moved her hand around to the back of his head and drew him towards her. 'Where were we?'

Thick lashes lifted again, his thumb moving to the corner of her mouth. 'Here.'

He kissed where his thumb had been, then lifted his head an inch and moved his thumb over her bottom lip to the other corner. 'And here.'

Clare didn't care how late it was, or that they both had work to think about when the sun came up—it didn't matter; the new day could wait. When she was eventually lying across him, with her head tucked beneath his chin, she lifted her chin enough to whisper up at him. 'Stay.'

'Here?'

'Right here.' She snuggled back into place, her palm resting against the steady beat of his heart. 'I haven't been sleeping so good.'

His arms tightened. 'Me either.'

'So stay.'

'Just so long as you still respect me in the morning.' He reached up for the throw rug she had tossed over the back of the sofa.

'Well, I don't know about that one…'

Lethargy settled over her as he smoothed his hand in circles against her back. 'Do you trust me, Clare?'

'You know I do.'

'You know I'd never do anything to hurt you?'

'I know.'

'But you know I'm not easy?'

She smiled sleepily. 'Spoken by the man sleeping over after our second kiss.'

'I need you to know what you're getting into. I'm not—'

'I know what I'm getting into. You said a while back that I knew enough. And I do.'

When he continued smoothing his hand over her back she felt herself drawn down into the depths of the kind of languorous sleep she hadn't experienced since he'd left; still smiling as she did.

She was going to give that six week deadline of his a run for its money…

CHAPTER ELEVEN

'DISCO BABIES?'

Quinn smiled from his perch on the edge of her desk as she pushed the filing cabinet shut with her hip and turned to look at him with enthusiasm dancing in her eyes. 'Yes. Parents bring their kids along and they all dance together and have a great time. It wouldn't take much to get it going. And it doesn't interfere with what you already do.'

It wasn't that he didn't think it was a good idea. He did. He just liked having Clare persuade him that it was.

When she attempted to get past he casually reached out, hooking an arm around her waist and spreading his legs to make room for her. She didn't put up a fight—she never did. Instead her hands slid over his shoulders and linked together at the back of his neck, her thumbs massaging the base of his skull so he automatically leaned back into the touch.

'You want to turn my clubs into kids' playgrounds?'

'No-o.' She smiled when he splayed his fingers on her hips. 'I want you to consider how much money parents spend, especially in a city with lots of rich parents...'

Quinn nodded. 'Uh-huh. It has nothing to do with the sight of all those dancing babies? The cute card isn't swaying you any?'

'You *like* this idea.' She turned her face a little to the side and quirked her brow knowingly. 'You know you do.'

It never ceased to amaze him how much her confidence seemed to have grown since they'd started dating for real. She'd blossomed before his very eyes. Not that she hadn't been something before—but now?

Well, now she was *something*.

And Quinn had real problems keeping his hands off her. For someone who'd never been renowned for being overly demonstrative in public, he'd gone through quite a transformation of late. He was holding her hand as they walked through Manhattan, kissing her at hotdog stands in Times Square, and randomly grinning like an idiot even when she wasn't there. She was shooting his reputation for cool, detached control down in flames. The thing was, he liked it that she was.

'It has possibilities.'

'See.' She sidled closer and leaned him back over the desk, her long lashes lowering as she focused her gaze on his mouth. 'I knew you'd like it. I'm getting much better at discovering things you *like*...'

Smiling at the innuendo, he removed one hand from her hip to brace his palm on the desk, lifting his chin. 'You think you have me all figured out now, don't you?'

'Oh, I still have a few secrets to discover; keeps you interesting, mind you...'

The thought of her finding out everything before he told her himself made his smile fade, and Clare immediately searched his eyes and saw what must have been a flash of doubt. Her voice softened in response.

'And I've told you a few million times now that nothing will change how I see you.'

With each passing week Quinn liked to believe that was true, but he'd wanted her to be more attached to him before he took the chance. The way he figured it, it was just a case of making sure she was insanely crazy about him first. With that in mind, he sat upright to bring his nose within an inch of hers, his fingers curling into her hair.

Angling his head, he examined her eyes up close, blinking lazily. 'Bring me any ideas involving pets and my clubs and we may need to have a serious talk.'

When a smile formed in her eyes he closed the gap and kissed her long and slow, until the hands at his nape unlocked and gripped onto his shoulders and she rocked forwards, pressing her breasts in tight against his chest. She was temptation personified. Resisting her was getting to be nigh on impossible. Slow and steady was a mammoth test of his endurance.

Quinn moved the hand on her hip around to her back, slipping it under the edge of her blouse so he could touch his fingertips to baby-soft skin. The fooling around they'd been doing had been escalating of late, and it couldn't happen soon enough as far as Quinn was concerned. He had only to think about touching her and his reaction was so strong and so fierce that it left his body in an almost constant state of pain.

She knew it too—the witch. Good little Irish girl, his eye. She'd been pushing him closer and closer to the edge for weeks.

When he slid his hand further up she made a muffled sound of complaint against his mouth and wriggled. 'Don't you dare.'

When she lifted her head he feigned nonchalance. 'Dare what?'

'You know what.' When she tried to wriggle free he dropped his hand from her hair and used the arm to circle her waist and keep her still. Clare laughed throatily in response. 'I swear if you undo that before my client arrives you're in big, big trouble.'

With a flick of his thumb and forefinger he unhooked her bra. Her hands immediately lifted to hold the material in place—cupping her breasts. 'I *hate* that you can do that.'

Quinn grinned. 'Old high school party piece.'

'Too much information, Casanova.' She mock scowled at him, her eyes dancing with amusement. *'Fix it.'*

'Say please.'

'Fix it or I'm telling Morgan and Evan you bring me daisies twice a week…'

'Yes, because my ability to charm you is something I should be ashamed of—obviously.'

'Fix it.' She leaned closer to whisper in his ear. 'Or I'm telling them you watched *Breakfast at Tiffany's* and *enjoyed it.*'

Okay, that one would run and run, so he placed a kiss on the sensitive skin below her ear before lifting both hands under her blouse to fix what he'd done. 'I might have to stop being nice to you.'

Truthfully, he probably wouldn't have enjoyed the movie as much if she hadn't loved every minute of it. But then that was something else that had crept up on him: his state of happiness being directly related to hers. The fact that when she smiled he smiled had always been there, even when they were friends—but it was so much more than that now. Some days he even wondered if all the touching they did had led to her emotions being transmitted to him.

Quinn grimaced at the effort it took not to laugh when she wiggled about, making sure everything was back in place. His voice was filled with husky-edged amusement. 'Can I help you with that?'

'No—you can go away. You have a meeting in fifteen minutes.'

'I have another ten minutes, then, don't I?'

'Like heck you do.' But she smiled at him anyway, leaning in for another kiss. 'Go.'

Quinn sighed heavily. 'Maybe for the best. There's someone confused enough by the writing on the doors to be one of your clients.'

When he jerked his head in the direction of the doors Clare turned and smiled encouragingly at the woman before glaring back at Quinn. 'How do you *do that*?'

He shrugged. 'I have amazingly good eyes.'

The woman pushed the door open just as Quinn let Clare loose, the turn of her body giving him enough cover to slide his fingers over the curve of her rear as he stood and walked past. When she jumped a little he smiled, leaned in and shook the woman's hand,

'Hi, there—I'm gonna leave you girls to talk romance, and Clare will fix you right up.' He winked. 'She has excellent taste in men.'

The woman smiled back. 'If she has a few more like you on her books I'll be more than happy…'

'Why, thank you.' He inclined his head, glancing at Clare in time to see her roll her eyes. 'But I'm afraid I'm temporarily out of circulation.'

The woman laughed girlishly while Quinn walked

towards the door, turning on his heel to walk the last few steps backwards so he could point a long finger at Clare over her client's head. 'Don't be late tonight.'

She made a small snort of derision. 'I'm not the one who's normally late for things.' She tapped her wristwatch with meaning. 'Would you go away, you clown? I'm going to find Marilyn the man of her dreams.'

Marilyn grinned at Clare when Quinn left. 'Boyfriend, I take it?'

It was the first time she'd been asked the question, and Clare hesitated on the answer. Telling the woman in front of her he was her boss would seem strange after the interchange she'd just witnessed. Boyfriend, however, suggested that it was something committed, and even though every bone in Clare's body ached for that kind of stability with Quinn she was still deeply aware of the fact they were in his usual honeymoon period. If she got past the six-week cut-off point she'd probably feel better…

One week to go…

It didn't stop her wanting to say it out loud, just the once while he couldn't hear her, as if saying it would make it more real.

'Yes.' For now anyway…

'He's gorgeous.'

He played on it no end too, the brat. But she was so completely wrapped up in him she couldn't call him on it. Everything was so *right* in so many ways. She'd honestly never been happier. It was why she'd decided to seduce him. Sometimes a girl had to do what a girl had to do. Not that she'd ever set out to seduce a man before, or had the faintest idea how to go about it with a man like Quinn. But they'd been fooling around long enough for her to have a fair idea of what worked and what didn't…

Linking arms with Marilyn, she guided her towards the seating area. 'Let's see if we can find you someone just as gorgeous, shall we?'

Someone Marilyn could love as much as Clare loved Quinn. Because she did; she'd probably been falling for him long before she'd realized it. The slow build had led to a deeper emotion than she'd ever felt before. It made the relationship she'd had with Jamie look shallow and pointless in comparison. But then Clare supposed there was no way to know if what you felt was real until the real thing arrived. *You just know*, they said. They were right. Clare just knew.

She was head over heels in love with Quinn. And he now had the ability to hurt her as she'd never been hurt before…

'Where are we going?'

'We're here. Close your eyes.'

'If I close my eyes how can I see where we are?' She cocked a brow in challenge.

'In the future when you complain about a lack of surprises can we remember how bad you are with them?'

The very mention of the word future was enough to earn a firm kiss, her arm lifting to wrap around his neck. 'But we're already here. All you have to do is yell "surprise."'

Quinn smiled indulgently as the door behind her was opened by their driver. 'You have to promise you'll close your eyes in the elevator when I say so.'

Intrigued, Clare slid across the soft white leather and swung her knees out. Lifting her head when she was on the sidewalk, she blinked at her surroundings, smiling when Quinn's fingers tangled with hers.

'The Rockefeller Centre? Isn't it closed at this time of night?'

Quinn leaned his face close to hers, his gaze fixed forward as he stage whispered in her ear, 'Not when you have the means to keep it open, no.'

They walked past the row of United Nations flags, Clare's eyes automatically seeking out the Irish one so she could smile its way. Then she looked at the golden statue of Prometheus and the art deco buildings surrounding them before she turned towards Quinn and lifted her chin.

'So what are we doing this time?'

The night had started with a limo at her door, progressing to a sell-out Broadway show and supper at one of the chicest restaurants in Manhattan, leaving Clare feeling distinctly like royalty.

Quinn chuckled, his smile lighting up his vivid eyes. 'Wait and see.'

She decided she liked champagne and caviar dates if he got so much enjoyment out of them. Not that she needed them every day, because she didn't. She was just as happy with a hotdog stand in Times Square, or sitting on the steps outside the house they shared eating bagels in the early morning after his run, or lying across the sofa watching a movie late at night...

But Quinn had excelled himself. She barely had words when they finally stepped out of the elevator at the Top of the Rock and he uncovered her eyes. The panoramic view of New York at night spread endlessly before her.

Hand in hand they walked to the edge, and she took

in everything from the Chrysler Building lit up in green through to the Empire State Building with its ethereal glow of white light. It was breathtaking.

'Over here.'

When she turned she saw what she'd missed: a small table set for two—candles flickering inside glass globes—smiling daisies in a vase. It was perfect.

Squeezing his fingers, she pressed into his side, her voice filled with awe. 'How did you do this?'

Quinn smiled lazily, his gravelly voice low. 'One of the joys of dating a rich guy.'

The very fact he'd spent what must have amounted to a small fortune to hire the place after hours—*for her*—made her want to tell him there and then how much she loved him.

'You don't have to impress me on a date any more, you know. I'm a sure thing.'

He stopped at the side of the table, turned and wrapped the fingers of his free hand around the nape of her neck, his thumb tilting her chin up so he could kiss her before mumbling against her lips. 'Sure thing, huh?'

She bobbed her head. And was rewarded with another kiss before he stepped back, freeing his hands so he could lift a silver dome from a plate. 'Caviar…'

Clare chuckled at his theatrics as he jerked his head towards the table. 'Champagne, naturally…'

'You've never actually done a champagne and caviar date before, have you?'

'Never let it be said I can't rise to a challenge.'

'This cost you a small fortune, didn't it?'

Wide shoulders jerked. 'Not all of it…'

Naturally it made her look at the table again. 'What's under the other dome?'

'Good of you to ask.' He reached forward. 'Didn't know how you felt about fish eggs…so…'

When he revealed the other plate she laughed. 'Apple pie, perchance?'

'Apple pie.' He grinned. 'Best of both worlds.'

'You hate fish eggs, don't you?'

'Can't stand them.'

She took the dome from his hand and set it down before insinuating herself under his jacket and wrapping her arms around his lean waist. 'Okay. So the apple pie would be for whom, exactly?'

'I figured we could share.'

'Sharing works for me. Did you bring ice cream?' Not that she had so much of a need for it any more.

'I did.' He leaned down and pressed a row of kisses up the side of her neck before whispering in her ear. 'Rocky road…'

'You thought of everything.'

Quinn kissed back down her neck, nuzzling into the indentation of her collarbone before surprising her by releasing her. 'Well, as it happens…'

When the haunting strains of 'Moon River' sounded over the whisper of city noises in the wind, emotion rose in a wave inside her, her voice wavering as a result.

'The *Breakfast at Tiffany's* music…'

He nodded, his gaze fixed on hers as he slowly made his way back around the table. 'Can't have you thinking I don't pay attention to the little details, can I?'

Heaven help her, he'd be like that as a lover too, wouldn't he? Clare knew it as instinctively as her body knew to breathe in and out. Never, ever had she wanted a man as badly as she wanted Quinn; all the patience he'd been exercising not to push her into sleeping with him was driving her crazy. How could he not know that?

He stepped backwards, drawing her into an open space before he wrapped his arm around her waist. When she lifted a hand to his shoulder and brought her hips in against his he began to sway them—oh, so slowly—and the softness in the vivid blue of his eyes was enough to bring tears to the backs of hers.

'Do I get to graduate from the school of dating etiquette yet?'

Clare had to clear her throat to answer. 'With flying colours.'

'Good.'

When he celebrated by whirling her in circles before dipping her backwards to kiss her breathless she looked up at him with dancing eyes.

'Where did you learn to dance?'

Dark brows waggled at her as he drew her upright and back against his body. 'My mother insisted all the Cassidy boys knew the basics. The dip and kiss I added.'

'Remind me to thank her when I see her.'

'And have her rub it in that she was right? I think not.'

Clare smiled softly. 'Anything else I don't know about that you want to tell me?'

The expression on his face changed in a heartbeat. 'Yes. There's a lot.'

She lifted her brows in question.

Quinn took a shallow breath and looked over her head. 'You asked me how I got started with the clubs.'

Clare kept her voice low in case she broke the spell. 'On the door, right?'

'Yes.' He frowned. 'But that's not how I ended up

buying the first one. I could never have afforded it on the wages I earned.'

'Okay.'

Thick lashes flickered as he watched a fine lock of her hair catch in the breeze. 'My old man left a life insurance policy. For a lot more than anyone thought he could; he couldn't stick to much of anything else, but somehow he kept up the payments on it his whole life…'

'He left it to you?'

'No, but I'd pretty much been the provider for the family since I turned sixteen—worked construction sites during the day—so my mother trusted me to put it to good use. When I talked about trying to get a mortgage for the club after it came up for sale, she staked me. I paid it back with interest.'

Why on earth hadn't he felt he could tell her that?

'He'd have been very proud of you, your dad.'

It was the wrong thing to say. She knew it the second his mouth twisted. 'He wouldn't have given a damn. It'd been twelve years since he bothered with his family. Dying and leaving the money was the best thing he ever did for any of us.'

The bitterness in his words sent a shiver up Clare's spine. 'I thought he died when you were little?'

Quinn frowned at her. 'Who told you that?'

'No one.' She floundered. 'I just—well, when you said about that fight you had—your nickname—'

His eyes widened. 'You thought I got into that fight to defend him?'

'Well, yes. Sort of. I thought—'

'Every word they said about him that day was true. What made me see red was the fact they said I was just like him. Apple never falls far from the tree, or words to that effect. The truth can hurt more than anything else…' He took a deep breath, held it for a moment, and pursed his lips into a thin line before continuing. 'I didn't want to be told I was like him. Problem is, I'm the walking image of him—the young version of him anyway. I see him in the mirror every day.'

Clare's eyes searched his, catching sight of an inner torture that made her ache for him. It made her fearful of knowing everything she'd wanted to know. But she knew what it meant for Quinn to let her in, so she asked the question. 'What did he do?'

'He was a drunk. A lousy one.' His arms tightened before he added the one thing he had to know Clare would feel the deepest. 'And he cheated on my mom from before I was born.'

Clare gasped, feeling the pain as keenly for his mother as she ever had for herself, maybe more. She'd met Quinn's mother countless times and adored her. She was one of the strongest, warmest, most caring women Clare had ever met. From the moment Clare had arrived in New York with Jamie—feeling more than a little lost and overwhelmed—Maggie Cassidy had made it her business to ensure she felt welcomed into their community. When Jamie had left she'd been the first to come and see her. Not once had she ever let on that she understood better than most how Clare had felt.

She shook her head, trying to make sense of it. 'But she had more kids with him. They must have—'

'Thought having each of those kids would save their marriage? They probably did. But it didn't. She put up with him for years, because she remembered what he'd been like when she fell for him. And she let him convince her time and time again that he could change. But he didn't change.' Quinn paused. 'He got worse.'

'My God.' Clare breathed the words at him. 'Is that why you were so worried I might think you were like Jamie? You thought because your father was a cheater…'

Was *that* why he never stayed in a relationship more than six weeks? Did he think if he even looked at another woman there was a chance he might stray, so rather than hurt anyone he cut them loose? It was a twisted logic, but it made sense.

Quinn's voice was fiercely determined. 'I may look like my old man, but…'

Clare slid her hand off his neck and framed his face, smoothing the harsh line at one side of his mouth with her thumb while she told him in an equally determined voice, 'You're talking about genetics, Quinn—not who you are inside. I *know* you.'

But he removed her hand from his face. 'For a long time I was more like my old man than I wanted to be. We're taught that growing up, people like you and me— aren't we? It's the Irish thing. We're taught how it runs through us, how it's part of who we are; the generations that went before run in our veins.'

'Yes, but not the way you—'

Just when she feared he was distancing himself from her, he caught her fingers in his and squeezed tight. 'I listened to that when I was a kid. I thought that his blood running through my veins and looking like him meant I'd end up exactly the same. I've spent a good portion of my life proving I'm not.'

He smiled a smile that didn't make it all the way up into his eyes. 'But I certainly had his temper. And that day in the playground showed me I could be just as quick with my fists.'

Clare's chest cramped so badly she could barely catch her breath—*no*. 'He didn't…?'

His gravelly voice said the words she didn't want to hear. 'Like I said—lousy drunk.'

'Oh, *Quinn.*'

Not her Quinn. Her eyes filled with tears. It all made sense to her now. He hadn't been able to defend himself against a grown up, but all the anger and hurt he'd felt had been directed at five boys his own age when they'd told him he was exactly like the man who'd caused him that pain. It wasn't *fair.*

Quinn smoothed his hand down her back. 'It only happened the one time. My mom had us all packed and moved to Brooklyn before it could happen again.'

Blinking the tears away, Clare found the strength to lift her chin. 'I'd have done the same thing.'

'I like to hope you'd have left sooner.' He smiled with his eyes before his mouth quirked. 'You're stronger than you give yourself credit for, O'Connor. I saw it that day when you had to go face those people and tell them there was no wedding. I don't think I've ever respected anyone more than I respected you that day.'

Untangling her fingers from his, she lifted both hands to the tensed muscles of his shoulders, shaking him firmly as she informed him, 'Listen up, Quinn Cassidy. You're *not* him. I know that. You know that. And you could have told me all of this any time and it wouldn't *ever* have changed how I see you. Nothing you do or say could change how I feel about you. I—'

The words were almost out before he interrupted her. 'I hope you mean that.'

'Quinn!' How could he think—?

'No, you need to know.' He took a breath, and then said the words that literally stopped her heart.

'I sent Jamie away that day.'

CHAPTER TWELVE

WHAT QUINN HAD SAID didn't make any sense to her. But as she searched his eyes she automatically stepped back, frowning when he set her fingers free, almost as if he'd known she would need space and been prepared for it.

'I don't understand. Why—?'

'Someone had to do something.' She saw a muscle clench in his jaw. 'I guess it was always gonna be me.'

'Someone?' He made it sound like—

Her brows jerked. 'Everyone *knew*?'

'That he was messing around? Yes. He didn't make much of a secret of it. He never did. He was one of the best friends I ever had, but on that one subject we never agreed; he was a player for as long as I knew him.'

Everyone knew? Having the man she'd followed blindly across an ocean cheat on her was bad enough on its own, but that everyone had known, and had no doubt been talking about it while she'd sailed through her fantasy bubble days blissfully unaware, was too much. It was like being slapped. She'd walked out there in front of all those people and they'd *known*—

She felt nauseous. 'You *all* knew and none of you thought to tell *me*?'

The sense of betrayal was overwhelming.

'It caused more arguments than we'd ever had before. But when it came down to it we didn't know you that well, and no one wanted to be the one to cause you that much pain. So I dealt with Jamie. *Him* I knew.'

'Draw the short straw did you?'

She saw anger flash in his eyes. *'No.'*

'Well, what then?' She flung an arm out to her side, humiliation morphing rapidly into anger. 'Because you're leader of the pack it was your job to fix things for the poor wee Irish girl?'

When he stepped closer she lifted her hands to his chest to push him away, but he grasped them in his and held on. 'Go ahead and let it out, O'Connor. Yell, shout, call me all the names you want. But I'd do it again.'

'You patronising, self-righteous...' She laughed a little hysterically, tugging on her hands. 'Let me go.'

He held on. 'I know you're hurt—'

'Hurt? Oh, hurt doesn't even begin to cover how I feel right this minute. I thought I'd made some real friends here—people I could *trust.'* She tugged again.

He still held on, looking down at her with an air of self-composure that made her want to lash out. To say things that would make him hurt as much as she did. Anything that might make him understand how much she hated him for bursting the bubble of happiness she'd allowed herself to inhabit—*again.* It wasn't that she saw him differently or loved him less; it was just that she was so very—

Hurt.

Just as he'd said—but she couldn't back down and tell him that. She didn't want to. He had to have known what telling her would make her feel. Why tell her now?

Why, when it was all behind her, had he felt she needed to know?

Was it a way to make her hate him before he handed her a little blue box? But that didn't make any sense. Why set up such an incredible night and open up to her the way he had if he planned on cutting her loose?

But she ignored reason, unable to focus anywhere beyond putting the final pieces of the puzzle together. 'What did you do, exactly? I want all of it.'

When he grimaced she tugged harder to free herself, stumbling back a step when he let go and said her name with a pleading tone. *'Clare—'*

'No—come on—you were so determined I needed to know, so tell me. What did you do? What did you say to plead my case for me? To try and get him to stay with me when he so very obviously didn't want to?'

Quinn's eyes flashed. 'He should never have brought you here!'

Clare flinched. So much for what he'd said about her making the right decision to stay, then. She nodded, biting hard on her lower lip as she began to pace aimlessly. 'Right. I don't belong here. Good to know.'

Quinn swore viciously. 'That's not what I meant. I meant he should never have brought you here when he had no intention of staying faithful to you. You deserved better. I told him that.'

She nodded again. 'And how long after I arrived did you tell him that?'

When he didn't answer she stopped pacing, the set of Quinn's shoulders and the clench of his jaw telling her he was fighting a silent battle.

'How long?'

His gaze locked with hers. 'A month.'

Wow, the truth really did hurt. To know she'd managed to hold her fiancé's attention for less than a whole month was a real kick in the guts. Even knowing he was lower than a snake's behind didn't help how bruised her confidence felt.

Dropping her head back, she blinked at the sky as she tried to control her anger, her gaze flickering back and forth while her mind searched for answers to what it was she'd apparently been lacking.

Quinn's voice softened, sounding closer. 'It wasn't anything you did or didn't do. It was him. He was a fool, Clare—I told him *that* too.'

'So basically you warned him off. Did what—? Threatened to tell me what he was doing?' She laughed as she dropped her chin and looked at him. 'Bit of an empty threat that one, wasn't it?'

'What was I supposed to do? Drop in for coffee and just land it in your lap? I didn't know you well enough for that. It was none of my business.'

'You *made it* your business!'

'Yes.' He nodded brusquely. 'I *did*. Someone had to. Up till then I was his closest friend, so I told him straight what he was doing was wrong. I gave him a chance to make it right. He owed you that.'

Clare still didn't get it. Quinn was right about many things; it hadn't been any of his business, she'd meant nothing to him back then—hell, he'd barely given her the time of day. Why would he take her part against someone who'd been one of his best friends for years?

Her eyes widened with horror. 'Tell me you didn't run him off because *you* wanted me.'

Rage arrived so fast she felt it travel through the air like a shockwave. *'What?'*

'It's what *he* did, you know.' She nodded. 'I was seeing someone—just casually, mind you—but we'd been dating for a couple of weeks until Jamie came along and launched his charm offensive. He used to joke that he stole me away, that it took strategy and a long term plan. Did *you* have a long term plan, Quinn? Is that what *this* is? I remember what Morgan used to say about you and Jamie always competing for the girls in high school. He said you were always rivals when it came to women.'

Quinn bunched his hands into fists at his sides. 'I'm back to being slime again, am I? I stepped up because what he was doing to you was *wrong*! He was about to make a commitment to you—a lifetime commitment. Not only did he make the promises to you, he dragged you all the way over here—away from your family and your friends—and then after you'd given up so much to be with him he…'

He had to pause for breath, turning his face away while he fought to keep his anger in check. Clare read every sign, knew everything he'd said was true. It was that honourable streak of his—it was his belief in right and wrong and his ability to care about the welfare of others…

They were all part of the man she'd fallen so deeply in love with. He'd championed her, hadn't he? In that old-fashioned knight in shining armour way that women dreamed of.

She just wished she'd known. 'You should have told me.'

When he looked at her with an expression of raw agony the very foundations of their relationship shook beneath her feet. When tears formed in her eyes, she wrapped her arms tight around her waist to hold the agony inside, her voice barely above a whisper.

'You offered me the job and a place to stay out of guilt, didn't you?'

Even the words left a bitter taste in her mouth. Their entire relationship was based on a lie. How could they ever come back from that?

'Clare, please—'

'Didn't you?' Her voice cracked.

'At the beginning, yes—partly...' He swallowed hard, and the fact that he was so hesitant broke her in two. 'He humiliated you publicly and left you in debt, but you loved it here. You needed a job and I had one. Then you needed a place to stay—and I had one. It made sense.'

Quinn stepped into her line of vision, her gaze immediately focusing on a random button on his shirt before working its way up, button by button...

'But, yes, I did feel guilty about what happened. I told Jamie to fight for what he had with you or leave. I had no idea he would wait till your wedding day to make a decision. If I had I wouldn't have let it happen. When it did I told him never to come back.'

Clare's gaze lingered on the sweep of his mouth before searching out the slight bump on the ridge of his nose, her voice suddenly flat. 'I bet you didn't say it as calmly as that.'

'No, I didn't.'

She nodded, somehow finding the strength to look into the reflected light shimmering in the dark pools of his eyes. 'Did you hit him?'

Out of nowhere she remembered the smudges of dirt on his suit when he'd come to tell her Jamie was gone. And when he sighed deeply she had her answer.

So she nodded again. 'Saved me doing it, I guess.'

'We said a lot of other stuff too; it got personal—and heated. We hadn't been seeing eye to eye on a lot of things even before you came on the scene.'

Because Jamie had been a player, and a man of honour like Quinn would have had problems with that. Clare got it now. If she'd known Jamie as well as Quinn had, she'd never have followed him to the States to begin with. But then she'd never have met Quinn…

She dragged her gaze from his eyes and looked out into the distance. 'Maybe you're right; I should never have come over here to begin with.'

'You belong here now.'

When she shook her head, the never-ending panorama of twinkling lights beyond the edges of the building blurred in front of her eyes and her lower lip trembled. 'I thought I did.'

'You *do*. This is your home.' His fingertips brushed against her cheek. 'You belong with—'

Clare's breath caught on a sob as she moved her face out of his reach. 'Don't. Please. Not now.'

From the fog of her peripheral vision she saw his hand drop. 'Don't ask me for space, Clare. I mean it. I didn't want to give it to you last time.'

Sharply turning her head, she frowned hard. 'So I'm supposed to do what? Pretend I'm fine with all this and just let it go?'

'I'm not asking you to do that either.'

'Then *what is it* you expect me to do?'

'Work through it with me!' His large hands rose to frame her face so fast she didn't have time to step away. Then he stepped in, towering over her and lowering his head so he could look into her eyes with an intensity that twisted her heart into a tight ball. 'You wanted honesty, Clare, and that's what I've given you. I want that for us. I don't want secrets. I don't want anything we can't work our way through—*together.* Because if we can't do that—'

With a calmness that belied the pain she felt, Clare peeled his hands from her face. 'This is a lot, Quinn. I can't—'

'Yes, you can.' The words were said on a harsh whisper. 'You just have to want to.'

It wasn't that she didn't want to. She wanted to with all her heart and soul. From the very second they'd started down the path they'd taken she'd known she didn't want to lose him. She still didn't. But she needed time to think, to piece everything together, to work her way through it all…

To find a way to get past her shattered illusions of the relationship they'd had—and the relationships she had with all the people she'd come to love as friends. He'd just shaken her little world to pieces.

She lifted her chin. 'Do you trust me?'

Quinn looked suspicious. 'You know I do.'

'Do you trust me to make the right decision for me?'

'Why?'

'Because if you do, you need to trust me enough to give me some time with this; it's a *lot.* You know it is. And you can't land it in my lap and not give me time to think it through.'

'Right, I get it.' Then he quirked a dark brow. 'So what's the time limit this time?'

Clare gasped. 'Don't you dare. You *lied* to me.'

'There's still no grey area with you, is there? I could have gone a lifetime without telling you this.'

'What I didn't know wouldn't hurt me?'

'*Yes!*' He threw the word at her in frustration. 'Because you'd already been hurt enough! You think I ever wanted to cause you the kind of pain he did? *Why* would I want to do that?'

'It wasn't pain.' Clare shook her head. 'It was *humiliation.* I got it so completely wrong, don't you see? I didn't know him well enough to follow him all the way over here, let alone marry him!'

'Then why did you?'

'*I wish I knew!*' Just like that the tears came. Clare moaned in frustration. 'Damn it, Quinn, that's exactly why I need to think this time. Don't you get it? I'm not some starry-eyed dreamer any more. If I was, let me tell you, this would have knocked it out of me. It's not just that you lied—you *all* lied. I've never felt like such— like such an *outsider* before. I need to deal with that. So, please, let me do it.'

'I'm just supposed to wait for you to make the decision for both of us, am I? If you say it's over then it's over?'

'Like you do in every relationship you've ever been in?' She'd said it in the heat of the moment. It was uncalled for and she knew it, but it was too late to take it back. Quinn shut himself off before her very eyes, the control she'd always respected in him sliding into place like a shield.

Only this time she didn't respect it—she hated it.

'This'll be a dose of that thing called karma, won't it?' He even smiled a small smile. 'Well, while you're going through that decision-making process of yours maybe you'll think about why it is I've laid all this on the line for you tonight. And why it is I'm trying harder to make this relationship work than I ever did any of the others.'

Clare folded her arms across her thundering heart as he carried on. 'There was never going to be a right time to tell you all this, and believe me I searched for a right time. But I can't change the past, Clare, even if I wanted to. I can't tell you I wouldn't do it all over again either. Because I would—every damn time.'

When she gaped at him he jerked his shoulders. 'I am what I am. You wanted to know me better—well, now you know it all: the good *and* the bad. If I'm not what you want then I can't change that.'

She watched with wide eyes as he smiled meaningfully. 'I'd have a damn good try at it, though, don't get me wrong. If I'd been the kind of slime you thought I was, however briefly, along the way then I'd have been doing everything I could to tie you to me emotionally and physically these few weeks. But I haven't made love to you, no matter how much I wanted to, because I didn't want anything between us when it happened. More fool me, huh?'

He turned near the steps to the elevators, taking a deep breath before continuing. 'I'll take you home. Or wherever it is you plan on going.'

After a long moment of silent defiance she unfolded her arms and walked over to him, carrying her chin higher, but watching him from the corner of her eye. She was in front of him when he added, 'And to think I did all this tonight to reassure you the six week cut-off doesn't exist for us. I got that one wrong, didn't I? Only difference this time is it isn't me ending it. Guess I won the bet.'

Clare stopped and turned her face to look up at him;

Quinn's gaze was fixed on a point above her head. She watched him blink lazily a few times, searched what she could see of the vivid blue of his eyes but saw nothing. She hated the fact that he could hold himself together the way he was. But then she looked down and saw the pulse jump in the taut cord of his neck and she saw a tremor in his breathing. It was then she knew he was hurting as much as she was. It was the worst argument they'd ever had.

When she lifted her lashes she found him looking down at her, and when he looked back to the point over her head she took a deep breath and told him in a low, soft voice, 'I won't hate you. No matter how hard you try to make me.'

She heard him exhale, as if she'd just knocked the wind out of him. Then his chin dropped while he took several breaths before raising his lashes. 'The driver will take you wherever you want to go.'

'I'm going to Madison's for tonight, to give us both time to cool down.'

'Right.'

'Because this is the worst fight we've ever had.'

'Yeah.'

'And right now we're just making it worse.'

'Uh-huh.'

She frowned at him. 'You're being like this because you're hurting from it just as much as I am.'

Quinn blew air out through puffed cheeks before lifting his chin and looking her straight in the eye. 'Are we done here?'

It was a loaded question. One she didn't have an answer for.

CHAPTER THIRTEEN

'YOU'VE REALLY MADE a mess this time, haven't you?'

Shouldering his way into Madison's apartment, Quinn ignored the other occupants in the room. 'Where is she?'

Morgan stood up. 'What do you want her for?'

Quinn frowned hard at him. 'Butt out, Morgan—*where is she*?'

'Not this time.' Morgan squared off against him, folding his arms and spreading his feet. 'Just how exactly are you planning on making this right? Do you have any idea how upset she was?'

'If she's here you know I'm moving you out of the way to get to her, right?'

Morgan jutted his chin. 'You could *try.*'

When Quinn sidestepped, Evan and Erin appeared, each of them assuming the same crossed-arms pose that said they meant business. Quinn practically growled at them, lifting both arms and dropping them to his sides before he asked in a raised voice, 'How am I supposed to fix this if you won't let me talk to her?'

'It took you all night to come up with a plan, did it?'

He glared at Evan. 'She needed time to *think*!'

Erin blinked at him. 'And her time's up now, is it? You're over here to bully her into forgiving you?'

Quinn scrubbed a large hand over his face and began to pace the room, grumbling under his breath. 'I don't need this.'

Madison's voice sounded from the door. 'It took from the early hours of this morning to talk everything through with her, you know.'

His head jerked up. *'Everything?'*

'Oh, she wouldn't discuss how she feels about *you*—seems you've infected her with that privacy disease of yours.' She shrugged. 'It took all that time for her to understand why none of the rest of us ever told her about you and Jamie. Worst eight hours of my life. She feels like we saw her as some kind of outsider. When the truth is we couldn't love her any more if we tried.'

There was a chorus of agreement from around the room, and then Morgan added, 'We all messed up. But she understands.'

'She does?'

'Jamie humiliated her on a grand scale—we should never have let it come to that. You were the only one who did anything about it.' Evan paused. 'We told her about the arguments we all had—how none of us could look her in the eye. And we told her you wanted her told from the get go.'

Quinn's eyes widened.

Erin confirmed Evan's words. 'We did. Though *you* could have told her that and it might have helped. But that's you all over, isn't it? We were the ones who told you to leave it alone—that it was none of our business. That made us guiltier of a lie of omission than you were. At least you *did something.*'

'*I had to.*' The confession was torn from so deep inside it came out in a croak.

'We told her that.' Madison's voice softened. 'She said she understood why. Don't suppose you want to tell *us* why, do you?'

Quinn shook his head. *Not so much.*

Morgan's large hand landed on his shoulder and squeezed in response. 'I think I know why.'

Erin ducked her head to look up into his eyes. 'Would it be okay if Morgan told us why?'

Quinn shrugged, despite the fact he'd just been spoken to as if he were a nine-year-old. 'If it's important you know.'

'It is. We do love you, you know. No matter how much of an idiot you can be.'

It honestly felt as if everyone on the planet was trying to rip his heart out with their bare hands. But Quinn nodded, the ache in his chest making it difficult for him to breathe, never mind find words. He just couldn't breathe properly until...

He lifted a fist to his chest and rubbed at it with his knuckles. And shifted his gaze in time to see Madison watching the tell-tale action. Her mouth twitched. 'Heart aching a tad there, big guy?'

He smiled ruefully. 'Where is she?'

'Went looking for you, funnily enough...'

Quinn's smile grew.

Erin laughed at his expression. 'You still here?'

Madison waited until he'd left before holding a palm out, waggling her fingers as a satisfied smile formed on her lips. 'Ante up, boys.'

Hands disappeared into pockets, and Morgan grumbled as he slapped a note into her hand. 'Never should've gone double or nothing on it being Clare he ended up with...'

Clare was sitting on his stoop when Quinn ran down the street, her knees drawn up high and her arms hugging them while she rested her chin. When she saw him she swallowed hard, her eyes following him until he stood in front of her. Chest heaving, he looked at her with an almost pained expression. Clare couldn't seem to find the right words, no matter how many times she'd thought about what she'd say when she saw him.

In the end he broke the tension. 'Hello, you.'

Clare took a sharp, shuddering breath, her vision blurring at the edges. 'Hello, you.'

'You scared me.'

The confession surprised her. 'Did I?'

'Uh-huh.' He nodded.

'You scared me by not being here. I thought you skipped town on me again.' Her brows wavered in question. 'Where were you?'

'Looking for you.' She watched his throat convulse. 'I needed to tell you something. But we need to talk about all this other stuff first. Lay it to rest.'

With some considerable effort she found a voice barely recognizable as hers. 'We do.'

Quinn took a step closer and hunched down in front of her. He nodded, he frowned, and then he studied her hair.

Clare couldn't help but smile affectionately at him, her voice threaded with emotion. 'It'll involve the use of words.'

Quinn grimaced. 'Yeah, well, I'm still not so hot on

those when it comes to the things that matter, so you might have to give me a minute. I already messed up royally last night; I don't want to do that to us again.'

'Would it help if I started?'

'Might.' He smiled a somewhat crooked smile.

'Okay…' she took a deep breath '…you should have told me you wanted to tell me about Jamie but the others convinced you not to. It might have helped.'

'They mentioned that when I went looking for you.'

'You went to Madison's?'

'I did.'

'Did they tell you we spent hours talking?'

'They did.' When his eyes shadowed she smiled a somewhat watery smile at him. 'They said it helped.'

'It did.' Her lower lip shook, so she bit down on it. 'I just needed to work it through with a neutral party. I'm sorry.'

'It's okay.'

She was never going to make it all the way through everything she needed to say if he kept looking at her the way he was. In all the time she'd known him she'd never once seen such intense warmth in his eyes. It made her want to crawl into him, wrap herself around him, and stay there until she didn't hurt any more.

'There were too many grey areas for there to be a right or a wrong. It was unfair that you were all put in that position in the first place. I know why you did what you did, Quinn.' She swallowed down the lump in her throat before continuing in a broken voice. 'You did it because you couldn't stand by and watch another woman treated the way your mother was. It was too close to home for you. Being so close to Jamie, you thought you could make him see sense. You thought you could fix it, didn't you?'

Thick lashes flickered as he searched her eyes, and then he nodded, almost as if he was afraid to say yes in case he got it wrong.

'When you couldn't fix everything, you gave up one of your closest friends and tried to make up for his mistakes by looking after me.'

'It might have started out that way, yes.'

The first fat tears tripped over her lower lashes and blazed a heated trail down her cheeks. 'It's what you do. It's not like I was your first damsel in distress…'

'You're the only one that mattered *to me*.'

'Once you'd had time to get to know me.'

'There was no strategy, I swear.' His mouth quirked. 'I wasn't anywhere near that clever.'

More silent tears slid free, and Clare saw the flash of pain in his eyes as he followed their path. 'You didn't like me much at the beginning, did you?'

He sighed heavily. 'I wasn't supposed to notice you at all. When someone's engaged to someone she's automatically off limits. I just didn't understand what you were doing with him, was all.'

Not that it would have made a difference even if he *had* noticed her; he would never have broken the code of honour that ran so deeply in him. Clare loved him for that—he would never, ever cheat on her, or so much as look at another woman sideways. When he made a commitment it would be for life, wouldn't it?

'I didn't love him, Quinn. It was…I guess it was just the adventure of it: whole new life, new country. I was very starry-eyed back then. But when I got here I was more in love with the city than I was with him. I think I knew I didn't feel enough when I was able to stand in front of all those people that day. It wasn't heartbreak I felt—it was just complete and utter humiliation.' She paused to take another shaky breath. 'But I don't think anyone really knows they're in love until it's the real thing. Then it's the only thing that really matters. I know that now. And I'm not sorry I came here...'

When he frowned she tried to find the words to make him understand. 'If I hadn't, I would never have met you. It's because of you I know the difference...'

Clare damped her lips, took another shuddering breath and felt another tear slide free. And while Quinn looked at her with intense, consuming heat in his vivid eyes, she let the words slip free on a husky whisper. 'I love you.'

It was as if a dam burst. Hiccupping sobs sounded and tears streamed while she said it more firmly. 'You really have no idea how much I love you.'

For a moment Quinn froze, and then his gruff voice demanded, 'Say it again.'

'I love you.' Somehow she managed to smile. It was weak and tremulous, but it was the best she could do. 'I can't breathe properly when you're not there.'

Large hands framed her face and he kissed her as a man would drink water after a long spell in the desert. The vibration of the groan that rumbled up from his chest awakened every nerve-ending she possessed until she ached from head to toe with the need to get closer. So she did what she'd wanted to do. She crawled into him, wrapping her arms around his neck and pushing her breasts tight to the wall of his chest as they slowly came to their feet. But it still wasn't close enough for

Clare—even when his hands dropped and he squeezed her waist tight enough to break her in half.

Her mouth followed his when he lifted his head and looked down at her with an incredulity that made her smile. 'Say it again.'

Clare's smile grew, her heart swelling to impossible proportions in her chest. 'I love you.'

The smile he gave her made her laugh. But instead of kissing her again he let go of her and tangled his fingers with hers, tugging her up the steps. 'Come on.'

Less than a minute later she was being steered across the hardwood floors into his study, where he pushed her into the leather chair behind his desk and hunched in front of her again.

'I've got something for you.'

Clare was vaguely aware of him pulling open the top drawer and reaching for something. But she was too mesmerized by him to look away. Too enthralled by how happy he looked. Too much in love to want to look anywhere else...

'Here.' Something was set into her hands.

When he looked expectantly at her she smiled and looked down, her gaze rising sharply when she saw what it was. 'You're giving me my goodbye gift *now*?'

'Open it.' He reached out and brushed tendrils of hair off her cheeks with his fingertips. Clare loved it when he did that.

She tugged at the white ribbon while still staring at him, only dropping her chin when she had the lid off. Inside was a smaller box covered in dark velvet.

Quinn smiled a smile that made the blue of his eyes darken to the colour of stormy tropical seas.

'Keep going.'

There was a slight creak as she opened the second box. Her gaze dropped as its content was revealed to her amazed eyes. Heart pounding erratically, she jerked her chin up, gaze tangling impossibly with his. And what she could see there stopped her heart, tore it loose from her chest…and allowed it to soar…

'My last Tiffany's box.'

Clare smiled dumbly.

The voice she loved so very much was impossibly tender when he told her; 'I love you back.'

Her smile trembled again. 'You never use that word.'

'I don't think you should unless you mean it.'

'I know you think that.' She lifted a hand and rested her palm against his face. When Quinn exhaled and closed his eyes as he leaned into her touch she saw her vision mist all over again.

His eyes flickered open. 'You crept up on me, and I like to think I fought a good fight, but I love you. I know they say that living together and working together is the kiss of death for a relationship, but I want to spend every minute of every day with you. And since I'm not good with words, I want to spend pretty much all night every night keeping you awake so I can *show you* how I feel—*lots.*'

A threatening sob magically morphed into a hiccup of laughter and she let her fingertips smooth against a hint of stubble on his cheek, turning her hand to draw the backs of her fingers along his jawline.

'And when I tire you out enough for you to sleep I want to wake up in the morning with you beside me. I want to be told off for not using a coaster and I want daisies everywhere, and I—'

She smiled at him. 'You had me at *I love you back*. Ask me the question.'

Quinn apparently felt the need to kiss her into a boneless heap before he did, just to be sure. So it was amidst a state of sensory bliss that she heard not a question, but another demand. 'Marry me.'

She loved him. She would love him till the day she died. He loved her. There was only the one answer. 'Yes.' The box still held firmly between her fingers, she wrapped the crook of her arm around his neck. 'And not just because I love you. But because I need you as much as you need me. It's your turn to be rescued this time. I'm rescuing you.'

'I'm okay with that.' He pressed a light kiss on her lips while reaching for the box to extricate the ring. 'And you're right, I do need you. You're so tangled up in my life now that I can't breathe right when you're not around either.'

The fact it was said with a husky crackling in his already gruff voice told Clare a million things about the depth of his feelings that words could never have conveyed. He needed her every bit as much as she needed him—they were a perfect match.

Using her right hand to tilt his chin up while he reached for her left, Clare informed him, 'It's a Lucida, by the way. The Tiffany setting you have that enormous diamond in.'

'You said diamonds were a girl's best friend. That's apart from me, obviously…'

'Obviously.'

Amusement danced in his eyes. 'You have all the Tiffany settings memorized, don't you?'

Clare bobbed her head. 'Pretty much. Everyone has a hobby.'

'I'm in love with a crazy girl.'

'And she's crazy in love with you.'

And there was no niggling doubt in Clare's mind, no fear for the future, and, yes, her starry eyes were back. But Quinn had put the stars there. He was her soulmate in oh, so many ways. The thought made her grin as he slipped the ring onto her finger.

'You know what this means, don't you?'

She leaned forward, placing her hands on his chest to push him backwards as she slid off the chair and onto him; stretching her body along the length of his.

'What does it mean?' Quinn smiled as he pushed long fingers into her hair and drew her face towards his, where Clare whispered the answer against his lips.

'I win.'

EPILOGUE

'HELLO, YOU.'

Clare grinned at Quinn's reflection as he walked up behind her, one long arm snaking around her waist while his head lowered to the hollow where her neck met her shoulder. 'Hello, me.'

Quinn spread his feet and pulled her against his lean body, pressing a row of kisses along the neck she angled for him. 'You ready?'

'Mmm-hmm.' She lifted her hands and set them on his arm, leaning her head back against his shoulder. 'You?'

He'd kissed his way to the sensitive skin below her ear before he lifted inky lashes and his gaze met hers, his rough voice vibrating against her ear. 'I love you.'

Clare smiled softly. 'Getting easier to say that word, isn't it?'

'Practice makes perfect.'

Turning in his arms, she stood on her toes and kissed him. 'Love you back.'

'Course you do.' He bent his knees and lifted her off the ground, turning on his heel to head back towards the door. 'I'm irresistible.'

'At the risk of making it difficult for you to get your head through doors I'm going to have to agree with that.' She wrapped her arms around his neck and looked down at him. 'So, are you telling them or am I?'

'I am. You can fend off all the hugs and kisses.'

'You're still a work in progress, you know.'

'You can work on me more later…' He set her down by the door and studied her incredible emerald eyes for the longest time. 'Do you need a minute?'

'No.' She kissed him again.

It never ceased to amaze Quinn, as he looked at her, how he could love her more with each passing day. He hadn't known it could be like that. But then he hadn't known anything about love until Clare.

It felt as if nobody had ever known him till she knew him, touched him till she touched him—loved him till she loved him. She was air to him now. Without her he wouldn't exist. Turned out he was a romantic after all.

'Okay. Here goes.'

With her fine-boned fingers tangled in his, they walked to the front of the room. Quinn eventually gave up on the waved-arm method in favour of placing his thumb and forefinger between his teeth and whistling. It got everyone's attention a lot faster.

When he looked down at Clare she was laughing at what he'd done, so he winked at her before lifting his chin and clearing his throat.

'Thanks for coming—especially those of you who travelled so far. We appreciate it.' His smile grew. 'But I'm afraid you're not here for an engagement party. You're here for a wedding…'

AUSTRALIAN BOSS:
DIAMOND RING

JENNIE ADAMS

Australian author **Jennie Adams** grew up in a rambling farmhouse surrounded by books and by people who loved reading them. She decided at a young age to be a writer, but it took many years and a lot of scenic detours before she sat down to pen her first romance novel. Jennie has worked in a number of careers and voluntary positions, including transcription typist and pre-school assistant. She is the proud mother of three fabulous adult children and makes her home in a small inland city in New South Wales. In her leisure time she loves long, rambling walks, discovering new music, starting knitting projects that she rarely finishes, chatting with friends, trips to the movies, and new dining experiences.

Jennie loves to hear from her readers and can be contacted via her website at www.jennieadams.net.

For David.

For the sound of your laughter, and your un-caffeinated morning voice. For the memories we're building, for the teasing and for your strength and your love and your vulnerabilities. For the best hugs in the world and for bringing me home the piece of my puzzle that I needed so much. I love you with all my heart. This one is for you.

CHAPTER ONE

A LITTLE tingle went down Fiona Donner's spine. It came from the impact of a pair of particularly appealing green eyes fringed with thick black lashes, focused utterly upon her as Brent MacKay made his job offer.

To compensate for that odd, unexpected reaction, Fiona used her best professional tone as she responded. 'Thank you. I'm thrilled to accept your offer and yes, I can start Monday!'

The famous, fabulous, talented, highly private and intensely focused millionaire landscape designer Brent MacKay wanted *her*. That was reason enough for a shiver or two, wasn't it? Fiona would be working with Brent for the next twelve months, with an option to extend if they were both happy with things by then. She knew already she would be happy. She'd just been offered the ultimate dream job!

Brent shifted in his executive office chair and his lean, tanned face creased into a smile. 'You may find the pace challenging at first. I work hard across multiple projects at once and you'll be providing input into all the major jobs I handle.'

'I'm not afraid of hard work. In truth, I can't wait for

the challenge.' She meant that with all her heart. 'A chance at a job like this doesn't come every day. It makes the past two and a half years of graphic design study worth every moment.'

And his offer was a true shot in the arm for her confidence in her artistic abilities. He wouldn't want her if he thought she lacked the talent. She would work on computer graphic design for work proposals and job outlines. Original landscape paintings for the walls of his clients. Specialised photography for advertising and more. Fiona couldn't wait!

See, Mum? I do *have what it takes to survive in this field.*

Fiona straightened in the comfortable black leather visitor's chair and tugged at the hem of the pink and white checked jacket that covered her generous—well, okay, *quite generous*—curves, and tweaked the matching skirt into place.

She was five foot eleven in her stockinged feet, and Junoesque to go with it. Well, at least in this outfit she looked as good as she could look.

'Here's hoping you still feel as enthusiastic after your first week or so here.' Brent's glance lingered on her for just a moment before it moved to the bench-top storage that covered two of the walls in the room. Regimented rows of work covered their surfaces.

Fiona followed his glance, and followed it further, to the view of a busy outer Sydney suburb business street outside the ground floor window. A view of working class Australia going about what it did best. Working, and living.

If he wanted to, Brent could be in the heart of the city

in a suite in a high-rise building with Sydney Harbour spread before him like an offering.

Instead, he was here in Everyman's territory. A place Fiona knew *she* would be very comfortable because she loved its reality. Fiona murmured, 'I will do everything possible to please you in every way.'

A beat of silence followed in which she realised her words could have been chosen a bit more carefully, and heat started to build at the base of her neck.

She hoped the blush stayed where it was and didn't give itself away all over her peaches and cream face. Fiona's hand rose to her high ponytail of blonde hair. She smoothed it in a nervous gesture before she could stop herself.

Her new employer stared at her intently before he dropped his gaze and said a low, deep, 'I'm certain you will be everything that's required.'

The fingers of his right hand drummed out a rhythm on the desk for a moment before he stilled them, became utterly still, and cleared his throat. 'To date I've worked very privately on my projects at grass roots level, but I'm ready for this step now. You come highly recommended from the graphic design centre and, now that we've discussed the work, I very much want to bring you on board.'

To share in his creative process. It *was* a rather intimate thing. 'I'll respect your privacy, Mr MacKay. However you want us to work together, I'll do my best to fit in.'

'That's appreciated, though I'm sure we'll get along…fine.'

A few words followed by a calm glance that gave away absolutely nothing of his thoughts and yet somehow seemed to reach inside to a core part of her and find a connection anyway.

There was no reason for gooseflesh to break out on her skin, but it did. What was the matter with her? 'I'll work hard—whatever you feel will be helpful to the business.'

'Thank you.' He drew a breath. 'I'd like to introduce you to everyone now. It's a small office staff. Only about twenty people. Most of my employees are out on ground teams turning my designs into reality. You'll meet one of the teams Monday, others as time goes on.' Brent rose to his feet, crossed to her side and when she also stood, cupped her elbow to lead her to the door.

He was a tall man. Around six foot two, and all of it honed without an ounce of fat to be seen. Broad shoulders, slim hips, dark hair cropped short and with a distinct wave in it. His mouth was wide with a full lower lip, his teeth even and white. He had a straight nose that flared at the end.

And those gorgeous green eyes beneath winged brows. Eyes that seemed to watch the world with a combination of intensity and guardedness that Fiona found…compelling.

Employee to employer, that was. She found him compelling as a *brand new* employer. 'It will be nice to meet everyone, Mr MacKay.'

'They'll all be excited to hear you're coming on board,' he said. 'And please call me Brent. You're going to be all over a work site with me Monday morning getting grubby, so I think we can do away with the formalities. I suggest you wear jeans for that, by the way.'

As he spoke, a worker stepped through the front door of the building. A brisk May wind followed the woman in. Winter would officially arrive in another month. Out here in this suburb, further from the Sydney coast, it would get cold. For now, the weather just had a slight edge.

Fiona glanced at her employer. He had dressed for that edge in a tan button-down shirt over charcoal trousers. Business-casual. He should have looked less compelling than he did, but an aura of leashed strength and intensity came from him, was stamped on his face.

Please let me be equally strong and focused so I can do well here.

At almost twenty-six years of age, it shouldn't still matter so much to Fiona that she be able to prove herself. Perhaps if her family had been a little more supportive, or believed in her at all, it wouldn't have.

'Thank you…Brent.' Fiona breathed in the sharp blue tang of his aftershave and tried not to notice the warmth radiating through her clothing from his fingertips.

Brent led her deeper into the open-plan office area. 'You'll want to move out here to live, I assume, rather than try to commute? From the address on your résumé, I gather you lived in central Sydney while you attended your course.' He paused before the first desk, introduced Fiona and waited while she exchanged a few words with another employee.

As they moved on again, Fiona nodded. 'That flat-share in the heart of the city was convenient while I attended the graphic design centre. But I'd prefer to live close to my work here.' She liked the idea of migrating to this outer suburb. It would be an adventure.

It would bring her closer to several of her friends who came from out this way, too. And of course it would take her further from her family, who were all based on Sydney's North Shore, but she couldn't do anything about that.

The thought gave her a hint of something rather close

to guilty relief. 'I'll start searching for a place immediately. Hopefully there'll be something available through a local real estate agent, or a listing in a shop window—'

'We'll discuss that once you've met everyone.' Brent guided her through the room, pausing at this desk and that desk to present her to his other employees.

She did her best to remember names and position titles as each person was introduced.

Finally Brent led her to the kitchenette at the rear of the open-plan area. Two men stood almost shoulder to shoulder there. The youngest wore a business suit, the older outdoor clothes. They both watched Fiona and Brent's progress across the room.

'Fiona, meet Linc and Alex MacKay, my brothers.' Brent gestured to each of the men in turn. 'Boys, I'd like you to meet Fiona Donner, the company's new graphic artist as of about—' he glanced at the watch on his wrist '—ten minutes ago.'

The way he addressed the men held pride and deep affection. She hadn't known he had brothers, but then her research for this job application had yielded very little of a personal nature about Brent MacKay.

'I'm pleased to meet you.' Linc shook Fiona's hand and let go. 'I run the chain of nurseries that, among other things, acts as Brent's key supplier.'

Linc was a tall man with dark hair, grey eyes and the same lean build as Brent.

No. Not the same build. He was deeper through the chest than Brent, thicker set all over. The impression of a shared leanness actually came from something in his expression, in a measure of guardedness in the backs of his eyes that Brent had also revealed.

Fiona murmured a greeting. 'I'm having trouble

guessing who's the eldest. You seem very close in age.' As she said so, the lack of true genetic similarities between the men occurred to her.

'Brent's the eldest. Most people don't pick up on how close we are in age...' Linc gave her a slightly surprised look as he trailed off.

Before she could think about that, the youngest brother extended his hand.

'I'm Alex. I run an export business near here, but I'm also a shareholder in Brent's company. I hope you enjoy working here.'

'I can't wait to start.' Fiona shook the young man's hand and released it. The third brother was substantially younger than Linc or Brent. Early twenties, she'd have guessed, though that was young to be running a business.

Blue-eyed like Fiona herself, Alex had a square-cut jaw, broad forehead and mid-brown hair and looked nothing like either of his brothers. He also had a glint in his eyes that probably had women chasing after him.

Fiona wanted to know the nature of this family, how they all fitted together.

As for eyes, and glints therein, she only had eyes for her employer.

Well, she meant she was only *focused* on him. She was focused on her new job! She didn't have 'eyes' for men generally, anyway. Her role was that of 'everybody's friend' and she liked that just fine. It was much less stressful than getting into a relationship that would only end up disappointing her. Or, worse, disappointing the man involved. Been there, not interested in repeating that. It was enough having her mother's criticism of all the faults in her ability to appeal.

Fiona turned to Linc. 'Maybe I could take photos at

one of the nurseries some time soon. I'd love to get some background material to use when I start working with my computer designs for Brent.'

Linc's shrewd gaze examined her as he inclined his head. 'That can be arranged for you.'

'When there's time for us both to go,' Brent inserted, and fell abruptly quiet. His head twitched to the right and a frown swept over his brow.

Linc's eyebrows lifted and Alex stared at his older brother before both he and Linc looked quickly elsewhere.

Brent's entire body seemed to freeze then.

Uncertain of what she was sensing in him, Fiona said slowly, 'I don't need to visit the nursery if that's not convenient. It was just a thought.'

'It's not a problem.' Brent pushed his hands deep into his trouser pockets. 'I was just—'

'Distracted,' Alex put in.

'He lost his concentration,' Linc said at the same time, and clamped his lips together.

'I was just *thinking*,' Brent stated, and frowned again. 'I'll make a day for us to visit Linc's nursery, Fiona.' Brent seemed to make a conscious effort to move on from whatever that reaction had been. 'I'll make sure you get to do that. It's a good idea for you to take those photos, and I visit the nurseries regularly anyway to inspect the stock, keep the inventory fresh in my mind and see what new things Linc's managed to find for me. It'll be convenient for us to go together, that's all.'

'Well, thank you. I'll look forward to that when it happens.' Fiona nodded and relaxed a little. She hadn't committed a faux pax…

Which meant Brent's reaction had been—?

Something she wasn't going to be able to figure out right now.

So leave it alone, Fiona. You don't have to understand everything about him.

In truth, she tended to want to delve too deeply into what made people tick. Well, her mother said so anyway.

A short silence fell before Linc cleared his throat and addressed his brother. 'Have you discussed accommodation options with Fiona yet?'

'That was next on my list.' Brent turned to her. 'You're welcome to do whatever you like about your living arrangements, but Linc owns an investment property you might be interested in renting. It's a one bedroom flat about a ten minute drive from here. The complex it's in has courtyard parking for a car, if you own one.'

'Are you serious? I thought I'd be looking all weekend and maybe end up staying in a pub or hostel before I managed to pin something down.' Fiona tried to stifle her grin, and failed.

A smile lurked in the backs of Brent's eyes in response, a beautiful, lovely smile. The man was lethal, and she didn't understand the connection she felt towards him.

Fiona drew a steadying breath and turned to Linc. 'How much are you asking for the flat per month? I'll have to stick to a budget.'

Linc named the figure.

'I'll be able to afford that rent.' That was a relief, and she simply needed to concentrate on the tasks and necessities at hand. Not on eyes that smiled at her through shields that made her think of her own life, its hurts and triumphs, and what Brent's might have been and might be now. 'When can I sign a lease agreement? I don't need to see the place first. If you recommend it, that's all I need to know. I don't want to miss out on the opportunity to pin this down, if that's at all possible.'

She smoothed her hands over her thighs and told herself to stop babbling.

Though Brent had remained silent during this interchange, his gaze followed the movement and she thought she heard him make a soft sound in the back of his throat before he glanced away.

If so, it was probably because she had drawn his attention to just how non-slim those thighs were.

On this lowering thought Fiona suppressed a sigh. Her body was what it was. There was no changing her build, or her height, or what she preferred to refer to as her curviness but her mother said was the result of far too much self-indulgence and couldn't Fiona try to eat less?

She didn't overeat. Her tiny mother couldn't see that, though. To Eloise Donner, Fiona was the stork among the pigeons and someone needed to shrink her somehow. Preferably while shrinking her into a far more practical mould at the same time.

And Brent had simply followed her movement with his gaze. It was completely meaningless. It wasn't as though her employer would be noticing her in that respect.

Which was a good thing, she reminded herself.

Linc drew a folded document and a set of keys from his back pocket and handed both to her. 'Once you've read the lease, you can go ahead and sign it and leave it with Jaimie. She'll pass it on to me the next time I'm here. Brent will explain where the place is and about getting you moved in, if you need help with that.'

The two brothers excused themselves and left then, and Fiona curled her fingers around the keys and lease and turned to her employer. 'That was generous of you and your brother. Thank you.'

'It was no trouble. Linc deals in a lot of that kind of property investment.' Brent watched his brothers exit the room and the building before he allowed his gaze to return to his new employee. He hadn't meant to follow the slide of Fiona's hands down her thighs moments ago.

He hadn't meant to notice her at all, but he had. She was a striking woman. Tall, beautifully built and curvy in all the right places. A woman who wouldn't blow away in a strong breeze, who a man could hold in his arms without fear of crushing her.

She was also femininity through and through. From the dark blonde hair tied back from her face in a high ponytail to the robin's egg blue eyes and fine arched brows, the straight nose and generous mouth, she looked softer than a flower, and equally as sweet.

The thoughts surprised him. Not the appreciation of her beauty. How could any man fail to notice that? But the intimacy of where his thoughts had taken him— thoughts of how it would be to hold her, of wanting to protect her from harm. Brent's life had been all about protecting himself, his brothers. His father had put him in a place where he'd had no choice but to be strong. To hide his flaws from the world so they wouldn't judge him as Charles had done. Brent hadn't reached out to a woman for the kind of intimacy that would result in wanting to protect her as well as protect his own interests in a long time. Actually...he never had.

He never would do that. His limits would forever

prevent that. And Fiona looked the kind of woman who would deserve exactly that kind of…care.

Which simply reminded him that he needed to appreciate her attractiveness from the distance of an unconnected observer.

Right. And he did. He'd simply become distracted for a moment. The same thing applied to the head twitch he'd experienced earlier. It wouldn't happen again in front of her. He'd make sure of that as he did in all other circumstances.

Brent nodded in a completely concise, controlled manner as he came to this conclusion. If he felt somewhat relieved to have arrived back at a more known, comfortable place in his thinking, he told himself this was a good thing, anyway. 'Let's take you to Jaimie so you can sign your employment agreement and leave the lease with her.'

Once Fiona had done that, Brent gestured to his office area. 'Would you like to hear about some of the projects I've got going? Some preliminary information to give you an idea of what's in store for you?'

'Oh, yes, please. That will give me a chance to think over the weekend before I start work officially on Monday.' Fiona half-reached one hand towards him, dropped it self-consciously to her side, and her face pinked slightly.

His gaze locked onto that blossom of colour and his breath caught…

He pushed the door of his office open and stepped through to open the adjoining door. 'You'll be working in here. It's a decent-sized room. I hope it'll suit your needs.'

His voice was deep. Too deep. He cleared his throat.

Fiona's gaze tracked around the long room, dodged

his. 'I'm sure it will. It's a generous working space. There's good light for my easel work, and plenty of desk space for computer monitors.'

'I imagine there'll be times when you'll need all of that space.'

'Is it okay to dress casually for when I'm painting? I realise there'll be times when I need to look smart. Client discussions…' A little ridge formed between her brows. 'Perhaps I should just dress smart all the time, and wear a smock or something when I paint. I'm inclined to be a bit messy during that process, but I could try to change that.'

'There's a dressing room. I keep clothes here. You can do the same. Messy is fine, anyway.' The thought of her using his changing room, shedding clothes and putting on new ones, wasn't a place he needed to go.

So get on with it, MacKay. 'On Monday we'll be helping to finish up a landscaping project, and I'll want you to take photos and think about a painting for the clients. They're an elderly couple, very agreeable. They'll be happy with whatever you put together. The photos will go into a Progress Album for the clients and our stock here for showing clients how we work. Nothing for newspapers or magazines, though. I accept the occasional interview to keep the media off my back but I'm selective, so if you're ever approached I expect you to shoot the enquiry straight to me.'

'I will do that.' Her expression showed she didn't understand the 'why' of it, but her acceptance was enough. 'And I can certainly take the photos and also use them to help me create an appropriate painting for the clients.'

Fiona gave him a pleasant but firm look. 'It's not

ideal to come in partway through and need to produce a painting in that way, but I'm sure that won't happen in the future.'

Brent liked a woman—correction, a *person*—with enough spunk to say what they wanted.

From the distance of an observer. You like it from that distance. 'Don't worry. You'll be included in future planning. In fact, I have a project that's been driving me mad for the last three weeks. The client won't settle on a design. I'm hoping if I pull you in on that one it might get me the breakthrough I need.'

'Okay, well, that's good then, and I'll be happy to try to help with your project.' Her expression held the slightest sheepish edge before she squared her shoulders and seemed to decide it was best she'd been clear about her expectations.

Brent went on to explain the problems with the project he'd mentioned, and to discuss some other issues. Work was easy. He always felt at home with his landscape projects.

An hour later Fiona stood at the door of his office once more, bag in hand, and thanked him for his time. 'I can't wait to start work Monday. I'll have some photographic equipment to bring out to the landscaping site, if that's okay.'

'That's fine. Anything you bring will be safe there, though we should get your equipment added to the business's insurance cover.'

'Shall I phone the details in later today? Model numbers and so on?'

'Do that. You can leave them with Elizabeth, my receptionist.' With this issue resolved, Brent went on, 'If you need help to move into your flat this weekend—'

Fiona smiled her thanks, but shook her head. 'I can get Tommy to use his delivery truck to help me shift the larger items. My friends all knew I was coming for this interview, so they've been on standby, half-expecting this.'

So 'Tommy' was simply one of those 'friends'? Brent couldn't explain why he suddenly felt…lighter than he had a few seconds ago. 'Okay, then I guess I should let you go so you can start making arrangements.'

Fiona made a little bouncing motion on the balls of her feet. 'A new home, a new job and a new part of the city to live in. I can't wait to take it all on. Thank you again, Mr MacKay—*Brent*—for this chance.'

'You're more than welcome.' Brent said his goodbyes and then watched her leave the building, hips swaying with each step she took.

And then he immersed himself in landscape plans, where he could line up his ideas in neat rows and spend as long as he needed on each aspect of his work. His head twitched sharply to the right, but he was by himself now. He didn't worry about trying to conceal the action.

At least the condition he lived with was good for helping him to focus on his work, and he had every right to keep knowledge of it from the world at large. It was in his best interests to do so. His father's past behaviour had made that abundantly clear.

Brent dug into his plans and put thoughts of Fiona Donner's lovely smile—of *his new employee's smile*—right out of his mind…

CHAPTER TWO

'A DOZEN shrubs for you, Russ.' A worker placed the shrubs on the ground and moved away to collect another load.

It was Monday afternoon, towards the end of Fiona's first day at the new job. Spending it out of doors helping to complete an actual work project as well as gather photographic resources for her painting and for the company to use to showcase its services had been a thrill. She smiled to herself as words continued to flow around her.

'Hey, Phil. Can I use that mattock for the next ten minutes?'

'Great job with the bougainvillea, Chelsea.' This was Brent's voice as he turned his head to check on one of the more junior members of the ground team. 'Keep up the good work.'

The sun was shining and the ten-acre work site on the edge of a newish Sydney suburb was abuzz with activity. Brent was motivated and positive and determined, and the ground workers responded to his authority and encouragement by giving their absolute best. He was at home in this, and Fiona...found that knowledge of him perhaps a little too appealing.

'We're going to finish this job on time.' The site boss, a man in his mid-thirties with a shock of carroty hair squashed under a baseball cap, paused beside Fiona to murmur the words. 'I knew we would. The company hasn't missed a deadline yet, even when things have gone pear-shaped, as they did with this project when some of the goods we ordered didn't arrive three days ago.

'That never would have happened with Linc's nursery supplies. I'm guessing in future Brent will refuse to buy from anywhere else, even if it means asking his brother to import or source what it is that he needs.'

Brent had pulled in about a dozen extra workers from other job sites to work on this project. Fiona had done her share of carrying and carting and planting and fetching throughout the day, too. She was 'grubby', as Brent had predicted would happen. Mostly around the knees and seat of her jeans, and it was all good honest dirt. She'd learned so much about his process by getting her hands into it, and she'd had a ball getting dirty at the same time! 'There doesn't seem to be a lot left to do now.'

'I'd say another half hour of work for everyone, if that.' The boss moved on, and Fiona planted the last shrub in her allotment and dusted herself off.

She watched as Brent lifted a plant from a wheelbarrow and placed it in a prepared hole a few metres away with an efficient movement. In the early days of his business he had probably spent a lot of his time on this kind of thing.

He worked with a focused, economical efficiency. Her camera lens had tracked that focus again and again throughout the day. She itched to photograph him again now.

For their office files, Fiona justified. She glanced

guiltily at the other nearby workers, but none of them seemed to be taking any particular notice of who or what she was studying.

Right now she needed to study landscape photo angles. She gathered her equipment. There should be a nice sunset soon, if she could find the right place on the property to photograph it. She fished her iPod out of her jeans pocket, placed the earphones in her ears and let the music and the lighting and the mood absorb her.

She truly was all about the work.

She was!

Brent found Fiona in a far corner of the property site, camera carefully placed on a tripod. She was waiting for something, he wasn't sure what. And, while she waited, her body moved unconsciously to music only she could hear.

In her jeans and fitted red shirt, with dirt smears on her legs and other places, and her hair ruffled and half-falling from her ponytail, she looked…lived-in, girl-next-door.

He almost managed to convince himself she looked quite ordinary, in fact, until she made a small sound in the back of her throat, leaned in and took several photos before she straightened with a satisfied sigh, pulled the earphones from her ears and began to dismantle her equipment.

Because the truth was Fiona dressed in this way was anything but ordinary, and with the flush of achievement on her face she was anything but comfortable or girl-next-door.

Brent drew a deep breath and stepped forward. 'Finished? Did you get the shots you wanted?'

'Oh!' Her hand rose to splay over her chest. 'I didn't realise you were there. I was photographing the sunset.

I've taken around two hundred photos today. Not all of them will be used, of course, but I think I've gained a good overview of what a team of people can achieve on a site in a single session. But please tell me I wasn't muttering or singing while I worked.'

'You were soundless, I promise. I didn't want to disturb your concentration so I waited, that was all.' Their fingers brushed as he reached to take the tripod from her.

Just that, and Brent's focus slipped. He froze on that slip. Came to a complete stop with his fingers closed over Fiona's. Only a beat of time passed before he moved his hand, but that one beat was a beat out of his control and that concerned him.

That Fiona now studied him with her head tipped to the side and curiosity stamped on her face bothered him more. There were certain things about him that he kept to himself. He'd learned from a master instructor that doing that was necessary.

Most of all it bothered him that this one woman set off in him things to do with his condition that very few other people could make happen, no matter how much they impacted on him. His need to protect his privacy about that rose even in the face of his awareness of her. It wasn't a comfortable combination.

'I think I got a couple of great shots just now.' She glanced up into the branches of the lemon-scented gum tree that towered over them. 'Ones with the light spearing down creating a dappled effect. I hope to base my painting on that concept.'

'That's good.' His thumb rubbed over and over against a ridged edge on the tripod. Brent forced the movement to a stop. 'I'm glad you got the material you wanted.'

'It only took a little while, a bit of waiting for that perfect moment.' Fiona seemed about to ask him something.

Brent braced, but her glance shifted around the vacant lot, past him, swung left and right and finally moved to the outside perimeter where all the work vehicles had been parked.

'I guess maybe I took longer than I noticed. The work's finished.' She seemed chagrined. 'They've all left. I was so focused on what I was doing that I didn't notice. How long did I keep you waiting?'

'Not long, and I didn't mind waiting.' He growled it in a tone that quite likely made her believe the opposite. The truth was, he'd got value out of watching her work. 'If you're done here, we can leave now.'

'Yes. I'm done. Thanks.' She hustled towards his utility truck.

Brent joined her, opened the passenger door for her and climbed in behind the wheel. 'The office will be closed by the time we get back, but we'll get anything from inside that you need. Then, if you're not too tired, I'd like you to join Linc and Alex and me for dinner so they can hear your impressions of your first day on the job.'

They'd planned for this—to get Fiona's impressions without giving her too long to think first and maybe fall back on more PC answers rather than simply giving her true impressions.

And it would be fine. Taking her to his brothers would be exactly what he needed to bring this— whatever it was that he experienced when he was near her—back into perspective.

It had probably just been too long since he'd spent

time with a woman. There were always offers. They never meant anything more than what they were, and maybe he was starting to feel a little jaded about that.

Brent pushed the thought aside, because there was nothing else for him. And he wasn't jaded, anyway. 'Linc and Alex and I all hold shares in each others' companies. So you'll be reporting to all of us.'

'I'd be happy to discuss the day with all of you. Actually, I'd like a chance to bat my reactions around with you, particularly.' Fiona glanced down at her jeans. 'I'm grubby, though.'

Brent drove into the traffic. 'That won't matter. We'll be eating at home, and Linc and Alex know we'll be coming straight from the site.'

'Then I'm happy to come to dinner and "report in".' Fiona smiled. 'Thanks.'

And Fiona was. Happy. Cheerful. Chatting about the other workers and Brent's work projects generally as they made their way back to their suburb, where she collected her car from all day parking and followed him to his warehouse home.

'It's this way.' Brent waited while Fiona exited her car in the large ground floor parking area and led her into the foyer of the converted warehouse building he and his brothers shared. It felt good to bring her into his home, and that was one more reaction he didn't want to have to deal with.

Fiona stopped in the centre of the polished floor and her glance darted this way and that. 'Oh. How gorgeous. And it's so big and very private. I never imagined from the outside…'

'That was what we hoped when we bought the place and converted it. An illusion of it being nothing special, but inside there's space and…we know we're not on display.' He cleared his throat. 'We like it, anyway.'

Brent laid his hand on the curved handcrafted staircase that led to the upper level, and watched her look her fill in this place where he felt…comfortable, where he owned his space.

One end of the foyer held a leather sofa and chairs. The art on the walls was bold and bright—blues and whites, yellows and greens and pinks on canvases large enough not to get lost on the huge walls.

Fiona's gaze settled on those artworks for a long moment. Finally she said, 'The colours and designs of those are fabulous. I don't think I know the artist…'

'Alex'll be pleased you like his work.' Brent was pleased. And proud. And way too conscious of her reactions altogether. 'Let's go find my brothers.' He led the way up the staircase. 'We all have separate homes within the warehouse. For tonight, we're meeting in the courtyard area upstairs.'

'I think it's wonderful that you're all so close.' Her tone held a wistful edge she didn't quite manage to conceal.

Yet she had a family, had referred to parents and sisters on the drive to the site this morning, and obviously, if they'd raised someone like Fiona, her parents must be special people.

Before Brent could consider that further, his guest made a beeline for the youngest of his brothers. 'Alex. Your paintings are beautiful—'

'Thanks.' Alex turned from the barbecue with a modest smile and a wry twist of his mouth. 'Brent brought your portfolio home over the weekend to show us. Your work is far better.'

'Different,' Fiona corrected. 'Not necessarily better.'

Linc placed a bowl of salad on the long table. 'Hiring a graphic designer was a big step for our brother. He's accustomed to working his designs through on his own, but he felt the company was ready for it, that it would be a good thing.'

'I hope it will prove to be.' Fiona's gaze encompassed all of them.

Brent glanced her way. 'I've seen enough of Fiona's work, and now seen her in action, to have no doubt I've made the right choice.'

At least she had managed that while she'd fought her reactions to this talented and complex man. And surely, in a day or two, when she'd settled into the job and become used to her employer, she would move past this consciousness of him.

'I appreciate your faith in me, Brent.' In truth it touched a deep place in Fiona's heart that had been chilled the day she'd told her family she'd decided to follow her dream career, rather than the logical, safe one they'd steered her into when she'd first left high school at eighteen.

They'd been equally unenthusiastic when she'd phoned to say she'd landed this job and moved out here. She might as well have said she'd got a good bargain on bread this week at the supermarket for all the level of excitement or support she'd received in response.

So Brent's attitude was a boost, even if her reaction to it didn't exactly help her to feel blasé towards him.

'It's easy to have that faith. You're talented, enthusiastic.' Brent's gaze lingered on her for a long moment before he gave a deliberately relaxed grin that soon became a natural one. 'The company can only benefit from your input.'

'Thank you.' For the generosity of his words and the sincerity in his eyes as he delivered them.

He was a complex man—there was so much beneath the surface. She'd sensed that from the first moment of meeting him. Now, she simply wanted to know him all the more.

And, because Fiona felt a little emotional about that, and about his praise, she quickly cleared her throat and smiled. 'It means a lot to work for someone who has such faith in me and who I can have total faith in as well.'

Fiona drew a deep breath and glanced at the feast spread on the table. 'The food smells wonderful. I confess I'm a little hungry!'

They all took their seats at a picnic style table with bench seating. Linc and Alex sat on one side. Fiona ended up seated beside her boss on the other.

Focus on the meal, Fiona. On being an appropriate guest, or talking about work.

There were vegetable kebabs made of cherry tomatoes, courgette, onion slices and button mushrooms marinated in a wonderful herbed Italian dressing and cooked to perfection. Steak and sausages—Fiona left those to the men. Whole potatoes cooked in foil and served with sour cream and fresh chopped chives. And delightful seasoned ground beef patties.

'Which of you is the chef?' The outdoor area was set up with potted small trees and plants everywhere. It was enclosed, no view, and the overall feeling was one of security and…intimacy.

In a purely familial context!

'I did the easy stuff. Rosa did the kebabs.' Alex's glance dipped to his plate. 'Rosa's our cleaner, mostly, but she does other things for us as well.' He hesitated and his brows drew together as he considered the matter. 'Sort of like a mother would or something.'

A mother these men didn't have? Alex's words made it sound as though they hadn't ever known that.

Fiona's thoughts returned to how dissimilar the men were. She shifted her gaze to Brent's face but his eyes were shielded with those long silky lashes again.

Perhaps they'd all had different mothers? Or fathers? Or some of both? Perhaps family life had been a little complicated for them? Well, she knew all about that from her own family. Though she was the only one who would say that situation was complex. Her parents and sisters would say it would all be just fine if Fiona would simply make an effort to fit in better. 'My compliments to Rosa, then.'

'So tell us your impressions from today.' Linc carved another piece of meat from his steak as he waited for her response.

'I have some photos now that I believe will be good for general marketing purposes.' She explained the thoughts behind those concepts, and was pleased when Brent started to nod and approval showed clearly on his chiselled face.

'I also have photos for the idea I want to use for a painting for the clients.' It was a great idea to add a painting into each landscape project, and Fiona was keen to get started on this one. 'If the clients hang the painting in their home and talk to their visitors about the landscaping work Brent's done for them, that can only be good for business. Working with my hands, helping to do actual planting, really helped me to get a feel for what Brent's work is all about, too. I...valued that.'

She felt as though she'd been given an insight into him. Fiona glanced his way and for a brief moment their gazes met and she wondered if he sensed that connection in the same way she did.

Seconds later he blinked and looked away and the moment was gone.

'I'd like you to create a better business logo for us, too.' Was Brent's voice a little deeper than usual as he said this? 'I think we're due for a change there. I've never been entirely happy with the logo we have. I want something timeless, with a style that won't date, but what we have now feels a bit too pedestrian.'

'I'm sure I can come up with some viable possibilities. You might want something with just a few bold lines. It's surprising how effective that can be.'

Brent's gaze narrowed as he considered the idea. 'Yes. I can see that.' Again, that smile kicked up one side of his mouth. 'I like the way you think.'

'Thank you.'

They ate and they talked and Fiona lost her over-consciousness eventually and relaxed and, before she knew it, they were batting ideas back and forth. So fast, in fact, that she was almost breathless with it.

The scent of barbecued meat and vinaigrette dressing and city in the evening filled the air around them and she leaned close to her employer and he leaned in close to her, two heads bent together in an almost conspiratorial huddle, until she realised just how close they were and her consciousness of him sharpened again.

As they fell silent and his gaze tracked over her and came back to rest on her eyes, a shiver similar to that very first one she'd felt tickled over her senses. There was warmth in his expression, and frank male interest...

Before he shut the latter down.

It stung. More than Fiona wanted to admit because she'd had this experience enough times in her life. She'd had it the one time she'd trusted a man enough to get truly close to him. That had been years ago now, but it had left its mark, had made her wary, and that wariness had proved accurate over the years.

And now her employer was doing the same thing.

But he *was* only her employer and that was what she needed to remember.

'I'm looking forward to tapping into your vision.' That was what they needed to talk about, to focus on. She swallowed. 'For your work. Tapping into it and learning how to present it in its best light for each project. The emotion you convey…'

His expression became a mask and the fingers of his right hand drummed out a staccato rhythm on the table.

Moments later that rhythm stopped.

All of Brent stopped, frozen in time for a long moment as his gaze searched hers.

Finally he said, 'All I do is make the best I can out of each project I take on. That's just…work. Any emotion you put into it will be your own.'

His belief in this was in his eyes, in the closed conviction on his face. Belief and self-protectiveness.

Why wouldn't he acknowledge that he poured himself into his work? It was so obvious to her.

She'd examined a lot of his projects over the past two years. Landscape design had fascinated her from the start of her course, and *his* work had held the most appeal to her purely *because* of what she sensed in it.

Strength and conviction, imagination and reaching out and…protecting himself. Oh, she had responded most of all to that. It was one of the things that drew her to him, even when she knew she shouldn't and mustn't allow herself to be drawn. She'd only get hurt and, anyway, he was the boss, out of her reach and her league!

'I want to draw out what you've seen, your vision for each project.' Fiona spoke carefully, took the diplomatic route in her reply. 'But I'm certainly happy to add my own layering to that.'

'That's the best way to look at it.' Brent seemed satisfied with this and the conversation moved on then, expanded to include all three brothers again.

After a time, Alex got to his feet. 'I have phone calls to make to one of the company's overseas contacts before it gets too much later. If you'll excuse me?'

Linc stood beside Alex and a frown creased his brows. 'I might head out to Cecilia's. I wasn't really satisfied with the discussion we had earlier today on the phone.'

Fiona watched the brothers disappear and turned to Brent with the quirk of one eyebrow. She asked lightly, 'Woman trouble for your brother?'

Brent stood and began to gather dishes and utensils together. 'Cecilia manages Linc's largest plant nursery. Who knows what the issue is this time? They're two strong personalities. They clash sometimes.'

'Ah.' Fiona got to her feet and helped gather the remainder of the dishes. 'Where are we headed with these?'

'My place.' Brent led the way out of the courtyard area and along a hallway until they came to a recessed door. 'It can all go in the dishwasher.'

'And then I'd better leave.' Fiona held the plates carefully and waited as he opened the door to his home within the warehouse building. 'I enjoyed the meal and our talk. I hope your brothers were happy with my first day reactions.'

She'd all but forgotten the presence of the others at times as she'd focused her attention on her boss. Fiona knew she had to do better than *that!*

'I think we were all more than satisfied. Kitchen's this way.' Brent strode at a brisk pace past a large living area and into a slate and white kitchen.

Was it the rich aroma of percolated coffee that drew him along so fast? She didn't get the chance to more than half-glance around her.

Fiona stopped at the edge of the kitchen and then she did let her gaze take in the sight of three different coffee machines on the counter, and a myriad of other gadgets beside them.

Her lips twitched. 'I take it you *really* like coffee. And gadgetry.'

'Different blends for different times of the day. The coffee is on a timer, so I can make sure it's ready for me when I want it. My evening dose is decaf.' A slight smile creased his lips. Then his expression sobered as he examined the rest of the gadgets. 'The way they all work interests me. I probably have bought more things than I really need.'

As though he'd said too much, he drew two coffee mugs from an overhead cupboard and raised them in question.

'Yes, please.' If it was decaf, it wouldn't hurt to have it. She was intrigued by this small revelation into his personality, too. She would have liked to pursue the topic, maybe tease him a little about having an obsession about the way things worked.

A small memory flitted through her head as she

thought this, of someone with similarities to her employer, but she lost it before it could fully form. 'The coffee smells far too good to be caffeine-free, you know.'

'It's an imported blend. A bit self-indulgent of me all up, I suppose. Overall, my curiosity hasn't always been welcomed, but I tend to indulge it nowadays, in my own setting, at least.' He cut off the words and then seemed to relax out of whatever place they had taken him. He poured the rich blend and passed her one of the cups.

'You're hardly self-indulgent, and I think curiosity is a good thing. How else do we learn?' The words emerged without her conscious volition. But he'd earned the money he had. If he wanted to import coffee and invest in gadgets he didn't necessarily use, why shouldn't he? Those things seemed very *small* indulgences and if he enjoyed exploring them at the same time… 'I mean great coffee is worth investing in.'

She put the mug to her lips and sipped, and the rich thick liquid slid down her throat so smoothly that she had to close her eyes and let a small sigh of satisfaction escape. 'Oh, that is *good*. I think for the pleasure of that taste alone, all your curiosity has been well worth it in this case.'

'You have a unique way of looking at things. Calling it that…' Brent fell silent.

'What else would it be?' She opened her eyes and caught his gaze on her. Unshielded in that first instance, and somehow almost vulnerable.

And…edged with a consciousness of her that brushed across her senses like a touch.

This time he didn't shut it down. Oh, he looked

away, but the awareness was still etched on his face when he did that.

It echoed inside her, too. Fiona dropped her gaze to her cup again while her heart inexplicably pounded. It was a foolish reaction. One that she needed to quash because, even if he did find her attractive right now, that could change. In any case, he was her boss and it would be really far less than sensible for her to allow feelings towards him or to start believing he had any towards her.

Maybe he simply found her opinions interesting and she was imagining anything else.

They sipped their coffee standing right there, leaning against the kitchen counter. When the silence stretched, Fiona turned her gaze to Brent's living room, to squashy chocolate leather sofas and chairs and long rows of magazines lined up like soldiers across a set of three coffee tables.

There were neat stacks of library books set exactly so, and other books and pieces of paper arranged carefully all through the area and beside armchairs positioned around the room.

'I see you like to bring your work home, and you're very orderly.' Was this why he had rushed her past the area? Because there was something quite *different* about the way he'd laid out all that work?

His office space was similarly regimented, and it *was* different.

He rubbed his hand over the back of his head. 'I sometimes have to work on projects until they're finished, whether that means bringing things home or not. Once I get started, I get very focused and I can't stop. I've always been that way. Some people...find that objectionable but it's how I am. Core me. It's not something that's going to change.'

'Nor should it.' If he changed, he might lose some of the intensity that made his work what it was. Why on earth would he even consider such a possibility—? 'I imagine there'll be times when I'll do the same. Get deeply involved in the work, I mean.'

He shifted on his feet, passed his empty coffee cup from hand to hand.

'It's time I went.' One part of her didn't want to leave, wanted to stay in his company longer.

To talk about work issues, she told herself. Instead, she put her empty cup down on the counter top and made her way towards the front door.

'I enjoyed our talk this evening.' Brent paced beside her. His words brought them back to business, and of course that was a good thing.

As she approached the door she noticed the photo-montage on the wall. It was positioned so it would be the last thing he looked at as he left his home each day.

Photos of him and his brothers.

Fiona looked, and looked again. And the story embedded in those images hit her so deeply her breath stalled in her throat and for a long moment she couldn't speak. She simply stood there, unable to shift her gaze.

When she finally found her voice it wasn't to state the obvious. Not, *You were all institutionalised.* Or, *There are no parents, are there?* At least not for a very long time. Or, *You're not biologically related.*

But, oh, they had created themselves into a family, first in that cold building in the background of several of the pictures, and later as they'd found their freedom and relocated here.

They were three men who'd *become* men before their time, and had stood up for each other. It was all there, captured in the stark stares and guarded expressions of young boys and the determination of young men, and the laughter and wry smiles and inner shields of the men they were now.

How had they all ended up alone? Parentless? In Brent's case, extremely private, and she imagined the others had their issues with privacy, too. Just look at where they all lived.

His brothers must have changed their names through legal channels, or perhaps they'd all chosen the last name MacKay and adopted it at some point? 'I thought from the beginning that you and your brothers were close. I hadn't realised all the reasons why.'

Fiona didn't have that closeness in her own family. It was a knowledge she lived with and tried not to think about. Right now it felt very blatant to her. Blatant and sad, and yet Brent and his brothers must have been through so much more. Indeed, the two things were incomparable.

'We're there for each other. The few people who've looked at those photos didn't even realise—' Brent opened the door.

'That you're a chosen family, not a "by birth" one?' They were proof the former could be as strong as any example of the latter.

'Yes. "Chosen" is the right word for it. For us, that's better than where…we came from.' He stepped out into the corridor with her. 'I'll see you back to your car.'

End of discussion, and fair enough. Though she might want to know more, he *was* a private man and this was obviously very private business to him.

They walked in silence. Moments later she stood beside her small car.

'We have a meeting with a client at her home tomorrow.' Brent rubbed his jaw with his hand. 'It's the troublesome client I told you about on Friday.'

Fiona mentally reviewed her wardrobe. 'I'll be ready for it.'

'Perhaps between us we can get her to stop blocking the plans at every turn.' Brent waited while she seated herself, and then he pushed her door closed.

She started the engine and rolled down the window.

He leaned in. 'Drive safely. I'll see you tomorrow.'

'Goodnight, Brent.' He'd given her some things to think about. The family he had built and her questions about where he might have come from. His emotional guardedness. That regimented work lined up in his living room and in his office. The privacy he sought in his home and his work.

'Goodnight,' he murmured.

With a final wave and an odd reluctance to leave him, and with myriad questions flitting through her mind and no answers anywhere in sight, Fiona drove away.

CHAPTER THREE

'MRS FULLER will either have to get on board during this visit, or we cut our losses and dump the project. The work is interchangeable with a dozen other projects that all need my attention. At some point I have to assess what's going to be best financially for the company overall and, right now, letting her mess us around further isn't.' Brent murmured the words as he and Fiona waited in the formal sitting room of the woman's ritzy Sydney home.

They'd been kept cooling their heels here for twenty minutes now with no sign of their hostess.

'I agree. This isn't a smart use of your time. The woman's behaviour is insulting to you.' And that insult made Fiona feel...protective towards her boss.

Which was fine, because she was his employee. She had the right to feel that way. Even if she had been somewhat too personally conscious of her boss initially.

The door to the room swished open and a maid entered with a tea tray.

Rose Fuller swept in behind her. 'Thank you, Lilly. You may pour and leave us.'

Mrs Fuller waved a slender, well-tended hand

towards the maid before she turned to greet her guests. 'Oh, I see you've brought an assistant, Mr MacKay?'

A very lowly one, her tone seemed to suggest.

'Mrs Fuller, meet my graphic designer, Fiona Donner. We were about to leave but, since you've managed the appointment belatedly after all, we'll do what we can in the limited time we have left.' Brent's voice held just the right amount of firmness. He got to his feet to shake hands with the woman and stepped back so Fiona could do the same. 'Fiona, meet Mrs Rose Fuller.'

The familiarity of name and face clicked into place when Fiona received a very practised smile and a rather limp hand to shake, though the woman had looked slightly chagrined by the end of Brent's speech.

Husband in politics. Big aspirations. Lots of media coverage as they did their best to climb the ranks.

Ah...

'It's nice to meet you, Mrs Fuller. I've been studying the project plans Brent has drawn up for you.' Fiona towered over Mrs Fuller by an entire head and shoulders. In the dainty room, with the maid pouring cups of tea into translucent china cups, Fiona had to fight off feeling oversized and, subsequently, unfeminine.

The two assessments did not necessarily have to go together, no matter what her mother may have said to the contrary at various times throughout Fiona's life. 'You must be pleased to have Brent on board for your landscaping work. He's the best in the city.'

'Well, of course I know Mr MacKay has a decent reputation, though he can be extremely elusive about contact outside of his work channels.'

'I apologise for turning down the dinner invitation,

Mrs Fuller.' Brent's smile didn't quite reach his eyes. 'I saw the write-up in all the major papers the next day.'

'Yes, we made quite a splash.' Mrs Fuller went on, 'I'm afraid I just can't decide on any one of the plans we've discussed. My husband is very exacting and everything has to serve our lifestyle and our business interactions perfectly.' Their hostess gestured for them to take their seats, did so herself and waited while her maid handed out the teacups and left the room.

'Of course.' Fiona took a deep breath and turned her attention to the view from the bay windows for a moment.

The house was elevated and the grounds rolled away to a seemingly endless stretch of Sydney coast. The scene from this window once the design work was completed in the grounds below would make an ideal painting for the client. If they could get the woman to start cooperating.

'Mrs Fuller, you've expressed what you want out of this landscaping project. Now it's time to trust us to provide it for you.' Brent placed his tea, untouched, onto the small table beside his chair and his fingers curled against his thighs as though he wanted to do something with them but was stopping himself.

Fiona took up the conversation where Brent had left off. 'The exciting news for you, Mrs Fuller, is that you'll be one of our first clients to have the benefit of an original artwork gifted to you at the completion of your project. I think a two metre by one metre canvas would work here. Of course, if you're unable to settle on our plans we'll need to move on. You'll understand my employer is highly sought after, and my paintings are award-winning works that will always find a welcome home...'

'That's a substantial-sized painting. I wasn't aware— What awards have you won?' The woman's eyes gleamed.

And Fiona ran with that. Just a little, and only because she truly did want her boss to get something back for the time he'd invested in this project so far. She named the prestigious awards.

Brent knew of them, of course. They'd been listed in her curriculum vitae and she'd included copies of the works in her portfolio.

'I recall now.' Mrs Fuller straightened her perfectly straight back even more. 'You're *that* Fiona Donner. One of the paintings was a landscape…'

'Yes. They both were. It's a favourite medium of mine.' Fiona could almost see the cogs turning in their hostess's brain.

She smiled at the woman. 'At this stage we are utterly one hundred per cent informed of your needs, Mrs Fuller. You've discussed them in detail with my employer, and he has explained everything to me. Now you can let it go, take that burden off shoulders that no doubt have many other responsibilities. Your husband, your social engagements.'

A suppressed hint of sound came from Brent that *could* have been a snort, though a quick glance his way revealed nothing but the blandest of facial expressions.

'It will be our pleasure to take care of the hard work and stress and decisions for you, Mrs Fuller.' Brent offered this assurance with calm confidence. 'All you need to do is enjoy the finished product when your landscape design is in place. Shall we discuss the original plans? I truly still believe they are what's going to be best to meet your needs.'

They talked. Or, rather, Brent did most of the talking in a firm, determined way. Mrs Fuller occasionally tried to get off track or waffle about some aspect or another she wasn't quite certain about. Invariably, Brent pulled her back.

Fiona sipped her tea until it was all gone while Mrs Fuller did the same.

Eventually, with all of his case put forward again as succinctly as possible, Brent leaned back in his chair. 'Well, Mrs Fuller. What do you say? Do we have a plan, or do we leave this here, cut our losses and both move on?'

'I'd like you to begin work, using the plan you originally produced, and providing a painting.' Mrs Fuller replaced her teacup in its saucer with a small click. 'It's a pity you weren't able to articulate things so clearly the first time…'

Several beats of silence passed.

Fiona didn't know she'd moved until she realised she was on her feet.

Brent whispered into her ear, 'Remember, the client is always right, even when she's not.' He'd risen with her and leaned in casually to give her those words while giving Mrs Fuller a businesslike smile.

Fiona bit her lip and bit back the words that wanted to pour out, telling Mrs Fuller exactly how offensive she had just been.

It would be unrealistic, Fiona supposed, to expect a *complete* turnaround from the woman and, in the end, Brent had achieved what he wanted.

So score one for Brent MacKay Landscaping Designs. With brief—and, Fiona thought in the circumstances, very constrained—goodbyes to their hostess, they took their leave.

Brent led the way back to his utility truck, opened her door for Fiona and got behind the wheel himself.

'You have excellent people-handling skills, Fiona.' A grin kicked up one corner of his mouth and spread until it reached his eyes. 'I had a much easier time of it with you there to help me out.'

'Oh, I didn't do much. You're the one who produced the ideas Mrs Fuller should have leapt at in the first place.' Fiona brushed aside her part in things and did her best to brush aside her annoyance at the same time. 'In the end it all worked out, I guess, and I think Mrs Fuller is someone who, despite all the difficulties with her up to this point, will talk your work up to the skies once it's done for her.'

Fiona was doing quite well being upbeat and positive until she added a muttered, 'I didn't appreciate her insulting attitude to the importance of your time or the way she insinuated that her mucking around for weeks was somehow your fault!'

Brent laughed. 'I caught that, and I appreciate you caring.'

He set the vehicle in motion. 'You *were* very diplomatic with Mrs Fuller. I think you'd even manage to tame the crowd of people just like her who attend the Landscaping Awards nights.'

'That's one event you do attend each year.' The words slipped out before she could consider how telling he might find them. 'I mean, naturally you attend whatever functions you're interested in—'

'And I protect my privacy the rest of the time.' He made no apology, simply stated it as fact.

'The Deltran Landscaping Awards are prestigious.'

'Yes, and I'm nominated for an award this year.' Brent glanced her way. 'I'd like you to attend the ceremony with me. It will give me a chance to showcase you as part of the company.'

'I'd love to go.' The invitation was unexpected, but her acceptance was instantaneous. Too fast, really.

Because she was a little *too* delighted. Because the thought of an evening out with him appealed a little too much. She wasn't supposed to be feeling that way about him any more. Not since she'd thought that all through and concluded that she wouldn't.

'Then you can consider it a date.' The moment the words left Brent, a frown creased his brow. He drummed his fingers on the steering wheel. 'Consider it a business arrangement, I mean.'

Right.

'I think it will be a very useful evening for the company.' And, for that reason, it would be good to attend the evening with her boss.

'Maybe I should do something similar for this dinner Mum's roped me into attending with the family.' There. That was good. A segue into a different topic by commenting on something that bore similarities to the first topic. 'I could go for "safety in numbers" and take a friend along.'

'It sounds like an obligatory family event?' This seemed to surprise him.

No doubt because his interactions with his brothers contained none of the difficulties Fiona encountered at family functions. Her family tended to find her far too different and 'out of the box' for their tastes.

Ironic, really, when Brent was the one with the unusual 'family' structure.

'I didn't mean to make it sound as though family events are a chore for me. Even if they were,' she added, and couldn't keep the doubt from her tone, 'the evening might be fun.'

Extremely doubtful, but in the end you never knew, right?

Brent drew the truck to a stop in its space behind their office building and turned to face her. 'I'll trade. You come to the Awards night with me and I'll be your "extra" for your family gathering. Assuming both these events aren't scheduled at once. When is your family get-together?'

Not the same night, as it happened.

Fiona was still shocked by his offer, even as she answered him. 'Th-thank you. I'd love to have you come along.' She stuttered out the details while Brent climbed out of the truck and led the way into the building and through to his office.

His face was tight. Maybe he regretted making his offer. Should she try to let him off the hook? 'If you don't really—'

'It'll be a chance for me to meet your family.' He picked up a handful of mail from his desk and began to sort through it. 'I'm planning to have you working for me for a long time, so it's strategic for us to do this.'

'Oh. Of course. Well, that's lovely, then.' And it was. Absolutely. Lovely, and practical and, for goodness' sake, why would she kid herself it was anything else? She would enjoy Brent's company as her boss meeting her family for a one-off occasion. That would be no biggie. Not at all.

This might provide a chance for your parents and sisters to see you actually have a serious job working for Brent, not some 'dangerously unstable artsy thing' as your mother dismissed it on the phone when you rang to tell her the good news that you'd got the position.

And maybe they'd see that she was making progress in that job. Yes, it was still very early days but Brent seemed pleased enough with her so far. It was about time her family acknowledged that her choices and decisions in life, though perhaps not right for them, were right for her and could even be quite successful.

As for the fact she hadn't entirely managed to quash her consciousness of Brent as a man…well, she would quash it.

Fiona hustled to the door so they could get on with some work.

'You're staring into space, Fiona! Do concentrate.' Eloise Donner's voice grated across Brent's nerve-endings as she addressed her daughter. 'You're holding things up.'

'I'm sure Fiona's just taking time to think through how she wants to answer the game question.' Brent battled to keep his tone unremarkable, polite.

He wanted to walk out, taking Fiona with him.

Her mother's niggling wasn't overtly vicious. In Brent's opinion, it was worse than that because it was subtle, ingrained and would be very difficult for Fiona to fight.

Particularly if she didn't want to get into an argument with her mother and have Eloise tell her she was over-stating the problem or making much out of 'nothing'.

Something told him Eloise Donner would be good at saying things like that.

It was Wednesday night, just over a week after Fiona had first started working for him, and they were at that obligatory family gathering he'd invited himself along to.

As her employer, he had wanted to meet her family. But curiosity had also motivated him.

He had wanted to see what her family were like. Maybe he'd wanted to be around a family that had parents in it, full stop?

You got over missing that a long time ago, MacKay.

His father had made that easy. Just dumped him and walked away…

Well, the answer to what Fiona's family were like was 'nothing he'd expected'.

With Fiona being so kind and sweet, he'd thought her family would be the same, people who would have brought out those things in her by their own example. Instead, they were clinical, critical, super-practical and unemotional people who almost seemed to lack…soul?

They certainly *looked* nothing like Fiona. Her mother and sisters were petite and brittle, where Fiona was tall and lush and vibrant. Her father was a 'medium' man. Medium height, build, medium brown hair, medium interest in life, it appeared. Fiona's inner beauty was something that had obviously come from the core of her and flourished *against* the odds of her family influence.

Fiona glanced at the card in her hand. They were playing a board game. A particularly stultifying one, Brent thought. There were eight people at the table. Fiona's family, Fiona, him, and a couple of extras.

Fiona cast an uncomfortable glance his way before she pinned on that smile she'd worked so hard to hold all night. 'I don't think I know the answer to this one, Mum. I'll have to pass.'

'You must know.' Terrence Donner cast a slightly impatient glance his daughter's way. 'None of the questions in this game are unanswerable.'

'For people who enjoy documentaries and non-fiction reading, perhaps.' Brent's knee brushed against Fiona's as he shifted in his chair.

The jolt to his senses shouldn't have happened. He'd made the choice not to notice Fiona in that way.

So why had he?

You've noticed her from the start. You've simply been avoiding your awareness of her.

Well, then, he could go on avoiding it. He had to go on avoiding it because she set off behaviours in him that he had worked hard for decades to subdue, and he wasn't about to reveal those shortcomings to her. He guarded those things.

'Nope. Sorry, Dad. I truly don't have an answer to put up at this point.' Fiona shrugged her shoulders and indicated they should move on to the next player, but her words were slightly breathless.

Brent reacted to that knowledge more than he wanted to.

The game ended. Brent got to his feet. He might not have all his answers, but he knew he'd had enough of this. And so had Fiona. 'It's been nice to meet you all, but we have a long trip to get home. I think it's time we left.'

When they emerged outside the family's house Brent breathed in the night air and thought of Linc and Alex and how lucky he was to have them. A chosen family, not a blood one. As if that mattered. He wouldn't trade them. The thoughts helped him regain perspective and that put him in a better place to care for Fiona.

As a colleague and someone he'd begun to admire in that capacity...

He helped Fiona into his truck and talked about this and that as they made their way back towards her home.

If he talked, maybe she would forget the unpleasantness of the evening. And maybe *he* would forget how much he wanted to draw her into his arms and kiss her to take her mind off the fact that her family didn't treat her the way they all should. *That* desire was not businesslike.

Words pushed past his lips anyway. 'What's wrong with them? They don't—'

'I'm glad you got to meet my family, that they got to meet my boss and hear a little about the work I'm doing.' Fiona spoke over the top of him. Her words were deliberately upbeat as he turned the truck into an empty parking space in the apartment complex's courtyard. Upbeat but edged with that same breathless quality as earlier, when their knees had brushed beneath the table.

She went on, 'I hope that will have made my goals a little more real to them, a little more understandable.'

A little more *acceptable?* Her family made her feel abnormal when she was a great person in her own right. And that was clearly something that had been going on for a long time. *That* was Brent's assessment and it was one that was…a little too close to the bone for comfort.

Brent turned off the truck's ignition and strode around the front to open her door and help her out. 'You have a good start in a job that's in your chosen field. There are plenty of people out there who never manage to say that much. Your family should be proud of the way you've pursued and begun to obtain your goals.'

'Thank you and…maybe they are.' She spoke in a way that seemed to try to keep the uncertainty out of her tone. And gave a soft smile, no doubt aimed at easing the moment. 'Well, I promise you I will do my utmost to support you in return when it comes time to go to the Awards dinner.'

'Your company on the night will be more than enough.' Brent all but growled the words. 'I'll walk you up.'

See her into her apartment safely and then leave. That was what he needed to do, not linger here wanting nebulous things he didn't want to name but knew would get him into trouble if he went after them. Things that had to do with odd notions, such as comfort and close-ness and acceptance.

What was the matter with him tonight? Where were these deep buried thoughts coming from?

When they reached the top of the staircase and made their way to her front door, Fiona put her key in the lock and turned to face him. 'They didn't pry too much into your business, I hope. When I was in the kitchen clearing away dishes.'

He pushed his hands into his pockets, frowned and took them out again. 'They didn't pry too much.'

She seemed to relax a little at that. 'Would you like a coffee or something before you drive on? I've only got instant—'

'No. Thanks. But I'll see you inside.' He had to know she was safely secured behind these walls. That was only common courtesy.

'O-okay.' She pushed the door open and walked inside.

Brent followed, closed it after him and glanced around.

A hand-woven rug brightened the floor. Those splashes of orange and sky-blue and red and green were echoed in throw cushions and the table lamp and an abstract Fiona Donner original on the wall.

She'd made a beautiful home, welcoming and indi-vidual and full of her life and vitality and sweetness. Brent wanted to sit on her sofa and just...be there among these things that held meaning for her. As though, if he did that, he'd...belong.

The inexplicable feeling washed through him, so much more than a simple awareness of her, even if that awareness had been causing him enough problems all by itself.

It took him enough by surprise that he hesitated in the centre of her small living room.

He should go.

He wanted to stay.

Since when had his emotions reached for such odd things? He didn't even do that whole 'feelings' arena. Linc and Alex—he loved them, but that was it. His inability to maintain a relationship with his father had taught him what his limits were. The autism—he hadn't been able to get past that. With Alex and Linc it was different, but they'd all come up together, had faced down their demons together.

With Fiona, Brent wasn't even prepared to let himself be attracted to her. He wasn't in the market for a relationship, and Fiona was someone who should be given that if a man was interested in her.

So say goodbye and leave. Do it now before any other temptation comes over you.

'Well, thanks again.'

'I should go.'

They spoke at the same time.

Fiona paused and her lashes fluttered over eyes the colour of the sky in the mountains on a warm summer day. Clear, sweet blue.

So lovely. He could appreciate the pure aesthetics of her, couldn't he? Just appreciate that?

Yes? And where was the distance to go with that kind of remote appreciation?

Brent didn't know the answer and, because he didn't, and because he couldn't quite make his feet take him to the door and through it, he addressed another issue that he did want answers to.

'Your family made tonight all about themselves.' Maybe she didn't want to discuss this, but what if she needed to? What if *he* needed to talk with her about the way her family had treated her?

His fingers reached out and brushed the back of her hand. She had smooth, soft skin like the petals of a rose. Too late not to touch her now. He'd done it. 'Your parents could have tried to be a bit accommodating of your tastes in terms of entertainment.'

'They think I need to fit in, be more like them, but I'm just…not. I tried that. It didn't work.' Her soft sigh was a whisper between them. 'But I love them, and they don't mean to make me uncomfortable.' She gestured with her hand to dismiss the topic. 'Thank you for your company, anyway.'

'You're welcome.' And he *had* to go.

Brent walked to the door and tugged it open and, with a low, 'Lock it after me,' he stepped through. On the other side, he waited until she did as he had asked, and then he walked to his truck and drove away.

What he thought about her family, about all this, didn't matter in the end. Whatever he now knew of her, whatever empathy he felt for her, he had nothing to offer anyone, and especially not someone like Fiona.

That was what he had to remember.

CHAPTER FOUR

BRENT parked his truck and made his way into the club. Fiona had left her flat keys on her work desk, half-hidden away between two separate messy piles of paper. He had discovered this fact as he'd cleared chocolate wrappers from her work area.

Not wrappers from chocolates his graphic designer had eaten from the stash in her bottom desk drawer.

But wrappers from the chocolates *he'd* eaten his way through while he'd examined her design program. He hadn't planned to eat the treats. He'd opened the drawer in search of a notepad and, though he'd told himself not to be tempted, somehow his hand had ended up in the drawer and the rest, as he focused all his attention on the nuts and bolts of her program and then on the work she'd done within it, had been, as they said, 'history'. He'd have to replace the candy stash before she got to work on Monday.

She was on the dance floor. His gaze locked onto her and he quickly forgot his thoughts. Dear God, she looked magnificent. A black skirt that came to just above her knees, high-heeled boots and a scoop-necked cream top that clung to her curves as she moved all combined to make her a highly irresistible package of appeal.

When the number ended, Fiona smiled at her partner and moved off the floor with him. She stood half a head taller than the man. At just about the moment Brent forced himself to acknowledge he felt jealous of that man, they joined a large group of people seated at some tables pulled close together.

The fellow put his arm around one of the women in the group and dropped a kiss on her cheek.

'Brent.' Fiona's exclamation came as he approached the tables. 'What brings you here—?'

'You.' The word was low, husky and far too intimate, reflecting thoughts that poured through him, pushed past his defences.

In her boots with the three-inch heel, she stood almost nose to nose with him. Brent wanted to trace all her dips and curves with his fingertips.

It had to be his autism speaking, a need for a tactile exploration to feed his thought processes the answers they sought.

Sure. You believe that, MacKay.

'Your flat keys. I found them on your desk after you left.' *That* was his reason for finding her here. Only that. 'You might have spares somewhere, but I didn't know.'

'I do have a spare set. *In* my desk at work. Oh, of all the silly things for me to do!' Her gaze searched his face. 'I'm so sorry you had to chase me down. I don't have my mobile turned on, either. It's a waste of time in here because I wouldn't hear it ring. How did you know—?'

'I heard you mention the name of this place when

you were on your mobile phone as you were leaving. There's no need to apologise. I couldn't have left you without your keys to get into your home.'

Fiona's mouth softened. 'Thank you.'

Just two simple words, and he leaned towards her. Brent straightened and his head tipped to the right. 'Ah—'

She was returning his glance, was as aware of him in this moment as he was of her, and Brent's need to protect his privacy fought with his need…for her.

But for what? To explore physical attraction with her? Because that was all he could want, wasn't it? For him, intimacy—true intimacy that involved opening up and letting someone else in was…out of the question.

And have you asked yourself why that is, MacKay? Why you're so determined to keep people at arm's length?

Brent knew the answer. He was different, and his 'different' wasn't something people, generally, would be able to accept. So he kept it to himself. He was happier that way. Comfortable.

Safe?

It wasn't about that. And he had every right to value his privacy, for whatever reasons he wanted to. And there was *nothing else* behind the way he felt. Nothing.

Fiona's gaze searched his eyes.

Brent stared into deep blue irises until he felt the stares of some of her friends *on him.*

She looked past him and seemed to force a casual smile. 'Everyone, this is my boss, Brent MacKay.'

A round of introductions followed. It gave Brent a chance to settle his reactions to her.

So why did they continue to simmer beneath the surface of every word, every exchange and glance?

Rejecting those reactions should be as easy as deciding they weren't in his best interests or, in fact, in hers. Brent had already decided that, so why…? 'I should get going.'

'Would you like to—?' She stopped, clamped those soft lips together.

Brent drew her keys from his pocket and, when she held out her hand, dropped them into it.

'Thank you.' Her fingers curled over the keys before she snagged her bag from the back of a chair and dropped them into it. 'Please, let me at least…I don't know… Can I buy you a drink or something? I feel awful, putting you out this way. We could go to the bar. I see a few spaces over there. Most people are on the dance floor right now, I think.'

The bar stretched across the entirety of the far wall beyond the dance area. It was further from the music than the tables here. Brent's voice emerged as a low growl of sound. 'A drink would be…nice.'

He'd led her halfway around the dance floor before he registered that his choice might not have been particularly smart.

When they reached the bar, they ordered drinks and Fiona watched Brent from the corner of her eye in the bar mirror and saw the way they looked together.

A dark head and a fair one. A lean, strong face and a soft womanly one. They looked right to her, side by side this way.

The image reached past her defences, left them in the dust, left her wanting deep silent things she couldn't want, couldn't let herself admit.

What did Brent want?

Nothing you can pin hopes on, Fiona. Remember that.

'I hope chasing me down with my keys hasn't interfered with other plans of yours.' She didn't quite meet his gaze. 'That is…it's none of my business of course… I simply didn't want to take you away from—'

A girlfriend? A lover waiting for him somewhere? The thought stung, yet it wasn't her business, was it?

'You might have come here with someone—?'

He spoke almost when she did, and then stopped, and their gazes met and held and the atmosphere between them thickened into silently acknowledged curiosity and a certain comprehension.

'I don't…'

'There's no one.' Fiona's heart began to beat more heavily in her chest.

They both lowered their gazes to their drinks, sipped.

Brent's face tightened as he looked up at her again. 'This—'

'I've been thinking about the Doolan project.' Fiona rushed the words out and took another fortifying sip of her lemon mineral water. If she made it all about work they could forget those moments looking into each other's eyes in a mirror.

Could forget the warmth and consciousness in their eyes, the desire that when they faced each other in reality, they both worked hard to hide.

A part of her wanted to see it again, even though following that path with him could only lead to hurt for her because he would do what every other man had done.

He would go cold on the idea of her sooner or later. He'd already shown the capacity for that.

So talk about work, Fiona, and ease through these moments and then let him go. 'I know the couple are at loggerheads with each other in their personal lives, but

I thought I might have an idea to keep both of them happy with our project plans.'

'Go on. I'm interested in any contribution you want to make.' It was clear he meant this.

And perhaps equally clear that he welcomed the change of topic to a work-related subject as much as she told herself she must take the conversation there.

The little sting of hurt was foolish and incidental, and she did her best to ignore its impact. 'If we use either of the couple's suggested overall ideas for the project, one of them is likely to resent the result.'

'It will be one more thing for them to argue about, and our company might get caught in the middle of that altercation.' His lashes formed thick crescents against his cheeks as he briefly dipped his gaze.

There was something almost vulnerable in that sight, and that made Fiona vulnerable as she softened towards him.

Maybe *they* needed to be at loggerheads so she could stop being so conscious of him as a man. Because, whether she wanted to be or not, she was, and, though she felt that same vibe back from him, he *was* her boss and he seemed determined not to notice her even if he *was* noticing her.

Oh, she had to stop this analysing!

Brent cast a wry smile her way. 'So do you think you and I could agree on something that might satisfy both of them?'

Far too easily.

So much for her idea of being at loggerheads for her own salvation. Fiona straightened on the stool. 'Yes. I think we could do it, for the sake of the project and for the company's overall good. It's simply a collaboration of minds, after all.'

'I couldn't agree more.' His nod was pure profes-
sionalism. The warmth in his glance was not, but he
masked that quickly and she told herself to stop
noticing. They sipped their drinks in silence before she
spoke again.

'To answer your question from earlier, I caught a lift
here with Stacey but I think she'll end up at Caleb's
place later.' The couple had been one of her 'fix it'
projects and had got back together after not speaking
to each other for three months. 'I'll head off myself
soon. I don't want a really late night.'

They'd finished their drinks. Somehow they were
both on their feet.

'Thanks again for bringing my keys to me, for taking
the time to do that.'

'Do you need a lift home?' He asked it in such a level
way, yet his gaze was not level. It was thoughtful and
cautious, offering and…almost braced for her to say no?

As if Brent MacKay would care whether she rejected
or accepted him in anything. He was a self-made, very
wealthy, highly eligible and extremely talented man. If
anything, he had the whole world at his feet.

*Yet that's not what you see in the backs of his eyes
at times when he drops his guard a little. That's not what
you saw in those photos with his brothers.*

Well, what Fiona looked for and believed she 'saw'
in those around her were things *she* had to guard. Her
family's discomfort with that side of her had proved
that. She tried to respond in kind. 'I left my car at
Stacey's place. I just need to get a taxi that far.'

'What suburb?'

Fiona told him.

Brent nodded. 'I'll drive you.' Decision made. 'It's

on the way. It would be silly for you to wait around for a taxi and have the expense of it when there's no need.'

'Thank you. I just feel guilty for bringing you out when you must have had far better things to do with your time than chase after a designer who can't even keep track of her apartment keys.'

'You're an artist. It is okay for you to forget things sometimes, you know. Some people would say it was almost obligatory.' They drew near the tables of her friends and Brent waited while she bade them all a quick goodbye.

Once they were outside he quickly hustled her to his truck and got them on the road. They didn't speak much at first. In the quiet of the night the truck's cab felt isolated and enclosed and…intimate.

If only she could be a little less conscious of him, but that didn't seem to be an option for her at the moment.

As he drove them towards her friend's home, she turned to him and searched his shadowy face. 'Were you at work late before you discovered my keys?'

'Yes. I got…caught up there.' His slight hesitation seemed to hold perhaps a hint of embarrassment. Or some kind of chagrin?

'Well, now I'm going to owe you twice as much of an effort when I attend the Awards night with you tomorrow night.' Fiona gave him directions as they neared Stacey's home.

He drove the truck into an empty space on the street and killed the engine.

It was a quiet residential street and she'd parked her car underneath a street light.

'Talk about your work for the company if that chance comes up. That's all I ask.' He climbed from the truck, crossed in front and opened her door for her. 'Let's see you to your car.'

When they got to her car she had her key ready and she turned to him and thanked him quickly and maybe that would have done it, except her nose bumped the side of his neck as she did that because he moved, and she moved, and she didn't anticipate his closeness and suddenly all the resistance seemed pointless because all the awareness was there, wasn't it?

He smelled good. Did she press her nose to his neck for the slightest split second?

Did he tip his head towards hers, encouraging that act?

Two deep breaths, one from him, one from her, and they were apart again, the silence an endless conscious-ness until his gaze met hers and she saw what had to be rare indecision inside him.

'I shouldn't do this. It's not smart.' His words were an echo of her thoughts.

And she wanted to know… 'Why do *you*—'

He shook his head. 'Maybe it's those long, tall boots. They're as good to blame as anything.' His hand closed around her upper arm. His lashes swept down over glit-tering green eyes that had gone from indecision to de-termination in…the blink of green eyes.

And Fiona's senses stalled and her heart stalled and inside her the war hit a new level of anticipation and concern, of need to engage and need to retreat and she thought, *Now. He's going to kiss me now.*

And it *was* what she'd waited for, hoped for without wanting to admit it to herself. Would it be such a bad thing, even if it might cause complications for them?

But he stood there very still, and his fingers tensed

where they held her. And his head twitched once, hard, to the right and the moment was lost.

Brent uttered a harsh, 'Goodnight,' and dropped his hand, and left her standing there while he walked away.

CHAPTER FIVE

'It's the autism playing out. Having that happen as much as it has lately in front of…other people makes me tense.' Brent muttered the words to Linc as the two men stepped out of his home the following night and into the communal corridor.

He tugged at the collar of the starched white dress shirt. 'You know how I feel about being in the public eye with that kind of thing.'

The loss of control of his condition in Fiona's company—he'd known it was happening from when he'd first met her. Because of that fact alone, he could forget any chance of being intimate with her. Not that he would have tried to pursue that. She worked for him, for starters, and she deserved better than he could give her.

Why was he thinking this way at all, anyway? He didn't want to examine his motives.

'Your autism is barely noticeable. Even when it does "play out", most people wouldn't figure out the source.' Linc drew a breath and his gaze searched Brent's. 'Are you sure that's what this is about?'

'What else would it be?' Brent spoke quickly, a little too loudly.

A murmur of voices sounded in the foyer below. Voices Brent recognised. His brother Alex.

And Fiona. Alex must have met her on the way in, before she had a chance to hit the buzzer.

He told himself he wasn't relieved to end the discussion with Linc.

'Good luck tonight, anyway.'

'Thanks.' Brent bade Linc a quiet goodbye and headed down the staircase.

When Alex spotted him, Brent's youngest brother excused himself from his guest, shared a brief word on the staircase with Brent and disappeared.

That left Brent and the woman at the foot of the stairs.

She was stunning. Utterly and completely stunning. The dress was creams and pinks and greys with a fitted top that left her arms bare and nipped in at her waist, then flared over shapely hips and thighs and fell to her calves in a soft swirl of fabric. It dipped into a discreet V front and back, caressing the curves of full breasts to perfection and revealing a lovely hint of the dip between her shoulder blades.

The dress showcased her beauty, but her beauty itself was what stopped his heart for a moment before a deep, warm feeling washed through him.

He couldn't explain it. Only that Fiona was soft and curvy everywhere. He wanted to immerse himself in that softness, body, mind and…something even deeper that he didn't fully understand that had something to do with all the softness there *hadn't* been in his lifetime.

Okay. So that was fine. Any man would want that softness anyway. It didn't need to mean anything particularly deep. Brent's body tightened.

'Good evening. You look wonderful.' Husky words, his gaze locked probably too intimately and directly on hers as he battled to pull his thoughts and reactions into place.

'Good…good evening, Brent. And thank you. I thought about not wearing heels but you won't mind if I'm eye to eye with you?' She stepped forward on the killer high heels in question.

Her hair was piled onto her head and pinned back with some kind of butterfly clip. Wisps kissed her nape, and she looked tentative and a little uncertain of herself, and the way she walked in those heels…

Why would she see herself as anything other than stunning? Brent's gaze rose slowly to her face and locked there. 'I won't mind.' He might go mad from the results of all that not minding, but no. He wouldn't mind.

Some of the tension seemed to leave her and her gaze shifted to encompass all of him in a swift examination.

Brent had just started to relax himself when she did that, and the blue of her eyes deepened. Her smile wobbled and she hesitated there in his foyer while a delicate flush rose in her cheeks. Desire flared, a small flame burning brighter, back and forth between them.

'*You* look wonderful, Brent.' Her quiet words held conviction, and unease, and a wary consciousness. 'I hope I'm not too early. Alex let me in. I've kept the taxi waiting, as you suggested.'

'The timing is perfect.' Everything about her right now was perfect and, because that was so, it seemed a good idea to get out of here and get his focus onto the business of the evening. 'I'm sure tonight will be a good PR exercise.'

'I'm looking forward to it.' Fiona chatted on about it as they made their way outside, almost as though she too felt the need to distract herself. 'The guest list should provide some opportunities to mingle both with industry professionals and also members of the public who appreciate what we do.'

'Those contacts will make the night worth it,' Brent agreed.

Worth stepping outside his usual guardedness, worth letting people see past his privacy and defences to a little of the man beneath.

Brent guided Fiona to the outer door with a hand on her elbow. She trembled beneath his touch, just slightly, just enough to make it impossible to think of anything but touching her.

When they climbed into the back of the taxi, closed themselves into the confines of that rear seat that somehow seemed so isolated despite the driver right in front of them, Brent noticed that intimacy again.

It was there in the knowledge of his body close to hers, their thighs touching where his legs sprawled and hers were folded neatly in front of her.

'I'm excited to have the chance to attend the Awards ceremony with you.' Fiona smiled as she turned her head to search his gaze. Smiled with an edge of awareness that he should have wished wasn't there.

Instead, a part of him that just didn't want to obey him revelled in her reaction, even as he thought of all the things he wouldn't like about the evening. 'I don't exactly adore public events, but this one is important for my work.'

'I could take them or leave them most of the time myself,' Fiona admitted, 'but I'm excited about tonight.

I want your nominated design to win. I've studied all the candidate works and yours is by far the best.'

Her faith in him made him smile. 'I appreciate your confidence in me, though there are several other very talented contenders.'

They discussed the other works and their designers for the rest of the journey. Brent talked, but he never lost his awareness of her. She smelled of soft woman's skin, of subtle perfume that made him think of a tropical stretch of beach at midnight at the height of summer.

As they arrived at the converted mansion that would house the Awards ceremony, Fiona vehemently assured him there was no chance anyone else would be the winner tonight.

Brent wanted so very badly to lean forward and kiss the passionate declaration right off her lips. He allowed himself one brief touch of her forearm with his fingertips instead and they climbed from the taxi and made their way past several function rooms to the largest one, reserved for the ceremony. He had to do better than this and yet, with each passing moment, his determination to keep at arm's length from her became more and more difficult to follow.

The venue was busy, with multiple functions taking place in a variety of rooms. Brent turned his attention away from all of that and focused on the woman at his side. *On their joint interest in the night's events, he meant!*

'Oh, why can't he stop droning on and hurry up and just announce it?' Fiona couldn't hold the words back any longer. She whispered them against Brent's ear where they sat at the table with a number of other guests.

Yes, she shouldn't have leaned in so close and let her

lips touch him that way, and no, she simply couldn't care about that fact right now.

They'd done all the right things all night, had mixed and mingled and every other thing they had to do. And all the while, through everything, the awareness of each other had simmered. Something had changed. Maybe it was Brent, maybe it was Fiona herself. Or perhaps it was both of them, striking sparks off each other in this different setting.

If he truly was attracted to her, if he was the exception rather than the rule…

A short bark of stifled laughter came from her employer's lips. He turned to smile at her, turned his head quickly enough that her lips brushed fully across his ear before she pulled back.

His smile turned to sensual consciousness between one breath and the next.

Fiona's senses fluttered as their gazes caught and held. A moment later she sat straight in her seat again and Brent sat straight in his and the keynote speaker continued his spiel about the history of the award. There'd been no break in proceedings, but her heart was pounding. That expression in Brent's eyes…

'The award.' She murmured the words beneath her breath. That was what was important right now. She shouldn't have said anything about the keynote speaker going on too much. She should have waited patiently and then she wouldn't have ended up with her mouth pressed to Brent's ear.

Well, right now patience wasn't her strong suit. Her senses were all out of whack because of what had just happened. And she wanted that award for her boss!

Are you sure you don't just simply want your boss?

Tonight, in formal suit, white shirt and bow tie, he looked better than James Bond. She could attribute his impact on her to the flattering clothing and the tie that exactly matched the colour of her eyes.

Her eyes. As though he'd chosen to wear it to complement her, not himself.

That's rather whimsical, don't you think, Fiona?

And attributing his appeal to any of those surface things simply wouldn't be honest, and she knew it.

Brent bent his head to hers and whispered, without getting too close to the shell of *her* ear, 'Whether I win the award doesn't matter one way or the other, you know.'

To a degree he was right. He would still be the highly successful landscape designer he was. But she wanted the industry recognition for him, believed he'd earned it, and wanted his peers and the various connections here tonight to see him win.

Fiona was about to explain those things when he reached out to cover her hand where it rested on the snowy linen of the tablecloth.

His deep voice whispered into her ear again. 'Don't stress, okay? We're fine here and look on the bright side. Whatever the outcome, we got a nice meal out of it.'

'We did, didn't we?' She laughed, as he had no doubt expected she would. And her hand turned. Her fingers curled around his and held on.

'For luck,' she murmured, and knew it was far more than that.

Brent made no attempt to break away from their joined touch. Instead, his fingers repeatedly stroked over hers as the speaker finally announced the third place, and a runner up, and finally, after a pause in which the whole room seemed to wait breathlessly…

'And the winner of this year's Deltran Landscaping Award is… Brent MacKay of Brent MacKay Landscaping Designs, for his design of Tarroway Gardens!'

'Oh, I *knew* they'd give it to you. I'm so proud, Brent. Congratulations!' Somehow Fiona ended up with her arms around Brent's shoulders.

By itself that would have been okay, but his arms closed around her in return and she felt the touch of his fingers against the flesh between her shoulders, the press of strong forearms covered in suit cloth against her upper arms.

The scent of his aftershave and his skin filled her senses and his mouth pressed against her hair. The moment of congratulation and excitement became something more, became a promise of what she had wanted all through this public night.

But people clapped, and the room and their surroundings came back. Brent got to his feet and gripped her hand and used that grip to tow her onto the podium with him. He introduced her and her role in the company, said a little about his work as he held their tucked hands at his side.

His acceptance speech was short and succinct and witty and wry. He stopped once in the middle and his shoulders tensed. His hand squeezed around hers before he seemed to relax and everything seemed all right again.

And then, award gripped in his other hand, he returned to their table and to a round of congratulations as the formality of the evening dissolved into industry talk, mingling and people drinking one last glass of wine while others lingered over pungent coffee served by waiting staff in smart grey coats.

There *were* some people like Brent's difficult client, people with certain aspirations, who now suddenly found Brent's business most interesting indeed.

Brent handed them business cards and let them know that if they wanted to book appointments to see him they'd be waiting at least a month. Fiona stayed at his side and simply gave herself the pleasure of watching people acknowledge his success. Pride in him joined other feelings and blended together inside her.

Finally they left the function room and made their way through the building's long winding corridors towards the front exit.

The doors to another of the function rooms just ahead swished open. Two men stepped through, one garrulous and talking a mile a minute, the other with his face turned half away, doing his best to ignore that man's effusiveness if his body language was anything to go by.

Fiona observed this and leaned on Brent's arm to peer across his body at the award statuette. 'It's a rather elegant tree, really. Sort of "eternal life-ish" in appearance, don't you think? I'd like to display it in a glass-fronted cabinet in the reception area at work.'

Brent seemed distracted by the men before them, but he forced a nod. 'We'll put *your* awards up at the same time—'

The men in front of them glanced their way as they drew closer. Probably they heard every word being said, but they weren't private words really so it hardly mattered, did it? So why did Fiona feel uneasy suddenly?

'Displaying all the awards would be nice,' Fiona murmured.

She would simply have walked on, but something

about the stillness of one of the men drew her attention and she looked his way just as Brent drew a deep breath and did the same.

As they all drew level, Brent wrapped his free hand around her wrist, a gentle touch that guided her to a stop, yet his expression when she looked into his eyes was not gentle, but oh, so determined and guarded and…braced. For what?

Fiona left her wrist in his hold. She wasn't sure if he even knew he had it clasped there.

Brent could have done without this, but he looked into the face of one of the two men before him and waited for recognition to dawn. Oh, not for himself. He'd recognised Charles immediately. But for the older man—God, for his *father*—it was apparently taking longer.

Memory hit Brent. Of his father frowning, pushing Brent into a car, muttering that he couldn't be the father of a freak. Brent had tried so hard as a child to control the outward signs of his condition. He couldn't remember any other way. Even now he could feel his body tightening, trying to make sure nothing of the autism showed.

Well, it had been too late then. Tight-lipped and silent, his father had taken him to the orphanage, signed him over and walked away.

'It's been a long time.' Brent was proud of the flat, even tone of his voice. He hoped that calm extended to his expression, even if his body was braced.

Charles was older, his hair was grey, but the dawning expression in his eyes was the same. Displeasure, discomfort, rejection.

For a moment Brent thought the older man might

simply walk on, not speak, and in that moment Brent knew he would not allow that. This time he wouldn't be ignored, brushed off. He opened his mouth to speak again.

'If I'd realised you'd be here—' Charles broke off, glanced at his companion and his frown deepened.

Brent recognised that look, too. It was amazing just how much came back to him. He'd thought it almost all forgotten. A twitch built at the base of his neck. He banked it down.

Fiona's glance made him wonder if she'd sensed that tension building. Her hand turned and her fingers closed around *his* wrist, and he thought she murmured, 'I know now where I've seen that before...' before she leaned into his side.

Then she gave a polite, plastic smile and said in a normal tone, 'Won't you introduce me, Brent?'

'Fiona Donner, meet Charles MacKay.' He didn't explain Fiona to Charles. He didn't explain his father's identity to Fiona.

Fiona's nostrils flared and the sparkle in her eyes flattened out until they were pure blue, expressionless chips. Her gaze turned to his and came back to his father and a thick silence fell.

Into that silence, Charles's companion spoke.

'You've won an award. Congratulations.' The man stepped forward and leaned in to examine the award, either oblivious at this point to the tensions in the air, or convinced he could actually do something about them. 'Oh, I see that's the landscaping industry award. I read about that in the club notices a few weeks ago. What do you think, Charlie?' He turned to address the question to the second man.

And what did 'Charlie' think? Was he surprised by Brent's success? Pleased by it? Discomfited by it?

Why care? His opinion means less than nothing. It's meant less than nothing for a long time now.

'The family resemblance is strong.' Fiona's words were low, the unspoken words written all over her.

This was the man who had given his son away. Somehow she understood so much. That knowledge hit Brent while a raft of emotions washed through him.

Old rejection. A need to understand.

His father's rejection, Charles's inability to love the child he'd helped create?

Brent pushed it all away before it could go any further. It was all past news. There was no point revisiting, though he couldn't be sorry this meeting had happened. At least he could say it was done now, and let go of the feeling he'd carried around of waiting to stumble across this man.

Yeah? So why didn't Brent feel any better or more resolved?

Because Charles was acting just the same, and some deep down part of Brent had maybe hoped, just the tiniest bit...

'Yes, we should be going, Fiona. I think we're done here.' As he spoke the words, Brent became truly aware of the curl of Fiona's fingers around muscles that had set like concrete. His free hand came up to close over Fiona's, to register the tension in *her* fingers.

She gave a sturdy tug, as though to shepherd him away from there, and her entire body pressed into his side.

The level of protectiveness he sensed in her in that moment stunned Brent and touched him in ways he couldn't define.

'Wow.' The jolly man's mobile face worked.

No doubt in another moment he would voice his conclusion that Brent and Charles were 'father and son'.

How would Brent's father explain that? He'd done such a good job of ignoring the fact that Brent had ever existed.

How *had* Charles MacKay dealt with that? An inconvenient accident that had taken his son so soon after the death of the older man's wife? If so, Brent was rather inconveniently 'resurrected'.

'If you'll excuse us.' The blandest of bland phrases. Brent decided it was somehow fitting.

He steeled his muscles to keep under his command. There would be no twitching of his head to the side, no drumming of fingers or anything else. Not in front of this man. No exposure. Brent started to turn away.

'Surely you'd have realised the major industry event in my calendar year was at this venue tonight.' His father's words stopped him. The displeasure and self-centredness in them was clear. 'You should stay out of the limelight altogether. I can't have—'

'I do what suits me. I've been in charge of myself for a long time now.' Anger made its way through Brent's reserve. That, too, he squashed down. It really wasn't worth it, was it?

Charles couldn't be proud of his success. The older man couldn't see past the shame he felt in Brent's existence.

You let Charles's shame impact on you, on how you live, how you present yourself.

Had Brent done that? Would he have looked at his autism differently if Charles had done so?

Well, Charles hadn't done, and that hadn't changed. Brent spoke with that thought fresh in his mind. 'If that doesn't appeal to you, you're welcome to stay clear of anywhere you think I might show up.'

As for Charles's business activities, Brent had little clue and planned to keep it that way. If they crossed paths again, so what? Brent wasn't about to actively keep away from anything for the sake of avoiding this man. What could Charles do, after all? Reject his son?

Been there, lived that, got the new and better, loving, close-knit family with Linc and Alex to prove it.

With that thought calmness came back to him. He *did* have Linc and Alex and they were what he wanted. Not the cold stranger in front of him.

'Good evening. Don't feel it's necessary to speak the next time we meet—'

'You must be highly medicated to succeed at hiding your flaw, even temporarily, for something like this evening.' His father's words held ignorance, accusation, harshness and confusion. 'I didn't know autis—'

'Obviously you don't know much.' Brent spoke over the top of the older man. 'Goodbye.'

He whisked Fiona away then. And he noted with some almost detached part of himself that his body responded perfectly to each of his commands.

Grip Fiona's hand. Lead her around the two men. Nod politely at the goggle-eyed companion in passing.

Stride away, relying on the length of those beautiful legs of Fiona's to allow her to keep up with his pace until they got outside and he sucked in a deep breath of cleansing air.

'There's a taxi. We're going. We're getting right away from here and from that—' Fiona's words were shocked, shaken. She flagged the cab forward with a hand that visibly trembled.

Brent turned his gaze to her and something deep and protective came to life in him. His voice was soft as he spoke, deep and gentle… 'Don't worry. Everything's fine—'

'No. It's not.' She shook her head, a decisive shake that said she wasn't about to be convinced.

And what else had she registered? Charles's final word? That Brent had autism?

Moments later they were ensconced in the back seat and her shoulder was pressed to his, their bodies tucked as close as she could get them as she gave her address to the driver without sparing him as much as a glance.

All her attention was for Brent. In part that made him uncomfortable, and yet…

'I should explain.' Brent cleared his throat. 'He's not… I don't…'

'What? He isn't important? You don't care that he rejected you because you're autistic?' The words burst out of her and then she chewed her lip. 'I'm sorry. I heard him, but I'd already wondered.'

It shouldn't surprise him that she'd come halfway to figuring it out. But now, thanks to Charles, Fiona completely knew the one thing that Brent had worked to keep to himself, where he could guard it and control it…and no person could judge him for it.

'Yes, I have a form of autism. It's less of a challenge physically or in other ways than many people live and deal with daily, but it's still an inherent part of me.'

The mix of emotions he felt as he told her this was difficult to define.

Fiona's face tightened and she whispered, 'How could he treat you like that?'

And Brent realised that for all he'd believed he'd

resolved this in his heart and mind long ago, there was still…something there. 'I—don't know. I don't know how he could have done that.'

The glitter in her gaze was anger and other emotions mixed. It made something inside him clench. He curled his fingers because suddenly he wanted to lace them with hers.

'This explains your ability to concentrate your focus so intensely when you're producing those amazing landscape designs.' Fiona drew a determined breath, deliberately seemed to calm herself. 'I've thought that was amazing. Now I understand it.'

She turned Brent on his ear by addressing his condition as though it were of benefit.

God, she was amazing, even if she wasn't seeing the whole picture. 'Well—' Brent realised he was simply sitting there, soaking in her warmth. He would have drawn away from Fiona then. He had to get this back to some kind of ordinary footing before his body started leading the rest of him, short-circuited what his brain knew he had to do, namely leave her alone, and got him in trouble.

'Please don't…shift away yet. I need…' Her words were low, a blend of anger and hurt and heart.

She had a generosity in her nature that Brent couldn't seem to help responding to.

'I know…that man revealed something about you that you obviously feel wasn't my business.' Her words were low, careful. 'He had no right to do that, but you can trust me with the knowledge. I'm just…furious about…'

'It doesn't matter.' Yet he couldn't deny his anger and old resentment. 'I don't need Charles MacKay's approval.'

'Maybe not, but you deserved his love and acceptance.' Fiona turned to fully face him and all her fury was in her eyes. Her fingers gripped his once again. 'You probably don't even want to think about him. We'll talk about the award. The night we had. It was a good night. You deserved to win. I said you'd get it, didn't I?'

She probably would have kept going, but he squeezed her fingers and laid them against his thigh and covered her hand with his. Set the award on the floor of the taxi so he could focus solely on her. 'I dealt with my father dumping me a long time ago.'

'What happened so that it was only your father making the decision to…stop parenting you?'

To reject Brent? Pass him off into strangers' hands because he didn't want to deal with a child who was different? 'My mother died. I was young. All I remember was he couldn't cope with my issues. Now he's got the problem that I grew up, made something of myself, and he doesn't want to have to acknowledge my existence.'

'He's the one who should be ashamed to exist.' Fiona uttered the words and let him see in her gaze all she was feeling. Her protectiveness towards him that was so sweet when he was perfectly capable of looking after himself.

Yet something down inside him admitted it would be nice. To have a woman's care.

Well, he couldn't do that, could he? He couldn't let himself care or wish to be cared for. Brent could take the hard knocks of life. But setting himself up for the embarrassment of rejection because of his condition—

That was one 'been there, done that' he didn't want to repeat.

Are you sure it's only about that, MacKay?

Tension pooled at the base of Brent's neck and he frowned. Of course he was certain. What else would there be?

'Here we are.' The driver's voice interrupted Brent's thoughts and he realised they'd arrived at Fiona's block of flats.

Brent still had Fiona's fingers pressed to his thigh, could feel their warmth. Her body remained pressed to his. Consciousness of her swept over Brent then, and pushed past his guardedness about his condition. His instincts took over and at this moment his autism didn't come into it. Brent's hand caressed over Fiona's. His fingers stroked hers.

A dozen different thoughts buzzed in Fiona's head, with as many accompanying emotions.

When Brent instructed the driver to wait, climbing from the taxi with her to start the short journey to her flat, those thoughts distilled into pure feeling. The touch of his fingers at her elbow as he guided her along the path, up the staircase and along the balcony that led to her flat.

The beat of her blood in her veins as she tried to decide whether to invite him in, say goodnight, talk about their night, the award, the good parts of the evening.

Of all of it, the trip back here in the taxi with their bodies close to each other had been the best. And for her, she had to admit, the most emotional.

His father had rejected him, abandoned him, all because Brent had a condition he had learned to live with and, indeed, to use to his advantage in business, in his work. His uniqueness only made him all the more appealing.

And right now he had his hand at her elbow and

Fiona's heart was beating a little faster because…she liked that touch.

Liked it too much for her safety? Attraction, that was easy to deal with, but was she more than attracted? Were her emotions involved? Because she really mustn't let that be the case.

He was her boss. She should say goodnight and walk inside… 'Brent, thank you for tonight—'

'Thank you for attending the Awards ceremony with me.' He paused. 'You got more than you bargained for with our exchange of a family night for the Awards night.'

'My family situation isn't even worth words in comparison to what happened tonight.' She shook her head. How could she even think her paltry difficulties with her family mattered now? 'Brent, I just don't know how to comfort—'

'Don't feel sorry for me.' Though he interrupted her, he did it gently, wrapping his fingers around hers where she'd been toying with her keys. 'My past is what it is. I've moved on from it.'

'Maybe, but you went on trying to conceal a part of yourself that you shouldn't worry about that way.' She bit her lip. Her breath stuttered in her throat and she whispered, 'I can't talk—'

About it any more? Brent certainly didn't want to.

'Then we won't talk.' He uttered the words with an accepting edge. 'I'd rather do this, anyway.' He bent his head to hers.

Touched his lips to hers.

A soft, seeking, giving and taking exchange. Lips to lips. How could it be all of this between them? And yet, somewhere inside herself, Fiona had wanted and needed his kiss and not even known how much she did.

Now she knew.

A taste of delight and sweetness and desire and pleasure. Her fingers wrapped around his forearms, and his hands were about her waist.

It felt good and right to have his mouth over hers, his fingers pressing into the soft flesh of her waist. For a few wonderful moments, she lived in the sensations of kissing him.

His mouth caressed hers as though he needed and wanted to kiss her this way. Their gazes were locked, his lashes dusky crescents that fanned against his cheeks as he focused wholly on her. And then those lashes swept down fully and her eyes closed too, and it was all sensation and feeling and the beat of her heart in her breast and the spread of such warmth all through her.

That warmth told its own story. She *had* invested emotionally in him, at least to a degree, even when she knew that was dangerous. A little hint of panic surfaced as Fiona made this realisation.

And the moment that panic hit, she realised something in Brent had changed as well.

He ended the kiss and dropped his hands away from her. Stepped back, and some kind of regret showed in his eyes. 'I shouldn't have done that. It can't go anywhere. You and I can never—'

He cut off the rest of the sentence, but he didn't need to finish it. Fiona could do that herself.

Now that he'd felt the reality, had *touched* the reality of her generous curves, he did not want her. The house of cards that had been desire and pleasure and closeness and a hope she should never have allowed, crumbled down.

Fiona tipped up her chin and told herself it didn't

matter. It absolutely, fiercely did not matter. 'Goodnight, Brent.'

'Goodnight. I'm—'

Sorry.

At least he didn't say it.

With one last glance from a troubled green gaze, Brent walked away.

CHAPTER SIX

REPEAT after me: I am a professional, I am a professional, I am a professional. I'm focused on my work, my career, my 'five year plan' and my goals for success...

Fiona attempted, yet again, for the umpteenth time, to figure out what was wrong with the feature plants in the painting she was working on. If she could feel settled or focused about anything at all, it might help her make a decent assessment of the problem.

And how could she feel settled when all of her was utterly distracted and had been since the night Brent had kissed her and walked away straight afterwards?

'Stupid thing.' She grabbed the open container of ochre paint from her work shelf.

Perhaps, if she blended a little white into it, she'd overcome the toning issue she had going on. If indeed the problem actually was a toning issue. The colour wasn't right. That much she'd known from the start. She just wasn't certain if that was the entire problem.

'I shouldn't call the painting names. I'm the problem, not it.' She muttered the words, set the container on a small work table and set about mixing the white in.

Overall, this painting was *not* going well. That much

she could say for sure, and that was a problem because the client expected to receive this artwork on Monday.

Brent was in the next room, working on something. Well, she assumed so. He'd had the door pushed across all morning so she couldn't be certain of anything, really, but she doubted he was having the same difficulties concentrating as she was.

In fact, he seemed just fine ignoring what had happened between them after the Awards night dinner. All of it. The revelation of his autism. The meeting with his father. Their kiss. His regret and rejection after it. Maybe it had been a sympathy kiss—for her sake. She had been very upset on his behalf and he was a kind man.

The thought made her cringe because to her it had been anything but that.

But he'd backed away from it, had clearly been put off by it. What other conclusion could she draw?

Fiona gave her paint one last vigorous stir. She would simply have to get on with her work, that was all. Take a leaf from her boss's book and only focus on the responsibilities they shared here. That was smart anyway. The only sensible thing to do, really, in the face of the fact that Brent didn't…want her.

So there. That was decided. Fiona snatched up her newly blended paint, briefly admired the glossy consistency of it and swung about to carry it to her easel.

'I need to go up into the mountains. This project—'

'I'm going to just focus on work… Oomph.'

As their words crossed each other, Fiona came up against a solid wall of chest. Paint hit that chest in a broad, gooey blob, slopped over her hand and splashed its way down until drips hit the floor.

'Oh, no.' The paint container wobbled in her hand. Fiona got it upright, but that was pointless now.

'I guess I should have knocked first or something.' Brent spoke in a slightly dazed tone while his fingers rose to his chest.

'It's my fault. I should have been looking at what I was doing.' Fiona's hand rose, too. She brushed at the dinner-plate sized splodge soaking into his shirt, sticking it to the firm muscles of his chest.

And then she stilled as Brent's fingers explored the paint, sliding back and forth through it, not to clear it off, but to get the full tactile experience of it.

The sight of that exploration was one of the most beautiful, sensual things Fiona had ever seen. Maybe he caught her staring because his fingers came to a stand-still and very green eyes searched her gaze while heat coated his cheekbones.

Embarrassment, but why?

Because that's his condition speaking.

'You must think I'm strange—'

'I'm sorry I stared. It was just that you looked so—' She couldn't complete the words. Couldn't tell him that his expression had made her imagine his hands stroking her skin that way.

'I…um…I've ruined your shirt.' Her mouth pointed out the ridiculously obvious while the rest of her tried to catch its breath. 'I was trying to fix a problem with this artwork. The colour change probably wouldn't have fixed it, anyway. I need to *see* the particular seed pod that grows on the plants I've used in the painting. The trouble is they don't go to seed pods until they're quite mature. I won't find what I need at any young plant nursery.'

Brent's glance moved to the half finished painting. 'What you have there looks...okay.'

'Yes, and that's the problem. Okay is synonymous with "average". It isn't good enough.' Fiona frowned at the painting. 'I need the real thing.'

He looked from her to the painting and back again. 'If you can't fix this it's going to drive you crazy, isn't it?'

'Yes, but how do you—?'

'Know how that feels?' He shook his head. 'Because I've just spent all morning working on a project and not getting it where I need to because the one part of it that's vital to the design I can't perfect until I study rock formations in the mountains. And, as it happens, the rock formations I have in mind are the only place I know of where you'll find your plants, complete with seed pods. It's where I spotted the plants before I incorporated them into that landscape design in the first place. They aren't normally stocked in nurseries. Linc sourced some young plants for me when I needed them.'

'If you could get me a look at some...' Without thinking about it, she took his hand in hers and used the base of his shirt to wipe as much of the paint off his fingers as she could. 'I hope that shirt didn't have sentimental value. I'll replace it, of course.' Her fingers worked at the buttons on the shirt. She got through three of them before he shackled her wrist.

'Don't—' He broke off. 'You'll get it all over yourself.'

'It's too late to worry about that.' It was too late to worry about a few things, Fiona realised, including the impact of revealing his chest to her gaze, even if she could only see a little of it. She dropped her glance so he wouldn't see the expression in her eyes.

He probably liked petite women with dainty feet who didn't have issues about plants, with or without seed pods on them... 'You should shower. There'll be residue soaking through onto your skin. At least it's not the most expensive brand of paint, but I'm sorry it got wasted.'

'Don't worry about that, and don't worry about the shirt.' Brent hesitated as he searched her face again. 'You've been putting in long hours, trying to get this painting pulled together. I shouldn't have asked you to produce something on demand for a project you weren't in on from its conception. I said I wouldn't let that happen more than once.'

'It's all right—'

'No, it isn't, but we'll make it right.' He wiped his hand on his shirt again. 'I came in to tell you I'm going into the mountains to study rock formations. Maybe you should come with me, see these seed pods, take photos, draw them, whatever you need.'

'A day trip.' A day to spend time with him. No. It wasn't about that. It was for work, had to be for that reason only. And Fiona had to look at it from that perspective. 'I'm a professional. I *have* to be able to produce the goods on demand, without special trips or anything else.'

'No. You don't have to be able to do that. I'd never expect that of myself and I don't expect it of you.' Brent's gaze became very focused as he said this. 'Finish up here in the office while I take my shower. When I'm done, we're going to swing by your place and my place for clothes and then we'll go. Bring the work boots you wore on site. They'll do for the trail I want to take you on.'

'O-okay.' What else could she do but agree? And be grateful, Fiona added silently as she glanced once again at her stalled painting.

'Good.' Brent gave a nod and turned away to head for the shower. 'Oh, and we'll be gone overnight.'

He walked off before she could even collect her thoughts.

An overnight stay in the mountains with her boss...

'And that's a square-tailed kite. See it?' Brent pointed into the branches of a tree to the left on the trail in front of them.

They'd been flora and fauna spotting for the past hour, indulging in guesswork when they didn't know what they were seeing, though in Brent's case he recognised most things, right down to a gold and white daisy Fiona hadn't seen in exactly its type anywhere before.

Fiona had photographed and sketched her seed pods. More importantly, she'd spent time simply studying them. Examining them from every angle, exploring the texture with her fingertips, feeling their weight and the roughness of their shells.

Brent's response to bush walking like this was very tactile, too. He would stroke his fingers over the spiky leaves on a bush, or stop to carefully examine a bottle-brush or some other native flower. That attention to detail carried through into his work as much as Fiona needed to carry it to her work. Fiona didn't doubt it was part of the reason his designs were so successful. She shouldn't wonder if that tactility would carry through into other more personal parts of his life, because those thoughts were adding to her consciousness of him.

His autism made him unique and special, and yet he

seemed determined to dislike it and hide its existence from the world if he could.

And Fiona needed to hide the existence of how attracted to him she was. She truly should have turned down the offer of joining him on this trip but, once decided, Brent had been set on the idea, convinced it would be good for both of them. And so far it had been. They were…enjoying themselves. It just worried her how much she struggled to do that without letting her emotions and feelings for him carry her in directions she shouldn't go.

'Is it really a square-tailed kite or are you making that up?' She was proud of the slight teasing tone she produced, the relaxed humour as she went on. 'I *think* I've heard of those, but I'm a city girl…'

'It really is one.' Brent's mouth quirked up at one corner, as though he understood that edge of humour and enjoyed it.

But their gazes caught in that moment and she lost herself in moss-green irises and in an instant the relaxed state of their interaction changed.

Part of her welcomed that, was fiercely glad that he hadn't managed to completely lose his awareness of her, after all.

The other part warned her not to think like that. She would only open herself to hurt from him all over again, though she knew he hadn't set out to hurt her.

Brent's head twitched to the side. It was only a little twitch in the scheme of things, but his gaze searched hers after it happened and suddenly every feeling she'd had the night they'd run into his father rushed to the surface to join with the rest of her confusion and interest in him that she needed to stifle, yet couldn't seem to.

'Families should love each other unconditionally.' The words burst out of her. 'There shouldn't be any question about it. That should simply happen as a matter of course. Your father was very wrong to reject you the way he did. He should have seen that you were unique and special, not less in any way.'

'Not less, perhaps, but I *am* different.' A lookout appeared on the trail to their left. He led the way down to it over steps hewn from dirt and rock and leaned his arms against the chest-high railing to look out over the gorge spread before them. 'I made a family for myself with Linc and Alex and I'm happy in that.'

Happy with his brothers—yes. Fiona believed that, and it was wonderful. 'It's just that you're very guarded—'

'An institutional training ground will do that. Linc and Alex are the same. I'm afraid that's something all three of us are going to be stuck with.'

'I can understand why that would be true, but people can change…' She was stepping over the line again, wasn't she? It happened because she cared about him, and that in itself was a cause for concern. Fiona turned back towards the trail and couldn't help her one final comment. 'Well, I believe your autism only makes you more special, and your work richer and more amazing for all you bring to it. I think that's something to celebrate about you.'

'You have…a very open heart and I appreciate you saying that.' Appreciated and felt disconcerted by her openness, if his torn expression was any indication.

They continued their walk in silence. Her outburst had probably been too much, she supposed, but his situation hit a particularly raw spot with her.

Because aspects of it bore an unpleasant likeness to

her treatment at the hands of her family. She'd said there was no comparison, but she couldn't ignore the similarities.

Fiona listened to the swishing of grasses and shrubs and the leaves of trees in the wind. Small birds and insects making their sounds, larger ones filling the air with clarion calls and sharp cries and warbles.

And she glanced at Brent and let the conversation move on because there didn't seem to be much choice. 'Thank you for this. I think I'll be able to do what I need to with my painting now.'

'I'm happy with my rock formation study, too. I consider the time well spent. We'll head to the house now.' As they completed their circuitous walk and approached his truck, he explained how he'd purchased the house in the mountains that he and his brothers now visited whenever they wanted to get out of the city.

'I'm looking forward to seeing the place.'

Brent started the truck and turned to face her while the engine idled and, oh, those beautiful deep green eyes were guarded and interested and thoughtful and self-protective all at once. Fiona longed to break through every barrier he had erected and know the man inside.

Yes, she wanted that even if it was dangerous to. Even though he had kissed her and then not wanted to be near her that way again.

'Seat belt.' Brent waited while Fiona strapped herself in. Her knowledge of his autism made him uncomfortable. He couldn't deny that. In his adult life, his brothers had been the only ones who knew of it. He didn't want Fiona to know of it, yet she did.

But it was more than that which had put lead in his

stomach. The sinking feeling came from a very old, very deep conditioning that his father had handed to him.

Brent forced himself to admit it. Charles had done a number on him and Brent hadn't managed to process and deal with that in the way he'd wanted to believe he had done.

'Sorry. I'm ready now.' Fiona gave a wry smile. 'I guess I was sitting there daydreaming.'

'It's no problem.' Brent's thoughts turned back to the woman at his side. Strands of hair lay in soft wisps against Fiona's face and neck. Their walk had put a soft flush in her cheeks.

She was lovely inside and out, and that *was* an ongoing problem for him. He'd helped her along the pathway and known he would have found some excuse to touch her even if there hadn't been a practical reason to do so.

Even choosing to bring her on this trip, he could have done things differently. He could have told her to forget about the painting…

He'd been a repeat offender where resisting Fiona was concerned. After the Awards night he'd kissed her. He hadn't even thought about not doing that at the time, let alone given himself a chance to decide against it. He'd simply leaned in and covered soft, warm lips and taken what, deep down, he had wanted from the first day they'd met.

He still wanted her. That was his problem. He wanted her and her gentle attitude about his autism, her determination to be accepting, even if she didn't truly understand the issues, didn't help him to resist. Brent's fingers drummed out a rhythm on the steering wheel.

'Is it far to the house?' Fiona gazed out of the window as they made their way along the road.

'Not far, but it's just as well we finished our walk when we did. Night falls earlier here, and there's often thick fog late in the afternoon. It's best not to be on the walking trails then.' He drew a breath. 'There's a small township between here and the house. We'll stop there and buy some groceries, and something ready to go to have for dinner tonight.'

They had to eat. It was too late to return to Sydney now. All he needed to do was treat the situation as though it were nothing out of the ordinary, and that was what it would be.

With this decision made, Brent drove them to the township. They shopped in one of those 'all things for all occasions' long narrow stores with foodstuffs lined along each outer wall and a single row up the middle. A barbecued chicken, a creamy potato bake and a big fresh salad air-sealed in a bag all made their way into the shopping basket. Breakfast items and fresh milk, and a glazed fruit and custard flan followed.

'I'll put on a hundred pounds if we add any more food like that.' Fiona made the comment half jokingly, but her eyes weren't laughing. 'Mum would have a fit if she saw—' She cut the words off.

But she'd said enough. Her mother had made a comment on the night he'd met her family.

I hardly think that's appropriate clothing for someone your size, dear.

Brent had assumed the comment was ill-thought out and something to do with fashion choices and Fiona being tall.

But it hadn't been that at all, had it? Fiona's mother

had been criticising her *size*. As though Fiona could do anything about being voluptuous.

As though she should want to!

'You don't need to worry about food intake. You obviously eat appropriately. Your size is right for you.' He growled each of the words more harshly than the last. And he piled apples and bananas into the basket, and some high nutrition, slow energy release snacks.

Fiona gave him a thoughtful, slightly arrested glance and then walked ahead of him through the store.

Brent dragged his gaze from the view of her bottom swaying in form-fitting jeans, tossed a few more items into the basket and followed her to the cashier's counter. His fingers drummed on the counter as the cashier processed his payment.

This time, he didn't even try to stop the incessant movement. Let Fiona look at it, think about what it meant.

She needed to start seeing his condition for what it was, not through rose-coloured spectacles, even if it was very kindly meant.

CHAPTER SEVEN

'I SHOULD set up my easel and have another go at this painting now.' The enthusiasm and inspiration was there inside Fiona, but she was also relaxed and mellow from the meal and the time spent chatting about nothing while they'd eaten.

She'd thought they'd be tense together but somehow they'd drifted into relaxation. Drifted in such a way that it was more dangerous than consciously thinking about it. 'I *think* I know where I want to go with the painting now. It'll mean starting over and I'm still considering a couple of aspects, but I brought a blank canvas—'

'Not tonight.' Brent's words were low, but firm. 'Rest tonight. Tomorrow you can paint.'

'What about your work?'

'I've got what I need.' He tapped his temple. 'It's in here. I'll let it churn in there for a day or two before I try to do anything more with it.'

And, when it had finished churning, something amazing would come out. His creative ability was something Fiona found extremely…appealing.

Brent seemed relaxed himself right now. Really

relaxed. Maybe that was because they'd done nothing but potter in the kitchen and get settled into their rooms before they stared out of the living room windows and watched the fog roll in until it obscured everything. Maybe Brent had relaxed because she'd stood back and left him to it while he'd organised their foodstuffs into regimented lines in the pantry and refrigerator just so.

Yet she got the impression he was deliberately allowing himself to do some of those things to prove something to her, rather than simply giving himself the freedom of them because he didn't need to keep secrets from her any longer.

'We could put on that MP3 disc you brought with you, listen to some music.' Brent raised his brows. 'If you want.'

'I would like that. I'll go get my music. I left it in my room in case I wanted to listen later when I'm going to sleep.' A little music, a little more relaxing. That would be a…nice way to round off the day.

A nice safe way.

She walked the length of the living room and corridor and went into the bedroom she'd been given, with its deep maroon and pale gold curtains. Fiona collected her music and went back out.

They sat on the sofa and listened and talked in a desultory fashion for the first hour. Made tea and drank it, and then the songs segued into a selection of dance tunes.

Two things happened. Fiona, who'd just carried their cups to the kitchen and left them there, danced her way back without thinking about what she was doing.

And Brent, who'd followed her with an opened package of cookies he'd placed away in the pantry cupboard, locked his gaze on the sway of her hips and a wave of male awareness rolled off him and over her.

'I…well…did you want to listen a bit longer or go to bed?' She uttered the words and then could have bitten her tongue out.

Oh, good way of putting it, Fiona! Heat blazed in her cheeks as she looked everywhere but at him.

She sank onto the sofa and lowered her gaze away from his. She didn't know whether to feel awkward for putting on that unplanned dancing display, or unsettled because her boss appeared to have enjoyed it. Or just purely embarrassed by what she had blurted afterwards.

'What I'd like is to dance with you to some of these tunes.' His words seemed to surprise him as much as they did her. He cleared his throat and took his seat on the sofa again and pushed his hands into his pockets.

Fiona understood that action now. If his hands were contained he wouldn't drum his fingers on things. How much self-control must it take *not* to do those things that must want so desperately to be done?

'I'd love to dance with you—'

'I don't often dance—'

Because of his autism? Did it cause problems with coordination? She hadn't seen that in other circum-stances. And she shouldn't have made it sound as though she was begging for him to dance with her. 'You don't need to—'

Brent stared at her for a long moment through a screen of silky lashes before he got to his feet and held out his hand.

Fiona rose and put her hand in his.

For starters she kept her hand in his while they moved a little to the music.

It was…nice. A thread of excitement ran beneath the calm and she let that be there and relaxed without meaning to because, in the scheme of things, what more was this than Brent enjoying himself and not seeming stressed and Fiona just wanting to enjoy the moment, too?

'I'm guessing you probably danced with several of the men in your group that night at the club.' His words were a quiet murmur. 'Really danced, that is. Not…like this.'

'I'm lucky that group all enjoys dancing with anyone rather than sticking to partners only.' She did feel lucky—and safe. Accepted for herself. Well, for herself and for lending a friendly ear to all their lovelorn problems.

But she didn't want Brent to think this experience was second rate. It was not. 'I'm enjoying this, too.' The words were perhaps a little breathless, a little more revealing than they could have been.

His fingers tightened over hers. That was all, and yet it felt like a complete change from where they'd been, to the promise of something more.

Brent left her for a moment to close the curtains. A moment later her hand was back in his—both her hands were in his and they were swaying to the music.

'The night I brought your keys to you, I thought you were with the guy on the dance floor.' As Brent spoke the words, the light overhead flickered once, and again.

They both glanced up just as the bulb died. The music kept going, but now the living room was nothing but shadows.

'I don't know if there are any spare light globes here.' Brent's words sounded deeper in the near darkness. 'I don't remember seeing any in the cupboards.'

'It might make more sense to search for them in the morning, anyway.' When it was daylight. Fiona went on. 'It's ages since I've danced in the dark.' A very long time, and never like this. She worked hard to hide the breathless edge in her voice that had nothing to do with exertion. 'I used to do it with my girlfriends sometimes in the "silly" teenage years. It was a way to dance however we wanted with nobody to judge or see.'

'Then dance in the dark.' He drew her closer until his hands were around her waist. 'And I'll…be here with you while you do it.'

Fiona's arms rose naturally to his shoulders. It felt… right to move closer, to sway in his arms while he held her. She let herself have the moment.

Brent's eyes had adapted to the shadowy dimness. Enough that he could read the dreamy quality in Fiona's eyes and the softening of her mouth that told him they had taken this to a place he shouldn't have allowed it to go. He knew what he could and could not have with her. This…closeness didn't come under the 'could have' category.

He should release her—now—and leave the room.

He didn't do that.

He didn't *want* to do that and, for once, he was going to give himself what he did want. For a little time, a safe amount of time. Five minutes. Ten at the most. What could that hurt? Just to hold her while she danced? That wasn't the end of the world. That didn't have to get them into any trouble at all.

And if his urge to hold her was more need than want—

It wasn't.

Of course it wasn't.

A twitch built at the base of Brent's neck, and that was something else he didn't want to think about right now. The manifestation of his condition that made him different from others. Instead, Brent focused his attention on the feel of Fiona's waist beneath his hands. He held her close and breathed in her scent and felt her softness and they danced. For that period of time Brent set aside his issues and just…*was.*

They danced for hours, or at least it felt that way to Fiona. Brent's gaze held hers in the dimness, unmoving, so focused.

The music slowed to a dreamy number and Brent took a step closer to her and murmured, 'You put your whole heart into it when you dance. It's…beautiful.'

His hand rose from her waist, up, until he had her hand clasped in his. He lifted her hand from his shoulder, moved it to his chest and cupped it there.

And, oh, it was the most wonderful feeling to have that one small connection with him and know he'd sought it, that he wanted it. That here in the shadowy room, for just a moment, he wanted this.

She curled her fingers into his and let the beat of his heart guide her while they swayed to the music.

Just trust me, Brent. Dance with me and trust me so you can be all of yourself with me.

Her heart ached with the need for him to do that. To relax with her and not modify anything about himself. And maybe she ached just as much for her own need.

'You dance beautifully, too.' She wanted him to pull her even closer so their bodies were flush against each other.

Yet keeping a little distance held a certain safeness for her because, even though she knew herself, knew her body size and her shape and her height and all the times she'd accepted she wasn't the build most men found appealing, if she and Brent didn't get *too close* then he wouldn't be too confronted by those things about her this time…

Oh, what a way to think!

The song ended and another began. A slow song from a popular romantic movie. Brent tugged her forwards and their bodies brushed and she *couldn't* think. Not while they were chest to chest, thigh to thigh and his arms were around her. They danced for real. Two people on a polished board floor in a living room in a house in the middle of nowhere in the mountains, dancing as potential lovers would.

How could she think of work in this moment? How could she see him as her boss when his arms held her and all she wanted was to lay her head against his shoulder and feel those arms close around her even more securely?

They danced like that through one song and another and another until Brent finally lifted one hand to the back of her head and spoke. 'I meant to stop after ten minutes. I didn't know I could do this at all. I thought—'

He'd thought he would do something that made him feel uncomfortable or embarrassed?

'I like the way you dance.' *I like the way you do so many things.*

He pressed her cheek to his and swayed with her to the music. 'I like this with you. *You* dancing.'

'Us dancing. Together.' There. She'd said it. Named it. And they were. Body to body, her heart to his heart as the music swept them away and she had what she had wanted. More closeness. A deeper closeness with him.

Fiona couldn't say just when they ceased to dance, or whose arms rose first to change the dance to an outright embrace.

It just happened and it felt right. Fiona didn't want to think about any of it or all the negative things her family had fed into her mind over the years about her size and her personality.

When she lifted her gaze to search his eyes, Brent let her see the glitter of need and awareness and attraction in their depths. There was a question, too, and she answered it in the tilt of her chin as his mouth lowered to hers, in the angle of her head to accommodate that melding of lips upon lips.

He stood perfectly still and kissed her.

His fingers dug into her back in a kneading motion, and he kissed her.

The pads of those fingers rubbed across and back over her upper arms beneath the loose sleeves of her shirt, and still he kissed her.

These were the reactions he worried about, that slipped through his control now, perhaps because he *wasn't* controlling himself.

To Fiona they were pure beauty because they told her he enjoyed touching her. She melted into his embrace and his arms and his mouth and his attention and loved all of it.

She lifted her hands and cupped his face with her fingers and breathed in the scent of him and wanted his kiss to never end.

When he drew her closer still, his body unashamedly craving hers, Fiona melted all over again.

'Let me…I need…' His words were deep, disjointed, hungry.

Anything. Whatever he wanted…

'Fiona…' He said her name and buried his face in her hair where it lay against her nape, and he breathed harsh and deep while a wave of tension built in his body, locked his muscles, even as he locked her to him.

'Brent.' She raised her hands to his back, rubbed them across those locked muscles and tried to soothe the tension from him.

His neck twitched. Once. Again.

He sighed and his hands tightened on the balls of her shoulders and he straightened and put distance between their bodies, and dropped his touch away from her.

Brent's guard went up, even as she watched him.

He closed his eyes and took in a single deep inhalation and held it. When his eyes opened again it was to look deep into hers before he spoke.

'You think you can accept my autism, but to you it is nothing more than a few random things that don't seem so unusual.'

'They're *not* so unusual. Lots of people have similar things about them.'

'You haven't seen what my father saw.' As though his words had surprised him, Brent stopped abruptly. 'I have nothing to offer in a…normal relationship. For my brothers I've found affection, appreciation, caring, but they have all of me that there is to give. I don't want to hurt you. That would happen if I…let you close and then couldn't give you those things. You deserve those things. This isn't because of you…'

But wasn't it? Oh, it was clear Brent believed what he was saying about himself, his capacity to care for others. Given his upbringing, the guardedness she'd seen in his eyes, in his history, Fiona could understand that. It was good that he could see this much of himself, that it went deeper than purely the fact that he had autism.

But in the end Brent was rejecting Fiona in the same

way his father had rejected him. She had no defence against that, other than to walk away from that aspect of him and her and…try not to look back.

'You're right. We wouldn't be suited. I can see that now. I'm…grateful you put a stop to things when you did. We'll both be careful to keep things strictly on a business footing from now on. That's all we need. And…to stay away from this kind of situation.'

She whispered goodnight, left him to worry about the stereo system and walked away through the darkness to her room at the end of the corridor.

At her door, she turned and spoke through that darkness to him one more time, with all her effort focused on how she needed to come across to him, whether she hurt down inside right now or not. 'I think I'll be ready to paint in the morning. That's why we came here, after all. That and for you to study rock formations so you could nut out your new design in your head. Maybe you'll get a long way with that now, too.'

In fact, Fiona knew she would be ready to paint in the morning. She was no longer blocked. Because she'd found what she needed. She'd found the emotions that needed to go into her painting.

She'd found warmth and pleasure and hope and connection.

Brent had tried to shut them all down, but they hadn't gone away for her. So she would take them to her art and release them there.

CHAPTER EIGHT

FIONA did get up and paint. She painted her heart onto the canvas and painted Brent's heart as she perceived it without censoring herself or trying to understand all of what it was she believed she knew of him. Only that he was complex and giving and guarded and restless and still and so many things all rolled into one, and that he had made his choice against intimacy with her, at least *believing* it was in both their best interests for him to make that choice.

He had probably saved her from a great deal of hurt further down the track by taking this step now.

Right. She should feel very resolute at this point.

So why didn't she?

Fiona handed the painting to the clients and they seemed more than pleased. A week passed. Brent spent much of it shut in his office or, when he wasn't sequestered in there, working from his home and leaving Fiona to her own devices.

Their personal situation was one thing. A good, workable business relationship was another and currently that relationship was suffering.

That side of things had to be addressed and Fiona was about to address it.

Well, if indeed he was actually ignoring her and not simply busy and focused and home surroundings were working best for him at the moment…

Fiona parked her car, hefted her half-finished painting in her hand and walked the short distance to the front of the MacKay brothers' warehouse home. She reached for the buzzer.

As she did so, her mobile phone rang.

'I've been working on my ideas for the project we discussed on the phone on Friday.' Brent's low voice filled her ear. 'I have the results spread out at home and I…would like you to take a look. Are you on your way to the office? Could you swing by here first?'

'Well…yes.' Most of Fiona's whipped up determination to force Brent past avoiding her evaporated. He'd probably just been busy thinking through project ideas anyway. Rather arrogant of her to put it down to him trying to stay away from her!

'I have a painting started that I want to show you for the same reason.' She cleared her throat. 'Actually, I'd decided to stop by with it. I'm standing outside your door now. I was about to press the buzzer.'

Given she felt a little silly now, she hoped he would assume it was nothing more than enthusiasm for the project that had driven her actions this morning.

There was a short beat and then Brent said, 'Good. I'll come down.' He let her in moments later and for one brief second his gaze searched her face and seemed to take in all of her at once.

'Come upstairs. I should have brought you in on this

last week.' He kept walking, didn't meet her gaze as he went on. 'I've needed your input.'

'We need to maintain a good working relationship.' Fiona forced the tentative edge from her tone. 'Anything else aside.'

'Exactly.' He nodded. 'All the rest…aside.'

And, that easily, Fiona felt so much better. Even though feeling better because he sounded as unconvinced as she felt wasn't exactly sensible.

They climbed the stairs and entered his home together. Brent had the materials for the project spread in a long, neat line from one end of the floor space in his living room to the other.

He stopped abruptly and ran his hand over the back of his head, frowned and then dropped his hand to his side. 'It makes the most sense this way.'

'And that's perfectly fine. It looks the same as the work laid out in your office.' She said it without inflection and was rewarded when his shoulders lost some of their tension.

'Let me take that for you. I want to see it, too.' He took her painting from her hands and propped it onto a lounge chair he turned to face them.

Then he stared at the work she'd done while she gave her explanation and the more she explained and he looked, the more he nodded and comprehension sparkled in his gaze.

He touched her for the first time in days, then. Pressed his fingers to her forearm as he smiled finally and turned her to look at the first of the materials spread across his floor. 'I *thought* I'd handled the concept the right way. Now that I've seen your painting, I'm certain of it. We make—'

He didn't complete the sentence, but Fiona looked at his work and knew what he'd been going to say.

They made a good team.

And they did. If only…

No. No *if onlys*. There was this, and it had to be enough. Fiona dropped to her knees on the floor to look at his drawings, the images he'd taken from books and arranged into a collage with notes between.

His entire vision was there, and her vision was there with it, the perfect complement to his work, and somehow that was just as intimate to her as anything that had passed between them.

She pored over his plans. That led to questions, lively discussion, and to her forgetting for a moment her other concerns as she immersed herself in the work, until finally she understood the entire concept—and was so impressed by his vision for it.

'I'm glad you can see where I need to take this, that you saw the same potential I have.' Brent held out his hand to draw her to her feet.

Fiona stifled a second set of *if onlys* and clasped his hand. She tried not to think of it as anything other than a courtesy to help her rise.

Her knees were all but numb and she glanced at the clock on his wall. 'I didn't notice so much time had passed. They'll be wondering at work where on earth we both are.'

Brent's fingers tightened around Fiona's hand as he helped her to her feet. She'd been crawling around his floor, automatically respecting his need to have his plans laid out in that long straight line he hadn't even thought about when he'd decided he needed her to come and look.

Had he really needed that so desperately this morning? Or had he needed this? He glanced down at their joined hands. This touch of her? This closeness to her? This re-connection through their work, through the emotions she took to her work and claimed he took to his work? He was starting to think maybe she was right about that, that he did, indeed, give parts of himself to his creative process that he otherwise tried to hold back elsewhere.

And here was Fiona, respecting his autism and the ways it affected him. And putting her whole heart out there as she always did, even while she tried to protect it.

He had to stay emotionally detached from her. He'd let down his guard enough with Fiona that he hadn't considered what she'd think of the way he prepared his materials, of his obsession with the project overall. That knowledge unnerved him.

It also didn't help him fight his growing attraction to her, and he didn't know where to go with this. The con-sciousness of each other remained, a constant ripple of unspoken thoughts and responses between them. They were both doing their best to ignore it. He'd told her he was determined to ignore it, but his actions weren't proving out those words right now.

He'd wanted to make love with her when they'd been away in the mountains. With Fiona it would definitely be too intimate and intense for him to be sure he could manage and control his responses.

And why was he thinking of making love with her anyway? That wasn't something that could ever happen.

Brent's lips tightened.

'We should head into the office.' He should probably not have asked her to come here, shouldn't have spent so much time with her, utterly absorbed in this one project and oblivious to anything else in existence. Except Fiona herself, and that was even worse. 'You'd probably like to get some other work done before the day disappears completely.'

'I think you're right.' She dusted her hands over her knees and gathered her painting. Perhaps she realised belatedly, too, just how distracted they'd allowed themselves to become, how easily they'd fallen into an intimate rapport with each other.

Yet they had to work together and do that well. Where did that leave them? He couldn't keep avoiding her the way he'd done in the past week. 'Fiona—'

'It's good that we're back on a better footing.' Her smile was full of determined good cheer that didn't quite erase the tinge of…sadness in her eyes? 'After getting slightly…off course while we were away. Circumstances, surroundings, can put people in that place, but we've sorted ourselves out now, haven't we?'

Right. And yet the attraction was still there between them. Still just as strong.

It would go away eventually as they both accepted what their roles with each other needed to be. Wouldn't it? He should be grateful for her determination, not feel as though both of them were somehow being short-changed in this.

'I'll head away now and see you when you get to the office.' Fiona moved towards the door and Brent…let her.

This was best, after all.

His mobile phone rang then. It would have been easy to ignore it but he'd trained himself to always check the number in case either of his brothers needed him. Brent checked and quickly answered. 'Linc. What's up?'

'There's a warehouse fire. I saw it on the TV Cecilia had on in the staff area at the nursery just now.' Tension edged his brother's tone. 'I couldn't tell for sure, but it *looked* like Alex's warehouse. The street and the location—I'm headed back to the city now, but it's going to take time for me to get in.'

'I'll go straight there.' Brent snatched his keys from the stand inside the front door and strode forward still talking. 'You've tried to contact him?'

'Yes, and I can't get him either at the warehouse or on his mobile.' Linc cursed. 'Look, I have to end this call. There's fog here this morning and I've already had one closer encounter with a kangaroo on the road than I would have liked. Even speaking on hands-free, I can't afford to be distracted.'

'Keep safe, Linc.' They ended the call and Brent was out of the door before he realised Fiona was right on his heels, painting clutched in her hands.

'What's going on?' she asked. 'We'll go down while you tell me.'

They hit the stairs at a ground-eating pace as he explained the situation. A ball of tension had lodged in his gut. 'I have to find Alex. I have to make sure he's safe.'

Nothing can happen to my brother.

The thought came to him uncensored, an outpouring of how much he needed Linc and Alex. Of how much he loved them both. They may not have been born of the same blood, but they were bonded in all the ways of family. There were two people in the world who hadn't rejected him, condition and all, and who let him love them just as much, and Brent... *needed them.*

Fiona doesn't want to care about your condition, either, and you know your *hesitations go deeper than that.*

Because, in the end, could Charles MacKay have rejected and abandoned Brent solely because Brent had what was for him a manageable condition that shouldn't have mattered to a parent? That in fact should have made that parent care for him all the more?

Something deep inside Brent shifted as he absorbed this thought.

And Fiona's history—her family not caring for her the way they should have? *She* was perfect…

'Hurry, Brent. We have to make sure Alex is okay.' Fiona climbed into the utility truck beside him and tossed her painting into the back with scant concern for its care.

He hadn't anticipated her company. Hadn't taken the time to think about it at all. Now, he turned to her while his heart seemed to soften at the expression of concern on her face. And his fears for Alex came back full force, driving, for now, everything else out. 'You don't have to—'

'Yes. I do.' Fiona interrupted her boss without any compunction whatsoever. She had to be here with Brent, to be at his side while he located his brother. That was all there was to it. She couldn't change what she needed. She wasn't about to be denied this, either. So he could just get over that idea! 'Drive, Brent.'

Brent drove, his hands gripped around the steering wheel.

There was such love for Alex in Brent's focus, and Fiona couldn't help but be moved by that.

Any time Brent was focused intently it seemed to come back to things that touched his emotions. Her boss might not want to admit that, but its truth spoke for itself. He *was* a man capable of deep feeling. This morning, for reasons she wasn't sure she should try to define, Fiona needed to know that.

'Alex caused me a few grey hairs when I first got him out of the orphanage. The moment he turned sixteen, he came to me. To me and Linc, but I was the eldest, and a bit better set up at that stage.' His mouth turned up in wry remembrance. 'Alex and his bags of attitude. He settled down, though. I've got used to things being easier the last few years. Financial security for all of us. Safety…'

Both those things would have been hugely important for three men who'd had little control over their destinies for many years. And they'd no doubt used their earliest resources to buy a home they could all share, so they could stick close.

Yes, they were a true example of how family should be and for Brent, at least, he'd built that new world over the top of some very unhappy ashes.

Fiona thought of her own upbringing. 'I wish I could say my family were like you and Linc and Alex, but they're not.'

Her family did lack what should be there for her automatically, simply because she was theirs. But couldn't it be there, simply hidden away? Maybe they needed a little more encouragement to come to realise she needed them to love her simply for herself? Maybe she just hadn't tried hard enough, reached out to them enough? If she poured out her love to them, surely they would respond?

Brent parked the truck and they climbed out.

They'd had to park some distance back. He wrapped his fingers around her upper arm and guided her at a half jog past bystanders, through the crowd of in-evitable onlookers.

As they drew closer, he sucked in one long, deep breath and blew it out. 'It's not his building that's on fire.'

He pulled his mobile phone from his pocket then and speed dialled it again as they hustled along. 'Still no answer.'

They reached the cordoned-off area in time to see several soot-smeared fire personnel emerge from the burning building. It was a terrifying sight. Men in full hazard gear, two of them with warehouse workers in their arms. Flames crackling, the roaring sound of a burning blaze as it consumed a path of destruction.

'There he is. Thank God. He could have been killed.' Brent uttered the words as he strode forward. 'This isn't the same as him listening for the rush of wind that comes before a train roars around a blind corner in a tunnel, giving you just seconds of warning to get out of the way. There's no predicting fire.'

He grabbed Fiona's hand and plunged them beneath the cordon.

'Alex did that?' she asked, but, from Brent's 'grey hairs' comment, she already knew the answer was yes.

Someone called for them to stay back, that they weren't allowed in.

If Brent heard, he ignored it. His focus was on his brother.

Alex had just finished giving water to a woman prone on the ground. His suit, face and hair were covered in soot. He laid the woman's head gently back down, spoke a few words with her and, when an ambulance officer approached, stepped back.

'You know most people undergo training before they

start rushing into burning buildings.' Brent's words were low, gentle and raw at once, though Fiona could see he was working very hard to hide the latter emotion.

Even so, he clasped Alex into a bear hug for a long moment before he held him at arm's length and searched his brother's eyes, face. 'You're not injured? How did you end up in there?'

'Should have figured you'd find me before I had a chance to clean up.' Alex gave a lopsided grin. 'At least you're not hauling me away from trains and tunnels—' He broke off, glanced sheepishly at Fiona.

'I just mentioned that to Fiona, actually.' Brent shook his head, but his eyes were warm as they searched Alex's face again.

Certain aspects of Alex's paintings, colour choices, style came to Fiona's mind—came together with those comments about trains and tunnels. Graffiti art... 'I think you gave your big brother some tough moments while you were exploring your...er...talents, Alex.'

'Something like that.' He ducked his head with a self-conscious cough that quickly turned into the real thing.

Brent gave the younger man's shoulders one firm shake. 'Have you been checked out by the medical staff?'

'Yes, and they said I have to take today off work, which is stupid. It's just a cough. All I need is a shower and change of clothes before I go back to it.' He paused and gestured towards the building. 'They have everyone out now, at least. They got the last two just as you arrived.'

'And now you need rest and...' Brent hesitated and his brows came down. 'Rosa. You need Rosa. She'll know what to do to look after you.'

A short debate followed about how much Alex did

or didn't need to be off work or babysat. That took them all the way to Brent's truck, where Fiona climbed into the back so the brothers could be together in the front.

Brent made the call, so whatever Alex wanted was apparently, at this point, irrelevant.

Fiona hid a smile.

She looked at the backs of those two heads; saw the set of Brent's shoulders and the way his head ticked to the right as he glanced once again at Alex, as though to reassure himself the youngest MacKay really was okay.

And emotion welled up out of nowhere and flooded through her. Emotion for this man who had made a family out of nothing, and made it work better than her 'real' one ever had. She didn't have a 'work only' attitude to Brent. Somewhere along the line that had changed, despite her belief that she couldn't allow that to happen.

And maybe she needed to at least admit that fact to herself, even if doing so couldn't change anything between them.

'Tell me how the fire started.' Brent dropped the topic of Alex's health as he headed for their warehouse home. 'And how you ended up in the middle of things like that. I'd like you to say you weren't even in the building but, from the look of you, I'd say multiple trips without any safety equipment or protective gear is more likely.'

'Half a dozen trips. I was careful.' Alex explained he'd spotted the start of the fire from his own office window, called it in and headed straight there.

And Brent listened and nodded and was clearly trying very hard not to let his head explode over all the things that could have happened to his brother and, thankfully, hadn't.

He drew the truck to a stop inside the warehouse's garage area and turned to Alex once again. 'I understand you couldn't have done anything differently. You no doubt saved lives today. How can I chide you for that? I'm just glad you're okay, that's all.'

As they all got out of the truck, Brent drew out his mobile phone and hit a speed number. 'Linc. Yeah. I've got him. He's got a chest full of smoke fumes and a couple of singed patches, but he's okay. Meet us at home, okay?' He ended the call.

Fiona hesitated as the two brothers headed for the staircase. 'I can head to work now, put in a belated showing for at least one of us since we haven't been in yet. I don't want to intrude on your family time—'

'Stay.' Alex uttered the single word while his gaze shifted from her to Brent and back again. There was something in his expression—a question and perhaps even hope—that Fiona didn't understand.

Brent's mouth tightened and he headed for the stairs. To Alex he said, 'Fiona and I were *working* on a *landscaping outline* here earlier this morning, so neither of us has been into the office yet.' He turned to Fiona and added, 'We might as well go at the same time when we do go.'

'At least my car's in all day parking.' Even if it hadn't been, Fiona would have forgotten about it one way and another this morning!

The change in Alex's expression was subtle.

The statement in Brent's was a little less subtle.

Fiona caught on at last and her face heated as she realised what their exchange had been all about. Alex had thought she and Brent had spent the night together and, from his expression earlier, he'd hoped that might have been the case.

Why?

Well, bachelors being bachelors, maybe she was better off not knowing why!

They went straight to Alex's home. He tipped out his smashed mobile phone from his trouser pocket. That explained the lack of communication earlier.

'Did you get cut when that happened?' Some deep ingrained mothering instinct rose up in Fiona as she waited for Alex's answer. She wanted to insist he go check on that right this moment.

Brent turned his head when Fiona asked this question and sharp eyes examined Alex once again.

Alex shrugged his shoulders. 'I'll check it when I clean up. Shame about the phone, though. I really liked that one.'

The door pushed open and Linc stepped through. He strode straight to the living room where they stood. 'Reminds me of the time we got locked into the orphanage while that fire raged next door. I thought we were all going to burn, shut in there, before they decided it was "safe" to let us out.'

As he talked, he examined his brother through shrewd eyes. 'You're all right, then?'

'I want him through the shower, cleaned up to get the smoke off him.' Brent uttered the words before Alex could respond for himself. 'When she gets here, Rosa can go in there and check—'

'No. Rosa can *not* go in there and check. Anything,' Alex added, and sighed as the door pushed open yet again and a middle-aged woman bustled through it, shaking her head all the way. 'And yes, Linc,' Alex added, 'I'm all right.'

'Alex, Alex. You look a mess.' Rose made a tutting

sound. 'Get those clothes off and take a shower!' She had a large carrier bag in one hand and headed for the kitchen with it while the men all sort of shuffled their feet and stood there. 'Well? Get going, Alex. I want you back out here by the time I've heated the chicken soup.'

Fiona stifled a smile in her chin, but Brent caught the edge of it as she turned her head.

'Rosa lives close to here,' he said, as though that explained everything. And then he fell silent.

Alex dutifully disappeared to shower. Linc filled the silence with his questions. What had happened? Was Alex truly okay? Had he honestly had appropriate medical attention?

When the youngest brother reappeared, Fiona couldn't help her words, either. 'Were you cut?'

'No cuts, just some bruises and, like Brent said, some singed bits. My hair, mostly.' He gave a weary, cheeky grin. 'I hate that. I have to look good for the girls, you know.'

Fiona laughed.

Rosa got a glint in her eyes and said she'd take care of Alex's hair problem. She fussed until Alex sat on the couch, and then put a bowl of fragrant soup into his hands with the promise that she would wield a pair of scissors on his behalf shortly.

The woman was a treasure. Fiona could understand why all three men valued their 'cleaner', who obviously had a wonderful mother's heart towards all of them.

'I'll be fine now.' Alex's embarrassment at being fussed over was clear on his face. 'Really. You should all go back to work, and Rosa, you don't have to stay. I might… I'll have a sleep or something.'

Somehow, Fiona doubted that, but she understood from his expectant expression that he hoped they would all clear out of there now.

'I will stay all afternoon.' Rosa indicated her cavernous bag again. 'I brought my knitting. I'll call you at the office, Brent, if anything worries me.'

'Right. Thank you. It's been a few years since we did this, hasn't it, Rosa?' Brent smiled and gripped his youngest brother on the shoulder. 'Just put up with being fussed on, okay? At least Rosa knows how to do that properly.'

'Yes, do take care, Alex.' Fiona turned with Brent.

As she turned away, Linc took his brother in his arms and dropped a kiss on the top of his head, as though he were a small boy, and as quickly pushed him away again.

It hurt, somehow, observing the love they all shared, the depth of it. The guardedness that went with it, and the reasons for that guardedness...

Because they'd been institutionalised. Because they'd been abandoned by the ones who should have loved them.

Brent had more to contend with than being autistic. His father's rejection, a whole history of things. *Could* he ever get past it all?

Did she want him to reach for that with her?

No. Of course not...

Because wanting that would be stupid, Fiona!

Anyway, Brent and his brothers treated Rosa's involvement in their lives as something exceptional and, in truth, what little involvement might they have had with women overall in any caring capacity over the course of their lives?

Could any of them be capable of that kind of love *with* a woman? Be able to learn how to give and receive it?

The thoughts were a little too deep for comfort—

And Brent hasn't given any indication that he is emotionally invested in you at all!

Nor was she invested in him that way. After all, it wasn't as though she loved Brent or anything. She liked him. She was aware of him as a man. Those were enough complications, thanks very much, and they'd drawn their lines anyway, so that was that.

With last words of advice to the man who really did not want to be an invalid but looked as though he needed to take care of himself for at least the remainder of the day, they all left.

CHAPTER NINE

'ALEX recovered without any difficulties, which is wonderful. He was very brave to go in to help all those people inside the building.' Fiona was in a coffee shop in the city with her mother and sisters. It was after working hours, Friday, a regular gathering for the women in her family, though it was a long time since she'd been invited along.

This time she'd invited herself and in a gap in the conversation had started to explain about her new job, her progress now she'd been there a while, how much she was enjoying the work. That had led to an account of Alex's involvement in the warehouse fire, but she'd lost them some time ago, really. The disinterest was on all their faces, and the joy went out of the telling for Fiona.

She had tried so hard during this gathering to make all the right connections, to make it clear how much she loved Mum and Kristine and Judy. And she had hoped to get something back other than their usual *Who is this alien among us?* response, but she hadn't.

Brent had told her he had work over this way for this afternoon. Fiona had made the decision to try one last time to connect with her family, if Brent didn't mind her taking that final hour out of her working day.

He hadn't minded, of course.

Well, her efforts had been a waste of time so far.

Fiona fell silent.

'I heard your old job at the Credit Union might be coming vacant again.' Her mother took a sip of her latte and examined Fiona over the rim of the cup with an expectant expression that was so devoid of any grain of true understanding of her daughter that Fiona stiffened all over before she could stop herself.

'I hope they find someone good to fill the vacancy.' She squeezed the words out somehow. Maybe it wasn't fair of her to feel that her mum and the others hadn't paid enough attention while she'd talked about her job, her employer and his family.

The difference being—your mother is trying to force you back into a mould more to her liking than the one that actually fits you.

Brent would be drumming his fingers if he were here. Fiona wasn't sure how she knew that, she just did.

Mum looked at her watch and gathered her handbag into her lap. It was a signal that she intended to leave, and Fiona sighed. She'd be standing outside waiting for Brent for a good ten minutes if they left now.

'Before you go, Mum, I brought you a birthday gift.' Fiona reached for the wrapped painting beside her chair and placed it in her mother's hands. She'd put her heart into the painting for her mother. A landscape of soft restful colours that would match the decor in her mother's living room. 'I know your birthday isn't until next week, but I wanted you to be able to hang it on the day—'

'You are somewhat early.' Her mother peeled back an edge of the wrapping. She glanced at the corner of painting revealed—less than a ten centimetre area—and covered it over again. 'Oh, it's one of your pictures. I don't know what I'll do with it…'

Hurt washed through Fiona. The urge to pull the painting out of the wrapping, explain it, point out its meaning and tell Mum the time and effort that had gone into it was strong. But she couldn't *make* her mother appreciate something like that.

Her efforts weren't ever going to be good enough, were they? Because they *were* different, and no one in her family wanted *different*. Fiona had tried to ignore and gloss over that fact for a very long time. How much more had Brent been made to deal with these feelings over his father? How could Fiona hope Brent would ever reach out for more when he had that hurt to contend with?

And, yes, a part of her *had* apparently secretly longed for that kind of connection with her boss…

Fiona forced a smile and stood as they all stood. She dutifully paid for her lunch at the register with them, and watched them hustle off in their different directions the moment they emerged onto the city street.

Her chest hurt. Right down inside where she'd been trying so hard for so long to ignore the fact that her family weren't exactly warm people when it came down to it. Well, they weren't. Not to her and, in reality, not to each other, either. It was just that they all felt perfectly secure in that emotionally stunted environment, while Fiona felt *in*secure and left out. At least she could now admit that fact to herself.

'Fiona?' Brent's hand closed over the ball of her

shoulder and his head bent to hers. 'I'm early. I thought I'd have to wait for you.'

'I didn't see you there.' She hoped he hadn't seen too much inside her in those unguarded moments just now. She didn't want to be caught feeling sorry for herself. She didn't know how to address what had just happened and where it put her in terms of how she felt about him either. 'You finished your business?'

'Yes. It didn't take as long as I'd estimated. I've been window-gazing since then.'

Fiona tipped up her chin and pasted a smile to her lips. 'Well, thank you for waiting for me. I'm ready to go now. Thanks for bringing me over with you so I could do this.'

'It was no trouble.' His voice was deep. Too deep. The kind of deep that said he sensed there was something amiss in her and that he cared about it.

That one grain of caring, not even openly expressed, went straight to that same hurting place inside her, and Fiona felt caught off guard all over again. She turned her head so he wouldn't see the emotion in her eyes. Instead, she started to walk blindly back towards his truck.

They walked the half block in silence and she used the time to try to pull herself together. She thought she'd done all right, too, until Brent spoke.

'So are you going to tell me, or do I guess?' They'd climbed into the truck, but Brent hadn't started the engine. He rested his hand on the steering wheel and searched her face and just…waited.

'Mum took a corner of the wrapper off the painting, glanced at it, covered it back up and made it clear that a more practical gift might have been good.' What was the point of hiding the facts from him? He'd already worked out something was wrong anyway. 'She also wasn't impressed that I pre-empted the actual date of her birthday by a week. Nothing I do "fits" with my family, I'm afraid. I'm too different from them and they can't accept that about me.'

'It was a good painting and it had your heart in it, and early birthday gifts are nice.' Brent's fingers drummed on the steering wheel and his head twitched once, twice before his mouth tightened and he said, 'Your mother should have liked it. She just should have—'

'Like your father liked and accepted all of you?' Fiona glanced towards the street at the small throng of people queuing to enter a nearby restaurant dance club. 'My family are all practical and they have a hard time relating to me because I'm…not, in a lot of ways. My choice of gift didn't appeal. I should have anticipated that fact and chosen something different. Next time, I will.'

She drew a tight breath. 'But, you know, I learnt a lesson just now. There are limits in my family. I have to accept that. It'll be easier for me in the future if I do.'

'That's not a lesson someone like you should ever have to learn.' His mouth was tight, angry and protective for her sake. 'You're soft, kind. You deserve for them to love you like they should!'

'Yet Charles's treatment of you has put you in the same place, only much more so. It's impacted hugely on core parts of your life, your outlook, what you'll—' She'd been going to say *reach for* but stopped herself.

Brent's expression was a combination of surprise, discomfort, comprehension and a certain kind of need that made her want to hold him for ever.

She wanted to bury herself in his touch and hold him and forget all of the world for a while. Because those feelings were intense and based in emotions she felt towards him that were far from safe and that *he* had denied *her* from himself, she did her best to let the topic go. 'Well, it doesn't matter. We should go.'

Brent hesitated before he gestured towards the club in front of them. 'Actually, do you feel like a meal? We're a fair way from home, and Linc's been to that club. He said the seafood is good. Fresh as an ocean breeze.'

If there had been even a hint of pity in his expression now or earlier she would have turned him down.

But there was only the desire to prolong their time together, even if he did feel uncomfortable about the need to do that.

And Fiona felt just restless enough to consider his offer, even if it might not be a smart thing for her to do. At least *he* wanted her company!

'Are *you* a seafood fan?'

'Oh, yes.' He nodded. 'Crab, lobster, prawns, mussels, you name it.'

'Then, yes. Dinner would be nice. Just because…we are quite a way from our homes and it'll be late when we get back.' They could spend time together and, no matter how guarded he was, he would never be *cold* like her family. And right now Fiona did long for warmth…

'Then we're agreed.' Brent felt the corner of his mouth kick up as he spoke the words. He was pleased, whether he should be or not.

But he wanted this time with Fiona. Just to be there for her, to be beside her while she adapted to this next step in the road when it came to dealing with her family. Brent could do that for her.

And for yourself? Have you adapted to Charles's rejection? Or have you just been avoiding it all this time?

Fiona bit her lip as though she wondered if her response had been too enthusiastic. But she'd said yes. Brent wasn't letting her off now.

So what if they ate a meal together? Tonight she needed company. He could be that for her. Why not?

'We're still in our work clothes,' Fiona pointed out, but it didn't matter.

Brent wore tan trousers and a navy shirt, and Fiona was in one of those silky, swirly skirts of hers and a pink blouse that hugged her curves. She looked—

'I guess we'd do, wouldn't we?' Her eyes shone with the beginning of anticipation. 'Unless you'll need a tie to get in…'

'I most likely will.' He reached over her and popped the storage compartment and drew out a navy tie, held it aloft. 'Emergency supplies. It's Linc's. He's always got his eye out—' He broke off and cleared his throat. 'He sometimes borrows the truck.'

He wasn't sure, but he thought Fiona hid a smile before she reached for the tie and gestured for him to lean forward. 'I'll do this for you, if you like.'

Brent liked.

The feel of her fingers against his neck as she tied the tie and settled it into place, patted it with an expression of satisfaction and an edge of consciousness of him.

Yes. He liked that, and he liked that she'd done it without thinking about it, let herself have the moment because that was part of what was inside her, a spontaneity and ability to reach for what she truly wanted.

You shouldn't be happy if you think she really, truly

wants you, MacKay. You should be worried about that and backing off.

Brent's brows drew down. He threw his door open and got out. This die was cast. They were going in. He didn't want to psychoanalyse it *or* overrate it. He just wanted to do it.

Minutes later, they'd entered the club and been shown to a dining table near the edge of the dance floor. The floor was empty, but Brent could imagine what it would be like later with people dancing. He could picture Fiona there, could imagine every movement, every motion as she gave herself to the beat.

'Seafood for two? There's a few different ones.' Fiona turned the menu to show him.

They bent their heads over the list until a waitress came along with her pad and a stub of pencil and her grey apron tied tight over fitted black jeans.

'This one.' Brent pointed to their selection, adding a distracted, 'Thanks,' as he turned his attention back to his—to Fiona. She wasn't his date.

No? Then what was dinner and dancing if not a date? And since when had he suddenly started to assume there'd be dancing for them?

A small slice of warning actually got through to him in the moment he asked himself that question. His body tightened in reaction to the corresponding tension that formed inside him.

But the reaction settled down a moment later, and he glanced up and smiled at Fiona. She seemed happier. That was the main thing, wasn't it?

Brent's gaze locked with hers and a silent communication passed between them that made Fiona's skin tingle

and her breath catch in her throat. She had so many con-
flicting emotions right now. Disappointment over her
family, thoughts about Brent's situation, happiness for
being in his company, warning bells because of that
same happiness.

He'd drawn back the last time. That night when he'd
kissed her. He hadn't wanted...

And if he wanted now? Would she also want? The
emotional risk of letting herself care about him when
she wasn't certain he truly could feel the same? If he
was attracted to her on some level, but in other ways
wasn't, did she want to have to deal with that?

*As though there's a choice, Fiona? As though you
can decide whether you want to have feelings for
someone or not.*

That system had worked for her until now. She'd
thought she was safe. She *was* safe. This was just
tonight, a one-off thing. He'd asked her because he em-
pathised over her mother's behaviour, and it was dinner
time, and they still had travel ahead of them. There was
nothing remotely romantic about any of that.

And, yes, Fiona might like to speak with him about
his own situation, try to get somewhere with that,
because she was getting more and more convinced that
he hadn't addressed it. Not truly.

'You love music, don't you? It's deep down inside
you.' Brent's words broke through her reverie.

She realised she'd been swaying in her seat, and
smiled and gave a slight shrug. 'I do love music. All
kinds from all eras.'

His gaze narrowed as he absorbed this information.
Then their meal arrived and Fiona laughed at the sheer
size of it, and he gave a wry grin.

'Don't say we'll never get through it. You haven't seen the amount of food I can put away.' His fingers toyed with the lobster-cracking tool at the edge of the tray. 'I don't think you noticed there wasn't a shred of food left by the time we left the house in the mountains after our hiking and painting trip.'

Fiona hadn't noticed. 'You must have eaten some of it during the night…'

'Yes. I'm a three a.m. grazer, I'm afraid.' He popped a Tasmanian scallop into his mouth. 'I get hungry a lot.'

'And eat people's chocolate stash.' The teasing words shot from her mouth and she bit her lip. 'I didn't mind, and I wouldn't have even noticed, except you bought some extras for me…'

His gaze locked on hers. 'I didn't realise what I'd done until the pile of empty wrappers impinged enough for me to notice them.'

'You ate them while you explored my graphics program?' She sipped her wine and wondered if he realised the significance of him discussing the impact of his condition with her this way. 'I should have walked you through the program when I first started there.'

'I enjoyed looking, anyway.' Brent did eat a lot of the food, and they talked while they shared the meal. It felt…good, and she relaxed and stopped wondering about what he might be thinking or not thinking, and just let herself enjoy the moment for whatever it was.

'Come and dance.' He got to his feet, held out his hand for hers and, when she placed her fingers against his, wrapped her up in the strength of long fingers and led her onto the floor.

Her senses were consumed in that touch, in the way

they matched each other in height as they made their way to a space on the floor.

Brent held her hands and they…danced. And, after a while, he rested both hands on her hips and stood almost still as she swayed in his hold with her hands on shoulders that flexed beneath her touch.

Fiona closed her eyes and let one hand slide until it rested over his heart. And she gave herself to the music and his heartbeat.

Only for a moment. That couldn't hurt…

CHAPTER TEN

BRENT'S hands flexed against Fiona's hips and he watched her dance with her eyes closed and all her enjoyment clear to see on her softened features.

She was so beautiful, and he…wanted her so much. He battled his way through some physical twitches that built in his body and lodged in his shoulders, and eventually got those under control and was able to enjoy her touch on him, the sight of her.

Her hair smelled of peaches and fell loose about her cheeks and neck in a glossy curtain. He bent his head just enough to inhale the scent of it and breathe it deep into his lungs. He liked her at the end of the day this way, with her lipstick long gone and a wrinkle or two in her blouse. He liked her dancing for him, and he liked her dancing *with* him.

Somewhere along the line, this evening had progressed away from his core plan and he had to admit he was responsible for that.

He might have stood and casually asked her to dance, but there'd been nothing casual in his need to hold her. He might have wanted to comfort her after her episode with her mother, but he hadn't said a word about that since they'd come here.

When Fiona's hand brushed his thigh as she moved, Brent drew her into the lee of his body. Not touching, not really. Just her hands against his heart and his shoulder, and his hands on her hips and a lot of…closeness.

But they were touching. He felt every movement she made, every sensual twist and sway through those points where their bodies did connect. Her eyes sparkled as she lifted her gaze to his. The rest of the patrons faded from his notice and his focus homed absolutely on the woman dancing with him.

'I like the way you dance.' Fiona spoke the words against his ear. Her breasts brushed his chest and Brent drew a breath and his arms somehow got all the way around her and held her close until they were both swaying to the music and he felt…as though he held home in his arms, even though he didn't know what home was, except for Linc and Alex and survival.

'I like the way you dance better.' His lips brushed her ear, lingered long enough to explore the feel of the soft, shell shape in a butterfly kiss.

Such a fine line. So easy to step over it because it felt so right.

The sigh of her breath brushed his cheek. That whisper was all about her pleasure in his touch, in what they were doing.

He wondered briefly how long it would be before he lost this calm feeling and had to work to keep his movements controlled again. For now he just…was in this moment with her.

It seemed right to hold her so their bodies brushed chest to chest and thigh to thigh as they swayed to the music. So he did. He wanted to close his eyes and feel her movements and just absorb them, so he let himself.

Somewhere between wanting to take her mind off her mother's hurtful behaviour and now, Brent had dropped his guard, had done it thoroughly, even if as quietly as a whisper.

The scariest part was that he couldn't find the concern over that which he should be able to find.

They danced, and Brent never did dance more than swaying his body while she did most of the work, but, oh, it was the best experience of Fiona's life. Because he danced with *her,* with his gaze fixed on her and never looking anywhere else. He danced with all of his focus, just for her.

It was probably inevitable that he held her closer, that she moved closer. That the songs went from slow to fast and back again without them changing their dancing at all until they were heartbeat to heartbeat with each other and finally, finally he pressed his cheek to her cheek and his hands stroked up her arms and over her shoulders to the dip between her shoulder blades and down to the dip of her waist.

The hurt of her mother's actions, of her own failure yet again to get what she needed from her family, receded to the background as Fiona lost herself in Brent's attention.

Doubts still hovered. They did. Because Brent's acceptance of her wasn't all-seeing, all-knowing and all-encompassing, either. He accepted her artistic side. Understandable, given he shared similar tendencies.

She liked to think he liked her as a person, overall. But he also held back from her. And seemed uncertain of whether he wanted to accept the attraction he felt towards her or not.

For now he was accepting it, and she was letting herself *hope* probably more than she should that he would continue to accept it. But she hoped anyway.

Fiona wound her arms more tightly around his neck. They didn't talk. They didn't say anything at all. Eventually their gazes simply locked and their dancing stilled and he clasped her hand in his and led her off the dance floor while her heart started a slow, deep rhythm in her chest and she couldn't catch her breath any more and could only walk with him into the night, to his truck, and get in.

He reached for her hand once they were on the road. Tucked it against his thigh and held it there.

'I set out to talk to you about your family—'

'Won't you talk to me about Charles—?'

He turned the truck into her apartment complex's car park and they both fell silent. The need to talk warred with other more instinctive needs. Fiona didn't know where to go with either instinct so she fell back on good manners.

'Thank you…thank you for a lovely evening.' Her fingers fumbled as she opened the truck door and climbed out.

Brent had taken advantage of an empty space towards the end of the courtyard parking. It was silent, shadowed, isolated.

He came to her side of the truck, pushed her passenger door closed behind her after she alighted.

'What are we doing, Fiona?' Did he open his arms?

Or did she step into them of her own accord? Did it even matter? Either way, it was inevitable really that she would melt into him.

'I don't know what we're doing.' She looked into his

eyes as she said it. 'You hold back because Charles rejected you. You give him power over you through that. It's not only about your autism. That side of you— it's just part of you. It's...a beautiful part of you.' Everything she wanted from him came out in those words—things she knew within herself and things she only knew instinctively.

Brent shook his head. 'The beauty is within *you,* within your generosity and your capacity to see the best in people.' Maybe Brent didn't want to talk about the rest. Maybe he reacted purely on an instinctive level to what she said to him.

Because his arms locked around her and his lips parted on a breath of desire and then there was no space between them, only his mouth on hers, taking and giving, offering and accepting as they both yielded.

Fiona acknowledged her need and held on. Arms around his neck. Body pressed close. Lips soft beneath his, absorbing and responding as his hands traced up and down her back, over the curve of her lower spine, and lower still. It was a kiss of tenderness and pleasure and sweetness, and she took it down into herself and held it there.

It changed so gradually. She was deep into that change before she even realised. Gentle kisses had become demanding, a play of tongues and desire that still somehow managed to coil around her emotions.

The strength of his body against her softness played through her senses and her heart whispered to be careful. Be so very careful because her soul could enter into this and what would she do if that happened?

'I want you closer. Closer.' Brent whispered the words and covered her mouth again, and his arms closed tight and strong about her and she felt safe with him. Safe and hungry and scared and desperate all at once.

She needed to be even closer, not only physically but to all that was within him. That truth was confirmed in each shaken breath she took. She'd sought such closeness from the start as she'd searched for his emotions in his work. Maybe even then something inside her had known she would come to care for him this way.

It was rumoured he was eccentric. Instead, he was brilliant, talented, unique, charming and intense and sweet and strong.

'Fiona. If I keep going with this I won't be able… I can't… I don't know…' He buried his face in her hair and his breath heaved in and out and his shoulders locked as he fought himself, fought what he wanted from her and maybe fought other reactions and responses in his physical make-up as well. 'I told myself this was safe. We're in a car park, for God's sake.'

It impinged on her slowly that they were. Right out here in the car park, which, while admittedly quiet right now, couldn't be guaranteed to stay that way.

And she had forgotten that, had lost all sense of time and place. Had immersed herself so fully in the moment and in his arms that she hadn't given a thought to their surroundings.

She should step away from him. Any moment now she would gather the strength to do that. Because…

Because they needed to talk. Didn't they?

Brent stroked his hands up the length of her spine and his fingers found their way into her hair and whatever reasons there might have been disappeared on the whisper of her breath.

Her mouth softened and her hands bracketed his face and if he had indicated in any way that she wasn't welcome...

A sound rose in the back of Brent's throat as his mouth covered Fiona's once again. She gave herself to the kiss in the same way she did everything—with generosity and openness. When he dipped his tongue into the cavern of her mouth, hers followed him home again, stroked, tangled.

He crushed her close and loved the way her body fitted his so perfectly. He couldn't get the thought out of his mind of her legs wrapped around him.

How they ended up outside her apartment he couldn't have said, but she had her bag in her hand and he vaguely remembered that ending up on the bonnet of his truck when he'd first taken her mouth out there.

Now she fumbled in the bag for her key while they snatched kisses, and a moment later they were inside her home.

A lamp burned on a corner table in the living room. That circle of muted light was the only thing that even half registered as he wrapped his arms around her and pressed his lips to hers.

Slow down. You have to slow this down.

But it was a train on a downward slope. Gaining pace and out of control.

How could he need this so much? Brent sought the answer in the warm recesses of her mouth, in the press of her lips against his, in the touch of her fingers where they stroked his arms, his chest.

His tie drifted from her fingers onto the edge of the sofa and slipped to the floor. Then *they* were on that sofa, arms around each other, mouths melding together.

He cupped her breasts through the cloth of her blouse, absorbed the softness and the shape of her...

Brent caught one glimpse of warm welcome in her eyes and wondered what she saw in him, and then he couldn't think any more, only experience and feel and need, with his senses and with pieces of himself that he'd worked so hard to protect from the world for so long.

Pieces that had taken the pain of Charles's rejection and buried it so deep that even Brent himself hadn't realised where he'd gone with all of that.

That one thought pushed through until it hit the surface of his mind and the warnings he'd tried to give himself earlier finally took hold. Brent's shoulders tightened as he faced just how much he was letting her in right now—he could not do that.

So totally couldn't do that. Tension criss-crossed his chest and rippled through his muscles and settled in his neck. Tension that he couldn't control. He broke away from her and his head twitched before he got to his feet in a movement that felt uncoordinated, uneven and aching.

He'd wanted to make love to her. It would have ended in that. The truth was in what they'd done, in the blur of blue eyes softened and confused and struggling to comprehend the loss of his touch as she, too, slowly rose from the sofa.

Everything in him ached to take her back, to hold her against his heart because there was a tension and lost feeling there that only doing that would ease, but Fiona couldn't be his saviour. He had to be that for himself, survive by himself, protect himself the way he always had done. Protect that part of him that Charles MacKay had done his best to crush so many years ago.

Brent had to do all that. Didn't he?

'I'm sorry, Fiona.' God. His voice was raw gravel. 'This...got out of control. I told you I wouldn't go here again. I meant that. For your sake—'

'Yes. You told me. Foolishly, I thought—' She broke off. Drew a breath. 'I should have learned the first time.' She took his tie from the floor, folded it, handed it to him and made her way to the door with steps that weren't as smooth or coordinated for *her* as they usually were.

She opened that door. Waited with her teeth over her lower lip and all sorts of defences wrapped around her, even as her arms wrapped around her waist.

'I don't know...' What she meant by her words. Why her dismissal of him felt like a dismissal of herself.

In this moment Brent knew nothing—how did he deal with that?

He hesitated and faced her. 'Fiona—'

'It's all right. You need to go. We both need for you to do that. This...' She hesitated. 'You thought you wanted me, but the reality... And I... It would be too much. I'm not ready.'

To deal with all of him? If not with the signs of his autism, with the emotional limits he carried that went far deeper than dealing with them?

How could he expect her to be ready to deal with such obstacles when he didn't know how to deal with them himself?

Brent crushed the tie in his hand and let his tension focus on crushing the fabric over and over.

And he searched her eyes one last time before he walked away.

CHAPTER ELEVEN

THEY worked. Interacted for the good of the company. Made progress on one project after another. Melded their ideas and their strengths and all they had to bring, combined, to the table.

Winter weather closed in. Chill winds and grey skies and morning rain. Fiona dressed warmly and worked as the consummate professional and told herself she wasn't unhappy, didn't feel unfulfilled, didn't need anything from Brent beyond their relationship as employer and employee.

And she decided she simply was best off just being 'everybody's friend', sticking to her known ground and not stepping beyond it where she couldn't feel safe.

She was good at being a friend. She did great pet minding and pot plant watering and advice to the lovelorn.

At that last thought, Fiona's mouth pulled tight. Some advisor. She certainly couldn't sort out her own issues. They were all still shuffling around in her head over and over.

As for her relationship with her family, she'd made her decisions about that. It would always hurt that they didn't accept her and love her for herself, but she could learn to be a step back from that hurt. She could protect herself.

If she needed to do that, how could she expect Brent to do anything other than protect himself in his life as much as he felt was necessary?

She rapped on the door of Brent's home inside the warehouse and forced herself to draw some deep even breaths as she waited for him to answer.

He wasn't expecting her but she couldn't do anything about that. The manila folder clenched in the fist of her left hand was proof of that. He'd left it in her car when they'd used it yesterday to attend an initial client discussion on site.

The file the client had given them held photos that covered the history of the area and its landscaping back over a hundred years, and Brent had told her he planned to work on that project, from home, all day today.

So…he needed the file.

And she was fine about delivering it.

Hand it over. Wish him a good day. Leave.

It wasn't her fault he hadn't answered his phone. At least she'd managed to slip in as Alex was going out. As though in response to her first thought, Fiona's phone beeped out a message and she drew it out of the bag slung over her shoulder.

Brent might not have been at home, of course, but he'd said he would be and maybe he had his mobile turned off and had let the home phone battery go flat. His receptionist was always at him to hang his cordless phone at work back on its cradle, not leave it lying on his desk.

Fiona thought she heard the click of a door catch somewhere inside Brent's home and turned her attention quickly to reading her phone message. It was from her mother.

I've spoken to the boss of your old job and she's prepared to take you back. Consider it, dear. Haven't you had enough of playing at this other career? You know it won't get you anywhere.

Anywhere except in love with Brent.
Oh, God.
Of all the thoughts to surface. Not, *It would get her where she wanted to be in her career path.* Not, *It was what she wanted to do.*

Not even, *I'm sorry, Mum, but this is me and I'm over you not accepting and loving me just as I am.*

All those thoughts were valid and real and true. None of them even compared to the one thought that filled her so utterly.

She loved Brent.

The knowledge hit her hard and deep. This was the reason she couldn't forget those moments that had come so close to a culmination in lovemaking.

'Fiona. Hi. I thought you must have been Alex and he'd forgotten something again…'

Brent's words trailed off and Fiona lifted her gaze from the message on the phone screen and stared with a brand new, shocking, devastating knowledge pulsing through her.

Brent was bare to the waist. That was what registered first. Steam wafted from the open bathroom door behind him. That registered second. Moisture beaded on his chest and his hair was freshly washed and still damp. He had jeans on with the top snap unfastened. She really shouldn't be looking but she had dreamed of him, of seeing him like this, and her heart was in her throat and her pulse and each breath she took.

Her gaze climbed his chest before it reached his face and looking into his eyes wasn't any better. They burned. A deep, slumberous green that sent hot and cold chills down her spine and fire licking along her nerve-endings, and all she could do was let love and need wash all through her.

'Um… Alex drove away.' Right. And that piece of information was completely vital, of course. As well as being coherent and oh, so eloquently put. She had to get hold of herself. Had to hide these feelings from him!

'Did you have a message for me?' Brent gestured towards the phone. His jaw was clenched. His gaze swept over her, from the hair in a ponytail high on her head, over the cream T-shirt and chocolate-brown pants. And returned to her face, lingered on her mouth, caught her gaze and locked there as though he couldn't stop himself.

Then why do you have to stop yourself, Brent?

She loved him. Was *in love with him.* She wanted the opportunity to express that emotion.

Even if he can't give it back to you? Even if, because of his father's rejection, he will always be emotionally unable to give all of himself?

But Brent wasn't asking for that from her…

'It's not a message for you. Mum said she can get my old job back for me.' She dredged up the answer from the part of her that had remained aware of anything other than how much she desired and wanted and… needed him. His arms around her, his mouth on hers. Her love being given to him.

'You're not taking your old job back.' His words were

anger and protectiveness wrapped into one. 'This job, working with me, it's right for you. It's the work you deserve, not some clerical job designed to turn you into the rest of your family. I don't want you to...' He stopped the words there, but his gaze expressed his thoughts.

Not only that he didn't want her to be hurt by her mother's words and behaviour, but that *he* didn't want to lose contact with her.

Because of the work they shared. She told herself this. It wasn't because he loved her, for goodness' sake.

Even so she told him, 'Don't worry. I signed a contract for the next twelve months with you, and I want even longer, a long-term career path with you, if that's possible.'

I don't want to stop seeing you, Brent. Not now. Not in the future. I have no idea how I could cope with that if it happened.

The discovery that she loved him was too new and raw for her to imagine not seeing him, career path or otherwise. How could she have let herself come to this? Have fallen for him so utterly?

Yet how could she have stopped it? She'd responded to his heart, in his landscaping designs that she'd studied, before they'd even met. When she'd met him face to face, some part of her deep, deep down had known that he would come to mean all of this to her. Otherwise, why would she now feel this utter acceptance, even in the face of all her uncertainties and fears?

But she did have those uncertainties and fears and, because of them, Fiona tried to pull herself together so she could deal with the reason she had come here, and take herself *out of here,* where she would have a chance to gather some defences and figure out how to go forward with these new feelings without revealing them to him.

She shoved the phone away into her bag and held out the folder gripped in her other hand. 'Anyway, that's not why I'm here. You left this in my car. You'll need it. I couldn't get you on either of your phones. Obviously you were in the shower.'

She passed her free hand down her thigh. Nervous gesture. She hadn't done that since she first started working for him.

'Thanks.' His hand closed over the folder. 'If I've made you feel awkward because I kissed you—'

'No. Oh, no.' Their kisses had unlocked things in her. She couldn't do anything about that but she couldn't regret it, either. Regret…just wasn't an option she could even consider.

'Good. That's good.' There was relief in his glance— more than relief—and somehow he was tugging on that folder and she still had her hand clenched around it and the momentum brought her through the door and into his home and he closed them in there while her gaze took in the extremely close view of a great deal of tanned male skin.

It was a very beautiful chest, the skin stretched tight over well-formed musculature, a light dusting of dark hair across it and arrowing down.

Not looking down again. That was a mistake the first time.

Brent seemed to become aware of his half-dressed state, too. He gestured towards the kitchen. 'You can get a coffee, if you like. I'll just…yeah, I'll be back in a minute.'

He disappeared into what must obviously be his bedroom and Fiona stood there with the folder still clutched in her hand because he'd left her with it, hadn't he?

What was she doing? What were *they* doing? Coffee while he threw some more clothes on? Would that help her at all, him covering up?

She walked to the kitchen and laid the folder on the bench and made her way towards his front door on wobbly legs, determined to get that wobbliness back to strength somehow. To leave before she did something that gave away how she felt.

Brent stepped into the hall from his room and she walked straight into his chest. Her arms came up, forearms against that chest, which was now, indeed, covered very discreetly with a button-down navy shirt.

That's right, Fiona. You notice that while you're staring stupidly at him and all your feelings are probably right out there for him to see.

'I don't know how to do this. I'm better in the "friend" role,' she blurted, and his hands made this odd *touch her—don't touch her* motion at his sides for a moment before they closed over her elbows.

He could have pushed her away. Maybe he intended to.

She could have used his touch to lever herself away. Maybe she might have.

But the irises of his eyes darkened to a deep, moss-green and his breath drew in on a sharp inhalation. 'I want—'

'Then take what you want.' The words burst from her because it was what she wanted, too, and couldn't he see that? 'Take what we both want, Brent.'

Her heart spoke for her, whether she could handle the fallout or not.

'God, Fiona. I can't fight this again. I just…can't.'

When his fingers tightened on her elbows, she leaned in to his touch, let it become an embrace, and breathed a sigh of relief and pleasure when he drew her in against his chest and cradled her there, heartbeat to heartbeat as his mouth came down on hers.

She had needed this, and her heart ached at the chance to have this. That ache warned her of all she would invest in loving him this way and of how much it could come to hurt her because, for her, it was love. For him...desire, need, perhaps, but those were all.

Even then, she could not turn back.

And Brent, oh, she hoped and prayed Brent would not turn back.

He gave her lazy kisses first. Long, slow, drugging kisses that reached inside her and let her immerse herself in pleasure.

He stroked his fingers up and down her arms, caught her around her waist and held her gently as his mouth took hers. Tremors passed through his body and for a moment he stilled, forehead to her forehead, as he breathed deeply.

This was his condition, and she stroked his back and murmured how much she enjoyed his touch, and he relaxed and the tension left him and he kissed her again.

And again and again.

He must have done this at other times, with other women. Yet she couldn't let herself think of those times, didn't want to think of her own past experiences, of trying to find a connection, only to discover there was nothing there.

With Brent it was all there. For her, it was, and she didn't think about what he might feel for her. Surely he must be in a better place within himself if he could reach for this with her this way…?

'You know what you want, what you're able to have.' She murmured the words and his gaze locked with hers and for a moment doubts bruised his eyes before they were blinked away.

So it was fine. Wasn't it?

They found their way onto his sofa.

Brent didn't know how that happened, only that he had his arms full of Fiona and his heart was hammering and when he drew a breath it was filled with the scent of her and he wanted to press his nose to her neck and just inhale the sweetness of her.

He did that, and she shuddered and a soft yearning sound came from the back of her throat and she tightened her arms around him and held on.

Just held on while Brent held onto her, too, and his reasons for holding back disintegrated in the face of his need for her. Was it necessary for him to try to reason through that, understand it or define it? Couldn't this moment be enough in itself?

'I need this with you, Fiona. This once, if you can allow it.' Just once. If she understood that at the start and he understood it…

Brent's expression showed his concern for Fiona, his confusion and uncertainty and, over it all, his need.

If he'd said he wanted this, wanted but didn't need, Fiona might have made a different choice. 'Then we'll have this, Brent.' It wasn't even a decision for her. It was a beat in her heart that matched the beat in Brent's heart. It was all of her that had to do this, to be with him this way.

If a part of her desired so much more than that, well, she was used to having less than she wanted. Life was like that. She would take this moment and immerse herself in it and live it and give all of herself to it, and that would be fine.

Just fine.

Fiona pushed the element of sadness away and focused her attention on the man in her arms. She'd sought his emotions. Maybe, in these moments, if she were very lucky, she would have them, even if they were only hers to keep for a very little while.

Brent took Fiona into his bedroom. His need outstripped his doubts and concerns. They were still there but, even so, he drew her into his arms beside the bed and looked deep into her eyes and let his touch and his reverence tell her all the things that were locked inside him, that he couldn't say and couldn't own and yet they were there.

They drew clothes from each other and tossed them on the floor until there was just them and the quietness and the sunlight slanting in through the gap at the edge where the curtains met the window.

His gaze roved her body and his hands followed, and he drew her onto his bed and touched every part of her until she took the foil packet from his bedside table and drew him home.

There was an aching need in the centre of his chest. Brent registered this as his body arched into Fiona's and longing and sensation rushed through him.

His throat hurt and he kissed Fiona blindly, emotions wrapped into it, control...lost with all cognizant thought other than to please her, to make this the best for her that he could. Somehow he crossed the line into instinct. The acceptance in her eyes took him there and he pushed back every other thought and made love to her with everything he had to give.

Not enough, his mind told him, and yet his body and his emotions told a different story.

No. Not his emotions. Brent pushed that possibility out, even as his hands worshipped her soft skin and his eyes gazed into hers, letting her in and taking her into himself in return.

At the last moment, she cried out and his control mechanisms fractured.

His body shook and he kissed her mouth and her eyelids and buried his nose in her neck and inhaled her scent. His arms locked around her, all the way around her shoulders and back and he…held onto her and his fingers stroked her damp skin.

Over and over and over.

She wrapped her arms around him, too, and her hands stroked over him and she made a sound that was pure pleasure. 'I love…your touch.'

And though Brent should assess what had just happened, think about his loss of control from the broadest perspective, think about a lot of things, her gaze was dazed and slumberous and he didn't let himself think about any of those things.

Instead, he made love to her again until they lay on the bed with streams of sunlight filtering onto the wall.

Only then did his actions begin, finally, to impinge. His fingers digging into her back in a kneading motion as he held her. Thumbs stroking across her collarbone repeatedly.

Burying his nose in her neck and inhaling the scent of her skin until his body was filled with it. 'I shouldn't have… I didn't expect… That wasn't what I wanted to see revealed.'

All the idiosyncrasies that went with his condition. All the…insecurities about them that Charles MacKay's words and actions had left Brent with for all these years.

Maybe she finally thought about that, too, about all the ways this hadn't been normal for him and…never would be.

Because she drew her hand away from his chest and sat up, took the sheet from the base of the bed where they'd kicked it and wrapped it around herself. There were shadows in her eyes as she got to her feet and started to gather clothes off the floor.

Brent also stood, pulled on his jeans and felt now even more vulnerable than he had at the height of loving her, when all his defences had been down.

Fiona pressed her clothing to her chest. 'This… I still have to go to work. I have work…'

She turned and shut herself in his bathroom.

Brent dressed and left the warehouse then. Just got in his utility truck and drove away because he didn't know what to say to her and he didn't want to face his thoughts and he wasn't sure where doing that would take him anyway.

He was still the same person Charles MacKay had rejected and he still didn't have enough to offer a woman and particularly one like Fiona, who deserved so much.

That was all still the case.

Wasn't it?

CHAPTER TWELVE

THEY'D made love. For Fiona it had been the most beautiful experience of her life...until Brent had come to himself enough to regret what they had done.

She loved him. Loved him deep inside herself in a way she knew she would never love again. All her life, she had searched the world around her for the emotion she needed.

Now she saw inside her own heart and knew that this was the one and only deep love she would ever have.

But Brent didn't share those feelings. He'd proved that through all the things he hadn't said at the end of their time together.

He hadn't even waited around to speak with her after she'd got dressed.

And she had to come to terms with that silence somehow and know how to go on.

She didn't want to lose his presence in her life.

Did that make her weak? That she couldn't imagine walking away from him, even if he couldn't love her or feel the things for her that she felt for him?

She'd gone straight from his home to work, and then she'd lost her nerve, made an excuse and gone from work up here into the mountains. She'd needed time to think, and hadn't been able to trust herself to do that in front of the others in their office space.

But eventually she was going to have to go back and face Brent. Somehow. Fiona didn't know how.

Oh, why couldn't he admit how much his past had hurt him? If he would accept that, maybe that could be the start of him being able to accept...her.

You're a fool, Fiona Donner. Making love is one thing. Yes, he seemed to enjoy that and seemed to be over any issues he might have had about your generous body size or anything like that, but he's not in love with you. Don't kid yourself into thinking otherwise. That was a one-off experience for him. No doubt he's totally over it already.

Right. And Fiona needed to be 'over it' as well. And just as soon as she got her emotions sorted out and felt she could face others without revealing them, she would be.

For now, cold stung her cheeks. Damp air filled her lungs and the scent of bush land closed around her. Fiona had the walking trail to herself and was photographing flora for a montage she wanted to use as a backdrop for her computer graphic work on one of Brent's projects.

If she focused her thoughts enough, she would make a success of this trip. It wouldn't be wasted. She wouldn't have to admit it had been as much about escaping having to face Brent as anything else.

Fiona worked on and eventually decided she had done all she could with the photography. The light wasn't as good now and there was a heavy stillness in the air that rather matched her mood.

Wetness formed on her cheek and her mouth tightened. She brushed her fingers over it, but other wetness caught on her eyelashes at the same time and she realised she hadn't given way to the emotion she'd been holding back this last week.

Snow was falling.

Unseasonably early, unexpectedly thick and getting heavier by the moment. White, pure flakes of snow that would obscure the trail she'd taken if it continued.

She had to get back to her car. Fiona packed her photography equipment into her backpack, gave thanks she hadn't tried to bring a tripod with her and began to retrace her steps.

Walking through that flurry of innocent-looking white flakes, Fiona told herself she would be back in the car park safe and sound in no time. And, if anything happened, the office knew her location. She didn't have her mobile with her. It was in the car in her bag. She hadn't wanted to carry any extra weight. Well, that had been a poor choice to make, but there was no point worrying about it now.

A bush parrot appeared briefly out of the flurrying snowfall and disappeared again. And Fiona hurried along and thought of Brent. Even now, she couldn't push the thoughts away.

For a short frame of time she had felt she'd held Brent's attention and focus and maybe even…his heart. That he had given all of himself to her, was trusting her with all of him. She had let her own guards down, all the way down, had believed, foolishly, that he could find as much fulfilment in her as she had found in him.

Obviously, that hadn't been the case and she understood his need to protect himself. She did! Within her family she had felt the same way. Not loved for all of herself, not understood. But the whole world wouldn't be like Brent's father to him. Fiona would never be that way to him.

The snow thickened and Fiona realised she could be in real trouble for other reasons. She had to get out of here before she lost the ability to see the trail. She put her head down and walked as fast as she was able and prayed she wouldn't end up lost in the bush...

'Fiona? Fiona!' Brent shouted Fiona's name again, and again received no response. He walked the trail in jerky strides while snow coated his back and shoulders and brushed against his face.

It was cold. The snow had been falling for over an hour. And Fiona was out in it. He had to find her. Already he was struggling to be certain he was still on the trail. If he hadn't walked it before...

Fiona had left her plans at work but Brent had stayed out of the office until well after lunch. He'd dodged making contact with Fiona, and this was the result.

All because he hadn't known how to address the concerns at war inside himself, but now he'd worked that out and he needed to speak to her.

He needed first of all to be certain she was safe!

Brent pushed on and tried not to imagine Fiona lost in this.

Please stay on the path until I find you, Fiona.

When the snow covered the path completely he started to call her name again in earnest. He should have called in a search and rescue team, not tried to find her by himself.

He shouldn't have walked away this morning and left her to find her way out of his home by herself, left things unresolved between them.

And do you know what you want now, MacKay? And, more importantly, whether you have the right to try to have it?

Brent didn't know. Not entirely. He wanted Fiona as more than an employee. That much he now fully understood and admitted. He wanted her…as a lover. For however long they could make that work. If they could make that work…

For now, he needed to make sure she was safe.

Brent hadn't imagined this snowfall. Who heard of this kind of snow at this time of year here? It just didn't happen.

But today it was happening.

'Fiona!' His voice echoed. There was no response.

Brent pushed on, decided he would give himself another ten minutes and then get on the phone to Linc, ask him to organise help.

When Fiona hiked out of the snow straight at him, her face pale and anxious, all Brent's well-considered thoughts about the future, about speaking carefully and working things out in some way to buy them some time together and avoid hurting either of them when that time inevitably came to an end fell away.

He simply snatched her into his arms. 'You're all right? I thought you might have gone off the path. It's completely obscured now.'

His arms shook as he held her at arm's length so he could examine her. Brent registered that knowledge and couldn't do a thing about it.

She had a coat on, no hat. Her backpack and hair were covered in snow and, as she stared into his eyes, her mouth trembled for a moment before she pressed her lips together and tried to smile all at the same time.

'I'm okay. I was hoping I wasn't too far from the car park, but I've lost track of where I am.'

'It took me over an hour to get this far.'

'I thought I heard you calling me once, but I thought I must have imagined it because I wanted—' She broke off and shivered.

Brent pulled her in close again to his body. 'You're half frozen. I have to get you out of here.' His head twitched but he managed to hold on to her through it, and then he covered her in the second coat he'd worn for that purpose and started back along the trail the way he'd come.

He had her hand. He wasn't letting go.

He never, ever wanted to let her go.

The thought washed over him right there, closed in with swirling white, and his fingers squeezed hers as he faced what was behind the desperation and concern that had driven him to rush here to find her when he'd heard the weather report for the region. More than the same concern he would feel for *just anyone.*

Because this wasn't *just anyone.* This was Fiona. And Brent had fallen in love with her. Fallen totally and utterly all the way in love with her, in the way people would do who wanted now and forever and a picket fence. The way people would who wanted *normal* and believed they could have it.

Brent had never been *normal.*

How could he have done this? How could he even know how to love her in such a way? *How could he make a success of loving her like that? How could he ever be someone she would be able to love like that?*

'I didn't notice what was happening with the weather.' Her teeth chattered as she tried to speak.

'It doesn't matter. I found you. That's all that matters.' He drew her alongside him and chafed her hand with his, trying to warm her while the knowledge of what was in his heart for her spread through him.

He couldn't live without her. Her safety and security meant more to him than anything else in the world. The feelings were more intense than the…love he felt for Alex and Linc, the only two people in the world he had ever connected with.

He'd bonded with Fiona on some deep level. He…loved her. But not even just in the way he loved Linc and Alex, which was more than he had ever loved any person.

He loved her man to woman. Wanted her at his side for ever—

Later, that knowledge would burn him as he faced the impossibility of it. For now, he had to get her safe from this storm. He had to focus on that! 'Save your energy for getting out of here, okay?'

She nodded and wrapped her arms around herself.

Brent couldn't have Fiona that way, should never have made love to her in the first place when he knew there was no way things could work between them.

How could he ever expect her to accept all of him? His own father hadn't been able to do that. His father had rejected him so deeply and thoroughly that there'd never been any going back. Going forward, for Brent, had been something he had to do alone when it came to relationships, other than with the two men who'd been through the same rejection Brent had been through.

Brent promised himself he would get her out of here, into safety, make sure she was well, and then he would step carefully back into the role of employer. He'd been tempted. He'd allowed himself to dream some big dreams, but those dreams were not realistic.

The snow got heavier and he was thankful when they reached the part of the track where the trail was hewn out of rock face. Tracking it with their hands slowed them down even more, but it kept them on the path and that was vital.

Finally they climbed the last steps into the tiny car park. Her car was there but he put her into his utility truck with the engine running and the heater on and a blanket wrapped around her. It only took a minute to stick a note inside the windscreen of her car with his phone number and the message that the car's owner was with him at his home. He grabbed her handbag and took it to her, laid it on the floor of the truck at her feet.

'I've caused a lot of trouble.' She glanced at the bag and away again. 'I should drive the car out of here.' But she could barely get the words out, let alone carry out such a task.

'I left a note. We'll get your car later.' There was no way Brent would allow her to try to drive in these conditions. On top of that, his arms ached to hold her; his whole system ached with that need. He felt out of control and words wanted to push up from inside him and burst out, telling her again how worried he'd been and how relieved when he'd found her and so much more. The *so much more* was the biggest worry of all.

Instead, he strapped her into her seat belt and tucked the blanket around her. 'Hold tight. We need to get out of here.'

The drive that should have taken ten minutes took

thirty, but they reached the mountain house and he turned the heating up high and brought out towels from the bathroom and warmed them before the heater outlet.

'I can take the wet things off.' But her fingers wouldn't work.

He brushed them aside and stripped her to her underwear and wrapped her in one of the towels. He took care only to let her feel efficiency in his touch, though he hated the knowledge of her chilled skin beneath his fingers as he helped her.

Brent took her into the bathroom and set her in the shower and adjusted it to slowly get her thawed out. She gritted her teeth against even the lukewarm water at first, but slowly she warmed up.

'Your hands are cold. You must be frozen yourself.' She clasped his hands to stop his movements where he'd been guiding the shower spray over her back and arms. 'Let me get out and you can get in.'

He searched her face for long moments. She had colour in her skin again, a soft flush in her cheeks that may have been from the warm shower or from the intimacy of what they were doing. Brent didn't know which, but the thought lodged in his mind and he became aware then of exactly how intimate this was.

To be bathing her, even if he'd left her in her underwear. Her beautiful body was still revealed.

'I don't need a shower. I dressed for the conditions.' Yes, his hands and feet were chilled but a few minutes in front of the heater would fix that. 'Come out and I'll dry you off.'

She submitted meekly enough to being towelled mostly dry and then she took the towel out of his hands and tucked it around herself and said, 'I hope you have some pyjamas here or something because I'm not staying in this wet underwear.'

And she said it firmly enough that some of his tension and worry about her eased. *Some of it.*

'Right.' He wheeled about and went to his room, ransacked it for something suitable, brought her a pair of drawstring sweat pants, boxers and a flannelette shirt and a thick cable-knit jumper and two pairs of socks. 'Do you need help to dress?'

'No, Brent. Really, I'm fine.' She half pushed him out of the bathroom and closed the door in his face.

Tension built in the base of Brent's neck then. He didn't have the capacity to control it right now. He submitted to the twitchiness and the obsessiveness as he changed into dry clothes himself and then paced the living room floor and told himself that now was the time to back off. To pull this back somehow.

The problem was he had a snowball's chance in hell of doing that. To quote the weather and the drive of absolute need inside him right now...

Fiona emerged from the bathroom just as he turned to pace the length of the floor again.

Instead, he froze in the centre of the room. She looked so beautiful in the borrowed clothes with her face shiny from the shower. She looked healthy, strong enough to fight off any after-effects of being thoroughly chilled.

She also looked embarrassed and there was something in the backs of her eyes... 'I'm sorry you needed to rescue me, but I'm glad you did. I don't know if I'd have been able to make it out on my own. I admit I was starting to get really scared, and I'd left my mobile in the car. That was a huge mistake.'

'You couldn't have known the weather would turn.' He explained why he hadn't known of her plans sooner. Almost, he could tell himself that discussion led them back to a more work-related basis.

Except it didn't feel work-like to want to pull her into his arms and never let her go. 'I shouldn't have walked away this morning, and I didn't do much rescuing just now. I just got in the truck and got on that trail and prayed you'd stay safe until I found you.'

'And put me through the shower when we got back here.' This time she dropped her gaze, didn't meet his eyes. 'I should have done that myself. You didn't need to see me. I know my body is larger—'

'I've seen you.' Every beautiful part of her. 'Fiona, you shouldn't ever feel—'

'We should focus on what happened today. I'm so sorry, Brent.' She tipped up her chin as though a brave smile was as necessary as a change of subject.

He wasn't sure which topic concerned her the most. Getting caught in such dangerous weather or the topic of her appeal. Maybe he should let that issue go, but how could he when he needed her to understand how beautiful he found her? 'Don't ever think you're less than completely—'

'I've caused you a lot of trouble.' She'd heard him. Her gaze admitted that, but it equally told him she didn't want to revisit how he might have formed his opinions. 'And all because I didn't stop to think I should get a weather report before I headed onto that trail. I wondered why it was completely deserted, but the solitude suited me and I didn't think…'

'How could you have known?' Brent left the other topic for the time being and focused on reassuring her.

He drew a deep breath and realised he was running his fingers repeatedly over the cable pattern on the shoulder of the jumper he'd loaned her. How long had he been doing that without so much as a by your leave?

Brent dropped his hand away.

And Fiona moved towards the door of the house. 'You have chains and four-wheel drive. The snow has stopped falling. It can't be more than six inches deep. We should get back to Sydney. I've caused enough trouble and I want to get back to my work.'

To forget all about them? Wasn't that the conclusion he'd come to eventually too? So why did his chest ache as though something sharp had been driven through it?

'We'll go.' There was no reason to stay on.

Brent turned off the heater and led the way to the door. 'Your car will have to stay where it is. It can be collected for you.'

'I appreciate that.' Fiona didn't argue with Brent. Her car didn't have four-wheel drive or chains on it. And she wanted to get back to the city.

So they went.

Fiona settled into her seat and pretended to sleep.

Brent might want to reassure her, but that made no difference to the fact that she loved him and he didn't return those feelings.

Well, she had survived today. She would regroup and survive whatever else was ahead of her, too.

CHAPTER THIRTEEN

'DO YOU WANT to tell me what's wrong with you, or are you going to just keep snarling at everyone who moves until you get it out of your system that way?' Linc tossed the question Brent's way while Alex turned his back at the barbecue and focused on cooking the bacon and eggs.

Brent rammed his hand through his hair and started to compulsively straighten everything on the table. It was Saturday morning. They were outdoors in the courtyard area of their warehouse home preparing a cooked breakfast to share.

Yes, it was somewhat cold this crisp morning. Yes, his brothers hadn't entirely expected him to bang on their doors and demand they come out and eat break-fast with him.

Brent hadn't cared. He'd wanted to eat out here where he didn't feel stifled and unable to breathe, and...he'd wanted Alex and Linc's company while he did it.

His brothers had looked at his face, donned jackets and said very little one way or the other.

Until now.

And Brent had deserved Linc's rebuke.

'I'm sorry, Alex.' When Alex turned his head, Brent met his brother's gaze and went on. 'Your company business is yours to run as you please. I've got no right to shove my opinions down your throat or say you don't know what you're doing. Obviously you do. I don't know why I ever got started on that.'

'If I thought your attitude was about me just now we'd have a problem, but I don't think that outburst had anything to do with me.' Alex put the cooked eggs and bacon onto the platter and carried them to the table. His gaze was shrewd, too knowing. 'I'd just like to know what it *was* about. Are you well? If your condition is causing problems—'

'Yes. We both want to know the answer to that, Brent.' Linc joined them there at the same time.

Both brothers stared at the plates, condiments and cutlery lined up like soldiers right along the centre length of the table.

'You haven't done that with the table stuff since that time in the orphanage when we were about eight years old.' Linc shook his head. 'What's going on, Brent? Do we need to be worried about you?'

Both older brothers had borne the strap over that performance at the orphanage because Linc hadn't let Brent take responsibility for it, had said they'd done it together, that they'd made up a game to entertain themselves.

Alex had been too young then. They'd all been too young, damn it. To be abandoned the way they had been, in Brent's case by a man who was no man at all, because what kind of man dumped his child that way and never looked back?

'They should have kept us and looked after us.' He uttered the words and realised Fiona was right about that. She was so right about that. 'Our families. They should have wanted us. Loved us exactly how we were.'

Fiona's family should love her that way, but they didn't. Why should Alex have been put into a shopping bag and dumped, or Linc knocked around and given up on? Why should Brent have been given up on because he had some perceived *fault?*

People lived with autism and didn't care who knew they had it. Brent had spent his life trying to hide it.

Trying to hide *from* it.

Wasn't that what he'd done?

He had, hadn't he? He'd held Fiona in his arms, had been given the gift of loving her, and all he'd done was worry about a condition he was lucky wasn't life-threatening. A condition that didn't limit his work capabilities, that was compatible with his design work. *That Fiona said only made him appeal to her all the more.*

She saw his autism as a gift, something that made him unique.

So he was different?

Fiona's family treated her that way and her only *crime* was loving deeper and more, living life with her heart open to others.

Brent had loved her in his heart, but he had rejected that love the moment he acknowledged it. He hadn't let her in. And, by keeping that door closed, he'd robbed both of them of any chance of being together.

What if she wanted that? What if he could convince her to take him on? What if the way she had loved him, given herself to him, had come from her heart as well as her senses? He *could* do this. He wasn't Charles

MacKay, nor should that man's attitude and behaviour decide Brent's future!

He'd made a huge mistake. Was it too late to try to fix it? How could he fix it? Brent's mind began to focus on the possibilities...

'What's going on, Brent?' Alex's broad shoulders hunched like the boy he'd been not so very long ago. That young-old child who'd got into trouble and needed his brothers so desperately, had needed to be out in the world with them, not in the orphanage waiting for Brent to get it together to rescue him.

Brent had done his best, Linc had done his part, too, and they'd all made it. What if Brent and Fiona could make it, too?

Linc leaned forward in his seat and his gaze searched Brent's. 'Alex is right. You've been a lot more off-kilter than usual lately. If you need a doctor—'

The worry in Linc's tone brought the words out of Brent when everything else wouldn't have. 'The only doctor I need is a "love doctor".' When his brother looked at him blankly, he went on. 'Relationship advice.'

Brent dismantled the items he'd lined up down the centre of the table, systematically set them back where they should be.

'You fell in love with someone.' Alex made a statement of the words, as though he wasn't surprised at all.

'Fiona. I'm in love with Fiona.' Brent stabbed several pieces of bacon with his fork and slapped them onto his plate, dumped some eggs beside them, then pushed the whole lot away from him.

'If you love her, you should go after her.' Linc leaned forward across the table. 'There's no reason why you shouldn't. Not a single reason.'

'What do I know about women or relationships?' What did Brent know about trust, or whether he could reach out? But he wanted to. Oh, he wanted to.

'You told us we could work it out if we found the right woman.' Alex pointed this out and pushed his hands into his pockets. 'We've had Rosa in our lives. She's a woman.'

'Rosa's great, but knowing her doesn't exactly qualify me for loving Fiona and doing a good job of it.'

'Everyone has to learn how to love.' Linc's words were surprisingly revelatory. As though he truly knew what he was talking about in this. 'We've all…loved each other. How we are hasn't mattered.'

That was true, and Brent had been stupid not to acknowledge that fully a long time ago. He'd let Charles's rejection of him convince him that no one in the world, aside from these two brothers, would ever be able to give and receive love with him.

He'd told Fiona that he and his brothers would always be guarded, but with each other they weren't. So maybe they wouldn't be with other people. Significant people. People they…loved.

'I never should have pushed you both out of that part of me. The autism. I shouldn't have worried about hiding it at all. It's not an indictment. It's just part of me.'

'At least you realise that now.' Alex clapped him on the shoulder. 'We have tried to show you that.'

'I know.' They'd tried, and he had pushed those efforts away until they'd given in and pretended to ignore the whole issue. 'I just didn't want to see. Now there's Fiona. I have to figure out how to do this, and then I have to go find her.'

He needed to go shopping. Urgently. And he knew exactly *where* he needed to shop.

Brent walked away without thinking to say goodbye. His brothers didn't seem to mind.

Fiona had been painting in her living room listening to music when she received Brent's mysterious call to meet him at the lookout on their favourite mountain trail.

Well, it wasn't *their* anything and she didn't know where that thought had come from. But Brent wanted to discuss a new project. Perhaps he needed to show her some local flora or something in relation to it. At any rate, she'd made the trip, had been grateful to see pale blue sky above and no sign of snow. And now here she was, walking towards the lookout in jeans, a soft pink blouse, cream jacket—and with her mobile phone in her back pocket because she'd learned that lesson!

Brent had come after her in these mountains, had worried about her safety. He'd been gentle and focused and she'd run because he'd seen her in her underwear and all her old fears and uncertainties had surfaced and she just hadn't been able to take it. She'd loved him too much. And he didn't care for her in the same way.

Fiona took a few more steps and contemplated turning around and leaving. It was Saturday, after all. She didn't *have* to work today, even if her boss had asked her to make an exception and give up this time for him.

Her heart hurt. She loved her boss and she wouldn't turn around because she worked with him, and she needed to be his employee and do a great job of that, just like being a 'friend' was something she did so well, giving out advice about relationships…

Well, she wasn't good at relationships and it was a wonder she'd ever thought she knew anything about them. She would resign from that particular position among her friends. From now on they would just have to work out their problems for themselves, because Fiona was *not qualified* to help them.

Fiona trod the final stretch of path and caught sight of Brent standing at the lookout railing, his face turned towards the view. At the sound of her footfalls, he turned to face her. One hand was deep in the pocket of his brown leather jacket. The collar of his tan shirt wasn't quite straight and he looked…both focused and uncertain at once.

'I wasn't sure if you'd come.' Brent's low words washed over her senses.

'You said you wanted to discuss a project.' Why discuss it here? Her heart couldn't define the answer, could only take in his presence as she joined him at the railing and a deep, strong beat registered in her chest, as though being with Brent had brought her fully back to life when she'd only been existing before.

'A project of sorts, yes. Did I disturb anything important when I rang you?' Brent's gaze searched hers.

Behind them, mountains and valley glowed in gentle winter sunshine. Mist particles clung to tree branches and bushes and hung in the air, turning the panorama a beautiful warm blue-grey. Fiona nervously ran her hands down her thighs and forced herself to stop the motion. 'I was just fiddling with a painting. If I could capture the beauty of this…' She gestured towards their surroundings.

'That's why I chose…here for this.' His gaze shifted to the view, and returned to her. 'I knew at this time of the day the colours…would complement your eyes and that it would be beautiful, like you, and it's quiet here, peaceful and tranquil, the way you make me feel inside myself.' He stopped speaking, couldn't seem to find what else he wanted to say.

Fiona didn't know what to say. His words made her feel beautiful.

A moment later he cleared his throat. 'Tell me what you were painting?'

'Nothing specific. I was just seeing what emotions I could get out onto the canvas.' So she could get them out of herself. And now he had said things that brought all those emotions to the surface once again. Her voice quavered a little as she went on. 'Why did you ask me to meet you here, Brent?'

Why here, specifically, as opposed to anywhere else? He'd said it was because of the colours and a lot of other things that didn't seem to relate to business.

And if they didn't relate to business—

'A similar reason to why you were painting.' He hesitated and his gaze searched deep into her eyes. 'Bringing you my emotions way too late and hoping… you might welcome them if I brought them to you here, where we could be by ourselves with nature and I could focus on you and be surrounded by plants and trees, things that help *me* feel calm and centred.'

'I don't understand.' Her heart had leapt at his words, but she couldn't rely on that particular part of her. It had led her into loving him, but it didn't know how to make her stop.

She didn't think she could stop.

Maybe he was finally ready to speak about his relationship with his father. That was emotional. Maybe

Brent needed to unload that and it had nothing to do with…them. If so, Fiona would still listen. 'Charles—'

'Hurt a very small boy deeply, enough that it almost crushed that boy.' Brent drew nearer, reached for her hands, gripped them in his and his thumbs stroked her skin over and over. 'Enough that when that boy grew up, he told himself he couldn't have normal relationships and blamed that on a condition instead of the hurt that was handed out long ago and *blamed* on that condition by the man who abandoned him.'

'Charles walked away because he was too weak to be a father to you.' Fiona's mouth trembled as she spoke the words and her hands gripped his. She couldn't help her reaction. She wanted to draw Brent's head to her chest and hold him. Just hold him. 'Not because he couldn't cope with your condition.'

Brent dipped his head in acknowledgement. 'That's right.'

'There's no reason why you couldn't have…all sorts of relationships.' She tried not to sound as though she needed him to think about a relationship *with her.* 'You can have whatever you want.'

He dipped his gaze to where his fingers stroked hers, clenched his teeth and stopped the motion. Only to shake his head and start it up again, as though he'd chosen to let himself, or to give her that touch that was uniquely his. 'There's only one person I want to build a relationship with now.'

'Who…who is it?'

'I think you know the answer to that, but I want to tell you anyway.' His voice deepened as he went on and he released one of her hands and pushed his into his trouser pocket. 'I don't know how to tell you how I feel, or what you might feel in return. I'll try to express it. I bought something…I'm hoping you might be able to feel *something* for me. I'm hoping you might be able, over time, if we spend a lot of time together and I work to show you how much I need you and love you…'

An insecurity of hers that she'd thought she'd conquered rose unexpectedly. 'My body shape and size… After we made love you didn't like…'

'I didn't like what I'd *done*. Losing control, exposing aspects of my autism. Those stroking and kneading motions, the way I inhaled your scent over and over.' His hand rose until it cupped the soft flesh of her upper arm in the most gentle of touches. 'But you…you were so beautiful. You *know* that's how I felt and what I saw. You have to know.'

Fiona looked into deep green eyes and wanted to believe him. Oh, she did. 'I'm large. There's no getting away from it. I'll never be dainty or petite or small. I try to dress in things that suit me, but Mum says—'

'Your mother's got no right to say anything other than how lovely you are, inside and out.' Brent made a sharp sound in the back of his throat. 'I don't want them to hurt you any more, Fiona—your family. There must be some way—'

'There is.' She'd been thinking about that, too, and she'd taken her first steps. 'I've called a family conference so I can tell them they're not…meeting my needs. If they can't hear that, can't respond as I need them to, I'll begin to draw some lines regarding my involvement with them. I've let that situation hurt me long enough.'

'I want to come to that meeting with you.' He wished he could protect her from having to do it, but he understood why she had to. And there was something he could do for her. 'When it's over, we'll have a meal with Alex and Linc. They will love you, Fiona. If you...can be part of us? Of *our* family? If you can let me love you with all my heart and soul?'

He realised he was getting ahead of himself and tried to explain. 'I want...all that with you. For us to be a family. When we made love, I didn't understand the feelings I had for you then, all the need and desire and tenderness wrapped up inside me and welling in my heart.' He stopped and shook his head. 'I lost control— because of the autism. Because I wanted you so much. I thought there was no way you could have...been okay with the repetitive touching, the way I smelled you.'

Brent drew a breath. 'Even when I thought maybe you were okay with those things, I thought back to how Charles had pushed me away. I got...angry. And resentful. All these old hurts that I'd never addressed rose to the surface and I realised I'd pushed them all down.'

'Maybe you should take some steps where he's concerned as well.' Fiona made the suggestion with gentleness in her gaze, with nothing but acceptance and, dared he hope, with total love?

Brent had made the same decision. 'There's no chance of reconciliation and, truthfully, I'm not prepared to open myself to him a second time when I see no chance of him changing at all. For me it's more about putting his rejection in perspective. He had no right to abandon me the way he did; I didn't deserve that. There's a service available for separated family members; it's government run. I'm going to make contact and book an appointment. I want the chance to tell him, that's all—'

'I'll go with you.' The words burst out of her. 'I'll go

with you and when it's over you'll come home to me, to be with me. I love you, too, Brent, with all my heart, with all my soul. I spent…my life looking for you. I looked in paintings and artwork and faces and the world around me. I think somewhere deep inside I knew what I'd found when I first looked at your landscaping work. I knew I'd found…what my soul needed.'

Brent squeezed her arm gently beneath his fingers, and his fingers shook as he touched her. His voice shook, too. 'I love you, Fiona. I love you with all my heart. I want us to be together. I want to be at your side for the rest of your life.'

He drew his hand from his pocket and there, at the edge of a lookout in the mountains, with towering trees all around them and mother nature providing a soft background of bird calls and the whisper of the wind rustling through grasses and leaves, Brent dropped to one knee before her.

Between his fingers he held a diamond ring. Behind them, as he glanced from the ring up into her face, the sun brightened suddenly and gilded the mist that filled the air and kissed the treetops until everything turned golden and the ring glittered and sparkled while Fiona held her breath and kept on holding it.

'I went to a jewellery store in the city.' Brent's fingers tightened on the ring and the green of his eyes deepened. 'That day I waited for you to finish visiting with your mother and sisters, I saw this ring in the window and thought how pretty it would look on your finger. The diamond…it's cut and set to look like a particular type of everlasting—'

'Daisy. The one we spotted here, with the golden spiky petals around the outside and the lovely white centre.' Fiona completed the sentence for him. Indeed, they had spotted exactly those flowers when they'd first walked this mountain trail. She'd paused to admire the tiny sturdy blooms that managed to look delicate and yet were so enduring.

'I wanted something that reminded me of you, and that would tell you how I feel about you.' Brent's gaze softened as he spoke the words. 'You're those daisies to me. Delicate and beautiful, steady and strong and I want to be what they represent, to you. I want to give you my love for ever, unfading, everlasting.'

'I love you, too, Brent.' With all her heart—for better, for ever—she loved him. Oh, she did!

'You're a good friend and a beautiful person.' He took her hand in his and laid her fingers in his gentle clasp. 'Inside and out. To me you are perfect.'

Fiona finally believed it. A soft warmth swept into her cheeks. 'I loved the things you…did when we made love. All those things. You don't need to worry about that because you entrance me. Your focus and all of those things that are unique to you.'

'Then…' He drew a deep breath and his gaze held hers, deep moss-green to her robin's egg blue. His fingers squeezed hers. 'Will you marry me, Fiona? And live the rest of your life at my side in all the ways there are? Will you wear this ring for me and wear a wedding ring for me, and let me wear a ring for you? I don't know how to do marriage. I don't know how to manage even a serious relationship, but I love you and I'll learn.'

'Oh, Brent.' Fiona stayed very still as he took in the expression in her eyes and slowly slipped the ring onto her finger and got to his feet still holding her hand.

She slid her arms up and her hands cupped the sides of

his neck and she sighed as his arms closed strongly around her. 'Yes. Yes, I will marry you and we'll learn together.'

The ring caught the sun's rays and reflected golden light from every facet of the diamond, and Fiona knew this was indeed the beginning of their everlasting love. Hers and Brent's together.

* * * * *

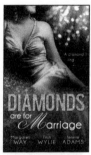
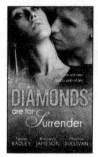

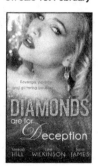
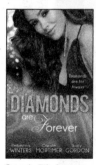

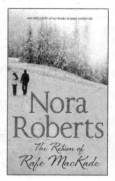

Have Your Say

You've just finished your book. So what did you think?

We'd love to hear your thoughts on our 'Have your say' online panel
www.millsandboon.co.uk/haveyoursay

- 🌹 Easy to use
- 🌹 Short questionnaire
- 🌹 Chance to win Mills & Boon® goodies